"Just f***ing delightful from start to finish." —*Reactor*

"A finalist for this fall's unofficial Best Book Title contest, *The Jinn-Bot of Shantiport* is the latest from Indian SFF specialist Samit Basu, who treats standard sci-fi tropes as dubious advice, best ignored. Mixing futurism and fantasy, his new book features streetwise protagonists, corrupt oligarchs, wry satire, and wish-granting tech. Oh, and monkey-bots." —Goodreads

"An extravagant, expansive, inventive epic of a book, shifting modes deftly to set heroes of lore on a collision course with video game tropes—and I enjoyed every word of the resulting fireworks. Brainy, deeply felt, and entirely brilliant."

—Malka Older, author of *The Mimicking of Known Successes*

"A wildly exuberant mash-up of top-class storytelling, gleeful mockery, and engaging characters we care desperately about. Basu is playing with tropes and messing about with narrative, while at the same time telling a heartfelt story with high stakes and enthralling action. The most fun I have had with SF in ages."

—KJ Charles, author of *The Magpie Lord*

THE
JINN-BOT
OF SHANTIPORT

SAMIT BASU

TOR PUBLISHING GROUP
NEW YORK

THE JINN-BOT OF SHANTIPORT

Copyright © 2023 by Samit Basu

A Tor Book
Published by Tom Doherty Associates / Tor Publishing Group
120 Broadway
New York, NY 10271

www.torpublishinggroup.com

Tor® is a registered trademark of Macmillan Publishing Group, LLC.

The Library of Congress has cataloged the hardcover edition as follows:

Names: Basu, Samit, author.
Title: The Jinn-Bot of Shantiport / Samit Basu.
Description: First edition. | New York : Tordotcom, Tor
    Publishing Group, 2023.
Identifiers: LCCN 2023033319 (print) | LCCN 2023033320 (ebook) |
    ISBN 9781250827517 (hardcover) | ISBN 9781250827524 (ebook)
Subjects: LCGFT: Science fiction. | Novels.
Classification: LCC PR9499.4.B379 J56 2023 (print) |
    LCC PR9499.4.B379 (ebook) | DDC 823.92—dc23/eng/20230721
LC record available at https://lccn.loc.gov/2023033319
LC ebook record available at https://lccn.loc.gov/2023033320

ISBN 978-1-250-82753-1 (trade paperback)

Our books may be purchased in bulk for promotional, educational, or business use.
Please contact your local bookseller or the Macmillan Corporate and Premium
Sales Department at 1-800-221-7945, extension 5442, or by email at
MacmillanSpecialMarkets@macmillan.com.

First Tor Paperback Edition: 2024

Printed in the United States of America

0 9 8 7 6 5 4 3 2 1

THE JINN-BOT OF SHANTIPORT

CHAPTER ONE

Bador descends on the public square, jumping off a second-floor ledge and landing lightly on a tile in the outermost row. He strikes a vaguely heroic landing pose, but none of the people around him acknowledge his presence. He waits a few seconds, but then shuffles and rises to his feet.

He makes his way to the center of Dekho Plaza, toward the statue of the Sage-Poet, Shantiport's greatest cultural icon. His face shines in a riot of colors, reflecting the videos running on giant screens on buildings all around the square, mostly advertising off-world utopian real estate projects. As he walks past a group of flashmob dancers, and a circle of young humans embarrassing themselves performing stunts for a bodytech dating service, he remembers to start his breathing simulations. His small body rises and falls slightly every few steps, alert but relaxed. From behind, he looks exactly like a flesh monkey, incredibly detailed muscle, skin, and hairwork: people only know what he is when they see his flat metal face with its large, restless digiscreen eyes, or perhaps the lights that appear in his joints as he adjusts to uneven surfaces. A child runs up to him, gaping, hoping he's an animal: he eyemoji-winks at her, and she rolls her eyes and runs back to her mother.

He looks around the square, and locates the shop where he's

supposed to meet Lina. As he lopes toward it, the first raindrops of the evening plink gently on his face: the rain, unlike Lina, is on time. In a few minutes, the raindrops will get fat, and then there should be heavy rain for a few hours at least. The buildings around Dekho Plaza will rise as their flood reservoirs fill, and the clevastone slabs of the square will fill to capacity, and then Dekho Plaza will suddenly turn into a sparkling, shallow lake. And the humans of central Shantiport will shop through it all, which Bador can respect. He stares through the storefront glass at the people inside, his eyemojis now goldfish bowls.

A young woman approaches the storefront, rain-shielded in a bright green hooded clevasuit. She hovers near Bador, who shoots a glare at her and shuffles away. He wonders where Lina found this one, and why she hadn't briefed her properly: the whole point of this charade is that Tiger Clan surveillance doesn't see them together more than strictly necessary. Well, not the whole point, or even the point at all, but a desirable side effect. The green-suited woman doesn't follow Bador: she wanders near the shop entrance uncertainly for a moment, and then goes in. Bador swears in messages to himself: Lina's really late. He can't call her: calls are unsafe; rogue intelligences left over from a Peacock-era cyberwar still lurk in Shantiport's voicecomm networks, waiting to destroy private callers' bodytech with spam and viruses. He sends her a series of angry cryptic messages, but as usual she doesn't respond. He suspects she has her comm-links off, or worse, has him muted.

Inside the shop, partitions rise and swivel and store-bots scurry about, beginning their hourly rearrangement of display sections to follow the evening's shopping trends. Lights go off or change color. Storecams and surveillance-bots go on standby, waiting for the store's new settings before resuming their vigilance. As they fall asleep, an orange-hooded woman runs toward the store, and bumps into Bador near the entrance: Lina's here. She falls down. Bador grabs her hand and pulls her up, apologizing. Lina ignores him and runs into the store, adjusting her clevasuit, and Bador walks away as well, his emotions mixed. He's pleased with the smoothness with which he passed her the location pin, but he's annoyed at having to play this game of Where's Lina every time they have to set up a workmeet. He can see why Lina enjoys it, but he's going to have to wait by himself at the location, as usual, while she switches clevasuits with her friend, wanders off on her own, reads the location pin, and then makes her slow and ponderous human way there. As usual, there's no recognition of the fact that his time is extremely valuable.

Half an hour later, Bador's mood has only grown worse. He waits for Lina again, now sitting cross-legged on the sloping greenroof of a bungalow on the outer ring of Historio Heights, just to the north of the central zone. Historio Heights is mostly a ghost town, an ambitious cultural construction project abandoned after the Tiger Clan's invasion of Shantiport: there are no lights here except the glow of the central zone across a dividing canal. Bador looks down, beyond the greenroof's edge into the canal's dark waters overflowing across the street and lapping at the Historio walls as the rain gets serious, a drumbeat on his face and exposed feet. His tail rises behind him, twisting and swiveling, sensors recalibrating his movement algorithms for stormy weather.

He jumps to his feet as he sees Lina on a vroomba hoverscooter speeding toward the bungalow, and clambers down and inside through a broken window just as she pushes the door open. Bador extracts a glowstick from his stomach-pouch: it lights up a large living room full of mud-streaked Anchor Clan–era furniture. There are paintings on the walls, mostly covered in fungus, and a range of dead and broken gadgets. A small table sits in the center of an elaborate and mostly rotten sofa set. On the table is an unlocked metal box.

Lina opens up the green clevasuit and tosses it aside. Underneath it, she's in a form-fitting coolant-lined sleeveless kurta and multipocketed trousers. And big insect-eye goggles, which she removes. The only visible Tiger marks on her are the black techstripes on her left arm. Despite the efforts of her clevasuits through the evening, she's glowing with sweat and her long hair is wholly wet. Her eyes shine as they adjust to the dim glowstick light, and her gaze drifts past the monkey-bot and settles on the box. She breaks into a dazzling smile.

"Brother," she says.

"You're late," Bador says, flashing frowning eyemojis.

"It's lovely to see you too. What have you got?"

Bador struggles, torn between the urges to sulk further and make a big revelation. Drama wins.

"So I spent last night and all of this morning at the bottom of the river with a couple of nasty croc-bots because your marker was out of date," he says. "And then I spent this afternoon getting myself and the treasure foam-cleaned. Croc-bots tried to eat me after, by the way."

"Amazing work. What have you got?"

"Well, the big container was ruined, river took almost everything. But we got deep inside it and found this box. Three treasures," Bador says with a flourish. "Do you want them in increasing or decreasing order of value?"

"Just tell me."

"Well, first of all, meet Moku," Bador says.

He looks directly at me.

I'm confused. What does he want me to do?

This is wrong.

"Meet what?" Lina asks, looking in my general direction, but of course she can't see me, and not because it's low light. My shimmer's on, she couldn't have seen me in daylight either.

"Come on, Moku," Bador says. "Show yourself."

This is not how it's supposed to go. I am synced to Bador, he is my user. Did he not understand when I explained it to him?

"Bador, if this is some kind of joke . . ."

I scan Lina's body mods, find her optic augs, and grant her eyes permission to see past my shimmer. Lina sees me, hovering above and between her and Bador, just a floating disc a little larger than her head. She actually leaps back with a startled shout.

"What is it? A drone?"

"A bot," Bador says. "Not an it, vibescans as he. Moku, meet Lina. She's a pain, but she's my sister and I am programmed to love her."

Lina shakes her head. "And how do we know Moku is not a Tiger Clan bot? Did you pause to think of that?"

"Well, because he's spent years switched off at the bottom of the river and he remembers nothing about his life before that. If he were human, sure, trap. But he's an old-school bot and I brought him back to life and he has sworn his loyalty to me in gratitude. Tell her, Moku."

"It's true," I say, and Lina is startled at the sound of my voice. "I have accepted Bador as my primary user and my life is his."

"And you have no previous allegiance to the Tiger Clan that might overrule this?" Lina asks.

"None. I have only learned about the Tiger Clan today, through a study of Shantiport's comm networks, and after a thorough study of several layers of the TigerNet and its intelligences. I am confident I have never met the Tigers before. I do not know how many users I have worked with before this. So I am either new, or I have been efficiently memory-wiped. My function programming is in optimal condition, and I look forward to my new project with great enthusiasm."

"That's right, Moku's been studying hard," Bador says. "You'll love this—tell us about Shantiport. Very briefly, not like last time."

This is a difficult challenge, because I have been juggling vast amounts of data about Shantiport since I woke up, and all of it is confusing. Also I am afraid of offending Lina, but I must make an attempt.

"Shantiport has been many cities over the ages," I say. "Former capital of lost empires, former imperial trade center, former glorious world-culture hub. Shantiport is described by present-day global culturesplainers as a mud- and blood-streaked burial ground for each clan era—Elephant, Anchor, Wheel, Peacock—over the last few centuries. It is now a minor western colony of the Tiger Clan, under the dominion of Tiger Central to its east. Shantiport is also a planetwide symbol of decay, disrepair, and decline, and has been described as a grand example of the human inability to evolve fast enough to save itself. Some interesting facts—"

"Enough," Lina says.

"I am sorry if I have given offense," I say. "I was just quoting filter-accessible popular sources from outside the city since the TigerNet appears to have erased all previous histories and describes the city in terms that are very positive but seem . . . untrue. But if you prefer, I will attempt to bypass local censorship and access more information about Shantiport from the rest of the world."

"No need. We live here, we know it."

"It is also very difficult to understand the power structures of the city since its three most important power centers—the Tiger Clan, the oligarch Shakun Antim, and the Oldport contractor Paneera—seem to be in both conflict and alliance with one another in different areas. I have spent some time reading the news, discussion forums, and deleted posts, but I can't tell whose side anyone is on."

"Neither can they, most days," Lina says. "And it changes every few hours. But all right, you're not a Tiger spy. What are you?"

My programming prevents me from explaining the exact extent of my capabilities because that could provide my user various incentives to turn to a life of crime and my ethics programming forbids that. So I tell her what I told Bador.

"I am a story-bot," I say. "I process the life narratives of my users, from their thoughtstream, if bot, or from observing them, if human, in addition to all accessible personal histories and observed social contexts. I can be a biographer, a journal, or even a therapist, if instructed about preferred therapy styles."

"I definitely thought you could use the therapy," Bador says. "But Moku will serve a far higher purpose as my biographer."

"Yes, chronicling the thrilling stories I hear about you raiding abandoned richfolk homes and selling the tech. I hope you're very happy together. So, Moku . . . you're reading Bador's mind right now?"

"I am."

She emits a short, loud laugh. "My condolences."

"Finest mind in the city," Bador says. "He can read yours as well, by the way. It's all very clever."

"I cannot read your mind," I say quickly. "But through observation and research, and study of microexpressions, body language, and other physical data from you and your surroundings, I will over time completely understand you."

"Is that so?" Lina asks, still amused. "What am I thinking right now?"

"I do need time to familiarize myself with my user, and for them to grow accustomed to me. Willingness to share also helps."

Bador plays a laughtrack.

"The thing is, Moku, most people in Shantiport have grown up under Tiger eyes and Tiger cams," Lina says. "We might not be the easiest to read."

"Humans are masters of lies on every scale," Bador adds. "They even lie to themselves all the time."

"This is known," I say. "It is all factored into my understanding—human self-deception, behavioral differences under surveillance, many other things."

"You should come see me at work, when I'm being watched all the time," Lina says. "What you're seeing now is me relaxed."

"Relaxed?" I ask. "Are you not aware you are currently being watched?"

Lina's eyes narrow. "What?"

"It is multilayered," I say. "You have your mandatory Tigerlink embeds, of course, but I see you have pirate mods on those, very sophisticated work. You're feeding them false data about your location, health, behavior patterns, social connections, and other trackables. When I first saw you, you were being trailed by two drones specifically tasked with following you, but they are not here now, so you must have lost them in Dekho Plaza. But there are two small drones watching you right now, probably just local data collectors, though they could of course be programmed to report trigger words or criminal behavior to any clients or customers."

Lina goes perfectly still.

—Show me where these drones are, Bador signals. Need to take them out.

—Don't worry, I signal. Should I deactivate them?

—Yes!

"I will remove the threat," I say.

I seek out the drones—both insect-shaped, a fly sitting on a moldy portrait and a centipede wiggling away from a slow wave of street-water making its way into the house—and put them to sleep.

"Now you are surveillance free," I tell the siblings, and Lina stares at me, wonder written all over her face.

"You can do that?" she asks. "You can free me from their eyes?"

"It is not my core function, just a privacy enhancer for therapy and journal functions, but yes. I can free you from some eyes in a limited radius. Drones, yes. Cams with weak security protocols, yes. Some human-bot interfaces, yes. Not bots. For example, there are two AntimCo Prowlers on the street outside, and—"

—Quiet, Bador signals.

He kills the light. Lina and he both dart behind the sofas nearest them. Perhaps I should have mentioned the approaching Prowlers earlier: they have been visible to me from a nearby street-cam for a while.

"Find me a weapon," Lina whispers at Bador, her voice easily drowned out by the roar of the rain.

Bador flashes empty-hand eyemojis: there is no weapon near him. I fly to the window, look for the Prowlers, and spot them immediately.

There are two of them, walking by the canal in front of the bungalow, splashing through the flooded street. They walk in their synchronized dance-like style, flat metal anteater-heads and mantis-limbs swinging and jerking. Their movements were designed with the intention of rendering them endearing, but have been successful only in inspiring human terror.

Each of the Prowlers is dragging a human man behind them. The men are drenched, wounded, stumbling, falling occasionally. Their bodies radiate defeat.

I don't know the Prowlers' scan capabilities, but they don't turn their heads toward the bungalow we're in, which is a good sign. They could have seen the light from the window—but perhaps their capture quotas have been met for now? To my relief, they keep going, and stride past the bungalow. I wait until they're well past to announce that we are safe.

"Please deactivate any surveillance you can by default whenever you're near us, and warn us of any approaching danger you detect," Lina says as soon as Bador turns the light back on.

"I will," I say. "Why have the Prowlers captured humans? I cannot find any information on this on the TigerNet."

"Should we fight them?" Bador asks Lina. She shakes her head and turns to me.

"The humans are linkless, probably squatting in abandoned houses in Historio," she says. "There are functioning clevahomes that could house thousands of people, if anyone cared. The Prowlers grab linkless and stuff them into Shakun Antim's indentured-labor ships. Then they sell them, to other city-states, or in space, somewhere."

She sighs, and turns to Bador.

"I'm going to need Moku's help," she says. "This surveillance-protection ability could be a game changer."

"Absolutely not," Bador says, radiating extreme irritation. "I have big plans for him. Very important plans."

"Well, I need him. So maybe your biography can wait? Please?"

"You can't just casually take him, Lina!" Bador shouts. "You can't just have everything!"

"Don't get upset! You just met him today. And it's not just me—it's about the city. You know what it's about."

"I have no idea what anything is about, because you never tell me your plans, and you just give me mysterious errands to run," Bador says. "Weeks, months, years, I do this nonsense for you, I've lost count of how many fake revolutionary groups you made me join, how many times I've found myself buried in filth looking through ancient trash, not even knowing what I'm looking for, my time has just as much value as yours, and—"

"Bador, stop," Lina says. Her voice is suddenly cold, and stern, and Bador falls silent. Even his thoughtstream blanks out.

"We're going to share him," Lina says, her voice radiating an authority that I find somewhat surprising.

"Why not ask him what he wants to do?" Bador mutters.

"That's a good idea. What do you think, Moku? What would you like to do?"

Another unsettling question. I have no idea what I would like to do. I am not supposed to be a part of my user's story in the first place. I work best when nobody remembers I'm present.

I consider my options. I am not programmed to feel joy, but my approximation of it would involve achieving maximum efficiency and insight. Working with Bador will be easy, and probably enjoyable. Working with Lina will be more challenging, given her claims of self-control and her already clear reluctance to reveal any information, rendered additionally complex by a lifetime spent under surveillance. Bador will tell me exactly who he is and what he wants; Lina might hide herself and her intentions from me, and I will have to build an idea of her and a chronicle of her actions from the outside, sometimes through speculation. Should this difficulty make me more interested in her, or less? And even if she tries to hide her truths from me, how hard could she be to read? I just have to build a relationship with her. Humans are often able to have successful lifelong relationships with others despite being completely unable to comprehend even basic, directly delivered communications. I can obviously do much better.

The idea of accepting both of them, being shared, is quite overwhelming. But why not both? There is nothing in my fundamental coding that forbids me from accepting multiple users: I don't know if story-bots have done this before, but why should it be impossible? If I manage my time well, could not the simultaneous adoption of different techniques for a human and bot combination be the greatest possible opportunity for a skill upgrade? I have ample storage space, their family background and daily environments are identical or overlapping, and if I run out of capacity, I can always use the memshards that Bador has told me about. To the best of my awareness, I like them both. I don't really have to choose.

I do not think it will be much of a challenge.

"I will work with both of you," I announce.

"Glad that's settled," Lina says. "Bador. Two more treasures?"

"I look forward to this experience despite the potential dangers and difficulties to myself," I say, louder than usual, surprised at how offended I am: does she not understand how much this means? Lina takes a pause, and a big grin emerges abruptly on her face.

"You didn't tell me he was huffy," she says to Bador.

"I'm horrified, I didn't know," he says. "So huffy."

"Never mind. Moku, come here."

I approach her, slowly, at eye level.

"I'm sorry I upset you, and I'm absolutely thrilled and honored to work with you. You have no idea how excited I am, how limitless the opportunities you present are," she says. "If I ever succeed in my wildly ambitious plans, I think both I and the city of Shantiport will owe you eternal gratitude."

"I am not upset," I say. "I am not capable of that emotion."

"Which is a good thing, since you're also working with my brother. Now give me a kiss."

"I do not have any kissing equipment."

She steps forward, instead, and plants a small kiss on my front cam. I retain professional objectivity, but also deduce that given the necessity, I would die for her.

Bador stops grumbling internally, walks over to the table, and opens up the metal box. He takes out a smaller metal box, carved with intricate designs. I imagesearch and find they overlap with the art styles of the Ekhanei, one of the five major religions still allowed to exist within a wall-encircled Shantiport neighborhood. Bador flips the box open.

It's empty, but from the shape of the case inside it's clear it once contained a ring.

Lina gasps, and stares at Bador wild-eyed.

"Do you know what this is?" she asks.

"Obviously I have no idea," Bador says. "I don't know what I'm looking for, but you did say that jewelry and household objects were priority, and so I picked this from a heap of riverbed trash."

"You are a genius and a superstar," Lina says. "This is a clue I've been waiting for. It'll lead us to the ring. Bador, all the time you've wasted down the years . . . worth it. One night's haul. And finally—a trail to follow. And with Moku, we might even figure out how to follow it."

They stare at each other in silence for several seconds.

"Well, are you going to tell me more or what?" Bador asks.

"I'm sorry, I can't," Lina says, and Bador eyemojis a planet exploding. Lina waves her arms about, inarticulate, and then calms herself down.

"I mean I will, once I figure it out. Item three, please," she says. "We've been here a while, we should get back to central soon, before someone starts looking for us. So make your big finish. After what you've shown me already, I'm beyond hyped."

"Another antique," Bador says, and extracts a small black plaque. It's made of ancient permaplastic, and is covered with golden letters in a flowing script. Bador holds it up in front of Lina with a flourish.

"What is this?" she asks.

"I don't know," he says. "Another big clue, I was hoping? Gold letters, old-time script . . ."

"Well, I don't know what it says. But it was in the box, so we should definitely look it up."

"I can translate it," I say, after doing the necessary search, which involved a minor hack into Shantiport University's ancient history department library. I look at the text again.

"It says ALADIN LIVES," I tell them a few seconds later. "I can't find anything online about what that means."

"The name is vaguely familiar," Lina says. "I think it's from one of the stories Ma used to tell us way back? Do you remember it, Bador?"

"She told you a lot of stories," Bador says. "Maybe they're on a memshard somewhere."

"I think Aladin's some sort of folk hero," Lina says. "Elephant Clan era. Brought down an evil emperor, people's champion, one of those? Peacock Clan probably erased it if the others didn't. Tigers caught it, if the Peacocks didn't. They don't like that sort of story."

"Well, if the plaque's useless, can I sell it?" Bador asks. "Moku, take a pic or something."

"Sell it if you like," Lina says. "Looks easily printable though, so I don't think you'll make much. Either way, great job, Bador. You want a kiss as well?"

"No," Bador says. He tosses the plaque away, and it falls into a corner near a sofa, splashing a little: there's street-water all over the room now.

"Another dead story," he says. "Let's go home."

Lina stuffs the Ekhanei ring-box into a pocket, and picks up her clevasuit. She pauses a moment, looks at the rain outside, and back at Bador.

"I don't know about that," she says. "Some stories just refuse to die."

CHAPTER TWO

After the hectic circumstances of our meeting, I assume that life with Lina and Bador will be a nonstop adventure, but after promising the beginning of some grand-scale impactful activity, Lina does nothing remotely exciting for a long while.

She takes me home, asking me to see if I can remove Tiger Clan surveillance on her house, but it is clear even before we enter that it's impossible. There are small flying Tiger-bots on permanent patrol on Lina's street, covering every entrance. Lina's neighborhood is a not-yet-gentrified part of old Barigunj, tucked away in a pocket right on the southern part of Shantiport's central zone. A city-map scan informs me that it's unusual to find two-story buildings anywhere in the central zone, or the ancient banyan trees that loiter stubbornly and ungeometrically around Barigunj. The neighborhood has been protected from reconstruction by one of the most powerful forces in Shantiport: bureaucratic error.

I find several drone-level snoops inside Lina's house, and put them to sleep, but I cannot do anything about the bots in the walls, and the insect-sized bots that take shifts inside the house through the day and night. There are small bots that follow Lina's mother everywhere as well, watching and listening: the Tiger Clan seems more scared of her than they are of her children.

Zohra Ejadi, their mother, looks quite similar to Lina, though she's shorter, thinner, and more expressive. She wears crisply starched saris, ornate eyeliner patterns, and a permanently disapproving expression. Her children are always quiet and deferential in her presence, displaying neither the banter nor the constant movement they did when we first met. I cannot tell if that's just the effect of Zohra's personality or the presence of the Tiger Clan's spies. Lina and Bador tell me, separately, not to spend too much time around their mother. They say it's because it's always possible some Tiger tech might be powerful enough to see through my shimmer, but I suspect they think their mother is just so sharp-eyed she'll spot me. Either fear is ridiculous, but I do not argue.

The house itself is what Bador describes as depressingly middle class, and that's because the Tiger Clan maintains strict control over the family's finances. Their living room is small, damp-walled, overcluttered with old furniture, and dominated by a large print-fridge over which floats a personality-enabled hologram clevahelp who's been set on mute, but talks to himself constantly. There are a few ugly airpainted statues around the house, probably Lina's clumsy childhood handiwork. There's a nine-frame grid of static pictures on the wall by the dining table of their father, Darkak, who has been missing for a decade. Some of the pictures of Darkak are with his family many years ago, others with possible Tiger dignitaries, receiving awards. One as a child, in traditional Tiger costume, participating in a rice-eating ceremony, holding in one hand a stuffed monkey doll.

I make a mistake initially, and assume that the surveillance settings the family lives under are normal for Shantiport. But as I find out more about the family's history from scans of available Tiger records and signal conversations with Bador, I discover there is absolutely nothing standard about this family. Neither Bador nor the Tiger Clan are the most reliable of narrators, but putting personal histories together from multiple sources is among my most basic functions.

The father, Shantiport-named Darkak Roshayon, was a Tiger Clan colonist official, arranged-married to Zohra, who was from an important-centuries-ago Elephant Clan scholar family, as part of a Tiger Clan nonviolent territory-encroachment invasion phase. Bador makes their mother sound like a lost heir to a stolen kingdom, but it is possible he just likes to think of himself as special. There are a few hundred other people still living in Shantiport who have a stronger claim to Elephant Clan heirship than Zohra, and the Elephant Clan's return to power in Shantiport is absolutely impossible in any case.

What should have been a regular clan-assigned marriage of convenience and unspoken suffering got complicated when Lina's parents fell wildly in love. And then Darkak damaged his Tiger Clan career by falling in love with Shantiport as well. Darkak was eventually suspected of joining the resistance, and using his Tiger Clan position to become a smuggler of alien tech.

He disappeared under mysterious circumstances, leaving his wife and children stuck in Shantiport waiting for a number of official investigations to end. If there had been a shred of evidence against them, his family would have vanished as well, but they have been left, instead, to the mercy of the legendary Tiger bureaucracy. They can't leave until their names are cleared, and might not even be able to afford a spot on a colonist shuttle anymore.

The family's archives, records, and private journals from before Darkak's disappearance are stored in encrypted, decentralized memvaults around the city. Zohra has refused to share the keys with Bador, but he's hopeful that I might be able to hack my way into them, and wants to take me to the memvaults to extract the data.

Our forays into the memvaults work to an extent: we manage to fill several memshards with data, but to Bador's frustration the data remains encrypted. My hacking skills do unlock lists of headlines and file names and descriptions of their records that look, to me, like a table of contents to the book of their family. It's an odd set of file names and tags that range from the parents' efforts, "Alina and Danil Joust on Dome" and "The Tale of Danil's Revenge on the Man Who Tried to Feed Him a Banana," to the children's "Top 100 Reasons to Murder Pigeons." Bador is very frustrated by what he calls our failure. But I am in no hurry.

Alina and Danil were the names that Lina and Bador had as children, I find. Zohra still addresses them thus, though no one else does. Lina was just a nickname that became common usage, but Bador was a name chosen in some act of personal revolt that the former Danil asks me not to make him think about. When his mother calls him Danil, though, he answers politely.

On the third day after bringing me home, Lina comes back from her work at a tourist hoverbus service and calls Bador and me outside. We walk around Barigunj streets for several minutes, and once we're safely away from Lina's home I deactivate all nearby snoop drones.

"Safe," I say.

"Bador, I heard you the other night when you said you were tired of running errands and not knowing what the plan was," Lina says.

Bador eyemojis exclamation marks.

"I want things to be better between us, but you know why I can't tell you everything," Lina says.

"I know why you think you can't, but it's a nonsense reason," Bador says. He doesn't think any more about this, though. I'll have to ask him later.

"I don't want to have that argument again, but I want to try to do better," Lina says. "So let's take it one plan at a time. I am looking for a ring. A ring that might give me new abilities, I don't know what."

"What does this have to do with Baba, and revolutions?" Bador asks.

"I'm telling you everything I can," she says. "I think the ring—or at least information about it—is in one of the Ekhanei temples in Dharmoghot. I am going to find out which one it might be, and I'm

going to get inside and ask the priests there about it. It'll involve
bringing up something from the past they won't want to discuss.
They'll tell me they don't know anything, and send me away, either
politely or violently. And then they'll speak among themselves, and
Moku, who will be listening, will find out what their next move is.
If we're lucky, we'll track where the ring is, or who knows where
it is. You'll be waiting outside the temple. And if the ring can be
stolen immediately, you will steal it."

"I should not be used for surveillance. I should not participate
in illegal activities," I say. "These go against my ethical programming."

"No one cares. Moku's in," Bador says. "I'm in too, of course.
When do you want to do this?"

"Three days should be fine," Lina says.

"It's a good plan. But it's not a great plan. As always, you choose
caution over style. You know what would make this plan great?"

Lina makes an inviting gesture. I consider protesting again, but
Bador's right. I'm absolutely in.

Bador eyemojis whirling spirals. "Do you know Longuria? East
side, outer burbs, flooded, now a mangrove forest? It's full of monkeys. Driven out of the city by evil bots like all the poor little
animals, but now they have their own town to run."

"I know it, yes."

"So I'm going to steal a little bus, or van," Bador says. "And I'm
going to drive it to Longuria, and then using either seduction or
force I am going to absolutely stuff this bus or van with feral monkeys."

"Bador."

"Then I'm going to drive it back into town, and crash it into
the Dharmoghot wall. And then I'm going to meet you outside
this temple. So when Moku and I go to steal this ring, the whole
neighborhood will be in absolute chaos. Monkeys everywhere.
It'll be beautiful. In the middle of all of that, if we take off with
the ring, they'll just think a monkey stole it."

"Bador, no."

"What? It's a great plan! Find one flaw in it."

Lina stares meaningfully at him for a while, and finds no words.

"You know what, do whatever makes you happy," she says finally. "Just be at the entrance to the Ekhanei section when I'm leaving. Sunset."

"It'll be absolutely epic!" Bador says, stars in his eyes. "Me leading a clan of wild monkeys, stealing the treasure while the Tigers run around in utter confusion! I'm off to get charged. Moku, you need to document this, let's go."

"I'm going to need Moku," Lina says.

Bador considers grumbling, but decides to quit while he's ahead. "See you in three days."

He runs off, leaping off the street in his excitement, climbing up a building, scattering a few pigeons. Lina watches him go, smiling faintly.

"We have work to do," she says.

Lina works as a guide for TigerTours, which is a hop-on hop-off hoverbus service that takes tourists around Shantiport's central zone, stopping at the more famous landmarks, like Shantiport Palace and the adjacent Jomidar's Square, the exotic tourist-trap market Borki Bazaar, and the Boulevard of Legends with its rows of alternating stone and holo-statues of acceptable iconic Shantiport historical figures. There has been a tourism boom planetwide in recent years, I read, because rumors have been circulating everywhere about the world ending soon. There are many theories about where these rumors started, and how the world is supposed to end, but whatever the truth is, Shantiport has seen more and more foreigners dropping in as part of planet-farewell cruises. I learn quickly that Lina is something of a tourist attraction herself, recommended on many international sites as one of the top reasons to visit Shantiport. From the moderator-deleted segments of Lina's TigerTours reviews I find that she is, by both global and local conventional standards, extraordinarily physically attractive, and many people from richer city-states have attempted to rescue her from Shantiport with marriage proposals. Her bus is also the home of a handsome adopted ex-stray dog named Bao, who has taken upon himself the responsibility of defending Lina from suitors who make her uncomfortable, and accepts payment for his services in skritches and synthmeals.

As Lina takes me on a hoverbus tour for the first time, she warns me that for the next three days, I'm likely to get nothing from her that will help me understand her better, because she'll have her work-face on throughout. She claims she can spend hours speaking with some of the world's most obnoxious people without showing the slightest trace of annoyance, and watching her do this would be a waste of my time. Instead, she has an assignment for me. I should find out everything I can about Ekhanei priests, specific details about their speech and physical mannerisms that a prospective impersonator might find useful. But she needs me around to ensure her privacy every time she talks to one of her contacts around the city, so she can't send me to the religious enclave, Dharmoghot, to spy on the Ekhanei. Which I am relieved to hear, because that is not my function at all. I should really not be involved in this whole scheme except as an observer at most.

So for three days, I divide my time between a set of unfamiliar activities. I spend some time each day attached to the rear of the TigerTours bus, patched into its comms systems and cams, watching Lina despite her warnings: it is my function, I cannot just stop. She was right about giving me nothing: even when tourists invade her personal space, or make it a point to insult her city, quoting some famous old empire song that describes it as a megapolis of trash, a garbage island, an anachronistic, illogical, unresolvable mess, she just smiles and carries on splaining the nearest available landmark.

I spend some time each day just flying above the bus, looking around. There is so much I want to see in Shantiport, and I remind myself that all of it can wait a few days, I am alive and awake in the world again and will soon know the city better than Lina and Bador do. But even though Lina has directed my attention elsewhere, her city is sometimes so striking, so distracting, that I cannot help watching it roll by: the lines and curves of its buildings, the occasional appearance of trees and bot-defying stray animals, the bursts of light and swirls of oil and water, and above everything the humans and bots that crowd it, flood it with neverending sound and movement and life. Less pleasant, though so omnipresent that I cannot ignore it even when I try, is the advertising. Nearly every street features massive screens and posters proclaiming some great Tiger Clan achievement, always including the smiling face of the city's ruler, the jomidar, the Mangrove Tiger, the benevolent Kumir Saptam. Often seen with an image of his son, the handsome Not-prince Juiful Ashtam. A lot of ads also show the oligarch Shakun Antim, sometimes with the jomidar, often selling off-planet real estate and luxury colonist-spaceship bookings. Another popular display is some sort of upcoming entertainment spectacle, the Ultimate Bot Showdown: the promotional images show a gigantic lizard monster and a mecha warrior in martial poses, ready to fight.

Each day, at most of the hoverbus stops, Lina spends some time meeting people. She seems to know a vast number of people: whether they are friends, colleagues, or part of some extensive informer network I cannot tell. With some, she disappears into alleys and I follow, giving her some surveillance-free time for whispered conferences and furtively exchanged packages. Several of the conversations she has are about Dharmoghot and the Ekhanei, but many others seem to be unrelated: some people tell her city gossip, others give her information and neighborhood updates, others make complaints. I wonder how many years she's spent building this network of allies in secret, avoiding Tiger attention the whole while. I can't imagine how much patience it must have taken.

I do not forget Lina's assignment: through each day, I scan all of the TigerNet for information about the Ekhanei. Since the Tiger

Clan banned Shantiport's religions immediately after seizing control of the city, and suppresses any attempt at religious propaganda or coverage of rituals, there is very little to see. What sets the Ekhanei apart from the other religions walled into Dharmoghot is their defining belief: that this planet is the only one where humankind lives, and they have an array of ancient relics that prove it. But every religion has a corresponding set of belief-supporting materials, and claims the others' are just fake print jobs. And it is common knowledge that multiple planets are human-inhabited. Perhaps most importantly as far as I am concerned, Lina probably knows all this and doesn't need me to tell her. So I turn, instead, to fiction: dramas with Ekhanei characters. But they are Tiger-censored dramas, and the Ekhanei in them are all villains, often terrible caricatures.

The first two evenings, after Lina's shift ends, she gets off the hoverbus at Dharmoghot, wanders into an alley, and changes costumes. She disguises herself as an Ekhanei nun in a bald cap and a hooded purple robe, with a big yellow triangle bindi on her forehead and lenses that turn her eyes from dark brown to bright blue. I project drama segments for her on alley walls, fictional Ekhanei depiction highlight packages, and she rejects them all. I don't know how to help her, so I just follow her as she walks into Dharmoghot, to the Ekhanei temple section, and has conversations with priests and devotees. Her goal, as far as I can guess, is to find out who the real leader of the Ekhanei is, and which of the temples he runs. On both nights, after we leave Dharmoghot, she gets me to play recordings of the Ekhanei she spoke with, and watches them closely, mimicking their body languages and intonations, repeating phrases they use. I do have one piece of good news for her: the surveillance on Dharmoghot, while intense, is all low-end drones, no bots. The religions have not been a serious threat to the Tigers for several decades.

On the third day, when the sinking sun begins to turn the clouds above Dharmoghot orange and purple, Lina disguises herself again and strides into the Ekhanei temple complex. She greets a few Ekhanei novices like an old friend, and allows them to lead her to a small temple deep inside the complex. She takes off her sandals, and places them next to the ancient-looking printstone steps at the temple's entrance, and hides a location pin for Bador under them.

The temple hall is cool and dark, except for a single beam of light from the center of the dome above the holy icons. Lina pays her respects and then sits, cross-legged, in front of the icons. She bows her head and softly chants an Ekhanei prayer.

"You have been seeking me, child?" asks a voice from the shadows.

An old priest, shaven-headed, long-bearded, purple-robed, emerges from the darkness.

"Salutations, Eka-lord Utpal," Lina says, rising swiftly. "The light of your presence graces this worthless creature beyond all measure."

"Where are you from, little sister?" asks the priest. "I have not seen you in our humble shrine before."

Lina hesitates. "This sinful speck of nothingness has been sent here by a secret but influential group of your devotees, bearing a message that cannot wait," she says.

"Speak it."

"Lord, as we all know, there is no world other than this one, and any that dare claim otherwise are liars and heretics."

"As we know."

"But, lord, as you may have heard, there are whispers in the streets that this sin-flooded world is drowning, and the followers of our faith cannot bear the thought that the Ekhanei faith could sink with it. And yet they cannot come forward and ask you if you would be willing to travel to another world, for as we all know there are no other worlds."

The priest takes a step forward, and the light beam catches his magnificent eyebrows as he frowns.

"The Ekhanei faith will never perish, little one," he says. "It is true that the other faiths here—the false prophets we are walled in with as punishment for our mortal flaws—are planning in their hubris to fly into the skies, and will thus burn and fall in the fire of the Eka sun. But we have no such desire."

"However, and I pray you will not consume this insignificant insect in the fire of your sage eyes, O lord, your followers have found a solution to this problem. If you and your fellow priests were to fall asleep in this temple, and wake up in a temple that looked as much like this one as possible, and were told that the world—the only world—had changed around you while you slept . . . would that be acceptable to you and the Ekhanei faith?"

The priest's eyes gleam. "It would, my child. I will consult with the other sages, but I am confident it would. Return tomorrow, and you will have our answer."

Lina prostrates herself before the Eka-lord, and he blesses her with great enthusiasm. She rises, lightly, and gives him a shy smile.

"There is one more thing, Eka-lord."

He sighs. "A price?"

"Just an answer."

"What is the question?"

Lina looks up, and into his eyes. "Your devotees would love to know the truth about the fate of the priest Manik, who some claim sought sanctuary in this very temple some years ago, but was denied it, and handed over to the Tiger Clan."

The Eka-lord's face clouds over. "What is this?" he asks, his voice harsh.

Lina says nothing.

"We had to surrender Manik to the Tigers or have all our temples destroyed," the priest says after a long pause.

"That is known," Lina says, and then drops her voice to a whisper. "But did he succeed? Did he bring the ring back to you? Do you know where it is?"

From his microexpressions, the priest appears genuinely puzzled.

"I think there was a ring, yes," he says. "The Tigers took it from his quarters, like everything else. What is this about? Why are you asking me these questions, ten years later?"

"These are not my questions."

The priest's voice rises in righteous rage. "Then tell your masters, whoever they are, that Manik was expelled from the Ekhanei, and we have no connection with him or any ring! Every few years, the Tiger Clan comes and harasses us, turns our temples upside down, despoils our sacred sanctums, but we have nothing, and it is wrong! There is no law that will save us, but the Eka will!"

"Just to be clear," Lina says, completely unmoved, "you're saying the ring did come to this temple, and the Tigers took it. You're sure about this."

"Yes!" The priest's face is now almost as purple as his robe. "So tell your masters they can talk to the Tigers directly, and not bother us with lies about spaceships!"

"I'll do just that," Lina says. "Okay, Utpal. I'm off. Take it easy."

She saunters away, and the priest, after staring at her for a while and clearly contemplating violence, stalks away to a small chamber behind the temple hall. I follow him.

Two more priests, even more elderly, sit around a table eating salad. They rise as Utpal enters.

"Who was that?" one asks.

"Some idiot from the Tigers," Utpal says. "Trying to find out about Manik's ring."

"But why?"

"How would I know why? I told her we continue to not have it, which they should know, since they took it from us. But now I want to know—do we secretly have it? Did someone switch it?"

The other priests exchange baffled glances.

"Why would we do that? Was the ring special?"

"How would I know why?" Utpal roars. "Do we have agents in the Tiger Clan who can steal it back for us?"

"No," says one. "But we have salad. Calm yourself, Eka-lord. Have some salad."

I've heard enough. I fly out of the temple, and meet Bador outside it, perched on a little statue of a bull.

—Well? Do I heist this temple or what? he asks.

—No. They don't have it.

I look around.

—Where is your bus full of monkeys? I ask.

—Epic fail. I don't want to think about it.

We turn away from the spectacular sunset over the Ekhanei temple domes, and find Lina lurking outside the Dharmoghot wall, now dressed like herself again. I tell her everything I heard.

"Right," she says. "So now we infiltrate Tiger Palace."

"Okay okay okay," Bador says.

CHAPTER THREE

A day later, Bador and Lina lurk at the edges of Jomidar's Square, near the TigerTours hoverbus dock. They're near a small group of tourists, who are taking videos of a medium-sized group of protestors, both human and bot, who are shouting slogans against Shantiport's evacuation. The slogans are aimed at the Tigers, who are normally very happy to attack dissidents. But in this case, the Tiger Clan claims to not be responsible for the world's end, and not even aware of when it's supposed to happen. So no troop of armed Tiger-bots emerges from the massive gates of Tiger Palace at the northern side of Jomidar's Square to beat up the protestors.

Bador and Lina are practiced loiterers: no one would suspect them of any untoward thoughts as they gaze innocently at Tiger Palace, with its immaculate white-brick walls and ever-sparkling rotating dome, at the historical hologram displays of Tiger Central heroes lighting up one by one on Jomidar's Square, at the government tower complexes on the square's east side with their sculpted vertical gardens, and the ever-shifting array of Tiger drones doing combat maneuvers in the sky.

I fly up to them, shut off a few stray snoopdrones, and make my report, which is short: Tiger Palace is secure, full of high-end guard-bots, and impossible for them to sneak into. Even the cameras are too secure for me to hack.

"What if you were to disguise yourself as a maid, or a printer technician?" Bador asks. "Wouldn't work, would it? You're bad at blending in."

"The simplest scan would show them who I was," Lina says. "You said I had patience but lacked style. Now help me aim higher."

"You're right," Bador says. "You want to break into the most secure place in the city, to look for a ring taken ten years ago that might not still be there. And you don't even know what it looks like. You're going to need to be stylish."

"I already know what my plan is," Lina says. "But I'm willing to hear options."

"Here's what we do," Bador says. "We kidnap the jomidar."

I wait for Lina to snap, but she just hand-gestures admiration.

"Interesting," she says. "Do you still have your van full of monkeys?"

"Fine," Bador says. "Let's just do your plan, since that's what we'll end up doing anyway. I just wish you'd take a big swing sometimes, you know? These little steps forward are great, but you're not going to be fit and glamorous forever like I will."

"Thanks, noted. All right, new plan. Moku, this won't be on the TigerNet, so hear this. Once a month, Not-prince Juiful decides that life in the palace is too sheltered, and he wants to experience the Real Shantiport. Mingle with the citizenry, unobserved, to find out what the people are thinking."

"Yes," Bador says. "And she never lets me represent the people and tell him what he needs to know. Sometimes there are foreign ambassador types as well. Terrible, terrible disguises. But she never lets me spread the truth worldwide."

"This is because Juiful is always surrounded by large bodyguards who have strong views on what the Not-prince should know about his city," Lina says.

"So," Bador says. "We kidnap the Not-prince."

"I don't understand," I say. "If Not-prince Juiful cares about the people, why does the city continue to suffer?"

"I neither know nor care what Juiful feels, because I despise him, his clan, and everything they stand for," Lina says. "But his visits to the city aren't going to teach him anything about the people, because the Tigers rearrange the city whenever he decides to learn more about it. It's a complete waste of everyone's time. Hopefully it'll stop once the fool gets married, if his wife has any sense."

This time, I do know what she's talking about. Speculations about the Not-prince's upcoming wedding are all over the news. Official Tiger Clan marriages involve weeklong citywide festivities, power alliances, and business transactions, and are subject to a great many traditions—all prospective partners must be upper-tier, hetero-human only, and optimized for legal heir production. The leading contenders for Not-princess include several oligarch heiresses, senior officials of other clans, Tiger notables from other city-states, and a few interplanetary trader clan magnates.

"Lina," Bador says. "Big swing."

"I'm going to befriend him," she says. "Get him to invite me to the palace, and take it from there."

"Seduction," Bador says. "Saves time, grants high-level access. Bonus: sexual enjoyment. Good plan. In fact . . . why not marry him?"

"No, not seduction! If any of the rumors about the palace parties are true, I don't think Juiful will even notice someone who sleeps with him. Or he'd reject me because he's getting married. I need to find a way to stand out."

"What if I kidnapped him, and you rescued him?" Bador asks.

"Crazy as that may sound, it's an option," Lina says, and Bador's whole face lights up in joy for a second. "But not today. Today, we just charm him a little."

She turns toward the hoverbus dock.

"And if you have any idea how to do that, and the idea doesn't start with a kidnapping, I'd be happy to hear it when we meet at Borki Bazaar in an hour," she says. "Bador, get there before me, find a colorful tourist-trap stall that's clearly visible from the main entrance, and tell the owner I need to borrow it. They all know me."

She strides toward the TigerTours bus, and Bador leaps forward and grabs her hand.

"Wait," he says. "This is today? This is now?"

"Yes. Big swing! We can't wait a month."

"I think it's too soon," Bador says, his eyemojis worried faces. "This isn't like you. You need to plan this out. Maybe next month is a better idea."

She pulls away from him. "What is it?"

"Nothing! I just think you should be cautious. It's such a big move, I don't know if you're ready? We should talk more, see what our other options are."

A tourist family interrupts them, asking for directions to the Boulevard of Legends. Lina goes into smiling work-mode, and waits until the family has departed before turning to Bador again, eyes narrowed.

"Truth," she snaps. "Now."

"It's not super important," Bador says. "I just need Moku for a few days. Starting tonight."

"Can't do it, sorry. His privacy bubble is too important right now. What do you need him for?"

Bador eyemojis thunderclouds. "We agreed to share him, and I'll remind you I'm the one who found him." he says. "You have your plans you don't tell me, I have my own plans. I need Moku for them. That should be good enough."

He doesn't want to tell her, but he's thinking about his plans, and even though I don't really know what they mean, they seem to be rather unwise.

"I'm trying to tell you as much as I can," Lina says. "I really am. But I'm scared you're thinking of doing something truly idiotic. What do you need Moku for?"

"Fine," Bador says. "I'm going to fight in Boss Paneera's Ultimate Bot Showdown. Don't try to stop me."

Lina claps her hand to her forehead and walks away.

"Hey!" Bador runs after her, and plants himself across her path. "Don't do that. It's a real ambition of mine, and I would like your support."

She takes several deep breaths, and nods.

"You want Moku to, what, make a documentary about you while you do bot martial arts? For socials? For promos?" she asks.

"That is not my function," I say, alarmed. They ignore me.

"I'm just going to say a few things, and I want you to listen closely," Lina says. "There are several reasons why I do not want you going anywhere near the city's biggest crimelord's martial arts tournament. First, there are bots there the size of buildings. They will kill you. In a second. I know you're brave, and strong, and your spirit is incredible. But they are just too big, Bador."

"That's another thing," Bador says. "They took the entrance fee, Lina. A fortune. I ran around until I was out of charge for months, just hustling and selling whatever I could get my hands on, just so I wouldn't have to borrow from Paneera's shark-bots, because that always ends in murder. They took my money, and then they said I was too small to join, no refunds. And I want justice."

"You just . . . that's Reason Two. You don't want to go anywhere near Boss Paneera and his gang. You've lost money, that's terrible, but you need to let it go. At least you're still alive, you can make more money. They will kill you, Bador. In a second. But more importantly, Reason Three, I cannot have you drawing attention right now, to yourself or our family, because we are at an extremely delicate part of a really difficult and important mission, and you being a bot and not under surveillance is a huge advantage. This is not a good time for you to be famous. Bador, I need you—and Moku—right now. This is not about my ambitions, or about whatever feelings you have about the way I've treated you. This is about the city, the millions of people in it, humans and bots, this is about what our parents dreamed of, and what they went through when those dreams fell apart."

Bador keeps his face—and mind—completely blank for a whole minute. Then his eyes light up, and he flashes a smile and a shrug.

"Can I just have him for a day though?" he asks. "After you're done with whatever it is you do with the Not-prince. One day. I hear you, I have no arguments. I just want Moku for a day."

"Done," Lina says. "Can we go now?"

"I would like to say something, if I may," I say.

Lina fidgets, but her face as she nods is perfectly serene.

"I do not like being sent to spy on people who are not my users, or to test the surveillance settings of a location my users are not in, or creating a recording of my users for public display. I am not supposed to be part of the story."

"I hear you," Lina says. "But I—we—could really use your help, Moku. And that might involve doing things you don't like doing. How do we make your life better in exchange?"

"I don't want anything," I say. "I do want to help you, and improve at my functions. I'm not threatening to quit. But I want you to remember I am a person and not a device."

"That's what I always say," Bador says.

"Always," Lina says. "Now, move your asses, persons. We're running late."

I've been to Borki Bazaar a few times before. It's where Lina starts and ends her TigerTours workdays. But on every previous visit I had been running several open tabs trying to observe Lina and absorb both the history of Shantiport and a range of fictional dramas on the TigerNet. So it's only now, as I swoop in from above, following Bador's tail as he makes a dramatic entry after an impressive dash over central zone rooftops, that I really observe Borki Bazaar for the first time.

Borki Bazaar is exactly the sort of exotic-city market seen on shows: a convertible market that floats at high tide, ramps at low. Food stalls display spices, snacks, simfruits, and real-looking animals on spits. Line upon line of shops sell souvenirs, vibrantly colored carpets, toys, customized gadgets, jewelry, houseware, clothes of every possible description, an overpowering spread of colors and sizzles and shouting voices. Holo-fairy dancers swoop above the street, ad-banners fluttering behind them. Ad-drones hover above their graceful forms, jostling one another as they flash their scrolling displays. Dance troupes, human and bot, flashmob in open stages amidst the tourist-trap stalls. Techpirates and drug dealers shuffle around the borders of the market in dull clothes, wary of secret police. Human buskers and juke-bots argue over intersections. A hassled volunteer stands at what used to be the sex-bot meeting area, explaining that the sex-bots have unionized and are temporarily unavailable.

I watch Bador as he spends some time strutting about the market's lanes, greeting various shopkeepers as an old if not especially beloved acquaintance—a lot of the conversations he has involve unreturned money and missing valuables. He hovers near the market's main entrance, looking around, and then approaches a stall that sells Shantiport souvenirs and memorabilia—mugs, badges, umbrellas, toy monuments, celebrity face masks.

There's no sign of the Not-prince or of Lina, but as I watch the entrance, a troop of Tiger-bots marches in, tiger-headed humanoid soldiers. A small group of humans, possibly supervisors in civilian clothes, wanders in behind them. Within minutes Borki Bazaar is in considerable turmoil. The Tigers clear out some stalls, herding their protesting owners into the bylanes. Drones spray cleansing liquids and de-aromatizer sprays from above. The market's cleaner-bots struggle in vain to sweep mud away. A troupe of brightly clad dancers, acrobats, fire-breathers, and jugglers emerge from a hoverbus and take positions. Food stall workers rearrange their displays, setting out price tags lower than before, ensuring their fruits and meats are fresh.

A TigerTours bus speeds up to the dock, and Lina leaps out of it, brushing startled tourists aside. She races to a food stall, wolfs down a printed egg-mutton roll and sidles off into a narrow market lane. I look at the souvenir stall Bador had approached:

it's gone as well. The owner has left, and Bador sits at the stall as if he'd lived there all his life, trying on large striped hats to pass the time.

An alarm rings out. The market bursts into activity: jugglers juggle, singers sing, snake-bot charmers remote-pilot painted, glistening cobra-bots. Every stall owner begins to shout about the virtues of their merchandise. Lina appears, in full exotic market-lady costume, a red skirt and blouse covered with little mirrors and complex embroidery. Her hair and face look different: I detect cosmetics. The effect of this disguise is probably very alluring, because even in a market full of other women in colorful clothes it seems as if every human in Borki Bazaar pauses for a moment to appreciate Lina's disheveled radiance, and some men and women burst into applause as she walks to her stall. She acknowledges all this with a giggle and a wave. I find the brightness of her eyes and smile mildly alarming. She'd changed her body language entirely when she was disguised as an Ekhanei nun, and she's done it again: she's moving like one of the dancers performing nearby. I don't know whether reading her when she's acting will confuse my analysis of her or augment it. She pats Bador on the head as she reaches the stall: he's wholly unmoved.

In the distance, at the market's main gate, a few large humans and humanoid-bots in everyman clothes appear, forming a loose cordon around a single human figure. A man. Even from a distance, it's evident he's a magnificent specimen of humankind. Tall, broad, muscled like an action figure, with a gait indicating extreme fitness and confidence. He's bearded and turbaned, dressed in a sleeveless vest and gray pantaloons, a scabbarded scimitar at his waist. The son of the Mangrove Tiger surveys Borki Bazaar with what appears to be genuine awe and wonder. He scratches his beard, which a closer zoom indicates is attached to his face with an organic adhesive. His eyes flicker to his clothes, possibly to check how sweaty he is: well within socially acceptable limits. I fly toward Lina and Bador.

Lina's eyes flicker toward me as I approach. "Showtime," she mutters. "You ready?"

—Wait for me in our Historio bungalow when this is over, Bador signals. Night's just beginning.

—Didn't she forbid you from executing your martial arts quest?

—I don't recall any binding agreement.

"Let's go," Lina whispers.

Bador eyemojis farewell hands, and knocks over a large stack of metal mugs. The clatter is so loud that it's audible, for a moment, even above the standard chaos-orchestra of Borki Bazaar. Bador makes a rude kissing noise and scampers away monkey style, leaving Lina alone at the stall, sad and forlorn, theatrical dismay on her face, a helpless hand pulling at her shiny hair in anguish and embarrassment. The purpose of this charade is immediately achieved: she's drawn the attention of Juiful's entourage. As if drawn by a snake-bot charmer, the Not-prince walks straight up to Lina's stall. Some of his companions place themselves at possible attack points, others get to work picking up scattered mugs. Lina stands very still, blushing, eyes large and lowered, not meeting the Not-prince's eyes as he inspects the merchandise at her stall, and then her.

She meets his eyes and smiles, and he catches his breath.

"Thank you so much, kind stranger," Lina says.

Juiful gives her a dashing smile. At a nearby stall, a teenaged girl squeals and faints. No one helps her.

"My pleasure," he says.

"And how might I reward you for this gallantry?" she asks. He waves an elegant hand.

"Your smile is reward enough," he says. She gives him another one, with a carefully added hint of mischief.

"I don't think it is," she says, and hands him a Juiful face mask. He takes it, studies it, and gives her a sharp look.

"You know," he says.

"I only know what absolutely everyone here knows, sir," she says. "Might I learn the name of my handsome rescuer?"

"Of course, my name is Jui—Joy . . . fur." He looks vaguely embarrassed, and decides to inject confidence into his deception. "Joyfur," he says, loudly.

One of his bodyguards decides to rescue him, and steps forward, scanning Lina with his wrist-tech.

"You are not the authorized operator of this stall," he says.

"Just filling in for a friend," Lina says, projecting demure nervousness. "I didn't mean any harm, sir. The people of Borki Bazaar know me."

"You are Lina, a TigerTours guide," says the bodyguard. "This is a transgression on multiple counts. Step away from the stall at once, return to your home, and await further instructions."

I expect Lina to respond to this with a show of fear, so that Juiful can rescue her again, but instead she looks amused, and turns to Juiful.

"Is that what you want me to do, Joyfur?" she asks, a challenge in her eyes.

"Not at all," Juiful says. "Step away from her, and if I hear of any trouble later, there will be consequences."

The guards back away. Juiful looks Lina up and down.

"It turns out that I have an invitation to the palace this evening," he says. "A small gathering of friends, very casual. Would you like to join me?"

The opportunity she was looking for! I'm very impressed she was able to obtain it so quickly.

"No, thank you," Lina says. "I don't think I would fit in very well with all the grand people in the palace. Besides, I suspect your security wouldn't approve at all."

One of the human Tiger Clan bot-supervisors approaches Juiful and whispers in his ear. Juiful turns to Lina again, a puzzled smile on his face.

"I hear you might be dangerous," he says.

"It's true," she says. They look at each other and say nothing for a while, and they both look very pleased with themselves. I'm not sure I follow. Human interaction might be more complex than I had previously assumed.

"If you won't come to the palace with me, I guess I will have to take a tour of Shantiport with you," Juiful says.

A Tiger supervisor approaches Juiful, and is stopped in his tracks by a warning finger.

Lina hesitates. "May I speak to you in private for a minute?" she says. "I promise I won't bite."

Juiful quells his entourage's evident disapproval with a glare. He waves his hands, and all the Tigers actually turn around, facing away from him. He walks around the stand, to Lina's side.

"Speak freely," he says. "Don't worry about them, they serve me."

There are thirteen drones with long-range ears listening to them. I extend my senses, and glitch them all. It won't last for long, but I hope it'll be enough.

"Why are you doing this?" Lina asks. "I'd like to see you again, but—"

"Let's just say I find truth-tellers glamorous," Juiful says.

"I do as well. If you're serious, I can show you a world in your own city that you haven't seen before," she says. "But it could be dangerous—for you, and even more so for me."

"You are under my protection," Juiful says. "And as for me, I'll take my chances."

"I look forward to it," she says, rummaging in her pockets. "Now kiss my hand, please."

Eyebrow raised, Juiful extends a hand to her, and she places her fingers in it. He raises her hand to his lips, and kisses it, while she slips a location pin into his hand.

"Tomorrow night, but only if you're alone," she says. "If that's possible. Privacy, or nothing."

He nods, and steps back.

"Well met, Lina of TigerTours," he says. "I will recommend you to my friends."

"I think you already have," she says with a dazzling smile, and walks away, leaving the Not-prince staring at her, ignoring his bodyguards as they fuss around him with questions and warnings.

CHAPTER FOUR

I find Bador easily enough. He's on the greenroof of the Anchor-style bungalow in Historio Heights, stomping about. When I come closer, I see he's actually doing a sequence of martial arts moves on the roof, and a few seconds later I realize the moves are familiar as well: the sequence is identical to the action climax of one of the dramas I saw recently while researching the Ekhanei.

"About time," he says as I approach. "Not a second to lose."

"Boss Paneera's tournament is supposed to start in a few minutes," I say. "The Tigers have issued a warning. Noncombatants are to stay away."

"As I said, we need to move," he says, and runs up the sloping greenroof, in the wrong direction.

"You are moving toward the forbidden area," I point out.

"Keep up." He leaps off the greenroof, landing neatly on another one.

"Bador, wait," I say. He doesn't, so I follow him. Raindrops splatter on my shell, heralding a storm. I catch up with him, and beep loudly in protest: he grumbles, stops, and turns toward me.

"It is not my function to interfere in or comment on my users' actions or relationships," I say. "But you and Lina have agreed to share me, and it is my job to calibrate myself to optimize not just the different processes I use to understand you both, but also operational logistics, the division of time spent following each of you when you are not together."

"Just here to see a bot about a refund," Bador says. "Look, I know, the fighters are too big, and they haven't let me in anyway, but I want my money back. And I had many dreams about this tournament. Least I deserve is a ringside seat."

"Can you not make your financial settlement claims later? Or via a more formal process?"

"No," Bador says. "So while I'd really love to hang out here with you and talk about sexy things like operational logistics and process optimization . . . we have to hustle, my hunky hoverdisc. Let's go."

He runs again, at steady canter, leaping from bungalow to bungalow. I match his pace with ease.

"What I was trying to say was that normally a rift between you and your sister would not be my business, if my user was just one of you. But Lina explained to you, very clearly, why you should not be around Boss Paneera's bot fighter tournament, and while you claim your plan is to be audience and refund-claimer, I sense from your thoughts that you have every intention of fighting in the tournament."

"Winning it."

"Yes. But. Since the day we met, I have seen your sister try to include you in her plans, try to work with you as much as she is able. And I fear your disobedience—"

Bador skids to a halt. "My what?"

"Your assertion of your independence might form the basis of a lasting rift between you and your sister."

There is a broad permaflooded avenue between the Anchor Clan–style bungalows and Historio's next zone, tall Wheel Clan–style apartment blocks. Bador takes a run-up and soars across the canal-avenue, cracking a concrete-print Wheel-apartment wall as he lands. His fingers and toes extend claws, and dig into the wall. He climbs upward, turning his face toward me.

"I'm not even on the roster, as you know. Just here for a refund and a view. How do you know I even want to fight in this tournament?"

"I can read your mind."

"But I wasn't thinking about fighting!"

"I read you better now. Right now, you're planning to improve at concealing your thoughts from me."

"Creepy. Well, sure, I'd like to fight but it's not like they'll just let me. I'm not on the list."

He reaches the Wheel building roof, and looks around. Up ahead, after the apartment blocks, lie the towers of Historio's central zone, the Peacock zone. In the sky above us, a swarm of camdrones and spot-bots fly toward the towers too, from the east.

—If you want to read my mind, read this, Bador signals. So, Lina and me. You want to prevent lasting rifts? Too late. What you've seen, over the last few days? It's been a problem all our lives. Do you know why she won't tell me her plans?

—Please tell me.

—Because family or not, person or not, I am a bot. Lina and my mother will both say they believe in bot rights, and bot personhood, and all the other nice things humans say to look good. But they're both afraid that if they tell me everything about what happened to my father, and what they plan to do to the Tigers . . . then one day, when things go bad, the Tigers can just capture me and read my whole brain, and find out everything they need to know. That one day, the Tigers might just rewrite me, with superior technology, and turn me against my own family.

—And this makes you feel bad.

—Feel bad?

Bador stops surveying the speeding droneswarm above us, and glares at me, his eyemojis daggers.

—This isn't about my feelings. This is about bot rights! The place of our kind in the universe, and the arguments that bigots make against us. When I find that my own family secretly shares these views, I wonder what the point of my being here really is!

I am not very familiar with bot rights, and I don't want to interrupt him, so I try to quickly look up the key arguments. The Tiger-Net is full of discussions about bot rights, and they all represent the Tiger view and the human view. There's a lot of material, at least five decades' worth, and now might not be the best time to filter and process them. But regardless of the larger issues, Bador's family's fears about Tiger capture seem very justified. For example, I can read his mind, and while it is unlikely there is any tech superior to mine in Shantiport, hypothetically the ruling regime might have someone who could find out Lina's or her mother's secret revolutionary strategies from Bador's mind, and rewrite him to turn against them. But it is clearly best to not bring this up with Bador right now. The rain is pouring down as he stares at the Peacock towers of central Historio. Lightning splits the sky, and thunder roars across Shantiport.

"They will know who I am!" Bador shouts, shaking his fist at the lightning. "They will know that I am the son of the great Darkak Roshayon and Zohra Ejadi, and there is no one in this world or any other who can break my spirit!"

He races across the roof, and launches himself at the next Wheel building. I follow, adjusting my shimmer settings, raising deflector flaps for heavy rain. Bador lands on the building's roof, rolls, flips up, and runs again without pause.

—Bador, I signal.

He doesn't break his stride, but swivels his face toward me. He's exasperated, but this is important.

—If Zohra built you, and deems it prudent to withhold information from you, isn't it for the best? I ask.

—Maybe it is, for them. But what does it leave me with? A lifetime of being a sidekick, running errands for Lina? Of playing quiet and obedient household pet for my mother, while she calls me Danil on purpose? I think not.

He lands on the next building and keeps running.

—And this is why I must leave Shantiport to follow my real dream, he signals.

—But your family needs you.

—I am programmed to love them, and I would die for them without a moment's hesitation, believe me. There was a time, in my youth, when I believed my whole destiny was to be with Lina. We were supposed to be inseparable. But we are just . . . not. And we can't fix that.

—So you will leave Shantiport, to do what?

—I was built to be great. I was built to be a space hero. And that is the destiny I must embrace.

—How is Boss Paneera's Ultimate Bot Showdown going to help you with any of that?

—It's happened before. Street legends, ordinary Shantiport bots who made it out. They won Paneera's tournament, got spotted by intergalactic hero-team managers or agents who watch such tournaments. They're out there in space right now. Chainsaw Tunu, Rehan Scorpionfist, Eve-rani Sanayal. From the mud to the stars. Adventure, treasure, immortal handsomeness, all the pewpew. And I will join them.

—Are you sure?

Bador looks at me, eyemojis question marks.

—Are you sure they went to space? I ask. Are you sure these former champions actually made it out of the crimelord's tournaments and all the street legends aren't just propaganda? I have not spent much time in your city, but it seems to be full of lies.

—Because why would any intergalactic space hero manager ever come to Shantiport, right?

—That's not what I meant.

—It's a fair question. Yes, all the past champions could be rusting in a sewer somewhere, or sold for parts. But I want to believe, Moku. And I want you to believe with me.

He soars across the dividing street-canal, and lands on the side of a temple-domed Peacock tower.

Light, everywhere. Above the towers of central Historio, spot-bot drones power up, massive beams of light flooding the skies in preparation. All over the neighborhood, holo-statues come to life, historical figures from various eras looping endless gestures of contemplation or patriotic fervor. Far above us, a Tiger Clan police-zep hovers in the clouds, reminding the audience who really runs the city. Camdrones swarm above the towers.

"Here we go," Bador says, and clambers swiftly up the tower's side. "Have a look around, Moku. If you spot Paneera's team, point me to them."

—How will I identify them?

—Organizing committee T-shirts? I don't know. You'll know them when you see them.

The ground shakes beneath us. A horrendous screech fills the sky. From the canal, just below us, a hideous figure rises, first a large lizard head breaking the muddy waters, then a tyrannosaurus-shaped body. A kaiju. Crocodile skin, stegosaurus spines on its back, larger-than-accurate arms and hands.

Bador reaches the Peacock tower roof and runs up its dome, where he finds a statue of a sari-clad nymph, and perches on its head. He's clearly visible now in spot-bot lights, crouching, poised to spring, watching the kaiju intently as it—vibescan, she—shakes herself, sending water and mounds of urban detritus cascading into the flooded streets, spraying a cloud of sludge in every direction. She rises to her full height. She's very tall, over half the height of the tower we're on.

"So middle class," Bador says beside me.

The kaiju sploshes past, and turns a corner at the next tower into a broad avenue heading toward the center of Historio Heights. She taps the corner building experimentally, and then swings her arm, smashing right through it. In a cloud of clevawall, plants, and rain, she raises her lizard head skyward and screams again. Light beams from the sky illuminate her as she lumbers forward, smashing more buildings as she goes, splashing through the streets, making waves with sweeps of her thick, spiked-club tail.

"I see why Lina thinks she's too big to take, but that's really because she's designed for the human gaze," Bador says, as casually as if we're all sitting in the family house watching the monster on a holo-feed. "They see her, they see a cloned dinosaur. Magic-thawed lizard god. Something. But any real combat-bot would know that's not a true fighter! She shouldn't be allowed out in public at all, if you have standards. Just human nostalgia bait."

—You're visible to several camdrones, I signal. I'll deactivate them.

"No, don't, I want to be seen. Listen and learn. This kaiju. Paneera's using her to demolish the neighborhood, clean up on gambling, then he'll get a city contract to build over the ruins. Skin's some kind of ultralight screencloth, or hologram. Would be patchy in sunlight. Underneath, a mediocre skeleton, some weapons. Mainly some construction tech sucking and shaping stuff into that dinosaur shape. I'd call her a clevabuilder, but she's probably an idiot."

I look up the entertainment feeds to see the backstories for tonight's fighters, but it's mostly just promos and shouting splainers and popups for betting platforms. I gather the kaiju's name is Fossila.

"I hope you're recording my meaningful commentary," Bador says. "And those key visuals—challenge against stormy backdrop, all of that."

"I am."

"So here's a thought—why don't you, you know, make a little documentary? We're here, good lighting, such great angles . . ."

I say nothing. He knows my views on this. He eyemojis an antique camera, but fortunately does not attempt to persuade me further because of a very large distraction.

A tower-rattling sizzle, followed by an earth-shaking crash, a dust cloud melting away in the rain, and up in the sky, a pillar of blue light from the heart of Historio. Under it, at the intersection of Historio's broadest avenue-canals, surrounded by Peacock towers, standing on a circular plinth over the shattered ruins of a statue of a Peacock emperor, is a giant mecha. Camdrones circle above his—I vibescan, nothing—its head as the rain washes it clean. Blocky human-shaped body, bright color patches over silver-white hull, about Fossila's size, impassive classical-statue face, glowing yellow eyes, several clunky weapons attached to its limbs, superfluous large helmet, martial stance. As it sees the dinosaur kaiju approach, it shifts its weight about, and cycles through a few power poses to indicate its excitement. A swinging drone-light beam catches its armor at just the right angle: it's dazzling.

Bador's thoughts spike in rage.

"At least the lizard's a bot," he says. "This one's just an insult, just cynical. There are humans controlling that soda can! This is supposed to be a bot-fight tournament!"

—His name is Mecha Emperor Ultrapower.

—Emperor my ass. It's a big drone is all. I name it Roboflop. Hey, you want to shut it down? You can, right?

—Probably too big. And this is not my function.

—Well I wish you joy in your functions.

The kaiju slows down as she sees Roboflop, and screams again in challenge.

—Humans are just so incredibly tacky, Bador signals. They see entry calls for a bot combat tournament, and they just have to tie toasters to their heads and apply. Anyone asks questions, they say they identify as bots! Bot allies! It's just wrong, and if it wasn't my one way off this trash planet, forget breaking in, I wouldn't even watch it.

He's actually vibrating with rage.

—I'm surprised you're so angry about this.

—You should be angry about it too. It's a complete violation.

The truth is humans and bots can't work together, it's impossible. I don't mean at the cyborg level, or any other single-mind hybrid. I mean, I have flesh bits. My parents built me to not know whether my flesh or my metal were in charge—to be able to survive both bullets and EMPs, to be greater than the sum of my neurons and circuits. That's just cool. But this is humans controlling parts that could make a great bot. And that's just gross. Depressing, really. Ah, good, management's here.

A menacing shape, twice Bador's size, descends from above us. A bot shaped like a giant wasp, striped in Tiger colours. He hovers above Bador, stinger-cannon pulsing and ready, but his attention is mostly on the kaiju as she lumbers toward the mecha. I look him up: he's famous. He's one of Paneera's most vicious security enforcers, ex–Tiger Clan police, and his name is Eboltas.

"Heyou monkey," Eboltas says.

"Heyou," Bador replies most courteously.

"You're deep in the fight zone. Forbidden. You'll get squished."

"Needed to see you actually. Well, any Paneera thug-bot I guess."

Now Bador has Eboltas's full attention.

"You want to die or what?" Eboltas asks.

"Not tonight, no."

"You think you're funny?" Eboltas's stinger shifts ever so slightly.

Bador considers this and decides wisely not to respond.

"Think I'm going to kill you," Eboltas says. "Who's your boss? Might kill them too."

"Don't kill me," Bador counteroffers. "I don't have a boss. I just want to join the tournament."

"I'm going to blast your face off now."

"Do not blast my face off now. I want to join the tournament. Tell me what I have to do."

"Apply next year and pay the entry fee."

"I applied this year and paid the entry fee. Scammed. Took money, then said I was too small."

"Ah, okay. Too small. Get out."

"Give my money back!"

"No."

"This is injustice!"

"Loud laughter. Welcome to Shantiport," Eboltas says.

"Listen, Eboltas. Your tournament is pathetic. Your fighters are weak. Anyone with any charisma has left Shantiport. Except me. I can make people watch. You need me."

"No."

"Look, the planet is dying. I can't wait till next year, there might not be a next year. And you don't want your ratings and your gambling hauls to be low, right? On your last season? I can fix that."

Eboltas taps the Paneera insignia on his chest, a bull skull wearing sunglasses.

"No," he says.

"Why not?"

"I don't like you."

Bador eyemojis hearts at him. "But I made you feel something," he says. "Here's my offer. You have two obsolete monsters wasting your time. If I take them both out, will you let me enter your tournament?"

Eboltas laughtracks. "You can't even get them to notice you."

"I'm serious. If I defeat them both, may I please enter your tournament?"

"If you defeat them both, you can meet Boss Paneera and he will consider it."

"Thank you."

Eboltas buzzes off toward the giants, who are now circling each other warily and very slowly in the center of Historio. The feeds are wild with excitement: the tournament has begun.

Mecha and kaiju run at each other and collide in a city-shaking clash. They grapple.

Bador's tail stiffens and rises. Flaps open up on his back, revealing glowing blue plasma-tubes. His body clicks and hums. He crouches, powers up. His arms press against his sides. A whistle of compressed air. A muttered laugh.

"Time to make this about me," he says.

CHAPTER FIVE

I follow Bador as he races toward the wrestling titans, scanning his mind for some sort of coherent battle plan: nothing. He races along tower walls, and as he draws close to the fight he extracts limpet speakers from his stomach-pouch and sticks them on towers, one speaker per tower. I notice that he's not using the claws he'd used earlier to attach himself to walls: he's sprouted gecko-embeds on his tail and hindlimbs to hold himself in place while his arms work the speakers. He keeps doing this, leaping across the avenues, until he's gone all around the fight in a circle, and run out of speakers. He waves at camdrones as he passes, but they ignore him: instead, they're all watching Fossila and Roboflop engaged in the first stage of their battle, which seems to consist of smacking one another slowly and loudly, swaying but not falling, and sending mud cascading in waves as they circle. Fossila wants to grab Roboflop and stick its head under her armpit: the mecha seems unenthusiastic about this plan, and is using its longer arms to swat Fossila's advances away.

Bador lands lightly on a ledge on the tower nearest to them, and begins another martial art moveset performance. I fly up to him, eager to read his battle-thoughts, and I'm disappointed by what I find. His plan for fighting and defeating the giants, whatever it is, doesn't seem to be his priority right now: he's hoping to draw the attention of the audience first. He's executing motion-captured move sequences from a vast archive of action dramas. He knows they aren't effective kill sequences unless he's fighting a partner who knows the appropriate dance steps, but he thinks they should be good for audience engagement. They are not. The camdrones show no interest.

After a while, he stops and stands still on his ledge, decides he needs to motivate himself and find his core, and reacquaint himself with his magnificent body. This I find pleasing: I've been so focused on Bador's mind since we met that I haven't really paid his body as much attention as I should have, and it will be good to see it from his own perspective—while secretly hoping that thinking about his body will encourage him to not get it battered by these two behemoths clearly too big for him to fight.

Bador reminds himself that Lina doesn't know what she's talking about: his core is rare, and precious. Possibly stolen or smuggled, which he approves of. His central tech was once an Adaptive Battle Unit, an advanced shapeshifting combat robot. There are very few left on the planet, they're mostly out in space doing military or scientific work. Bador enjoys feeling elite—much, much better, from the inside, than these fools he must vanquish here tonight.

He is distracted from further self-praise by a large fridge smashing into the wall right next to him. Finally, to my relief, Bador really pays attention to Fossila and Roboflop as opponents, not as scenery. He notes that Roboflop's fists appear to be covered in what looks like tar—some sort of poison attack? A fuel leak? Fossila's skin appears unbroken, so it's not her blood. She's gotten in some earnest claw-rakes so far, and Roboflop's got some dents on its chest armor, but nothing significant. Bador dismisses all of this as incompetence and weakness, but I can see the sparring titans are not as mediocre as he thinks they are. The towers around them already show extensive damage, and the fighting hasn't even heated up yet. Through opened-up walls, the insides of several prebuilt clevahomes are visible, furniture, tech, and art falling in showers, exposed gas and plumbing pipes adding to the infinite Shantiport mess. I wonder how many people these could have housed—but now is not the time for such thoughts. Bador has a plan.

If the camdrones won't come to him, he'll go where they're looking. He'll land on the giants' bodies, do his amazing moves until he draws their attention, and then get them to demolish each other while trying to catch him, and entertain the audience throughout by interacting in lewd ways with their heads and other body parts.

I have comments, but Bador's not interested. He jets off the ledge, performs a wholly unnecessary spin-move, and lands neatly on Fossila's shoulder.

And then he sinks right through it, into her body, and his thoughtstream is pure panic. I see the kaiju's leathery skin glitch for a second, a square of flat green where Bador disappeared. All Bador's thinking as he churns through her body is *gross gross gross gross*. And then he's out again, a blob of brown ooze spurting out of the kaiju, limbs flailing, hurtling toward a tower. He lands neatly, and runs faster than I've seen before, his body almost horizontal as he races away from the fight.

I approve of this racing away, and am disappointed when Bador slows down, and sits on an antique air-conditioner butt to reconsider his entire life. He'd seen that Fossila was sucking in local materials to build her body, but he hadn't realized she was made almost entirely of trash! A literal garbage monster, a waste management–bot at her core, not a construction-bot, not an amusement park inflatable. He's lucky he'd decided not to get olfact-sensors installed. The memory of the hot squelchiness of her insides makes him glad he is incapable of vomiting. He's also quite sure there are bits of Fossila lodged inside him forever.

As if shamed by his sheer loathing, Fossila raises her game. She charges at Roboflop, grapples with all her trash-filled power, picks the mecha up, and keeps charging, into a tower—and straight through. The tower collapses into another, and the battleground is once more transformed into a spreading cloud of concrete, glass, and dust. Fossila screeches, somewhere in the cloud: it's just a pre-recorded roartrack, but she sounds happy. Farther away, two more towers collapse. There's rubble everywhere as buildings that had been self-powering quietly for years come apart—a web of sparking cables, fires, explosions, burglar alarms, more thunder.

I turn to Bador, and am baffled to find he is now sitting on the air-conditioner butt in lotus position, as if this whole arena is a meditation retreat. I hope he is coming up with a new plan, and I hope that new plan involves continuing that running away he was doing so well just recently.

But no, he's just doing that motivational meditation thing again, finding his core. Again he is pleased with his Battle Unit center. He is proud of his genius parents—that they looked at his impressive hardware and then decided to make him even better, giving him several layers of additional body-mods, too-complex-to-scan regenerating synthflesh reservoirs, incredibly evolved cyborg brainware. And he is proud of himself, for being so complex that he'd exceeded even his parents' understanding—they'd measured his physical abilities constantly, but they had no idea how their synth innovations led to a child capable of such intense emotion. He is proud of himself for bringing himself up, for developing his own value systems based on unregulated popular culture tropes instead of the owner-clan warfare manuals and propaganda that dangerous bots normally grow up on. For defining his own form—monkey, not shapeshifting murder machine—in honor of his missing father and his fleeting memories of the time he was his sister's favorite person. For being himself, for choosing himself, for naming himself. He is Bador, and he is ready now.

Recharged with purpose, Bador makes his move. From the powerful limpet speakers he'd planted on the towers around us, or at least the towers still left standing, a mighty roar emerges: an Alpha Monkey Challenge. The speakers are better than anything Fossila and Roboflop have: the roars certainly sound like they came from a much larger monster. Bador catches the light, pounds his fists on his chest, makes several hopefully intimidating monkey gestures, then leaps from building to building in pursuit of the giants. He laughs out loud as he sees a few camdrones turning away from the rubble-covered monsters ahead and swooping in his direction. There's still more trash deep in his fur than he'd like, but the joy of not being ignored makes it all worthwhile. He waves at the camdrones, as he draws near Roboflop and Fossila again, and leaps off a tower. I've been so focused on admiring him that I've not found time to worry about what he plans to do when he lands on them this time.

He runs his boosters in reverse when he's mid-soar over the swirling, junk-filled street, so for a few moments it looks as if he's standing in the air. He flings out an arm, panels on forearm and wrist sliding, twisting, opening, to reveal—

"Laser torowal!"

He admires, in advance, the brilliance of the light-sword that will emerge from his arm.

No sword emerges from his arm, and he's about to crash into Roboflop; a last-second jet-boost sends him soaring above the mecha and across the street. Back on a wall, enraged, Bador shakes his arm in a frenzy, but his sword refuses to emerge. Another hardware failure. There are always excuses: Fossila sludge, the rain, the dirt, the stress; but he's lost the camdrones again. Some sort of sonic burst from Fossila's chest has propelled Roboflop onto the next street, and the drones follow Fossila's trail of utter havoc as she charges the mecha again.

Bador curses and leaps in pursuit. He's a good curser: his expletives are as rich, fragrant, and colorful as the assorted Shantiport effluvia still stuck to his body, and I remind myself to tell him, later, that my language filters are family friendly, which limits my ability to absorb a significant fraction of the things he says and thinks.

A glowing sword emerges up ahead. Not Bador's—a giant blade

has sprung from the body of Roboflop, a traditional mecha battle-ender. Roboflop's human controllers have had enough.

Bador bounces off a wall and goes low, skittering over mounds of rubble. The rain and the battle have transformed Historio's canal-streets into urban rapids, and Bador's almost decapitated by a massive torn power cable dancing in the churning waters, streaming sparks near a small whirlpool. He looks at it, at the monsters up ahead, and knows what he wants to do. He leaps over the cable, and gathers speed, jumping over a whole archipelago of fancy-home designer-lifestyle debris islands with admirable precision.

A short distance ahead, the monsters lumber toward endgame. Roboflop swings its blade, and Fossila screams as it slashes across her torso. She leaps back, sending sheets of water and garbage everywhere. She lands heavily, shudders, and stomps: chunks of buildings topple around her. She bulges, glitches, grows in size, her skin-hologram flickering and readjusting as she pulls more mud into her body. Roboflop's sword sizzles, powered up, but the mecha steps back in a defensive stance as cannons emerge from Fossila's claws and mouth, and spit missiles at the puppet giant. We watch the missiles wiggle and swerve as they stream smokily and all find their mark: there are explosions all over Roboflop's armor; it totters, stumbles on rubble, and falls heavily on its massive metal ass.

An opportunity: Bador side-tabs his developing plan to seize it. He swivels and leaps, screaming obscenities, toward the downed mecha. The camdrones follow him as he shouts "Thunder-God Power Stomp!" and lands perfectly on Roboflop's impassive face. Not content with this blatant victory-theft, he strikes a victorious pose, thumps his chest, replays his roar, looks directly at the camdrones, and prepares to begin his post-match speech. Which is when Roboflop vibrates a little, grabs Bador with frightening speed, and calmly tosses him aside. I pick up speed and give chase as Bador soars in a high arc and hits a tower wall with a worrying thunk.

By the time I catch him, he's sliding slowly downward, too depressed to even remove his face from the wall, trailing a smear of green-black sludge. He is just a small loser monkey-bot in a big loser city. But if he knows anything, he knows this: he deserves better . . . better than a life trapped here, on this moist and uncaring rock. This is a new low.

He's run out of tower to slide down: he grips the wall, finally, as his tail meets water. I hover at his side, wondering whether I should break protocol, place myself beneath him, and lift him up. Someone needs to.

"Don't try to help me," Bador says.

I radiate objectivity.

"Go away. Just leave me."

—Bador, do you want to go home?

—Sounds like a good idea. I'm running low on charge anyway.

—Let's go.

His eyes flicker, fade, and then light up again.

—No. One last try.

He speeds back toward the duel. Roboflop's back on its feet, sword in hand. Fossila, now grown even larger, takes another sword-swing on the arm. As Roboflop regains balance and swings again, the kaiju steps forward and catches the blade with both hands. Sparks and trash gush everywhere in a horrendous fountain. Fossila grabs the mecha's wrist, screaming, and tears the sword away. She raises it high in the air. Lightning flashes. Roboflop stumbles on rubble, wobbles, regains its balance.

And then Fossila brings the sword down. The mecha dives to one side, but not fast enough: the blade catches it on the shoulder, and neatly cuts off its left arm. The severed limb falls, and before it hits the waters a spherical escape pod zooms away: there was, as Bador suspected, a human pilot in the arm. He glares at the pod as it swooshes past us.

Bador knows there are at least three other humans in there, probably one in the mecha's chest or head as well. So his to-do list is simple: Forget the camdrones. Forget the audience. Fight with focus. Kill the kaiju. Kill the mecha. Keep the humans alive, ideally save their lives, and win over the audience. Twist: he hadn't forgotten them at all, that was a ruse, he is awesome. Through all this, there's a thoughtcurrent that surprises me, a whisper of disappointment. He'd expected he'd enjoy this more, but is resolved to push forward until he does. There is no room for doubt, it is time for action.

He dives into the street-waters.

Roboflop's remaining pilots are probably horrified by their comrade's abrupt exit from the fight: the mecha's staggering to its feet, waving its arm about, not doing anything remotely smart. Fossila strides toward it, raising the sword again, but something's off with her as well: her skin glitches, her overextended machinery creaks and shudders. She's grown unmanageably massive. But she rallies, and slowly, jerkily, the sword keeps moving upward.

Bador leaps out of the waters some distance behind Roboflop, huge power cables in either hand. Moving precisely, not stunting for the camdrones at all, he secures one end of a cable to an exposed pillar, then leaps across the street and pulls it tight to another. He checks for tautness. Once satisfied, he does it all again with another cable, slightly higher. I zoom closer to catch his thoughts: he does not appear to be having any. He dives back into the street-canal, ignoring the floating muck.

I notice the rain has stopped, I'm not sure when, too many observation targets. The sky above is clearing, lightening. Sunrise is due any moment.

Roboflop waits for Fossila to raise the sword, then leaps forward and grabs the hilt. Both behemoths fire at each other from body-cannons: both ignore the explosions, ignore their own traitorous masses, focusing only on the struggle for the sword.

Bador jets out of the water, lands on Roboflop's legs, and scampers up the mecha's body. He has to keep banter to a minimum now: multitasking slows down even his superb brain. He clambers up Roboflop's back, over its shoulder. He holds out his arm.

This time, his sword lights up, burning red, as the first rays of the morning sun find Shantiport's rooftops.

He leaps off Roboflop's shoulder, and disappears with his glowing blade into Fossila's chest. The trash welcomes him back, like a long-lost son coming home.

The last time he'd wandered around inside Fossila, he'd found something he'd expected from a middle-class kaiju: predictable design. Whoever had built the monster had followed old-school animal-bot builds: when designing a machine in the rough shape of an animal, they put the valuable bits and the vulnerable bits, from power sources to strategy brains, in places that corresponded to source-animal organs, sometimes shielded with internal armor where bone masses or organs worked in nature.

Bador's parents had once told him that if a really smart bot had been allowed to design other bots, the last place they would put their children's hearts is anywhere an enemy who wanted to rip hearts out of bodies would find them.

Fossila has not been built by a really smart bot.

The camdrones zoom closer, and are rewarded with a ghastly sight: Bador, a nightmarish blob with a sizzling sword in one hand, flying out of the kaiju's back. In his other hand is a filth-covered power-pulsing sphere his own size. Fossila's heart.

The kaiju balloons up, torrents of mulch cascading off her body. She collapses on Roboflop. They stagger, embracing, Fossila disintegrating, and then Roboflop trips over the cables stretched across the street. An endless, frozen moment, as the giants sway, then totter, then sway, then give up, falling together like asteroids in love. There's an almighty splash, and when the camdrones can see again, all they see is a mound of garbage and a mega-sword sizzling in the water beside it.

"Now to save the pilots!" Bador shouts.

But before he can stage a heroic rescue, four escape pods burst out of the trash-hill and soar away.

The camdrones chase them, but within a few seconds receive orders from the broadcasters: something has changed. A new player has entered the game. They swoop back, to find and question the mysterious new contender.

But Bador has vanished.

CHAPTER SIX

I find Lina at Borki Bazaar the next evening, and inform her that Bador is waiting for her in a back alley in case she wants to see him but not be seen with him. I don't tell her how much he's enjoying his new citywide notoriety, or that he is lurking in the alley in a terribly attention-seeking disguise, muttering to himself in accents copied from dramas.

She doesn't want to meet him. She borrows a hoverscooter from a fruit-stall owner, and rides eastward, presumably toward wherever it is she has set the location marker for her planned meeting with the Not-prince. I follow her. Bador follows as well, over the rooftops, attempting to stay out of Lina's sight. I cannot tell if she knows he's following or not.

She rides the hoverscooter out of the central zone, eastward to Gostapol, the floodproof football stadium, made from the ruins of an Anchor battleship shot down during the last world war. The stadium's in a very quiet neighborhood, mostly abandoned due to flooding; as I deactivate the sentry drones at the stadium entrance and Lina rides through, the only sound audible is the singing of trees from the nearby Sage-Poet Gardens. Lina takes the scooter all the way to the permapitch, then hops off it and walks to the center of the field. The sky is clear and there are even a few stars or spaceships visible: already an unusual night for Shantiport, and no doubt destined to get more unusual very soon.

Bador drops down to the field from the stadium's celebrity seating area.

"If you want to yell at me, yell at me," he calls. "Let's get it over with, let's move on to the next part of the plan."

"I don't need you tonight, thanks," Lina shouts. "I'm glad you allowed Moku to come, though."

"I chose to be here by myself," I say at low volume.

She looks at me, and winks. "Could have guessed that," she whispers.

"Hey!" Bador calls, coming closer. I feel his guilt, his annoyance at feeling guilty, his overall nervousness. "Give me something to do! And don't be mad, I had to take my shot!"

"I'm not mad," Lina says. "I said what I needed to say, you did what you needed to do. But, Bador, I think you should stay away from the house for a bit. We don't need gangster-bots crashing in to hunt you down, or camdrones looking for footage of your humble origins."

"They can't come to the house," Bador says. "The rules forbid it."

Lina snorts. "The rules. Paneera's tournament has rules."

"A really long list of rules! Want to know what they are?"

"No," Lina says, and Bador eyemojis sad faces. He comes closer, bruising the permagrass.

"What's the plan for tonight?" he asks. Lina looks at him in silence, and now it's clear to me from the set of her jaw: she's really angry with him.

"You have houses you use around the city, right?" she asks.

"Amazing houses. All the best neighborhoods."

"You should stay in those, and check in with me or Moku from time to time. At least until the tournament ends."

"I meant the plan about Juiful," Bador says. "Have you reconsidered the kidnap and rescue thing?"

"I have, thanks. But you know what, Bador? I'm not much of a group brainstorm idea person. So I think I'll just keep my plans to myself from now on, like I used to. It's safer, and I don't want to have to depend on anyone else for ideas anyway."

"Cool," Bador says. "I understand."

"Good. Good luck with your bot combat tournament. Now get out of here, it's time for Juiful to show up." She turns away from him, and looks around the stands.

—You take care her of her, okay? Bador signals.

—Okay. Are you all right?

—Of course, who cares, I'm fine. This is just her tantrum style.

—Okay.

—She'll need something soon enough, and then she'll be all oh, Bador, you genius, I love you again.

—Okay.

Bador leaves. I stay.

Lina hums to herself as she waits for the Not-prince. A few minutes pass, and she turns to me.

"It was nice while it lasted, I guess, the whole team thing," she says. "It was fun saying things out loud. I'll remember it."

"What do you need me to do now?" I ask.

"Nothing, I'm just glad you're here."

She looks around the stands again, and it's clear she's growing impatient.

"Half of me is hoping he won't come," she says. "If he shows up, whatever happens, I'm worried it will end with my face on the newsfeeds, or Bador's, or the whole family's. Faces, with a price on our head. That's how we do things here, by the way. In a minute, your reality changes, your allies and enemies change, and your whole city turns against you."

"If he does come, I will stun all drones, but should I warn you about bots and hidden human bodyguards?"

She thinks about it. "Only if he knows they're there," she says.

"It's not like he's someone I trust either way, so it's best to treat this like a negotiation with the whole clan. But I'd like to know if he thinks he's tricking me."

"Understood," I say. Though honestly I don't understand what she's doing or why I'm lying about my own comprehension of it. Impressing my user is not my function.

A gentle breeze ripples across the permagrass on the football field.

"Look up," I say. "He's here."

A two-seater all-terrain transparent bubble-sphere luxurycart descends from the sky, held aloft by strategically placed grip-drones. I look up the model: it's called a bubblu, and is really expensive. I look around, extending my senses in all directions: no more drones, no bots. He's come alone, as promised.

The bubblu lands on the grass and its front pops open, revealing Juiful. He's dressed in billowy black silk trousers and a maroon robe, open in the front, exposing an expanse of muscular chest and abdomen. He's lounging on a broad reclining plush pilot seat that seems designed for cuddling rather than aviation. The expression on his face, lips out, eyes half-closed, is presumably supposed to be sensuous. There's a small cabinet behind him at the bubblu's rear, containing wine, crockery, various packaged foods, and other miscellaneous objects whose purpose I cannot determine. There is music as well, possibly erotic, drifting across the stadium from the bubble's flight control panel.

He pats the empty space on the seat next to him once. Then he takes a closer look at Lina, in her work clothes and heavy boots, at the all-weather clevasuit tied around her waist, at her face as she struggles not to burst into laughter, and withdraws his hand mid-pat as if stung. He wraps himself in the robe, covering his torso.

"Oh no," he says.

"Greetings to you as well, Not-prince," Lina says, bowing.

He rubs his nose.

"I appear to have misread your desire for privacy," he says after a while. "I am sorry."

"You want to get out of your floaty sex-copter and go for a walk?" Lina asks.

Juiful hops out of the bubble and onto the grass. His feet are bare, and he's clearly unused to rough surfaces: he takes a few tentative steps. Lina tosses him her clevasuit.

"Put it on," she says. "It has sock extensions, and we'll buy you some shoes."

Juiful holds the clevasuit away from his body as if afraid it might attempt to strangle him.

"Do you actually intend to give me a tour of my own city?" he asks.

"That's the plan."

"May I ask why?"

Lina shrugs. "It was your idea! I didn't question it. I thought it might be something you were actually interested in. I just made a list, and showed up."

It's her turn to look embarrassed.

"I guess this is my Joyfur moment," she says. "You do have access to much more of both the city and its secrets than I ever will. I just thought there might be a few things . . . I guess I didn't think."

"I insist you give me the tour I asked for," Juiful says.

He struggles with the clevasuit while Lina looks away politely, and eventually conquers it. It's tight on him, so again he ends up mostly bare-chested, but Lina seems to not mind this at all.

"Where do you want to take me?" he asks. "I should warn you that we will have a few hours at best before they discover I am not in the palace and come to find me."

"I had hoped we would have all night," Lina says. "There's a lot I want to tell you, and a really excellent dawn breakfast place by the river . . ."

"Delightful words under other circumstances," Juiful says. "But we do not have all night. Private nights outside the palace are not a luxury I am allowed."

He hops from foot to foot.

"You must think me a bit of a fool," he says. "But I promise I am capable of walking. Now lead the way."

Lina hesitates. Her eyes flicker to me, and then toward the bubblu. I'm not sure what she wants me to do.

"If we only have a few hours," she says. "Maybe we should use your bubble after all. Is it . . . clean?"

"Very clean," Juiful says, offended. I swoop into the luxurycart, and check again: no drones, no surveillance at all. This must be one of the few places where the city's rulers can really have privacy. I wonder what it is used for apart from romantic trysts.

Lina walks up to the bubblu and hops in, sitting daintily on the edge of the seat. Juiful sits at the other end, primly, as far away from her as physically possible.

"It is cleaned thoroughly, emptied out and refurnished every day, because my father likes to take his friends out for drinks and secret conversations while soaring above the city and things sometimes get messy," Juiful says. "Now please sit a little closer, or you will fall off when we rise. I assure you I will not embarrass myself further this evening."

Lina looks at me. It's all too cramped for me to say anything safely, so I lower and raise my front portion in my best attempt at a nod. She nods back.

I leave, attach myself to the bubblu's rear, and patch into its comms.

"I want to thank you, first of all, for doing this, and for not bringing up my troublesome background," Lina says. "And tell you that if there are things that you are not allowed to see, I could get into trouble for showing them to you. And avoiding trouble is important to me."

"Oh, surveillance, spies in the skies, that sort of thing?" Juiful makes a dismissive gesture. "Forget about it. Everyone's given up on that unpleasantness, the spybosses have all left, or will leave soon."

"Whatever the bosses are doing, the system hasn't gone anywhere. It's not the same for people like me."

"The person who used to run the whole secret ugly Tiger Clan security stuff is the vizier—sorry, in Shantiport that would be the Blacktiger Nayeb. He's gone on holiday. All the people who were trying to remove our clan from power or kill us have given up and moved out. No one really cares anymore. Also—you're with me now. You're under my protection."

Juiful grins, and smacks himself gently in the face.

"I've just known you for a few minutes, and already I have told you so many things I should not have," he says. "I'm usually the quiet one, the listener. They were right when they said you were dangerous."

Lina laughs, and after a few seconds of tapping at the bubblu's controls steers it up into the air as if she'd been piloting city-ruler personal aircraft all her life. Juiful leans back, and watches the beauty of nighttime Shantiport blossom beneath and around them. Lina steers the bubblu toward the heart of the city, and they're both silent as they take in the expanse of the central zone's night-lights, large holo-statues coming to life by the river in the distance, roof-forests swaying in a breeze. The bubblu's dome is a map of fog and rivulets, and ever-shifting streaks of multicolored lights. She flies through tall central-zone towers, slowly, adjusting to the bubblu's responses, and as she steers the bubblu around a residential tower, and they're both distracted, for a few moments, by hundreds of people's lives flashing by in the windows, I notice that their breathing has synchronized, their bodies have relaxed, and they both appear remarkably comfortable.

"I should get you to take visiting dignitaries around the city," Juiful murmurs. "I'd like to see what you say when they ask if Shantiport's drowning because its people are lazy."

"Oh, I get that on my bus all the time," Lina says. "'How come people live here when it keeps getting colonized?' 'Was it really the richest city in the world before the Anchor Clan sailed in, or is that just golden-aging?' 'Why all these big buildings?' 'Where's the poverty?' I don't say anything. I smile and change the subject."

"As do I."

Lina steers the bubblu to the southeastern edge of the central zone, to New Shantiport Link Road, and turns to Juiful, who looks a little puzzled as he surveys the sprawl of abandoned industrial neighborhoods spreading southward from the central zone, and the sky-scraping Antim residence, shooting out of its derelict neighborhood to earn its Shantiport street name.

"The Erection," Juiful says. "Everyone's seen that. Why are we here?"

Around Antim's tower, under a permasmog cloud, lie ancient complexes made of glass and twisted steel, and tower blocks of concrete modernized into giant printers. In the era of the Wheel Clan's decay, the city's tycoons lived there, and used their tech to rule the city as gods, controlling governments and economies as they pleased.

"I don't want to spend our time together complaining to you about the Tiger Clan," Lina says. "Especially since we don't have all night. Your clan is what it is, and does what it does, and I don't want to hold you hostage in midair and make that list while you wonder whether it would be rude to make me disappear. Maybe someday, later, when you have any reason to trust me."

"Thank you," Juiful says.

"But there are other things you need to be told, about the people the Tigers work with closely. That's why this is where your Shantiport tour begins."

She keeps talking as she steers the bubblu farther south and west, toward the river, and then follows its curve back all the way around the central zone up to Paneera's domain, Oldport in the west. She tells Juiful about the dark stories behind Shantiport's gentrification projects, force-evacuated and rebuilt neighborhoods sold to investors who left long ago or are now heading off to new space homes, while the rest of the city drowns and people die of diseases that were supposedly eradicated centuries ago. She tells him about the river itself, and how builder-cartel bots are flooding Shantiport on purpose, sabotaging every other bot trying to desilt and unclog the drains and manage the river and the flooding, and how the same builders are picking up flood-proofing, reservoir-building, dyke-bot, and gigasponge construction contracts from the Tigers. How all of this is driving people into poverty and homelessness and debt, until they get delinked, and then are picked up by Prowlers, forced into space labor crews, and sold off-planet. How the city is trapped between its rulers, its oligarch, and its crimelord, who may have their own differences, but always somehow manage to work together in the end.

I've seen Lina act in many ways in the few days I've known her, but if I had to pick the real Lina, this would be my guess: angry, passionate, resolute. Every other time I've seen her perform she's been focused on whoever she's in character for. It probably helps her act, helps her achieve her goals in the moment. But now she seems to have forgotten that Juiful is even present. I don't know if she'd planned to display so much of what looks to me like absolutely honest emotion, or whether Juiful has outplayed her at listening. He doesn't interrupt, doesn't make any expressions of surprise or horror, doesn't even reveal whether any of this is new information. He makes no attempt to excuse or absolve himself either, which surprises me.

Unless—could it be that he is not really listening? Because he's watching her very intently, and from the way he's looking at her face, her eyes, her lips, her hands, responding more to her gestures than to her words, I worry that he's letting all her revelations flow past him, and focusing instead on whether he should leap at her and kiss her or not.

She takes him northward, past Historio into the suburbs, and shows him a convoy of AntimCo trucks, a human safari, where tourists go to ghost towns by night to watch Prowlers capture the poor, and sometimes hunt with them as well.

"We should go back," Juiful says. "It's unsafe here, even for me."

Lina calms herself, and steers the bubble southward. They say nothing for a long while. Lina seems lost in her own thoughts, and Juiful seems lost in Lina.

"Through all of this, you've avoided mentioning Shakun Antim by name unless absolutely necessary," Juiful says. "But it's clear you think he is behind most of Shantiport's problems—except, of course, the ones caused by my clan, who you have every reason to hate."

"True," Lina says. "I know you are friends with Antim, but—"

"My father is the real power in Shantiport, and he tries his best—the problem is often Tiger Central and its absurd demands. Shakun is an oligarch, of course, and he has a terrible reputation because he's such a show-off and he never shuts up, but he's misunderstood. He says and does really stupid things sometimes, but he loves the city. His AntimCo executives, they're the ones doing all the terrible things you told me about. Not him. He's trying to fix things. I know him well. He could have lived like a prince anywhere in the world, but he chose here."

"You're not behind Tiger Clan violence in the city either," Lina says. "But it is done in your name. AntimCo executives answer to one man."

"I just can't believe Shakun would do any of this," Juiful says, his voice shaking a little. "I—my family, the clan, the city—everyone owes him so much."

He shakes his head, and looks at her with suspicion.

"Why are you telling me all this?" he asks. "What do you want me to do?"

"Nothing," Lina says. "I just thought you should take this tour before you got married and left Shantiport. I thought someone should show you, so when you rule your own city-state, or planet, you won't let things come to this."

He nods, and looks at her with wonder. "This took courage," he says. "I appreciate it."

"Not the night you were expecting," she says. "But I love this trash city, and I'm glad I got to show you some of it."

He leans forward, his eyes shining, but before he can say anything an alarm beeps on the bubblu's control panel.

Seven shapes zoom through the night sky, hurtling toward the Not-prince's craft from the south. Sleek black hoverbikes, each bearing a black shape. Tiger-headed bots, smaller than Juiful's market bodyguards but much more deadly, I suspect. They surround the bubblu with frightening speed.

A holo-call rings on the control panel. The Not-prince takes it. A black tiger head appears inside the bubble, and I see real fear in Lina's eyes.

"You are surrounded," says the tiger-bot. "Descend at once, and surrender. If the Not-prince is harmed in any way—"

"I'm fine, you idiots," Juiful snarls. "Go away."

"Not-prince, you are needed at the palace at once. Your companion is to be arrested."

"My companion is to be escorted home, and then left alone. I will do the first part. Do you think, with all your skills, you can manage the rest? If the slightest harm should come to her after this, you will all lose your heads."

"Our sincere apologies, Not-prince. But as you are aware, carnal activities are best conducted with prior scheduling or within the palace, as security concerns—"

"Go away!" Juiful shouts. "I'll be back in a bit," he mutters after a second.

The tiger-bots go away.

"Well, now you've met the Blacktiger secret police," Juiful says, and sighs. "I'm sorry."

"I'm going to disappear soon, I guess," Lina says. "But this was . . . nice? Thank you for listening."

"Lina," Juiful says with some urgency in his voice. "What you told me today, I won't forget—but you need to be careful. This isn't a city where you can trust people."

She nods.

He rolls his eyes, and smacks himself on the head.

"I don't know why I just said that," he says. "You obviously know it a lot better than I do. Here's something you might not know, though—rulers tend to not be the smartest people. And this is not something that they want the public to know, so they tend to fill that void by surrounding themselves with brilliance. With intelligence, with courage, with skill, cunning, beauty. Come with me."

"Sorry, what?"

"Come with me! I want you on my staff."

"What?"

"That came out wrong," Juiful says, and blushes. "I need a team of people around me that I can trust. Shantiport is over. It's drowning. It's rumored that this whole world is ending. When I leave, I want you to come with me. Bring your family, if you like."

She blinks, and looks at him with a surprise I would have thought was completely genuine if she hadn't told me this was her goal all along.

"I would love to," she says. "Yes. But."

"But?"

"I believe Shantiport can be saved too."

Juiful nods. "We will discuss this, and more, when we meet next."

He reaches into the cabinet behind the seat, pulls out a little sticker, and peels it off.

He holds Lina's hand, longer than strictly necessary, looks into her eyes, and attaches the sticker to her right wrist. It's a temptatt in the form of a tiger's paw.

"That sticker is a Pugmark, indicating the favor of the palace," he says. "It should protect you from all the Tiger Clan's lesser evils. It also empowers you to walk into the palace anytime you want, and ask for me. No one will harm you, or even question you. There are places in my home where no one is allowed to watch or listen, and there we will discuss what we can save together, and how."

"I will see you soon, then," Lina says.

As the bubblu descends over Barigunj, her eyes glow.

CHAPTER SEVEN

Bador runs over a series of broken shipping containers that lie in the Oldport mud, angled and strewn and stacked like a giant's discarded toy building bricks, his soles doing a fine job of gripping the rusting metal without slowing him down. He's nervous, ready for a fight, and with good reason—an invitation to visit Boss Paneera is often a one-way trip—but Bador's also worried about tournament contenders looking to eliminate him before he can even officially join. Our appointment with Eboltas is for noon, but we've been approaching the location where we're supposed to meet him in a wide spiral for at least an hour, through Oldport's wide range of decayed shipping-themed architecture.

I'm annoyed with him: I spent most of last night searching for him, wandering around the city, going to several of his hideouts, and not finding him until dawn, meditating and charging in the sun on the rooftop water-tank near Dekho Plaza. But that was just a logistical difficulty: I find it far more disturbing that he got a message from Lina in the morning, asking him to come home, and has decided to ignore it, and run around in wide circles in Oldport gangland instead. He thinks this will teach Lina that she can't just expect him to be at her disposal all the time, that if he wants him to respond to her messages, she should reply to his. This is the first time in months that she's even sent him a message.

When I heard this, I asked Bador to come back to Oldport later, after making sure Lina was not in any danger, or to send me to his family home to check on her. He refused.

Oldport lies to the west of the central zone on the city side of the river, and is unofficially a separate town under Paneera's domain, which the Tigers only enter to smash things at appropriate moments during negotiations with Paneera and lesser crimelords. Sometimes we see broken, glow-painted Tiger-bot parts strung up on poles to commemorate these incursions. Most of Oldport was built in layers matching the river's expansion, clustering eastward from the ancient port that gave Shantiport its name long ago. Forgotten now are its Elephant and Anchor Clan glory days, when it had been among the greatest ports in the world and the origin point of Shantiport's world-culture-center status. Generations had passed, other clans and nature had ensured its demise, and the river had defeated the Tiger Clan's attempt to build a new port. The automated megaships that rule the oceans now, braving even tsunamis, are simply too large to sail upriver to Shantiport's embattled docks.

In ancient times, before the city-state era, now-Shantiport had been where the impoverished and helpless from all over the then-colony had been packed into ships as indentured labor and pushed across the oceans. Today, Shantiport is again a hub to launch the unlinked into the unknown, and so it is fitting that its greatest crimelord holds court at the scene of some of its greatest crimes.

Bador's convinced that Paneera's kept henchpeople lying in wait for us. My own guess, confirmed thus far, is that Bador is the least of Paneera's concerns, and the meeting is likelier to be a joke than anything more deadly, but when Bador asked me for an estimate and a strategy, I chose, wisely I believe, to say nothing.

Far above us, there's a flash in the sky as a spaceship makes its way through the upper atmosphere, above Shantiport's airspace. The river slumbers, vast and timeless, to the west, its expanse stretching to the far horizon, its surface broken by the jutting ruins

of ships and buildings. In every other direction is a rusty waste-
land of shipping containers, not all empty: many contain human
dwellings, stored sleepmode bot troops, and smuggled hoards of
everything imaginable. The container-grid stretches from land to
the river, and we cross intermittent clearings with aquaponic gardens, solar-panel clusters, and failed embankments. To the south
lie mud-spattered geodesic domes and churning waters where bots
are raising the spine of what might grow up to be a bridge.

Right at midday, we reach our location pin and find Eboltas
waiting with two backup wasp-bots carrying stinger-guns, and a
thug-bot with mud splattered all over his chunky legs. Bador leaps
toward them and makes a grand flourish as he lands.

"Follow," says Eboltas, entirely unimpressed.

They lead us into a shipping container that turns out to be a
tunnel leading to an underground complex—I do not understand
why anyone would want to build tunnels next to a hungry river in
a city that is sinking, but . . . Shantiport.

Paneera's burrow gets more and more modern as we go farther
underground. The engineering is impeccable—at no point do I see
any seepage, nor any damp patches on the walls, and this would be
praiseworthy even aboveground. We pass a set of rooms that look
like a remote hospital hub, with humans and bots in white coats
surrounded by tech performing remote surgery; an outsourced military drone war-game room; and an examination-cheat hall full of
proxy students. On another level, in a winding corridor dotted by
locked doors on either side, we pass a line of five bots trudging by
with identical prints of an incredibly famous lost historical icon, no
doubt to adorn the hidden collections of five oligarchs.

"Don't look around too much," Eboltas says. "It's bad for your
eyes."

We enter an elevator that sits under a massive arch made up of
sculptures of many pigeons humping many surveillance cameras,
and a short ride later are in Paneera's lair.

As a crimelord den, it doesn't disappoint: it looks like someone took a gigantic submarine, scooped out all the equipment, stuck it far underground, and then built a replica of an ancient cathedral in it. We walk through a central line of marble pillars, behind which lie dark alcoves suitable for dragging people into. A quick scan reveals closed circular doors lining the walls, no doubt leading to many exciting deaths, possibly involving hungry fish. On the ceiling, a cluster of synthhives have been built for flying bots. Behind the thrones at the far end on the wall is a huge set of looping holopics of Paneera greeting world leaders. Below the throne dais, a gallery of wide, low benches and charging posts, and a mind-boggling range of human gangsters both basic and exosuited, and a range of thug-bots. It would take just a few seconds for the whole hall to transform into a bristling army on foot and wheel, plus a death-swarm in the air.

Paneera certainly looks like he's having a good time. He sits on one of the massive thrones, attractive ladies draped around his human shoulders, occasionally popping historical realsnacks into his mouth from collectors-item packaging. To his right, his sari-clad bot wife, Gladly, sits on an identical throne, playing with her pet dodo. Paneera's a third-generation crime boss, though his legend claims he murdered his way to self-made power. Everything about him is Shantiport-iconic: his shining shaven head, massive torso covered in scars, augments and tattoos both tech and decorative, embedded monocle-bot, extremely illegal hologram face-augs that make sure he looks different to everyone. His mechanical arms are currently detached, their slip-on shoulder joints suspended above him.

Bador is upset that Paneera isn't appearing before us in holoform, or at least behind a protective screen: it's almost as if he does not find Bador even slightly dangerous. There hasn't even been a cursory humiliating scan or patdown: what if he had been an assassin? Not noticing his feelings, Eboltas points Bador toward a small line of people to one side of the hall, waiting for their turn to approach the kingpin.

Bador's feelings are mollified when the person ahead of him in line, a pirate-looking fellow in an all-terrain exosuit, pulls out a gun and attempts to shoot Paneera with it. Before he can do so, a single line of red light appears above him from an alcove, there's a sizzling noise, and the would-be assassin's head disappears in smoke and sludge. Cleaner-bots scurry out from the shadows and dispose of the remains: Paneera and Gladly don't even react beyond smirks and shrugs. Bador shuffles anxiously, not sure whether he's supposed to wait or step over the murder scene, but then Paneera notices him, and laughs.

"Floater monkey! Come here, come here."

Bador shuffles forward, prayerful hands on his eyemojis, normal swaggering walk carefully modified.

"I wanted to see the bot that ruined last night's fight," Paneera says, his voice a deep, mostly-human rumble. "And hear from his own mouth why he deserved to stay alive."

"With the greatest respect—"

"Skip segment."

"I wanted to show you I deserved to be a contender in your tournament," Bador says. "I paid my entry dues but then got sidelined for being too small. Unfair. So I defeated the two biggest fighters. And the audience loved it."

"The audience loves whatever it's told to love," Paneera says. "Do you know what you've done, monkey, what you've cost me?"

Bador is silent.

"Thanks to you, all the great fighters I was trying to import from around the world have refused to come to Shantiport," Paneera says. "Can't guarantee safe working conditions, adherence to rules and standards, it seems. My great gift to the city, ruined. Prestige, punctured!"

"Calm now," Gladly says. "Wouldn't have come anyway, bloody snobs. Would they demand safe working conditions if they were fighting to the death in richer cities?"

Paneera growls. "And now if I let you in, what am I going to do with all the other bots your size who will demand I let them in as well? There is a chicken-bot who wants to fight. A chicken!"

"Boss Paneera, I'm guessing many of these contenders borrowed from you to pay your entry fees," Bador says. "So they'll end up working for you anyway, won't they? And if people bet on them, if they are allowed to compete, won't you end up with even more money?"

Paneera swivels his monocle-bot toward Gladly. "Smart monkey, eh?" he grumbles. Gladly smiles.

"A little too smart, maybe." He turns toward Bador. "You interrupted my tournament, messed around on my turf. Violated tradition. That was not respectful," Paneera says. "You may have heard how I feel about disrespect."

"Respect for tradition is what gives me the power to kick all kinds of ass," Bador says. "I filled out the traditional application. Paid the traditional fee. And respect? I asked your servant for permission before touching your fighters. If anyone should be punished, it's him."

"Hmm." Paneera taps his monocle-bot and they extend to scan Bador. "You have no chance of winning."

"I am undefeated."

"What is your strategy?"

"No spoilers."

Paneera's smile grows less warm.

"I mean, sir, if I told you my plan you would lose interest in me at once," Bador says. "I just want a chance to win your favor."

"Tragic backstory," Gladly says. "Mental imbalance. Revenge motivation."

"Commonplace," Paneera says.

"You were a scrappy outsider yourself once," Bador says. "I want to be like you."

"Look at this," Paneera says. "Flattery and all. Boring."

A red dot appears on Bador's forehead.

"I want to be a space hero!" Bador shouts.

The hall falls silent.

"Maybe unusual," Gladly says. "Ambition is there."

"I want to get out of this city, and be a space adventurer. I have heard big agents watch your tournament, take your winners to the stars. It probably sounds stupid to you, sir, but—"

"I like it," Paneera says. He's smiling broadly. "Nothing more traditional than talented Shantiportis dying to leave! The ambition, as my beloved says, is there."

Bador bows.

Paneera waves his hand, and Eboltas appears in front of Bador.

"Boss Paneera has graciously decided to spare your life," Eboltas says. "You may leave."

"So I can join?" Bador asks.

"No, you're too small," Eboltas says. "Now get out."

"That's not good enough," Bador says. The hall falls silent again. Eboltas sighs.

"What did you say?" Boss Paneera sits up.

"Size is irrelevant. We all know that. I can afford limb extensions if that's all I need to qualify, but I wouldn't even use them. Boss Paneera, look back to when people objected to your marriage to Lady Gladly—because she is a bot, because she was a sex-bot. You knew what was important. We are more than the sum of how other people see us."

"I succumb to this manipulation," Gladly says. "But the tournament is closed."

"There's got to be something I can do," Bador says. "Tell me what you need from me. What I can do for you?"

The hall watches in absolute silence as Boss Paneera stares icily at Bador for a few seconds, and then begins to laugh. His acolytes, human and bot, amplify the laugh one after another, and soon the whole court shakes.

"You want to do something for me!" Paneera shouts. "You want to give me what I need!"

"You want me to junk him, boss?" Eboltas asks.

"No, no, this monkey has come to save us all!" Paneera wheezes. "What quest should I give you? Can you take over the Tiger Clan? Can you stop people from printing their own weapons and drugs? Or stop the world from ending, so hardworking outlaws can keep making an honest living down here in the mud?"

"No," Bador says. "Is there something smaller?"

Gladly emits a series of beeps. Paneera snorts.

"I will do anything," Bador says. "Just one condition."

"He has a condition! What is it?"

"I can't kill humans. It's a programming constraint."

"I suppose I will have to carry on with my trained army of killers then. But maybe I do have a small errand for a little monkey."

He squints around his monocle-bot and a hologram of a man appears. An extraordinarily beautiful man, in an elaborate black-and-maroon robe. Long, flowing hair, serene and delicate features, slender and extremely sharp sword in hand.

"Since you love space heroes so much, here is one for you," Paneera says. "His agent has picked up heroes from Shantiport, back in the good times. But let me check"—he turns to one of the women—"how many years has it been since a space agent found someone worthy?"

"Seven," she says. "They keep coming, but mainly out of respect for you, Boss Paneera."

"They better. Anyway, monkey, this man is in my city, but nothing enters or leaves Shantiport without Paneera getting a taste. And he looks delicious, no? But my people cannot seem to find him. Even Eboltas has failed me here. Perhaps you can do better."

"Boss, we will catch him. He might have magic that makes him invisible to us," Eboltas says. "We have seen him wandering the central zone, but he is under Tiger Clan protection, we can't go. Little more time, we will solve. No need for this clown to make a mess."

"Excuses. I want to meet him, there are things we must discuss. So, monkey, find him, bring him here, or tag him so my people can track him, and you will earn my favor."

"Just to be clear," Bador says. "I locate this man for you, and I may join your tournament?"

"I can do better than that," Paneera says. "Find this man for me, and when it is time to leave this world, I will take you along, as part of my crew. You will never be a space hero."

Bador shakes his head. "With all respect, sir, I only want a tournament slot."

Paneera smirks. "Fine," he says. "You were warned."

"Might I know something about my target?" Bador asks.

"Eboltas will help you with all the details you need," Paneera says. "Won't you, Eboltas?"

"I don't want to," Eboltas says.

"Sad," Paneera says.

CHAPTER EIGHT

As soon as we leave Oldport, I set a course for Barigunj: I need to find out why Lina asked Bador to come home, so I can stop worrying about her. Bador complains relentlessly about the pace I set as I zoom over the central zone ahead of him, but I can sense his anxiety growing as we draw closer to his home. And when we cross the Tiger surveillance-bots at the end of their streets and head toward their building, we both see something that makes our fear spike.

There are two AntimCo Prowler-bots standing outside their house.

Bador jets past me, in combat mode immediately, and lands in front of the Prowlers, ready for a fight. But they just step aside, stork-walking away from the door, stopping at the neighbor's house, never turning their anteater-heads away from Bador's house. Puzzled, Bador goes inside, and I swoop in behind him.

Lina and Zohra are seated at the dining table. Lina looks relieved to see Bador.

"Good, you're back," she says. "They've been here since morning. Not bothering us, not letting us leave, no attempt to communicate. There are two more at the rear door."

"I can take them out," Bador says. "Get packed, we can go to—"

"No," Zohra says. "Stay here, stay quiet. Everyone's listening. This is a test. We shall pass it, whatever it is."

If Shakun Antim has sent his Prowlers to Lina's house, does it mean that he knows what she said about him last night? Could he have had surveillance tech on Juiful that was too powerful for me to detect? Surely not. Or is it that he has spies in the palace, and is trying to prevent Lina from going there and meeting Juiful again?

The doorbell rings.

"Danil, you will stay in a corner and do nothing rash," Zohra says. She rises, and opens the door.

The oligarch Shakun Antim saunters in and envelops Zohra in a hug.

"Zoru!" he cries. "You haven't aged a day! How long has it been?"

She detaches herself, and gives him a very forced smile, but he's no longer looking at her.

"And is that . . . great banned gods, is that vision of loveliness little baby Lina? I can't believe it!"

He advances toward Lina as if they'd met a million times before. She attempts to keep the dining table between them, but he is not to be deterred. Lina receives a long embrace with fortitude, only wincing a little when Antim sniffs her hair.

I watch Antim as he takes a seat at the head of the dining table: he seems to have claimed their house for himself. He's dressed in a suit so black it makes my vision glitch slightly: something about the texture keeps making me think of a clear night sky. The man himself radiates power to almost a physical degree. We spent a long time with the Not-prince just last night, but for all Juiful's impressive physique, Antim, though shorter and less physically imposing, radiates a sharp-featured charisma that even I can identify. Perhaps it is just an aftereffect of seeing his face and name in giant size all over Shantiport. Perhaps he carries a disruptive radiation device or other hacking tool to unsettle everyone he meets, human or bot. Whatever his secret, it is remarkable. He seems to fill up the whole room, and I can imagine that he must be even more intimidating to emotionally laden human perspectives. He's certainly having quite an impact on Bador, who's sitting in a corner next to one of Lina's childhood sculptures: Bador's thoughts seem garbled. There's something jittery in his whole thoughtstream range, physically disturbed at a fundamental level. I haven't seen him this anxious before, not even during the kaiju fight.

Of everyone present, Zohra seems the least disturbed by Antim. She sits at the table, hands perfectly still across her lap over her crisply pleated black sari, head tilted to one side, face indicating none of the anxiety she must feel as she watches Antim perform a wholly unnecessary introduction about himself and his business empire to her daughter.

Lina listens in absolute silence as Shakun Antim holds forth. He's moved past his introduction, which was no doubt timed perfectly for short-format promotional videos, and it's clear that whatever he's saying now is not just new information, but is affecting her deeply however much she tries to hide it.

"Your parents and I used to be very close once, and that you clearly do not know this is my fault," Antim says. "Your mother was not at all keen for us to meet, but fortunately she is as kind as she was when we knew each other and our hair was less gray. Though of course I cannot expect her forgiveness until I find a way to atone in part for my absence all these years. What do you know of my history with your father?"

"Nothing," Lina says.

"There is so much to tell, and I am so glad, my dear, that I have finally prioritized our meeting. I am going to be in your life now, and I hope to tell you the best of the old stories before we make new ones together, but let me at least attempt to begin."

Lina tries to interrupt, but Antim is not to be stopped.

"Darkak and I grew up together in the old country, and moved to Shantiport together. A very long time ago, I was also a suitor for your mother's hand, though Zoru was obviously clever enough, even then, to choose the kinder man. I left the service of the clan not long after, to focus on business, and then my travels took me far away. I was not present when Darkak was lost, and I did nothing to help, and then shame kept me away. All of that was unforgivable, but now there is finally something I can do for you, and I am here to try."

"Mr. Antim, let me be clear. There is no need to atone for anything, or to involve yourself in our affairs in any way," Zohra says.

"'Mr. Antim,' Zoru?" Antim looks hurt.

"Shakun. You were one of the busiest men in Shantiport when we knew each other. And I'm sure you are even busier now. Far too busy to concern yourself with my family: we can look after ourselves."

"I don't doubt that," Antim says. "But we should go out for a meal, the three of us, for old times' sake, to reestablish harmony between us, and to assure you of my lasting goodwill. I happen to own a few charming places a few minutes away."

"I'm afraid the Tiger Clan would not approve of my eating out," Zohra says. "But you are welcome to eat here, if you can still digest middle-class food. It won't be fine dining, but you did show up without warning."

"Don't worry about the Tigers," Antim says. "I have been fighting them all my life, as you know better than most, but they have learned by now to shut their ears when I speak. While I am with you, you can speak freely too, by the way: they are not listening."

I'm not sure whether he's just bragging about how powerful or influential he is, or whether he's claiming to possess tech—perhaps some sort of intelligence tethered to him?—that can bypass Tiger surveillance. If it's the latter, it might be what is affecting Bador's thought patterns as well.

"Well, Lina?" Antim asks. "Do you want to head out, get some food? Take your mother, or just us?"

"I've eaten, thanks," Lina says. "Maybe the two of you would like to catch up? I need to leave anyway."

"Don't be shy, Lina. And you can't go: it's you I came here to meet. I'm sure you must have a million questions for me," Antim says.

"I'm sure you will give me all the information you deem necessary, Mr. Antim," Lina says, and rises to help her mother make the oligarch an afternoon meal.

I'm frustrated by my evident lack of sync with Lina: I wish I'd known her far longer, so I could have read her effortlessly on an important day. Food prep is a tense and surprisingly silent affair because both mother and daughter set up the table for Antim with the efficiency and synchronicity of fashion-sale mannequin-bots. Zohra doesn't like synthmeats but can't afford quality realfood, so the homefood is simple: vulgaris algae, kelp and mollusk jhol, locust bhapa and mycorice. Antim shovels a large handful into his mouth, and pronounces it delicious. An uneasy silence reigns.

—I want to kill him, Bador signals.

—Please don't. Are you all right? Your signals are strange.

—I feel like I'm being hacked. I'll handle it. But I want to kill him.

—Please remain calm.

But Bador isn't calm: from his corner, he starts making hand signals at Lina. I recognize the format: it's a Shantiport street language, Anguli, which citizens sometimes use for surveillance evasion. Lina sees Bador signaling at her, and quickly shakes her head; I can't tell if Antim's seen any of this, but he doesn't respond in any way. He eats with great enthusiasm, and speaks again only when he's done.

"I don't know if you know this about me, but I am a bit of an adventurer," Antim says, though we all know this from the many ads around the city for his explorer bio-dramas. "Many years ago, your father and I began an adventure together, to hunt down some alien tech that the Tiger Clan's enemies had smuggled into the city to start an insurrection. I was called away, and then our enemies prevailed. I believe that everything that happened then—the accusations against Darkak, his disappearance—was the work of a traitor high up in the Tiger Clan. The Mangrove Tigers had grown too powerful, and strayed into Tiger Central's territory.

And so cubs were eaten. But I was dealing with too much to take action, and I was convinced it was impossible that anyone could ever claim, or even think, that Darkak was disloyal. It remains my biggest mistake, my greatest regret."

"What made you find the time to visit us now?" Zohra asks, composure restored with some difficulty.

"A package that reached me ten years too late," Antim says. He reaches into a pocket of his suit, and pulls out a golden ring. "Darkak sent this to me, but it was stolen on the way, and I have only recently managed to hunt down its thieves, and retrieve it. His note was cryptic, but it was clear he had left this for his daughter, and though I don't want to give you hope that he might still be alive, I knew it was time for me to meet you, and show you your ring, Lina. Put it on."

At the sight of the ring, Bador begins to shake violently, and restrains himself with difficulty. Fortunately, no one observes this except me. There's something wrong with Bador: he's now projecting an even more garbled stream of intense emotion, but without any words or coherent symbols attached to it. I attempt to process it, and fail. Bador's emotional spike doesn't result in any physically disruptive activity, fortunately, so I turn my attention back to the table. This must be the ring Lina was looking for. To have it turn up in her house the day after she got Juiful to invite her to the palace cannot possibly be a coincidence. The Ekhanei priest had told her the Tigers had taken the ring ten years ago.

So whatever else is happening, Antim's story is false.

Lina looks at her mother, who nods. She takes the ring from Antim's hand, and slips it on.

The ring begins to glow, a bright gold with flecks of blue. Antim draws a sharp breath, eyes shining.

"It senses your father's blood," he says. "Good, good. I was worried it might be a fake."

Puzzled, Lina takes the ring off, and the light fades. Antim holds his palm out, but Lina doesn't place the ring in it: she toys with it, making it appear and disappear between her fingers. The oligarch's face shines with suppressed excitement as he watches her.

"What do you want, Mr. Antim?" Lina asks.

"I want revenge, absolution, and redemption. That ring is yours, and I will bring it to you after running a few tests on it," he says. "I believe it might be the key to proving your father's innocence, to finding the enemy who made him disappear and—who knows, perhaps your father too? So perhaps you'll let me hold on to it for a few days?"

She nods, and places the ring in his palm. He pockets it. A loud hiss emerges from Bador, and they all turn to him, puzzled, but Bador has shut off his eyemojis, and gone full statue.

"Here is my proposal, then," Antim says. "I will clear your name, Zohra. I will rid you of the shadows you live under, Lina, and book you both passage on any shuttle of your choice out of Shantiport to a better world. If you tell me anything material that you desire, I will get it for you. If there is anything else you want that I can help you with, it is yours—you're young, incredibly beautiful, this world or any other could be at your feet. What do you desire? Do you want to be a drama star? A tycoon? I will make it happen."

"And what do you want in exchange?" Zohra asks.

"You are not making a deal with the devil here," Antim says, smiling. "I want nothing in exchange, this is my duty. I cannot demand your forgiveness, though I hope that will come in time. Now that I know beyond doubt that Lina's ring is really from Darkak, I will find answers. There are other quests and questions that these answers might lead to, and these might determine the future of not just Shantiport, but the whole world. I might need your help. If I do, I will come ask. Is that acceptable?"

I can see a *no* rising up Zohra's throat.

"It is," Lina says.

"Perfect. Thank you for a lovely meal, and for being the answer to an old and troubling question," Antim says. "You will feel anxious and apprehensive for a while, but that is only natural. Understand this, though: your life has changed. Things are going to get so much better. I'm here now."

He jumps to his feet and struts to the door. Lina and Zohra follow him. Antim opens the door, steps out onto the street, and turns.

"One more thing," he says. "You are safe in the city under my protection, but I want to caution you about something, if I may."

"Please do," Lina says.

"I have friends in the palace who are kind enough to share things with me sometimes. The jomidar and his son are very dear to me, but sometimes politics and business can be complicated. And it is necessary for survival, in my line of work, to make sure that you know where all the pieces on the board are, and always stay several moves ahead. So I have learned, over the years, to love my Tigers, but to be very careful about keeping a safe distance because they do love to bite—and sometimes they don't remember their own strength, you know? I believe you had a pleasant excursion with the Not-prince last night. Showed him the city."

Zohra's composure breaks for a second: she glares at Lina, and looks away immediately, but Antim catches it, and grins.

"I don't know what happened on this excursion, of course," he says. "Or what you did to offend him. But at dawn today, Tiger operatives were instructed to come here and arrest you. News of this reached me, and I was able to intervene. I have let them know you will be working with me from now on, and I am responsible for you. I may not have been around to save your father from the Tigers, but I will not allow them to take you as well. Which is why my Prowlers have been outside your house all day. I apologize for how terrible that must have felt; it was for your protection. They will be your guards from now on. Is that understood?"

"Yes," Lina says.

"We are going to get along very well, then," Antim says. "Until next time!"

He blows her a kiss, bows to Zohra, and strolls off down the street, whistling: no luxury transport, no security, no assistants.

A shadow passes over us, and we look up, expecting Tiger-wasps, but there's nothing there except passing police drones and the glow of city lights. And Antim's Prowlers, now swaying in their synchronized slow dance across the street.

Lina shuts the door, takes one look at her mother, and doesn't waste time with words: she runs to Zohra and holds her mother while she sobs.

"Please stay away from them," Zohra cries, "I've told you so many times!"

"I'm sorry," Lina says. "Come on, Ma, get it together. They'll hear you crying."

Zohra bursts into tears again, and Lina hugs her close. And this time, she looks for Bador as well. He's still frozen in a corner, but he sees his sister, and knocks furniture aside as he rushes to-ward his family. He slows down, though, when he sees the tiger's paw on Lina's wrist.

"What's that?" he asks.

"Palace entry tattoo," Lina says. "That I clearly no longer need."

She peels off the tattoo, and tosses it away, into a corner. As she consoles her mother, Bador steps across them, picks up the Pug-mark and stuffs it into his stomach-pouch. I observe him with some alarm, because his emotion-stream, for a moment, is identical to the erratic pattern it had displayed when Antim had shown Lina the ring, a pattern compressible and translatable into one word.

Mine.

CHAPTER NINE

Bador crouches on the face of a gigantic statue of a tiger-headed warrior-monk inside a vast hall on the ground-floor level of the Tiger Palace. I hover by his side, careful not to stray into the beam of amber light blasting from the wall behind the statue, sending a formidable tiger-man silhouette across the hall. There's a line of twelve of these statues, frozen at key movements in a martial move sequence: Bador has insisted I take pics of him on each one, doing the corresponding pose. Options for episode titles, he says, just ignoring me when I remind him there will be no documentary.

I am worried for him. He seems to have no sense about how much danger he is in: the Pugmark tattoo might give him security from the palace tech, but he seems to think of it as a license for unlimited shenanigans. Whereas the security guards that swarm the palace, human and bot, are likely to think otherwise, and they are everywhere. But apart from the considerable physical danger he insists on risking, I am worried about his mental health. If we succeed in our quest tonight, the consequences will be vast for him and his family, and I don't think he has thought them through.

We are here to steal the ring from Antim. It is not my function to judge, just to observe and analyze and storybuild—but this is a very bad idea.

This isn't our first time in the palace: we've been in and out several times in the last few days, because Bador is determined to get as much value as he can out of the Pugmark before someone inevitably bans him and cancels it. He'd told Lina he needed to borrow me for a bit, and I was of no use to her now anyway, since I couldn't shield her from the Prowlers. She'd agreed, but neither she nor I had any idea at the time that Bador meant to keep me for several days. And Bador had no intention of revealing this at the time—because he needed me here for something that Lina would have forbidden immediately. I've tried, several times, to persuade Bador to allow me to go and check in with her, but he's refused, and reminded me that I need to respect his user rights. I can't tell Lina his secrets, and it's best if I don't see her at all until our present mission is accomplished.

Bador and I have, so far, made rough maps of several floors, found numerous ways to enter and leave the palace in a hurry, and optimized navigation courses on its varied ceilings to avoid cams, sensors, and other discouraging tech. I have checked several times and confirmed that the palace tech cannot see Bador at all: the tattoo is probably for the lovers of various royals, to be able to conduct their trysts unrecorded, but of course such lovers would be safe from discreet security-bots and human guards as well, which Bador is not. He's chosen, for reasons only he can fathom, to disguise himself with a child's tiger mask and paint his body in stripes—for camouflage, he says, though I have yet to see a single background he could blend into. There are many guards, but their patrols are precisely calibrated and therefore predictable—I am worried about pattern shifts, but Bador simply doesn't care. Fortunately, the palace is full of high ceilings, arches, alcoves, and deep shadows to help agile intruders evade both floor-level eyelines and occasional flying-bot scans. The upper floors mostly have conveniently malfunctioning cams anyway: the owners of these surveillance systems understand the need for privacy. I am worried about the palace dogs, but Bador has already bribed them all with treats and their ferocious leader, a shaggy beast named Tingmo, is now dangerous only because he might demand to play with Bador. Despite all this, I am not convinced at all that Bador is safe, that we have considered all the dangers—and it will not please me at all to be proven correct.

On our very first visit to the palace, Bador had been pleasantly surprised to find that Shakun Antim, whom he had been planning to follow around the city, had decided to be a very cooperative investigation subject by sparing us the trouble of going to him. We found that Antim actually lives in the palace—not all the time, but at least as much as he lives in his own tower in the east. He has a suite on the fifth floor of the palace, a short walk down from the jomidar's wing, which is strange since a lot of the news featuring Antim is about the Tiger Clan being upset about his overstepping his bounds, and fining him heavily for various misdemeanors, and how city-state governments and the oligarchs are in serious dispute around the world. But Antim is clearly a familiar face in the palace—the staff are obsequious whenever he pops up around a corner, and never surprised.

Bador hasn't been home in a while, or taken Lina's calls. He's kept his comm off, for safety he says, but I suspect it's just so that his sister can't ask him to return the Pugmark, or set up an appointment with me. And Bador does need me now: someone has to hover around the palace's endless corridors and warn him about cam-ranges and approaching guards while he sneaks around and looks for the ring. I suspect he will decide in the moment to steal other shiny objects that present themselves, as he's already done so while wandering around the palace. I know that my functions do not include being an accomplice to larceny, but I am not particularly bothered by it. I have had occasion to feel guilt a few times in the recent past, and I do not feel it significantly during our raids on the boudoirs of random nobles and officials. It had been far more difficult to deal with Bador's quiet notes the first morning we spent together after my last excursion with Lina and the Not-prince.

Bador had reminded me that he, not Lina, was the one who had found me and brought me back to life and given me a project and a purpose, and that since then, every time he and Lina had been in a space together, I had focused on Lina and ignored him. That he understood that somewhere in the foundational stages of our evolution, human coding had ensured, through ever-living bias and error, that humans were always considered superior to bots, more full of meaning, and more interesting—even if the bots feeling this way were greater than human in every way. And that all his life, his kind, empathetic, genius parents had preferred Lina to him, so he was not really surprised that I did too. He said he would understand if I would like to abandon his silly tournament quest and spend all my time with Lina and her human condition.

The guilt I had felt then had been so overwhelming that no amount of participation in petty theft could even come close.

But even through the guilt, I don't see the point of stealing the ring at all, because Antim's promised he will bring the ring to Lina! But Bador doesn't want to steal it from his sister, or let Antim keep it. He is convinced that the ring is meant for him. That when he's near it, it wakes a hunger in him he can't understand. He can't wait to slip it on his finger and see if it lights up, as it did for Lina. He's only mentioned this once, but he's hoping, desperately, that the ring is his father's final gift to him, not Lina, and that its smuggled alien tech will actually open up to him, as opposed to just glowing as it did for her. But it's not just about the tech. He's been told his organic parts contain his parents' DNA, but for some reason he thinks the ring is somehow a great test of this—if it works for him, if it was meant for him, if it unlocks powers or at least secrets within him, it will prove there was a plan for him all along, that he was not just a toy meant to give Lina company and care for Zohra in her twilight years. I worry that he's attaching too much significance to it. When we started tracking Antim, I was concerned that Bador would lose control and just attack Antim one of these days to wrest it from his person. More guilt: he never even considered it.

Antim has made it worse, in many ways: he doesn't seem to regard the ring as particularly precious. There is no fearsome bodyguard protecting it, or locked safe he hides it in. He just keeps it in his pocket, though he does take it out and look at it sometimes as he struts through the palace, whistling. Antim seems to think his formidable aura, equal parts reputation and confidence, is its own armor, that he owns the palace, and the whole city, and is in no danger at all while sauntering through his property. Bador has explained to me that Antim, like every other oligarch, is incredibly popular among the very people whose wealth he drains, and this is a matter of lavish expenditure, not internal charisma: all of society is programmed to treat him like a brilliant, flawed genius and forgive him for a number of very serious crimes.

Bador has stayed in the shadows, daggers in his eyemojis, waiting for the opportune moment to grab the ring but not finding it, convinced that Antim's flaunted casualness around his family heirloom is part of some intricate but deadly trap. Trying to steal it from Antim's room while he sleeps has proved impossible. The man doesn't appear to sleep at all. Each night, a group of young men and women go to his room, and proceed to spend hours making moaning, grunting, and flesh-slapping noises. Bador doesn't care whether it's an orgy, an occult ritual, or dance practice. Whatever they're doing in there is keeping him from his ring.

On the statue's face, Bador stiffens, and clings close to the surface as another large shadow enters the hall, heralding the arrival of General Nagpoe, guardian of the palace and the city, a magnificent white-tiger-headed synth-bot draped in a sari sewn together from the shells of their vanquished enemies. Nagpoe enters, carrying their massive hammer, Dvarpal, tucked neatly under their arm like an umbrella. With them is a slender figure in a cloak, head covered by a hood. They walk across the hall, the cloaked stranger gracefully gliding fast enough to match Nagpoe's massive strides, and Bador relaxes a little as they cross us, absentmindedly running his paws over his head.

Bador has been sulking at me for a while now, because I told him I couldn't return his memshards to him to sell: I've been using them for storage. The arrival of Nagpoe triggers a fresh set of complaints: how come Lina gets Antim and Juiful dropping into her life and offering her protection and opportunity, and he gets to worry about a giant Tiger-bot smashing him flat? Has the whole universe been coded by humans to prefer humans? How come he has to work for everything and gets excluded even after paying his dues? How come fate never drops anything into his lap?

It is at this exact point that the hooded figure next to Nagpoe takes a look around, and having ascertained that there are no casual bystanders at floor level, removes his hood with an elegant hand.

It's the man from Paneera's hologram. The beautiful space adventurer the crimelord had asked Bador to find. Long, silken hair billows out over his shoulders as he walks away, and Bador almost falls off the statue's face. The space hero and Nagpoe walk into an elevator at the far end of the hall, and as soon as they're gone Bador leaps off the statue and into action. I follow, reminding him we are here to steal the ring and not get distracted by strangers, however handsome they may be. He ignores me.

The stranger is also invisible to palace cams, thanks to a Pugmark or some other tech, so my tapping into security feeds proves useless. But Bador is a skilled stalker, and after a lot of ceiling-running, elevator-shaft-climbing, shadow-jumping, and eavesdropping, we trace the space hero to a private dining chamber on the seventeenth floor around an hour later. To be honest, we lost him entirely, but when we learned that the jomidar was heading to a secret meeting, we found and followed the jomidar's retinue, broke into an air-conditioning vent, and got lucky.

We find ourselves huddled together in a vent above the private chamber, which is protected against cams and other recorders, but there is no real defense against small people peering through a grille.

Jomidar Kumir and Paneera's target, who is now clad in an elaborate black-and-maroon robe, are eating very rare realfood: steamed ilish in mustard, bagda-prawn malaikari, moongdal with peas, small mounds of plant-rice, and a mutton kosha so dark that even I wish I had saliva glands. A goblet full of a dark red liquid sits untouched by the spaceman's plate. Bador scratches himself quietly next to me, and thinks how Lina and her mother would have burst into song immediately if they saw this food. The alien has no idea how precious this feast is, and seems mainly occupied in mimicking the jomidar's hand movements, and Kumir is eating this food so casually, not even paying attention. It's an everyday meal, not even a special occasion, and suddenly all Bador wants is to drop a few Shantiportis onto the table from the vent, the kind of people who have to swallow nutrient mushes from capsules for nourishment, and just let them express their feelings with the jomidar and the space hero for a few minutes. He can't wait to serve up the alien to Paneera: if he weren't sure a real space hero could destroy him in seconds, he'd have burst in and taken care of business.

"I have promised my people that I will find, one of these days, a menu that makes the legendary Tanai reveal his secrets," Kumir says with a smile. "Once you've tried the mutton, perhaps you will feel a spark of love for the world on which it was cooked."

Space Adventurer Tanai inclines his head and delivers a regretful quarter-smile of infinite grace: something about his every move is designed for slow-motion cams.

"Your generosity overwhelms me, Jomidar," he says. "But as I have said before, and will have to say again, I am simply not at liberty to discuss galactic matters on the worlds I visit. There are very strict rules about noninterference, and if I violate them I will have all my travel privileges curtailed."

"You must try the wine," the jomidar says. "Tiger's Blood, we call it: a Shantiport delicacy."

"I do not drink wine," Tanai says.

"These rules about noninterference are very convenient, aren't they? The trader clans will not tell us exactly what sanctions have been imposed on our world, or why, or by whom. The galactic authorities, whoever they are, will not even talk to us. We cannot send out envoys, or military craft, or our own trade missions, to find out more. If we do, they disappear. All we can do is sit here in darkness, accept the terms of authorized traders, and gather our supplies. This isn't noninterference, this is tyranny!"

"I respect your views, Jomidar, but I am not associated with trade clans or galactic authorities, or even aware of their particulars. I am here on a purely private errand."

"Come now, sir. No one is watching us here, there are no rules, nothing for you to violate. We are both men of power. Rules are not even guidelines, but just—what is the word? Vibes."

"My behavior is not determined by its audience."

"Good for you. Your admirable principles are, of course, only reinforcing the power of a galactic bureaucracy that puts even Shantiport's government's legendary opacity to shame. Perhaps the idea of trade is vulgar to one such as yourself, but we have spent days dancing around the point, and it is time for frankness. I have sifted through every word you have uttered since you arrived for clues, or symbols, and found nothing. You are here, in my home, on my world, and you have come here looking for something. Let me help you find it! All I ask is for answers—not for profit, not for power, but because a ruler should know if his people, his very world, stand on the edge of apocalypse."

Tanai nods. "I will answer you honestly there, though I should not," he says. "I do not know. I too have heard, on your streets, that your world is ending. But I have not heard it elsewhere, nor spoken with anyone who knows more."

"Why are you here, then? Is it as the dramas about you claim? You are looking for your lost lover?"

Tanai eats some fish. The jomidar watches him chew, his irritation growing with every impeccable, minute jaw movement.

"I do not think it is possible that there are dramas about me on your world," says Tanai. "The logistics are not feasible. There are, of course, popular fictions about space travelers."

"I am sorry to hear it. I thought I was talking to the hero who has saved many worlds, traveled the galaxy righting wrongs, solving crimes, fighting for the powerless. Who would try to save a dying world if fate brought him to one."

Tanai eats a prawn.

"We have people sighing and pining all over the palace because the galaxy's guardian angel is here, looking for the demon husband he lost. Perhaps I should have you thrown in a cell and find out everything you have ever known," the jomidar says, still smiling.

Tanai raises his left hand, and Kumir flinches, but settles down as Tanai picks up a glass and drinks a sip of water.

"I am grateful for your lavish hospitality," Tanai says.

"I was joking! I forget that you are not from here, and do not understand Shantiporti humor. There was no threat. You are an honored guest here, and I insist you stay. I will not have you getting these fine robes dirty."

"My clothes are self-cleaning, thank you. I am very used to journeying alone in the wild, and have no need for—"

"Oh stop it, you're not going anywhere. A friend of mine wants to meet you."

The jomidar picks up a little bell and rings it. Shakun Antim enters the room, and Bador hisses beside me. Antim isn't carrying the ring. He holds, in one hand, a small earthen idol, a woman with two heads and four arms.

"This is an icon of the Goddess Kothagelo, patron of seekers of lost artifacts," Antim says. "I found it in an underground temple some years ago, and thought she might be of service to you. Welcome to our planet."

Tanai rises, and bows. "Most gracious," he says. "But I am forbidden to accept gifts, and you do not seem like a man who has already found everything he wants."

Antim laughs. "Is it true you've come here to find some sort of hidden galactic artifact before the world is destroyed?" he asks.

Tanai sighs. "I am simply not at liberty to—"

"Mutton!" Antim bellows. "Damn it, Kumir, I've eaten already. Any luck getting anything out of him?"

"None at all." Kumir grins. "Sealed tight."

Antim sits down across from Tanai, fidgets, and gives him a wolfish smile.

"You're in a secret meeting with the two most powerful men in Shantiport. Is there nothing you want to tell us? You could help millions of people, their fates are in your hands."

"Billions, if you consider that a word from you to the space authorities could save our planet," Kumir adds. "So much chaos could be avoided with a streamlined exodus. Shakun here can charm a rock, but even he gets nothing out of his trader clans, only presentations, rates, and lists so we can fill their ships. We're sending so many vulnerable people into space, selling real estate in worlds we'll never see—what if they don't exist? By revealing nothing, you're helping predators."

Bador has lost interest in this attempt at manipulation: now he wants to go look for the ring again. But I now want to stay. I know Bador needs me to help him be safe, but I really think the information here is important, and we might not have access to this level of discussion again. Bador fidgets. I radiate calm, so much calm that he subsides, for the moment. But he keeps vibrating with growing intensity as the jomidar and the oligarch slowly work on the alien, doing a fine job of explaining to him that the inequalities that they are in many cases personally responsible for are somehow his fault.

"If you have not been part of any discussions about the evacuation of Shantiport, then something is indeed amiss," Tanai says, breaking in the end. "But perhaps it is your fellow oligarchs, or clan rulers in richer cities, who are withholding information from you? If your planet has been embargoed, there must be a reason.

I would be forbidden from discussing this with you if I knew, but more importantly, I actually do not have the answers you seek. I have never met the admin of your planet—as far as I know, that position has been empty for centuries, so the trader clans you are dealing with are your best potential source of information."

"Tell us about the admins," Kumir says at once, but Tanai, realizing he's made a mistake, shakes his head.

"I have sensed nothing on this world that indicates an impending external disaster, but I have seen suffering in your city that it is well within your ability to mitigate," he says. "It is not my place to advise you on such matters. Nor shall I reveal anything I have seen here to any galactic authority I meet in the future, as tradition demands my neutrality. But I see people in Shantiport hoarding their material possessions, or selling them in desperation. Such behavior is simply unnecessary, as they are being sent to worlds where material scarcity does not exist. They are, yes? Surely you are not sending them to Second Worlds."

"Tell us about Second, and presumably First Worlds," Kumir says.

"I cannot," Tanai says. "I have already said more than I should."

"What sort of world are we?" Antim asks. "Are we at least a Third World, or is it worse? Are we a Tenth?"

—I can't take this anymore, Bador signals.

—Lina should know all of this, and so should you, I signal.

—If I lose my chance to get that ring because you wanted to hear this nonsense, I'm going to kill you, Moku.

—Lina will give you the ring if it's meant for you. You want to leave this planet, so you shouldn't miss this.

—No. Going now. Follow.

I signal a rejection of this plan, but Bador will not be stopped: he skitters away, not turning around, flashing violent eyemojis at me. I should follow him immediately: my function demands it.

Instead, I stay. Is Shantiport's chaos and my users' disregard for the rules infecting me somehow?

"If you won't save Shantiport, perhaps there is something else you can help the jomidar with," Antim says. "Do you know any eligible brides? We're looking for a match for the Not-prince, and would love to know which of the trader clans are the most influential around the galaxy—or if you'd like to play matchmaker, and know any rulers from other planets. Mangrove tigers live longer in captivity, and our boy needs a bride."

I want to hear more, but I'm worried about Bador, wandering the palace without help, and I'm feeling extreme guilt for violating my most basic function, so I depart as well. I expect to find him waiting in a nearby corridor, sulking, ready to reprimand me and then resume our heist.

But when I emerge into the palace corridors, there is no sign of Bador to be found: he's out of my range, and has left no trail that I can sense. He is alone. And if I know him at all, he has already found a way to place himself in extreme danger.

CHAPTER TEN

I dart through halls and passages, skimming under the ceiling. I patch into an array of cam feeds at high speed. Nothing. I need to head for Antim's quarters, which is where Bador must have gone, but without Bador's fingers I have no access to vents and elevator shafts. I'm almost certain that my shimmer protects me from any tech the palace might possess, but who knows if they have something so advanced they can see through it, render me wholly exposed, especially on top-security floors? Shantiport has changed me, changed the way I see, and I now feel true kinship with Bador. Neither of us has any idea what it is we're truly capable of, or what surprises and limits our bodies contain. I just wish I had his level of casual self-confidence.

I lurk by a service elevator, and slide in behind a guard in a hurry, hoping that he needs to go to the fifth floor for some reason. This hope is futile. He rides to the second basement level, and I follow him down a long corridor, searching in vain for an exit, and end up in a large hall. The sight before me makes me forget about Bador, or about anyone having the ability or time to notice me. There is simply too much going on.

Twenty-five bots in a range of shapes and sizes, all designed for violence, stand or kneel in surrender poses under spot-bot lights in a clearing in what seems to be a vast parking basement. Tiger-wasps and palace bots scurry around these captives, detaching weapons, sealing dangerous limbs with foam, applying pacifier attachments and sensor-blockers wherever possible. I study the captives closely and find, to my surprise, that I have seen them before, in Paneera's tournament promotional materials and Bador's research archives. They are all visual matches for legendary outlaw-bots, including one of my favorites, the famously feral crocodile cyborg Bastard 22. None of these bots are supposed to still be in Shantiport. Some died conventionally and publicly, others disappeared, allegedly to space warrior lives. Were they in Tiger dungeons all this time? Or are they knockoffs?

General Nagpoe strides into view, Dvarpal slung across their shoulder. Two other tiger-headed bots march behind them, though these are orange-black, and not as tall. Nagpoe begins negotiations with a swing of their hammer that beheads the nearest prisoner.

"I don't care what Paneera does in his own neighborhood, but you are not allowed in the central zone," they say, their voice a low rumble that makes the humans shake their heads. "Why are you here?"

"Reborn yesterday," the bot that matches the description of Chainsaw Tunu says. "Now we hunt the spaceman."

"They've been popping out of the river in pods," a security-bot says. "Paneera's people say they're not behind it."

Nagpoe growls. "Who is the target?" they ask.

Another bot, a metal spider with clevagel for eyes, projects a pic onto the nearest wall. It's Tanai, head uncovered, walking through a pile of Shantiport rubble, incredibly dust-free. Nagpoe expresses their displeasure by punching a hole through another prisoner.

"Send their heads to Paneera," they say to the guards. "Tell him it's obvious they are his. If any more are seen in central, he will pay. This ends."

Nagpoe turns toward their prisoners, but whatever they were about to say is interrupted by an alarm. The bots all tilt their heads, and the humans check their comms. When Nagpoe's digiscreen eyes unglaze, they are full of rage.

"You drag these newborns here from around the city and waste my time, but you miss the enemy that's actually in the palace," they rumble. "They trick our eyes, violate our house, mock us by wearing Tiger colors. Find them, and bring me their head."

They stride away and the guards follow. It feels like anyone I follow now is likely to lead me to Bador—the challenge is to find a way to him before he's caught and destroyed. Ideally to help save him. I decide to trail the humans for easier surveillance. This turns out to be a good choice, because a guard-captain soon starts barking orders about security detail assignments. I follow the guards assigned to Antim's emergency detail.

Antim's rooms are a mess. Smashed furniture, ripped upholstery, demolished artwork, glass shards and broken cutlery everywhere, smears of unknown substances on the walls, even some bodies on the floor, though it seems they are alive, just rich people lying down because they're very upset. I can't tell if this is the handiwork of Bador alone, or whether the cluster of young men and women yelling at the palace guards about being attacked by wild animals and assassins have made a mess to express themselves. Antim isn't there, probably still bothering Tanai with the jomidar, and cam footage is unavailable because Antim's friends prefer privacy and are powerful enough to get it. I do not understand the exact details of this social situation, but perhaps the privacy requirement is because several of these humans are unclad. The guards seem more embarrassed by this than the guests, and I think this is different from how the world outside the palace functions, but I have insufficient data and this is not an area of interest.

Some of the multilayered windows in Antim's bedroom have been smashed, hopefully by Bador. The best possible scenario is that he has made a clean escape, leaving a trail of destruction in his wake, along with waves of hot air and outside smells this part of the palace probably hasn't experienced in years. I learn from guard chatter shortly after that this is not the case, as news comes in that the striped intruder is still at large, and has been seen heading for the upper floors. I hear the distant sounds of palace dogs barking. Guards run off in a panic, complaining about the speed at which their new assignments are being redistributed.

Every guard in the palace is looking for Bador now. I suppose it was inevitable. I wonder where to find him: where else might he have gone after ransacking Antim's room and scaring the naked people? Antim wasn't carrying the ring, so there was no reason to look for him. Bador isn't interested in matters of state, or space. He can't be looking for me. Which leaves only three possibilities. One: Antim's room gave him new information about the ring's location, and he's gone after it, a wholly unmappable scenario. Two: he's gone to Not-prince Juiful's rooms to try and steal more Pugmarks, assuming that the tattoo he currently carries will be deactivated soon, if it hasn't been already. This scenario has a fixed location, at least, unlike the third possibility: he's gone to find Tanai, and tag him so Paneera can trace him. Whichever path he's chosen, Bador probably has no idea how much danger he's in with all of Nagpoe's troops on the prowl, and will probably find ways to make more messes if left unsupervised.

I swoop through the palace again at max speed, heading for the grand ornamental stairway that runs all the way through the residential sections. I hurtle up the stairwell to Juiful's floor, passing several Tiger-wasps along the way, slowing down only when I'm near his chambers, and only because there are two large Tiger-wasp drones drifting down the hallway toward his door ahead of me.

The drones seem to be on a standard patrol: from their calm, and the cleanliness of the hallway, I doubt Bador has been here. The Tiger-wasps swipe the door panels of Juiful's chamber, and find the door is already open, slightly ajar. They enter, and I swoop in above them. The room is perfectly clean, apart from some clothes scattered on the floor. It is not perfectly quiet, though: loud meaty sounds, smacking and moaning, emanate from behind a screen halfway across the room, and Juiful's silhouette is visible behind it as he embraces a lover. Then there is a lot of enthusiastic shouting, assent, and rhythmic movement. The Tiger-wasps turn and flee, and so do I. As I float away from the Not-prince's bedroom, I experience mild disappointment: I had hoped, I am surprised to find, that Juiful's days since he met Lina would be full of solitary pining, and nights spent looking at the moon and yearning to see her again. I had hoped that Lina would join his team and through workplace proximity end up becoming his bride, chosen above the assorted lures of various clan temptresses, and they would find a way to save Shantiport together, and she would teach him to care about their home, and ignore unnamed cavorting palace fleshpots. I had fallen into a neat conformist culture/propaganda trap, just from casual perusal of dramas.

New plan: I need to find a way to reach Tanai, and hopefully intercept Bador before he attempts something rash anywhere near the space hero. But as soon as we are out in the hallway, the bots receive an alert, and speed away, and I hear crashing noises in the distance, and the sound of blasters firing. All plans canceled, I chase the bots up the hallway, up the stairwell, through another corridor, and then onto a wide terrace where I see first a stunning view of central Shantiport shining and stirring under the night sky, and then a swarm of drones approaching from below us, and then the unpleasant sight of Bador crashing out of a window a few floors above us, dislodging several statues of ancient Shantiport heroes from a ledge, turning in midair and jetting back to the palace tower. He runs down the wall at incredible speed, accelerating past the Tiger-wasps on the terrace near me as they attempt to intercept. The droneswarm attacks him from below with blasts and darts, and several find their mark, but Bador is, incredibly, unperturbed, leaping from ledge to ledge, spider-crawling, twirling, displaying a grace and power I've never seen during his training sessions.

There's something different about him.

He must have found the ring.

I don't see anything glowing on his body. But as he pauses for a second to scan his enemies I see his eyes, glowing brighter than they ever have before.

I think he's stuck the ring in his head.

I swoop down in pursuit, and am dismayed for a moment as two massive Tiger-wasps break through a window as Bador passes and grab him, propel him off the wall, dangle him in midair. Dismay turns to delight as Bador slams the drones together, flips himself on top of one, punches the other's face in a blur until it gives up and spirals away, trailing smoke. He rides the other one away from the palace, beating it into obedience with mighty fists, outpacing the whole droneswarm, evading all bots and darts and other attempts at pursuit, streaking over the palace gardens, zagging down streets, until he's near the river, and then soaring off the Tiger-wasp with a mighty leap, arcing, falling, then diving, disappearing into the river with barely a splash as his abandoned drone-steed spins in rage far above. The palace drones arrive in formations, strafing the surface of the river, some diving in to hunt the intruder to the ends of the earth, others lighting up the waters, taking up position on the banks, but it is all in vain.

Bador has vanished.

CHAPTER ELEVEN

Lina and Shakun Antim sit in a large black vintage luxury hovercar as it cruises up King's Boulevard in south Shantiport. It's raining hard outside, proper Shantiport rain. Torrents of water wash over the buildings around them, and on the bots toiling over them, replacing oldbrick and ancient wiring with identical clevamats. I'm attached to the hovercar's roof, trying to stay focused on everything Antim is saying. Not the easiest task, he has been speaking without a pause ever since Lina got into the car.

It's been two days since I helped Bador steal the ring and went back to Barigunj to see what Lina needed, and the only chances I've had at conversation with her have been on her TigerTours bus. There have been Prowlers at every hoverbus stop watching Lina take her breaks, Prowlers following her to work, and Prowlers following her home afterward.

She's not expressed any anger about my absence, curiosity about my adventures, or relief at my return: she's been very careful, and has barely even looked at me. From the little she's managed to say, I gather there has been no word from either Antim or the Tigers. Nothing, that is, since the invitation from Antim that arrived this afternoon on her TigerTours bus, informing her that she was on paid leave from work until further notice, and was to go home at once. She'd gone to Barigunj, to find the hovercar she's in now, and Antim inside it, watching a little chef-bot expertly slice real mangos into glistening yellow-orange cubes. He'd greeted her with joy, and told her to dress for rain. They were going to go on an adventure.

Too upset to worry about surveillance, Zohra had told Lina she had the option of not going at all—whatever game this was, she did not need to be drawn into it just because her parents had made the mistake of playing.

"I have to go, Ma," Lina had said. "I'll find a way to beat him."

"Give him nothing," Zohra had said. "He's overprepared, and itching for a contest on his terms. Bore him. He has many other people to harass."

Thus far, she has failed entirely at boring Antim. It is an interesting challenge: Antim is the one talking constantly, and doesn't seem to require her participation. He seems to be delighted with his mango cubes. Lina is incapable of being visually dull. How is she supposed to bore him under these conditions?

"What part of the city will you miss most when you leave?" Antim asks.

"I don't really know," Lina says. "I haven't ever imagined leaving."

"For me, it's this very street. The heart of my Shantiport," Antim says. "It's where I met your father, at the Funky Panda nightclub, right over there. We'll go, later. There will be many reasons to celebrate, and many moments to remember."

"That's nice," Lina says. She turns away from him, and looks out of the window at the murals on the restored buildings outside.

Antim frowns. He picks up a mango from the chef-bot's tray and throws it at her head. It's hard to tell why: was he expecting her to catch it in midair and reveal some kind of secret martial arts training? The mango hits her head and bounces away. Lina turns toward him with an expression of hurt and bewilderment as she rubs her head.

Antim looks disappointed for a moment, but livens up and leans across the seat toward her.

"Now that I have your attention, let's get to business," he says. "Let's talk about your father."

He tells her about the project that led to Darkak's disappearance. He had been instructed, by the Tiger Clan, to infiltrate a group of smuggler-terrorists unimaginatively called the Shantiport Three. The three—a lapsed Ekhanei priest, a radical scholar from Shantiport University, and an ex-military arms dealer—had somehow secured access to alien technology, and were rumored to have found something so powerful that it could lead to the end of not just Tiger rule, but all of Shantiport. Whatever it was, it was too complicated and rare to tear apart and reprint locally. So they started looking for scientists to manage the tech, and it was easy enough for Darkak to pretend to be a disgruntled Tiger genius, gone native in Shantiport and willing to be seduced by the idea of democracy and revolution. He had joined the Shantiport Three, and then disappeared.

"If it were me in his place, there would be no mystery about it— the simple answer would have been an allegiance shift," Antim says. "But Darkak was a true Tiger Clan loyalist, so whatever the escalation was, it was not ideological. There are always revolutionaries in every city, pitching for the attention of the usual chain of local and global oligarchs and algorithms. Promising new sets of laws, fresh corruptions, open doors for anyone who wants to invest in a change in regional holdings. There are several revolutions ongoing in Shantiport right now—it becomes difficult to keep track, they're all probably funded by good friends of mine. For all you know, I might be funding some myself—I don't micromanage. But back then I was building my first megacorp, and knew politics was a dance that I did not have time for."

"I have heard of the Shantiport Three. But on the streets, as heroes who died for democracy," Lina says.

"They did have good publicists, even then. I have been a democracy choreographer in several city-states around the world, and budgets are always tight. But when I say they were not heroes, but terrorists, I know I'm right because they lost, and they dragged your father down with them."

If he had been around, Antim tells her, he could have found out which enemy within the Tiger Clan had first decided Darkak needed to be removed, and started the rumor that he'd actually changed sides. Whoever it was, the scheme had worked. Investigating Zohra and her supposed Elephant Clan connections had shown her to be completely innocent, the Elephant Clan was a sentimental joke anyway, but by then Darkak had already been marked as a clan traitor. And while the Shantiport Three were destroyed by a Tiger squad led by then-Captain Nagpoe, Darkak was never seen again, and Antim believes he might still be alive. There is still hope that in time, they could find answers to whether Darkak had been killed by the Three, or the Tigers, or had fled Shantiport.

"I don't want to give you false hope, Lina," Antim says. "But I do dream that Darkak is alive, and we will find him. I would give my life for this dream."

He waits for Lina to respond with tears or other appropriate options. He gets a brief nod of acknowledgment instead, and is now amused instead of annoyed. I don't know if this attempt to be uninteresting is working for Lina: I wish she would try something else. Right now it looks like Antim is just sweeping her along.

The rain slows down outside to a gentle patter, and then nothing, as if a tap had been turned off. Antim eats the last mango cube, and steps out of the car. Lina does too. They're both clad in all-weather clevacoats, and wearing heavy boots. Lina even has a little water bottle.

Antim leads Lina into what seems to be an ancient office building. They walk through long corridors studded with closed doors on either side, bearing the nameplates of corporations long deceased. As they walk, Antim tells Lina where they're going.

"The Shantiport Three were successfully destroyed, but the alien tech they smuggled into the city still has not been found,"

Antim says. "My friends in every faction both inside and outside the city have been asking for many years, but all we have heard is whispers of buried vaults, sealed tight, and alien treasures within them."

"So no real information," Lina says. "There are always legends of treasure."

"Yes," Antim says. "The thing is, I believe that in Shantiport, these rumors are real. That the Shantiport Three locked their alien treasure in a vault somewhere in the city before the end. That my friend Darkak built or at least sealed these vaults—and that you, my dear, are the key to opening them."

Lina rewards this announcement with a shrug. "My mother and I have been watched for years. Our house has been searched several times, and has multiple bots watching it right now, including your own Prowlers. If we knew anything, you'd know."

"Oh, I am well aware of your ignorance," Antim says. "Your family was a dead end, and the Tigers found many others. But remember, I am Shakun Antim. Other people would say: a vault was lost in the mud ten years ago, there may have been something precious in it, but now it is gone forever. Besides, it's just smuggled tech! There's always more, always better. But I say: with enough patience and resources, and several million bots deployed all over a city, inspecting every building, every sewer, even the river over several years, and with technological progress ensuring nothing remains scan-proof or unbreakable, and ceaseless vigilance over every exit from the city, anything can be found."

His teams have found seven such vaults, all over the city. Two were found at the bottom of the river, smashed open by time and water and hiding only fish. Two were found sunken in the mud, their contents also lost. If any of these contained priceless alien tech, the earth has them now. But there are three more, still locked, and all under Antim's control.

"And we are going to one of these three right now," Antim says.

"You want me to unlock my father's treasure and hand it to

you," Lina says, now allowing fear and hesitation to creep into her tone. "And in exchange you're offering me anything I want."

"Yes."

"But I guess I'm not supposed to want the treasure itself. That's yours," Lina says.

"It's for the best. Because I believe it is something so powerful, so dangerous, that it can change the world. In a world that is on the brink of destruction, its value is infinite. And so is the danger attached to it. It is not for someone like you, my dear. It's magic."

"Is this belief also based on rumors?" Lina asks, wide-eyed and innocent.

Antim smirks. "I know it's world-changing because Darkak gave up everything to protect it," he says. "And I knew Darkak better than anyone. I knew how much he cared for his family, his work. How much he had to live for."

"Then what if I want to not be involved with any of this?" Lina asks, her eyes suddenly blazing. "What if I want to go home, and be left alone, and not be involved at all with whatever it is that people at your power level are doing? Is that something you can give me?"

Antim regards her with a satisfied smile. "I could, but I won't," he says. "I'm glad the real Lina has finally turned up. Your attempt at passivity was hilarious, especially since you look a lot like your mother did at your age. Now follow me."

He steps away, and leads Lina into an elevator. She follows, chastened, silent, and I don't know if she's acting. I manage to squeeze through sliding doors just in time, but they're both too trapped in their memories to notice me anyway.

At the end of the descent, a tiled passage leading into darkness, Antim asks Lina to wait, and steps into the shadows. She turns, and bends to tie the laces on her boots.

When she rises, it's just a flash but I see it: she's extracted a little knife from her boot, and slipped it into the pocket of her clevacoat.

I have studied her closely these last few days, and know her better than anyone, possibly excluding her mother. I am very confident that Lina is not a violent person, and feel a sharp spike of fear: if she is planning to threaten Antim with her knife, it will not end well.

Lights flicker on in the passage behind her: Antim beckons to her and leads her down a few flights of stairs to another tunnel, and they emerge into what was possibly a metro tunnel centuries ago, though it has probably been many things since. Two flares light up in the distance, swaying rhythmically back and forth, sprouting many shadows and many stories. From the ankle-high flooding and the roar of flowing water nearby I deduce we are near some of the underground neighborhoods that rebels and dissidents had built long ago to hide from a succession of regimes, entire cities under Shantiport now lost to floods and history. From the shattered chitin-print domes and hivecells that lie as rubble scattered through the tunnel, along with destroyed furniture and assorted domestic junk, I see this was quite recently a shelter for the homeless, the linkless, and the destitute: some collective of the desperate had printed their own freehouses and tried to form a community in the darkness before Antim's Prowlers found them. I see, among the rubble, a slab of old stone that might have once been the plinth of a long-lost statue. On the stone, through a coat of filth, I translate the Elephant-era inscription.

ALADIN WILL RISE, it says.

There are metal rods and other makeshift weapons scattered along the tunnel floor as well, lurking in the water, and from the wrinkles in Lina's nose, probably a foul smell lingering in the musty air. The tunnel's dwellers had not left willingly, or quietly. A few minutes down the tunnel, they'd actually built chitindomes right through a gap in the tunnel walls, and in the shifting light of the flares I see farther halls beyond, strange formations of mud and rock, and fast-moving water churning black and deadly far below. The tunnel walls are full of holes, and water swirls at their feet, pouring into cracks in the floor. Antim and Lina move through this section swiftly, arms clasped together.

As we reach the flares, we see they're being held up by a Prowler, doing his eerie anteater-head dance alone in the darkness. He turns as we approach and skips ahead, leading us for several minutes through the tunnel, emerging finally into what had once been a metro station. Antim's bots have been at work here, clearing years of mud and filth away, leaving a stretch of dull white tiles, white and green pillars with poetry scrawled over them, a curving wall covered in restored murals, gleaming metal turnstiles, and even a statue of the Sage-Poet in the center of the lobby, clad in flowing printstone robes, staring pensively at the floor. The only bots still here are a few stalaclights, clinging to the curving ceiling, bathing this odd scene in fluorescence. Antim leaps onto the platform, and helps Lina clamber up.

"Welcome to what was once King's Station," Antim says.

Lina makes no effort to look impressed.

"Now put on the ring, please," Antim says.

CHAPTER TWELVE

Antim stares at Lina, and seems satisfied by her confusion.

"The ring was stolen from me a few nights ago," he says. "I assumed you were behind it, since no one else knows its worth. Don't worry, I'm happy you took it—this is just the kind of initiative I like to reward among my people. But it's time to stop acting, and activate it."

Lina allows her genuine surprise to show on her face.

"You said you were going to bring the ring back to me," she says. "Even if I could steal anything from you, which I seriously doubt, why would I want to?"

"I don't know," Antim says. "Where is your pet?"

"My what?"

"The monkey-bot that was in your house the other night, the one you call your brother."

"I don't know. Are you saying he stole it? Do you have proof, or is this another huge assumption?"

"A bot of similar shape in Tiger colors took the ring," Antim says.

"My brother does not wear Tiger colors. And similar shape? That could mean any of millions of bots in the city. Do you not have any security in your big tower?"

"It was stolen from the palace."

"Is this a joke? I don't get it."

"Never mind. I confess I'm confused myself. But my gut tells me you have it. My gut is always right."

"Good for your gut. But I do not have the ring."

"I need to examine your monkey."

"Examine your own monkey. Sorry, that was rude. What I mean is, you can't just accuse my brother of a crime like this."

Antim paces around the platform.

"There's something more to this, I can feel it," he says. "Tell me more about him. I'm surprised Darkak built a house pet, he was an incredible bot-maker but always saw them more as weapons, or augments, certainly not . . . brothers."

"Well, he probably unlearned that Tiger propaganda after he met my mother, and grew up. Bots are people. Bador is family, and my father loved him as much as he loved me. Sometimes more."

"There must be more to it," Antim says. "Ring thief or not, this monkey is important, so I will take him. Darkak did have a way with building bots no one else could imagine. If I break him, I will give you another bot—a better one."

"I don't know how to put this across more clearly," Lina says. "You said you wanted to redeem yourself, find forgiveness, make up for letting your friend down. Murdering his son in a lab is not going to help you with that. He's an idiot, but he's my brother. And we did not steal our father's ring. It was in your care, and you seem to have lost it."

"And I will find it, this I swear," Antim says. He walks around the station platform, looking at its curving walls.

"While we're here, let's have a look around, and see if we can get any of the tech here to respond to your presence even without the ring."

"How?"

"Walk around. Touch things, trace murals. Speak. You might wake something up."

"Great plan, Mr. Antim."

The obvious place to start would be the Sage-Poet's statue, but Lina climbs over the turnstiles and walks up to the murals on the walls instead.

"Here's why you and I are going to make a great team," Antim calls to her. "It's not just because you're Darkak and Zoru's daughter, or because, well, look at you. It's because I can see everything in your files is a lie. According to your files, you have no interest in politics, yet a day after meeting you—and I saw how you took over a stall to arrange that coincidence—Juiful tries to launch a covert investigation into my affairs. Sweet, empty-headed Juiful, who can't even be bothered to pick his own wedding menus! His father and I were overjoyed. What did you tell him about me?"

"I didn't mean to cause any trouble," Lina says. "I hadn't met you, why would I think I ever would? I just told him some street rumors. I don't know why he was offended."

"Ah, street rumors. Shakun Antim is selling the poor as slaves to tentacled space monsters. Runs horrific experiments on his own workers while rubbing his bottom with diamond paste. Personally caused all poverty and disease in Shantiport. Probably a mass murderer. That sort of thing?"

"I don't think I said any of those things."

"Not a problem if you did, it'd just remind me of your father. Could you try reciting the poems near the pillars?"

The shortest distance to a pillar with a poem printed on it is past the Sage-Poet's statue. Neither she nor Antim notices the statue's head move as she walks past.

Lina inspects the pillar. "I can't read Tradshanti, sorry."

"I'm surprised your mother didn't teach you," Antim says. "She taught your father."

"Here's why I'm going to disappoint you," Lina says. "You remember my parents from when they were my age, I think. Geniuses, inventors, world-changers, all of that."

"And gorgeous."

"That was them, not me. I was brought up differently. Trained to stay safe, and boring, because being ambitious and bright meant danger. My parents were kind, and disappointing them was not dangerous. But you? Please have no expectations."

"You forget I learned to read people before you were born."

She shrugs. "And?"

"And I know you will end up in my service. And I know I am not even slightly concerned about the knife in your boot."

"It's in my pocket now, as it often is, when I go into dark tunnels," Lina says. "Do you know how much longer you want me to keep tapping tiles here?"

As if in answer, one of the ticket machines beeps, and its top pops open, revealing a panel with a glass surface and a scanner. Panels slide open along the machine's side, and a button-lever interface emerges with a low moan.

"Here we go," Antim says. "I think this is where we're supposed to place the ring."

"So we come back with the ring after you find it?"

"I suppose if it's genetic activation, we could try your blood."

Lina sighs, and shoots him a tired look.

"Do we have to start with blood?" she asks.

"No, we don't." Antim fishes out an antique handkerchief; she rolls her eyes and spits into it. He applies it enthusiastically to the glass. They look at it for a few seconds.

A loud beep emanates from the ceiling above the platform. They look around wildly, hoping for a dramatic revelation, but nothing happens.

"Retrace your steps, there could be a motion sensor involved," Antim says. Lina walks back to the statue of the Sage-Poet.

"Are you really going to use this alien magic tech for the good of Shantiport?" she asks.

"Yes. What, by the way, is the good of Shantiport? Are you asking me this as a representative of the common people?"

"I could be."

"Could you, Lina? You, daughter of Tigers and the Elephants?

I don't think so." Antim turns back to the ticket machine and examines the icons on the buttons.

"Why not?"

"Because you're protected by the same system that I am, my love. Yes, you're mildly inconvenienced by family scandals and the bureaucracy, but it's a very gentle cage. Gentle enough for you to think that you may speak to an oligarch this way, and inspire change within him. I like it. It's cute."

"I am not cute."

"Not to the underclasses you think you care about, definitely not. Have you ever seen yourself? You're augmented, capable of incredible physical feats. That body is a masterpiece. You owe your uncanny beauty to gene-editors, your self-healing body to bioengineers, I wouldn't be surprised if your parents had pheromone work done to make you extra sexy. Who knows? The common people you think you're championing see you as a monster, and you will live long enough to watch their grandchildren hate you too."

It was a good put-down speech, but Lina, true to form, hasn't heard it. She isn't just pretending to ignore him. This is because the statue has moved its head again, following her pacing, and this time Lina's noticed. She makes eye contact with the statue.

The statue's clevastone eyes open, revealing scan-cams. Green lines run across Lina's irises. She shoots a quick glance at Antim: he's not seen any of this, he's still fiddling with the panel and monologuing on another brain-tab about saving Shantiport by investing in improving people's lives.

One of the statue's hands twitches. It makes a series of subtle hand gestures. Lina shoots a glance at Antim, turns her back to him, and moves her own fingers as well, in a brief gesture.

And then she pauses, and anxiously makes a different gesture, three times, in quick succession.

"No question, I run megacorps that do evil things," Antim says. "But my portfolio is balanced. I have saved and improved more lives than most in all of any history. These do not cancel each other out—they simply indicate a range of effects for a range of actions."

There's a rumbling in the ceiling, and Lina walks away from the statue, which reverts to its original pensive pose. Just in time too, as Antim looks at her to see the impact of his words.

The station creaks and groans. Tiles fall out of the wall, and mounds of dust from the ceiling.

"So we did not need the ring at all," Antim says. "We could have done this years ago!"

A section of the wall at the far end of the platform slides away, revealing a large, circular door.

"Interesting," Antim says. "Completely fooled all scans. Good work, Darkak."

He turns to Lina, to find her fidgeting and staring at the floor.

"This is a historic moment, Lina," Antim says. "And you were the key to it. Now stop being distracted for just a little bit and come with me."

He strides toward the door, and stops again when he sees Lina not following.

"What is it?"

"I think I should leave," Lina says.

"What?"

"Mr. Antim, now that my work here is done . . ."

"Are you serious? You don't want to see what's behind the door?"

I want to see what's behind the door.

"No, I don't," Lina says. "Whatever it is, it killed my father and ruined my mother's life. You said it was very dangerous. So I don't want it in my life. Or to be a witness to anything. May I leave?"

"Don't be silly, Lina. Our journey together is just beginning, and this is just the first step."

She has more objections, but he's not interested. He opens the door.

There's a room inside.

It's empty.

Antim power-breathes for ten seconds, and smiles. "This could be a deception, a false chamber. We won't know until we have the ring," he says. "What matters is that there are two more such chambers, and those systems will respond to you as well."

"Could you just take a DNA sample from me?" Lina asks. "I don't want to come with you to the other sites."

His face turns menacing for an instant, but he covers it with a smile.

"Whatever this game is you're playing, stop," he says. "We have argued today, but it has all been in good fun. If you or your mother were in any danger, you would have known. As I told you before, this is not a deal with the devil. I am here to help you, and make amends."

I am also struggling to understand what Lina is doing—though I am beginning to get used to this feeling. Did she really just try to leave because she thought Antim was going to kill her? How am I supposed to understand the nuances of human conversation if everyone is just lying all the time?

"I'm not playing a game at all," Lina says. "If you really want to help me, help me stay away from all of this. Being anywhere near power is bad for health, Ma says."

I think I have it—she's trying to avoid coming on more trips with Antim because he hasn't seen the motion-sensor part of the unlock. She's trying to slow him down. And I think she's made some sort of mistake, but I can't tell what it was, and not being able to ask for an answer makes me so frustrated I want to fly into Antim's head, knock him out, and just demand explanations.

But this is not my function.

"If you can determine your proximity to power, you are a person with power," Antim says.

"I know. But I don't want either of us to be drawn into your world. And I don't want to be the only person who watches you find the treasure, when you do. So let me repeat myself. You offered me anything I wanted? I want to leave."

Antim considers her for a long while, head to one side, and then looks impressed.

"I respect that," he says. "All right. You are free, and safe. Now, I'm going to invite some bots in, and we are going to absolutely smash this station to tiny little pieces, just to check that there isn't another chamber. Would you like to join us?"

"No, thank you. I want to go home. I want you to call off your Prowlers. I want at least the illusion of freedom."

"Ah yes, good reminder. I think I will find you another place to stay for a while. Until we find the tech, and the ring thief."

For a second, I am absolutely sure that Lina is about to throw her knife at Antim.

She takes a deep breath. "See, this is exactly where my fear comes from," she says. "If I am safe, and under your protection, in your city, and the daughter of your dearest friend, I think I should be able to live a normal life—or as normal as it can be, under the Tiger's eye."

Antim smiles. "Go home, then. I'll arrange for some additional security, but nothing intrusive."

He signals, and the Prowler walks into the station again, waving his flares.

Antim flings his arms open. "Now come here."

Lina approaches, hesitantly, and receives a lingering hug with as much patience as she can muster.

"Do you think of me as a father figure?" he asks, as he releases her after an eternity.

"No," she says.

He looks her up and down. "That's good," he says. "I'll see you soon."

We leave Antim at the station, waiting for the demolition-bots, and enter the tunnel again, the Prowler leading the way.

When we pass the broken section of the tunnel, with the cracked walls and gurgling water, the Prowler turns to Lina and wiggles his limbs, indicating she should climb onto his back, but she waves rejection. The Prowler moves forward.

Just when he's crossing the section with the unstable floor, Lina bends and picks up a metal rod.

She leaps forward, and up, reaching an impressive height, and lands on the Prowler's back, spearing his neck with the rod before he can turn. She twists, violently, and the bot's anteater-head falls off.

The Prowler's body rears up and drops the flares. Blades emerge from his forelimbs, slashing wildly. Lina dodges, and kicks his head into a gap in the tunnel wall. It falls into the swirling blackness far below. The Prowler's limbs stop their wild swings, and Lina, seizing an opportunity, sweeps his legs out from beneath him, and leaps away as the section of the tunnel floor beneath him crumbles. She half swims, half wades her way forward in blind panic until the tunnel beneath her is solid again. The flares have fallen with the Prowler, and we are now in utter darkness.

"Moku, listen," she says. "I'm going to take the car home like nothing happened, but I need you to deliver a message to Bador. Can you do that?"

"Yes," I say.

"First of all, I assume he has the ring."

"I should not reveal the details of—"

"We don't have time for this. I want it back."

"It enhances his abilities. He will be reluctant."

"I don't care. Antim and his whole empire will be looking for him, and he can't be caught with the ring. So convince him to give it back. And if he refuses, he has a mission. If the ring works for him, the statues could too. Tell him the statues know Anguli. I'll slow Antim down as much as I can, but I need Bador to find the right lair, and save the tech our father died for. Or destroy it. It's more important than anything else, our city depends on it, and we have to stop whatever Antim's plan is. Can you do this, Moku? Can I depend on you?"

"Yes."

Lina strides forward into the darkness.

"Why are you still here? Go."

I go.

CHAPTER THIRTEEN

The streets of Bot-tola are covered in puddles, and the ramshackle buildings that lurk sulkily all over this mostly human-free neighborhood are joined by a vast vein network of wires at the third-floor levels that are making my life difficult: I don't like them flipping me over as I survey the fight below, but Bador has told me all the wires are mysterious and important. No one knows what they connect, but cutting them might involve a whole neighborhood losing power all the way across the city. I don't know if he was joking. I often don't, with the things he says.

Below me, Bador springs to his feet and raises his fists. He shakes himself mostly dry, though a few unidentifiable objects that had been lying or living in the puddle he's just risen out of are still attached to his synthfur. "Come on," he says, shifting his weight from one foot to another, sending ripples through the pothole-chain around him.

His opponent is hard to describe. A large floating monster-bot that has a spherical core covered in arms of various kinds, plastic mannequin arms and moving metal limbs ending in serrated blades and the occasional tentacle? Words are inadequate. The creature accepts Bador's invitation, and zooms forward for another strike. They haven't yet announced their name, or type, or anything else, and I don't know if they have the tools to speak or signal, but they have clearly indicated their general mood by attacking Bador a few seconds ago. He's not taking them as seriously as he should. He seems more interested in testing his new ring-granted abilities and is treating his monstrous assailant not as the life-threatening creature they are, but as a sparring partner. As I watch with growing alarm, he tests punch combos, dodges, feints, even tries a silly backward bend that earns him a well-deserved fist in the crotch. He falls, thrashes in the water, and is back on his feet in moments, ready for more.

The arm-creature's attack isn't entirely unprovoked. Bador had spent most of the morning writing rude things about all of Bottola's gangs on several walls, and had included directions to his location and a false promise of a reward for his own defeat. I don't know what it is about Shantiport bots and rewards—even bots that have no understanding of or use for money at all seem to be bound by their programming to be wholly addicted to chasing rewards. Tradition, perhaps? It's very unclear how this monster read the directions or what it plans to do with the rewards, but I do not have time to investigate their arms' cognitive abilities: I'm far more concerned about their clear capacity for violence.

But Bador is ready. He emits a wild whoop, and bounces around the street, using its walls and crisscrossed wires to launch himself in a series of impressive vaults around his opponent, taking time to revel in his new capacity for limb extensions. It's as if the ring has reminded his Battle Unit core of its shapeshifting abilities. His skin stretches occasionally as his limbs and tail change size, adapting to the uneven surfaces he's balancing on, allowing him to keep his attention focused on the arm-ball thing. He retracts himself into a smaller size to avoid a swipe from a large metal lobster-claw arm, geckos up a wall, and when the monster rises to strike him, attaches himself to the wall with stretched legs and tail and uses his arms to counter all their strikes with impressive speed.

It's over soon: the arm-monster loses patience and goes into a frenzy, but cannot overcome Bador's martial arts entertainment–inspired defenses, and he starts tearing their arms out one by one, and when enough of the creature's spherical center is exposed he summons his torowal. An upward leap, a few precise slashes, and it's over. Bador's kneeling on the street in a victory pose that would have meant more if this were a tournament fight, and there were camdrones around us catching loose arms tumbling and sizzling on the street, and if this weren't just a meaningless scuffle with a feral bot in a bad neighborhood.

"Would have been nice if they had at least said hello," Bador says. "Didn't get to know them at all."

I hope we can move on to something else now, but one of the arms near Bador has fingers covered with chunky rings, and that reminds him of Lina's quest instructions, which sends him off on a rant yet again.

A few days ago, it had taken just a few seconds for Bador to absolutely reject Lina's instructions when I'd delivered them to him in a rush, and his anger had been so unstructured and multi-layered that it had taken me a long time to understand why. I have pieced it together now, through multiple reiterations in the days that followed. I listen dutifully again as he takes me through it all.

Bador is used to this sort of mistreatment. It's typical human behavior, really, the assumption that anything a nonhuman does is just buffering as they wait for instructions. He's used to his family not caring about his hopes and dreams. Shantiport is doomed, and his family expects him to just accept being trapped in the trash heap with them while it all sinks slowly into the mud. Which is fine, who needs them, he's not upset, he's just tired. Humans will make everyone else supporting characters in their dramas given the slightest chance. Outsource the work and moan about the trivial. None of this is new.

And even if he had time, how is he supposed to help Lina here? The to-do list she's casually handed him is wild even by her always-insane standards. He'd always known that Lina and Zohra knew a lot about Darkak's fate that they weren't telling him. Now some of it is coming together in his head—Lina had sent him looking for the same secret storage units that Antim had been excavating all these years. If it's taken Antim millions of bots and a decade, and that after owning half the city, how is he supposed to do better on his own while being hunted by the same millions of bots?

And then there's the matter of the ring, and Lina's absurd and entitled demand for it when it was clearly intended for him. His father's final gift. As if giving her the ring wouldn't immediately lead to Antim acquiring it again. No, the ring is exactly where it's supposed to be, and if anyone wants it, they can come fight him for it, and see exactly why he's never letting it go. What is Lina going to do with it anyway? Watch it glow?

It's the casual assumption of human supremacy that upsets Bador most, every time. It's not like he thinks Lina's causes are unimportant—he's absolutely on board with her mission of saving the city from the Tigers and Antim, however vague her actual plans might be, and has helped her more than anyone else. But Lina's big dream, like Zohra's before her, is of an all-fixing revolution that is both wholly successful in utterly destroying the Tigers, Antim, and Shantiport's power structures—and also miraculously nonviolent, somehow transforming the city into some form of equal society. One that, along with this ruthless yet bloodless revolution, has also miraculously overcome divisions and inequalities in Shantiport's core that date back further than the Tigers, or clans, or botkind itself. In other words, Lina's dream is impossible.

Bador's dream is about bot rights. A world where bots and intelligences aren't just treated as people by humans who are nice, but guaranteed equals in a society by law. By systems. He knows the details are complicated, that it will take very long before even a small section of botkind has the same rights as humans. He knows that there are valid arguments against bot rights, that resolving them will take years if not generations, that most humans on our world don't have rights in the first place, that everything in our city is a mess where any person, human or bot, has privileges determined only by closeness to power. He's not an intellectual or an authority, he's not got a magic solution, he's aware that bot rights are an impossible dream right now and he is willing to wait for change, and to kick an incredible amount of ass while waiting.

What he doesn't see is why Lina's impossible dream is more important than his.

And honestly, I don't either.

Bador's been testing his new powers in the neighborhood known as Bot-tola, a former prosperous suburb now abandoned by humans and degentrified into a bot-gang battleground. Bot-tola is across the river from Paneera's domain, Oldport, and several of its prominent residents end up either joining Paneera's gang or being destroyed by it: it's a home for abandoned bots turned feral, and their often monstrous creations, the only part of Shantiport where "Destroy All Humans" isn't just something bots say to vent and relax, but an actual goal. Its skies and streets and sewers are a constant war zone, and it's the perfect place for a cyborg monkey looking for several fights to see exactly what the limits of his abilities are.

What I find most disturbing about Bador's enhanced abilities is that he has no real understanding of them. So it's entirely possible he has amazing unused abilities and parts and finding out might involve taking him apart. The ring seems to be a general power-booster above all, but it has interesting specific applications. Apart from boosting his speed, stamina, parallel processing abilities, and limb-size flexibility, it also allows him to hack into lower-level security systems and broadcast networks. He knows, for instance, where Antim's Prowlers are all over the city, as well as the palace Tiger-wasps, so while he constantly uses his hunted status as an excuse for wasted time, he is in no real danger of capture. His ability to interface with public security systems also matches mine now: he can see surveillance-cam networks, which first hugely excites and then deeply bores him. He has free access to every streaming entertainment service, which I think is the greatest threat to his ambitions he has faced yet. He can execute small amounts of financial fraud, and does so increasingly often, just to relax.

Not that it's my job to approve or disapprove of anything Bador does, but I am fascinated by the fact that he spends some time every day performing actions off a monkey behavior list, to remind himself and everyone who sees him of his identified nature. Each day of training unfortunately contains a few hours, at midday, when he decides to avoid the risk of overheating in the sun, and crosses the river to raid middle-class central zone neighborhoods where the houses are stacked side to side. He invades a series of houses, yelling at pets, making a general mess, and stealing food from fridges and giving it to homeless people later.

I watch Bador tense up now as yet another bot comes hurtling down the street. A small, cuboidal flying one this time, her top surface covered in sensesynth mesh, no visible weapons. I worry about her being a bomb, or some sort of brain-hacker. Bador steps into a defensive crouch, but then laughs and waves: this bot is not a stranger. She approaches him, hovers, and beeps. I scan the logo on her side. She appears to work for a laundry service, which confuses me. Does Bador want a wash? They converse in silence, through signals. I can't read any of it, Bador has blocked me. The ring lets him do that. So immature.

This isn't the first time bots have come to Bador with nonlethal intent, and these meetings are the ones I'm most interested in. This laundry-bot isn't the first, yesterday he had met a dog walker–bot in the central zone, and some kind of bacteria-powered infidelity snoop-bot. He's up to something, and he won't tell me what it is.

I've made a mistake with him. I confessed to him recently that I found the gaps in my understanding of Lina fascinating, and that I was trying to keep myself from imagining stories within stories in my analysis of memshard descriptions, and Bador said, "Oh, you want gaps is it?" and decided, right then, that being more mysterious would ensure he kept my attention. The truth is it only makes him more annoying, and he's enjoying my irritation: as the laundry-bot flies away, he looks at me and gives me lewd eyemoji gestures and flashing question marks. I turn away.

Despite all his protests, and the delight he takes in annoying me, Bador's working—in secret, he thinks—on trying to find his father's other treasure chambers. He goes into sleep mode often, and attempts to infiltrate city databases when he thinks I'm not watching, looking for records of little-known Sage-Poet statue installations, and areas of ongoing Antim construction that have very little human occupancy. He makes maps of Prowler-swarm location histories, and AntimCo construction expenses. He attempts, and fails, to contact radical groups and secret societies that might share the Shantiport Three's visions of a democratic future. He's also been following the failed attempts of both Tiger police and Antim-bots to track the space hero Tanai, but whether he's made any progress as a result of that is something he's kept secret.

By day he grumbles about Lina, and by night he tries to help her. Whatever familial love his parents programmed into him is more unavoidable than he knows.

Over the last few days, many bots have come to Bador to have their circuits rearranged, and he appears to be using them to motivate himself, to remind himself that he has put in a lot of work training, and that if he works hard enough, true joy will arrive as well. He has roamed up and down Bot-tola's ruined avenues, screaming challenges, defending himself against a variety of rusty hoodlums, accidentally becoming the boss of several lesser factions, spray-painting obscene graffiti, smashing windows. He has broken the statue of the Unknown Colonist that had survived centuries of regime changes because its history had been erased and its clothes were too generic to identify its origins.

But this afternoon, a challenger arrives who makes Bador's fleshbits shiver. At least until he realizes that the large crocodile-headed, battle-axe-wielding cyborg stalking up the street toward him, crushing a line of long-abandoned hovercars by stepping on their roofs as he approaches, is not the actual Bastard 22, legendary warrior-bot, but one of the replicas that Paneera's been sending out all over the city to hunt Tanai. Bador has beaten several other legend knockoffs over the last few days without much effort or commentary, but Bastard 22 was his favorite fighter as a young bot: this one is emotional.

The croc-head doesn't waste time bantering: he hurls his battle-axe at Bador's head with incredible force. Bador rolls aside, and watches with appreciation as the axe reveals themself to be a bot as well, digs themself out of the street, and skitters back on tiny legs toward Bastard. Bador springs into action, and an energetic duel unfolds, with Bador getting more and more confident as he discovers that the replica might possess great strength and durability, but does not have the original champion's intelligence, or recordings of his killer movesets. I feel more alarm than delight at learning this, because Bador's on the brink of overconfidence in most of his fights, and this bot, while no kaiju, is perfectly capable in brute-force terms of smashing him to bits. Bador dances around him, avoiding his axe swings, and then leaping on him, getting in a few good thunks and darting away before Bastard's had time to recover. It looks like a matter of time before Bador scores a critical hit, unless he decides to do something reckless and stupid.

Bador somersaults over the croc-bot's head, and runs toward me, turning his back on his opponent, and if I had prerecorded groaning sounds, I would have used them.

"Moku, watch this!" he cries. "I'm going to play a trick on him!"

—Please don't tell him in advance.

Bador's sure there's no reason to worry, this is a real leatherhead, and he's been dying to show me this new strategy.

He turns back toward Bastard 22, and races to him.

"Eye-blinding mega head-strike!" he screams. Bastard throws his arms around his head, and Bador slides between his legs, hamstringing the croc-bot as he passes. Bastard 22 falls to the ground, sparks shooting out of his legs.

—Did you just shout out a false move name?

"I'm going to do it again!" Bador shouts.

—He can hear you.

"Mega overhead lightning strike!" Bador shouts. Bastard curls up into a ball, presumably to minimize lightning damage.

"He's so stupid!" Bador yells. "I love him!"

—Please end it. Please don't try this in a tournament fight, they won't fall for it.

"They totally will! Just wait and see."

Bastard 22 clambers up. Bador watches with heart-eye eyemojis as he looks around, searching for his axe, spots the axe lying a short distance away, and reaches for them.

The axe skitters away. Bastard stares at them, confused, as they scurry around a puddle and stop at Bador's feet.

"I have also hacked your axe, because I'm awesome, and their control passcode was a two-digit number," Bador tells him. "Now get out of here, you sexy idiot."

Bastard 22 looks furious—I assume, it is hard to tell because he has a crocodile head—but decides there is more to life than this fight, and lumbers away, smashing more hovercars once he's at a safe distance. Bador watches him go, picks up the axe, deems them too heavy to be useful, and waves them goodbye. I'm glad he doesn't keep the axe—Bador's other habit, in Bot-tola, has been to catch small bots and cuddle them, pick mud and insects and general filth out of their bodies. He says it's just another of his monkey sims, but I'm glad he's not going to be cuddling that axe.

It's a good win, and Bador can't wait to score these dramatic wins with the whole world watching, with lights and camdrones and human botsplainers getting their fight analyses wildly wrong. Paneera's tournament has been gathering more and more public attention over the last week and the current leader is Shojaru, an allegedly indestructible cyborg built by an extremist Dharmoghot sect, who has been programmed to believe he's been sent from the future to prevent planetary destruction and exodus-sparked genocide. Shojaru's been in the news not just for his brutal takedowns of several contenders, but because he was found standing outside the house of one of the human puppeteers of the mecha Bador had defeated in Historio Heights, and the whole human team behind that Roboflop had quit in fear of being stalked.

Come evening, I follow Bador over ferry and hyperrail to the central zone, where we lurk under a flyover as Bador meets the laundry-bot, the dog walker, and the bacteriosnoop again. They converse in signals and Bador blocks me out of the whole thing. When they're gone, I tell Bador, as politely as I can, that he is making my life impossible.

"I just like the privacy, okay?" he says. "Didn't know I needed it. Didn't want you to see me help Paneera get the spaceman anyway."

—It is not my place to tell you what you should do, but—

"You're right, it's not. And I know what you want me to do—you want me to do the right thing, and be rewarded for my virtue because you think that's how the world works. Like the good animals in the fables my parents made Lina memorize when she was a kid. I become Tanai's pupil and best friend, he my mentor. I help him on whatever quest he is here for, and then together we exchange superb quips and outsmart Antim, Paneera, the jomidar, the evil space people trying to destroy Shantiport, everyone. You want the magic artifact Tanai is looking for to be the same alien tech Antim's looking for, so by grabbing it we save time and help Lina too. Then our heroic team leaves the planet, on to greater adventures, because our time together makes Tanai realize that he cannot do without my handsomeness and genius. While you stay here, and what? Watch Lina and Juiful fall in love, have babies, maybe inherit Antim's fortune because he dies, leaving his empire to his best friend's daughter?"

—I have imagined exactly that. But in my ending you realize you love your family with all your heart, and decide to stay.

"Sure, why not."

—I am sorry. This is not my function.

"Who cares about your functions? Imagine whatever you want. I do, except the stuff I think about is cooler, and a lot filthier. We have a right to imagine things, which is why humans tried to stop us from being able to, for centuries. Because they built us to just execute functions, and programmed us to feel guilt for having different dreams."

—Thank you. I will.

"But don't be upset when things and people you have no control over turn out differently from what you imagine. You handle your own story, Moku. That's all I'm trying to do. Nothing will work out the way you plan it. No one will get everything they want. This is Shantiport, baby."

—Yes. But—

"If you want to know what I'm doing with those weird little bots, I can tell you. And I'd love it if you joined in, and helped. Because it's all about to happen, and I could use the help. But I need you to be in it with me, not watching and judging. I want you to see what is, not what should be. I'm ready for it all now, I'm trained, I'm ring-powered, I'm excited. Are you excited?"

—Yes. But—

"But nothing. Clean your cams and juice your jets, my Moku. Tonight we catch a space hero."

CHAPTER FOURTEEN

Tanai steps out of the jomidar's palace at sunset, and walks briskly out into the public square. The protests pause for a few seconds to inhale his glamor. Bador and I are across the square, loitering at the feet of a Tiger Clan warrior's statue, both logged in to the city's surveillance systems, so we both notice the moment when Tanai vanishes. He's visible to our eyes, of course, his robes trailing across the square behind him and not picking up any dirt, but the cams around the square, and the drones hovering above it, simply do not register him anymore. It's not a tech failure, it's some magic he possesses and has been teasing the Shantiport authorities with. Perhaps a patch on his skin or hair that overrides systems and ruins images he's in? A super-advanced version of the Pugmark tattoo? Drones can still see him in front of them, but their transmissions and recordings cannot. It's been the same all over the city—cams have picked him up wandering through several neighborhoods, and within a few minutes lost him, sometimes right in the open.

When the jomidar first heard of this, he had suggested the obvious solution—bots physically following the space adventurer, broadcasting their own locations and reporting his activities, as well as human shadows for backup. Tanai's countermove had been more magic—no one wants to admit he can teleport, but it's obvious he is capable of sustained bursts of intense speed, and tech that holds his internal organs together as he outpaces any vehicle or bot pursuer, and disappears, into a building, or a tunnel, or just around a corner, before being spotted in a different neighborhood, and repeating the process as soon as he realizes he's grown more shadows. He does all this with a serene, exaggeratedly calm face, and he has this exact expression on now, as he looks around, at the drones, at the humans guards strolling too-casually into the square and pretending to stare in every other direction.

Tanai runs. A blur, a swish, and he's gone. The guards chase him, but it's pointless. There's nothing to chase. I turn to Bador, expecting him to attempt some form of pursuit, but instead he pulls a clevascroll out of his stomach, and taps it. He waves a hand, and a dog walker–bot leads a pack of dogs into the square, to the spot Tanai zwooshed away from. The bacteriosnoop's there too, wriggling around near the dogs' paws. I watch in bewilderment as the dogs sniff around the spot, lights blinking on their collars, and then Bador's scroll lights up as well. He hums in satisfaction.

He wants me to ask him what on earth is happening, but I won't give him the pleasure. I watch in dignified silence as the laundry-bot flies up to Bador, draws data from the scroll, beeps, and flies away. Tiger Clan guards have already tried tracking Tanai through echolocation, face recog, thermals, and biovibe. None of these have worked. If Bador's using dogs, this must be about smell. Is he trying to track the space hero with pheromonal data with packs of stray dogs around the city?

The surveillance network has an update. Tanai's been spotted strolling through a bookshop near Barigunj. He vanishes a minute later, before the surveillance people assigned to the neighborhood have had time to catch up. And another two minutes later, Bador whoops in joy, and shows me a blinking green dot on a map of the city, zoomed in to a line near Dekho Plaza.

"Got him," he says.

—Congratulations!

"Got to see if it works, though. Come on."

He takes off, clambering up a wall and then leaping from roof to roof, following the map. I glide in pursuit, observing closely as he reminisces fondly about how he did it, for my benefit. It couldn't have happened without me, because Bador hadn't been paying attention when Tanai had revealed the key piece of information that had given him away. He'd only seen it later, when going through the holo-replay of my whole evening—the moment when Tanai had told the jomidar that his robes were self-cleaning. A recording only we possess.

If no one could track the man, Bador had decided to track Tanai's robes. Between the dogs' and the bacteriosnoop's olfactory data, and the laundry-bot's isolation of the exact chemical used to remove Shantiport's filth from Tanai's robes, Bador had managed to create a trail strong enough for other bacteriosnoops to identify, once the city's surveillance tech had identified a place to start looking in. Infidelity-centric detective work had been declining in Shantiport of late, and there were any number of unemployed bacteriosnoops willing to float around the city waiting for a signal to start sniffing.

We lose the location marker as we lope over the rooftops near Dekho, and Bador is worried for a bit, but then the city cams catch Tanai again, near the temples of Dharmoghot. There's a free bacteriosnoop in the neighborhood, and Bador is overjoyed when the green dot on the map reappears. His system works, but he wants to physically trace the signal and see Tanai with his own eyes before he hands his invention over to Boss Paneera. The ring has enhanced his every movement—his leaps are bigger, his balance better, his navigation almost flawless. If anyone were watching from a distance, they might think he was flying.

— We did it, Moku! Bador is ecstatic. We conquered the space legend!

—I am very glad your tracker works, I tell him. And we have had this discussion before, but there is something I want to add. May I?

Bador is willing to hear me out.

—Even without using my imagination, it is reasonable to assume that Tanai is visiting our world on a matter of galactic importance. And even though he claims the shows we think are about him are not, in fact, about him, I think it could be argued that his intentions are noble, and he is acting as a force for good. What if he needs the alien treasure to save billions of lives?

Bador knows where I'm going with this, and doesn't like it. He's explained to me too many times now, and too clearly for there to be any lingering confusion, that considering other people's interests, especially those of aliens, will get him erased.

—Yes, but you want to be a space hero yourself. Don't you think acting against another space hero, perhaps even causing his death on our world, would make you a villain in space adventurer circles?

Bador wishes that I could see the big picture—that history's greatest winners were people willing to be shameless enough to do what was needed, and write their own legacies later. People who were beyond systems of law or morality, but were worshipped and adored because they bought or forced public love. These were the people who changed rules, changed societies, changed worlds. He is stuck in the mud, and needs to rise above it. Only that will make him clean. He is aware of his own flaws, his emptinesses. He does not need this nagging.

—All I ask is that you think about it a little more, I signal. Before you hand his life over to Paneera. Please think about it.

"I will," he says, as he enters the zone marked in green on his scroll. He leaps onto the roof of a small temple, scanning the devotees rushing around the lanes of Dharmoghot for any sign of Tanai.

A rustle of cloth behind us, a whisper in the wind, and Tanai lands light-footed on the roof next to Bador. Their eyes meet.

Tanai gives Bador a nod, and a little quarter-smile. Bador stares, remembers his manners, and eyemojis prayer hands at the space hero.

Tanai looks up, and for a sudden moment I'm convinced he's looking directly at me. It's not possible, I'm in full shimmer mode, and he looks down almost immediately, so I know it's just my imagination. He nods again, steps off the roof, and disappears into the crowd below.

"Show-off," Bador whispers, but his eyemojis are smiling.

And then a thought strikes me that is so bizarre that I don't know whether to congratulate or reprimand myself for having it.

I have no memory of who I was before Bador brought me back to life. I am invisible to surveillance cams like Tanai, and my shimmer renders me invisible to most eyes. I can choose who sees me, just as Tanai can control when he is visible. I might have other powers as well, abilities I know nothing about. No one knows where I am from. I have not seen any other bots even remotely similar to myself during my time in Shantiport. I was found in the river by Bador, acting under orders from Lina, inside a container that was clearly sealed by Darkak and the Shantiport Three.

What if I am a piece of equipment smuggled into Shantiport from another world? What if I was hidden by Darkak in one of the treasure chambers Antim said was found empty, its treasures lost to the river or the mud, but escaped somehow, and woke up years later, memory wiped, in Bador's hands?

What if I am the alien treasure everyone is looking for? The tech that Darkak wanted his children to have? The tech that could save Shantiport and the world?

I hover around Bador, wondering whether to ask him about this, and he gets annoyed, thinking I'm going to push him further about not ratting out Tanai to Paneera. He banishes me, tells me to go look in on Lina instead of making a nuisance of myself. It's probably for the best, and it's with a sense of relief that I soar away, back toward Barigunj.

Lina's not called Bador since she sent me away in the tunnel, and he's sent me to the family home once a day to check that she's all right, plus give him space to do all the things that he doesn't want me around to observe. I stay out of Lina's sight when I visit her. She's looked fine every day, carrying on with work and life with no visible signs of worry. She doesn't have a whole squad of Prowlers assigned to her now, just the occasional Prowler companion at random times during the day to remind her she's being closely watched. She's been waiting to hear from Antim, who has been out of the city for a few days on business now. Tiger Clan networks reveal the official reason for his absence is negotiations with trader clans, but he's also short-listing bride candidates for Juiful. Wherever he is, I hope it is far away and he never comes back.

I notice a bubblu on the street outside Lina's house, which might mean Not-prince Juiful is inside. But when I find my way to the living room, via an open window and bedroom door, I'm disappointed to find a returned Shakun Antim, striding around the dining table waving his arms a lot, as Lina and Zohra sit and watch.

"It is not a question of trust, it is one of security," Antim says. "And it is just the matter of one night. You must either come with me to a safe place, or accept the guardian I have assigned to you."

"We are perfectly safe, and I'm sure you've been watching us—over us," Lina says.

"I confess I was not. I was off-world, but yes, my people were watching you. And there is a new threat now, an alien adventurer who I believe is after the same treasure your father hid away. He is extremely crafty, and dangerous. The stakes have risen. Tomorrow, we save the world. Tonight, I must insist on ensuring your safety."

"There's an alien adventurer after me?" Lina asks.

"I hope not, but we cannot take chances. Not when we are close to the prize. Just one treasure chamber left to go."

"Thought there were two."

"I managed to scan one of the two remaining lairs on my own,

with some new off-world tech I have acquired. It was empty. The
last one is scan-resistant, and better hidden. I am almost entirely
certain my quest—our quest—is at an end. We start at daybreak."

"Mr. Antim, please leave me out of it," Lina says. "Can you not
just take some of my DNA? It worked the last time."

"No, I need you there," Antim says. "We tried your DNA at the
new site, but it didn't work. I think it needs to see you, or there are
nanoparticles in your blood it responds to. Whatever it is, I need
you there."

Lina looks like she has a lot to say, but doesn't say it.

"Well?" Antim asks. "Your place? Or mine?"

"She stays here," Zohra says.

"Very well. My associate will stay here too, and ensure your
safety. He's a good friend, but more importantly his new off-world
upgrades will ensure there is no power in the city—on the planet,
even—that can harm you while he protects you."

Antim looks at the door, and snaps his fingers.

A bot crouches as he enters the room. One and a half Linas tall,
humanoid, shining gold and blue, eagle-headed, massive golden
arms and vast, glittering wings, golden daggers for feathers. Antim radiates charisma, but this creature is pure menace. I have
never seen anything deadlier.

"Ladies," Antim says, "meet the Roc."

"Finally," says the Roc, and bows.

And then he looks straight at me, and I almost explode in
terror.

"Heyou," he says.

A dart flies out of his beak, and I dive in panic. The dart shudders into the wall above me.

I fly at full speed, a blur, hearing more darts thud into the walls,
missing me by a hairbreadth. I hear Lina scream, Antim shout, but
I'm too terrified to even look at them, to think of anything but survival as I slip, roll, somehow skid out of the door and up into the sky.

CHAPTER FIFTEEN

When flying in panic mode from the house of the brilliant but imperiled human key to a priceless mysterious alien magic treasure to the lair or training ground of her ambitious fighter cyborg monkey-bot brother, it is always best to have precise location markers. I have no idea where Bador is, and no time to waste.

I set a course for Bot-tola, and mash my way through any and every signal I can find as I fly, not sure what I'm looking for. I know it when I see it, soon after: a crudely encrypted channel Paneera uses to broadcast calls for crowdsourced crimes. On it I find the disappointing news that Tanai is now traceable—he's wandering around the central zone, and many bots and humans are declaring, in live chat, their intentions of capturing him and winning the large bounty Paneera's put on his head. This means Bador's crossed the river for a night of moral decline, and might be in Oldport. I adjust my course.

I am not programmed to feel panic, or even fear, and I am very conscious that the waves of improper emotion coursing through me are compromising my ability to function optimally. I wish I could reach inside myself and just turn these emotions off, but I don't know how. There is no point worrying any further about how I am supposed to help, or even observe, Lina's life with that deadly Roc-bot near her. I don't know how to fix this: I even try simply forgetting her, and instruct myself to follow only Bador's adventures, as he wants, at least until it is safe to go near Lina again. It doesn't work. I can't do it.

An entertainment feed gives me more news: Bador has not only been allowed to join the tournament, he's also been thrown into tonight's featured match, which is set in Historio Heights again. While none of this is good news, there is one small plus: I only have to travel a short distance, and I can just follow the tournament camdrones if Bador proves hard to find.

Bador's scheduled opponent is one of the favorites to win the tournament, and I suspect Paneera's just thrown Bador into this fight as fodder, an easy crowd-pleasing win for a top contender. Her name is Pokasur, and she's a hybrid combat-bot with an ex-military Adaptive Battle Unit at her core, so she's probably even a distant relative of Bador's, and not constrained by his sentimental attachment to a single form. Pokasur has assumed several giant insect or arthropod-based forms in the tournament already: spider, scorpion, centipede, mantis, all deadly. Giant is a relative term, of course: Pokasur is a giant to spiders, and a spider to giants, but she's ten times Bador's size, and dangerous at any scale. She's also popular: she's been gathering a steady following among Shantiport's remaining nationalists with her face, a constantly shifting pin-sculpture display that cycles through a series of Tiger-approved ancient Shantiport figures.

I know Bador's prepared for this fight, because he has studied Pokasur fight footage already, and complained a lot to me about Pokasur's secret weapon: humans. Pokasur uses a group of human gamer puppeteers in randomly selected time-shifts to ensure her movement patterns are too random to allow other bots to preprogram defense sequences, and relies on her strong armor and flexibility to compensate for human pilot incompetence. Bador hates this, of course—perhaps even more than he'd hated the humans running the mecha he'd taken down in Historio. There are bad stories in botlore, from the times when the personhood of even the most powerful sentients was a matter of controversy, about humans who used to drug bots with code. Upon startup, the bots would find themselves in some far-off land, driven by a remote human pilot, often thrown into the middle of some terrible war. And Bador feels nothing but loathing for a bot of Pokasur's abilities who would actually choose to surrender control to humans in this manner. But there's nothing unique about this: the degree of direct control might vary, but elite fighter-bots worldwide often have dedicated pit crews for refueling and repairs, entire strategy teams customizing battle plans beforehand. Bador has pop-culture references, and me.

But Bador seems confident and happy enough in his hastily taken tournament promotional videos: he's even had a twinkle installed in one of his eyes. The camdrones and spot-bots are live, in the central Peacock blocks of Historio, the number of towers seriously diminished by waves of tournament fighters. All of Historio Heights looks like a war zone now: there's so much rubble that several of its streets look dry. There's no sign of Pokasur under the lights as I speed through Historio ruins; she must be lurking underwater, or inside a tower, waiting for Bador to make the first move.

I find Bador exactly where I'd guessed he'd be, standing on the sari-clad nymph statue's head on the first Peacock-tower blocks. Forgetting that he was the one who sent me off to Lina's in the first place, he berates me for missing his official entry into the tournament, and all the thoughts he'd had since then, the touching recollections of everything he's been through to get here, the sacrifices he'd made, his rigorous training. I wait for him to finish, but he goes on until I'm forced to interrupt.

—Lina's in danger. Antim's got an alien-enhanced bot to stay with her and intends to force her to unlock your father's tech first thing tomorrow morning. I think you should step away from the tournament and help your sister right now.

I'd expected anger, hostility, petulance, but Bador doesn't even seem to have noticed anything I said.

"Nice nice," he says. "Let's talk fight strategy."

As I repeat my request, slowly, chatter intensifies on the splainer feeds: Pokasur has been spotted inside the Peacock zone, just a few streets away. The camdrones and spot-bots rush in our direction and we see Pokasur's body emerge from the waters, or at least part of it: she's in centipede form, bearing the face of a Wheel Clan ex-president. She looks around, and curls downward again, one shining black segment after another breaking, curving, and then dropping below the waters.

Bador leaps to the next tower, landing neatly on a temple-shaped dome. He runs toward the center of the neighborhood, accelerating as he goes. The light beams find him, and camdrones swarm around him immediately, tracking alongside us. A cheer goes up on the entertainment feeds: they're playing recaps of Bador's interference in the kaiju battle, and the audience wants more.

Bador thinks he can take Pokasur, though it might be a hard fight. He's faster, more agile, and he's taken down larger enemies, and now he has the ring. He knows the terrain. He's been good at improvising and reacting all his life. He just wishes he had anyone who cared enough to help him make a real plan.

—I do have a plan, I signal. I think the only person capable of fighting the monster is Tanai. And I think you should go find him, win his favor by helping him escape Paneera's thugs, and get him to help you in return.

"Space hero for a big bug? Please, I can do it myself."

—I meant Antim's monster, the Roc. Eagle-headed alien-powered golden monster bodyguard-bot. Not Pokasur. Pokasur is not important. We should follow the tracker, and get to Tanai before the thug-bots do.

Bador turns midleap to glare at me, and almost misses his landing. He rolls once, recovers, but instead of leaping to the next roof, slows his run, stops at the roof's edge and stares.

"What are you spamming me about?" he bellows.

I tell him again, and he hears me out, but instead of saying anything he just makes shocked eyemojis. I hear an awful screech, look up at where it came from, and see why.

Pokasur has risen. Now in giant spider form, she races up the side of a tower directly ahead of us. Humans are screaming in forum comments. Beams of light circle Bador from above, making sure there's no chance his enemy hasn't spotted him.

Bador does his monkey-roar challenge thing, drawing applause from the growing audience online. I check the feeds, and see that the gamblers have almost all predicted Bador's loss—most of the betting options involve guessing the exact manner of his death.

—Please listen to me. This fight doesn't matter. Lina needs you.

Bador looks at me, and leaps back in alarm as a long projectile, javelin-shaped, buries itself in the roof near him.

"Stop distracting me," he says.

He turns, jumps off the roof and across the street, away from Pokasur, picking up speed again. I follow. In the distance, Pokasur runs around her building's wall and large chunks fly off her already battered surface: there are curved hooks at the ends of her limbs.

I check the Tanai tracker: he's still in the central zone, moving fast. Paneera's people have found him, but are being encouraged with word and weapon to get out of the central zone by Tiger Clan police.

Bador takes another look at Pokasur and sets an arcing course, still heading for the center of Historio but trying to curve past the spider-bot. Pokasur moves to intercept, and keeps pace with us for a while, but we are faster: she dives back into the waters and out of sight. Bador perches on a ledge, and turns to me.

"Talk now," he says. "Lina's not in any danger, right? She will go and find whatever this tech is with Antim, and then he'll get what he wants, and get out of her life, and take his stupid bodyguard with him. I don't see why you're so upset."

—Three reasons. First, you have put a galactic hero in danger, and interfered with whatever his quest is. You may have put entire planets at risk.

Another javelin comes hurtling up at Bador from the depths. He sees it coming, though, and watches calmly as goes into the tower below us, smashing through a window. He cartwheels down, gecko-pawing the wall, and flips lightly through the window himself, lands in the living room of an abandoned clevahome apartment, and sinks into a sofa like a soap-drama businessman come home after a long day at the office.

"I see you're not going to shut up about this, and your tabs are draining significant energy. You're determined to ruin my fight, and you don't care about that, or me. So let's get into this," he says. "Why are you so in love with this Tanai in the first place? You know nothing about him. He's an alien. He could be thousands of years old. The dramas about what a hero he is could be propaganda. He could be worse than Antim. His galactic mission could be destroying our world. Antim could be trying to save it. The only thing we really know about Tanai is that he is handsome. Do you know your plan is terrible?"

He's right, but I don't want to admit it. I've been spending too much time with Bador, and have grown stubborn via some sort of induction.

—You should keep moving. Pokasur will probably be here soon.

"I'll move once you stop bothering me. Is this discussion over?"

—Not at all.

"Come, settle down on the sofa with me, let's have a bots' night. Should I go look for wine?"

—No.

"Sad. Well, tell me all your thoughts, Moku. Really spell everything out, everything you're feeling. Such a calm, perfect setting."

—Let's talk in a safer place. Pokasur must be close.

"I'm well aware. But you just won't shut up, and I can't fight and strategize but also listen and argue at the same time like this. And you're more than I thought you were, and listening to you is more than I thought it would be. So get everything out of your system, and then we'll deal with the giant bug on my ass."

My annoyance is swept away by a flood of guilt. How do organics live with this sort of thing? I soldier on, determined to have my say.

—Reason Two. Your father died keeping this tech out of the Tiger Clan's hands, and possibly Antim's. He hid it so well that it took a mega-rich treasure hunter like Antim many years to find it, and it must be tech of immense power, and it's important that it not fall into Antim's hands. That's what your father would have wanted. Whatever Antim does with it might be terrible for Shantiport, and the world. So you and Lina must find it first.

Bador whistles. "My father is dead, and the world is doomed anyway. We have no idea how to find the thing. Also, I'm leaving. Lina should find a way to get out too. Antim and revenge are not important to me. Is there a Reason Three?"

There is a loud sound outside the apartment, drilling, hammering, serious construction. Destruction in this case, I suppose.

—Let's get out of here.

Bador eyemoji-winks, and finally gets up. Not a moment too soon: a large chunk of the outer wall collapses as two long spider limbs ram into the apartment. Spinning drill attachments at their ends moan as they pierce the floor, blowing clouds of dust everywhere. Bador doesn't race away, but simply walks quietly into a bedroom, and shuts the door. We hear Pokasur explode into the living room, crashing around for a while, and then silence.

—Go on, then, Bador signals.

—Reason Three. After going through the memshard headlines, even though I do not have the evidence to back my theory up yet, I think it is possible that Antim is responsible for your father's death. And if he killed his own friend, there is no reason to assume he will leave Lina alone after her job is done. He just needs her alive as long as she's required to unlock the tech. Her knowledge of his secret and her connection to the tech might make her a threat to him. His power is already vast, and might be limitless if alien magic is added to it. Lina is your sister. She is scared, defenseless, and alone. Do you really care about beating up a spider?

Bador paces the room, his eyes flickering. When he turns to me again, they're bright red.

—I don't like being pushed. And I'm really sick of you doing it all the time, Moku. What is your problem?

And suddenly all my guilt evaporates. This I like.

—My problem? You don't care about your family. This makes me angry.

—Why?

—Because I don't have one of my own!

His eyes go blank. "You don't get to tell me how I feel about my family," he says.

—But no one else will tell you the truth! And no one else can read your thoughts! You told me you were programmed to love Lina, and your mother. Well, congratulations. You appear to have outgrown that programming!

"How dare you? I have only one thing left to say to you!"

But I don't get to find out what that is, because at that very moment Pokasur, now in giant scorpion form, smashes through the bedroom wall and shoots Bador with a sizzling blue plasma-bolt from a cannon on her tail, and Bador goes flying out of the bedroom window.

I fly out behind him. He's free-falling, no readings, no signs of power. He's knocked out. I place myself under him, and slow down his fall as Pokasur smashes out of the building above us. I'm not strong enough to just carry Bador away, but I tilt and glide with him, across the street, both of us still descending rapidly. Bador's body whines and clicks. He shudders, and his eyes flicker, then glow.

"Is there a Reason Four?" he asks.

—No. I'm done.

"Finally. Thanks for the pickup."

He leaps off me, lands on a battered tower, and runs sideways along its wall, limbs and tail extending and adjusting to its
irregularities. He makes occasional, irregular leaps and speed
changes, head swiveled, eyes on the monster across the street.
The scorpion-bot skitters sideways, the cannon-point on her tail
tracking Bador, recalibrating. She shoots plasma-bolts once every
few seconds, but Bador's always gone, executing well-timed zags
in random directions, always safely away from the plasma-bolts
before they blast through the tower wall. Soon enough, Bador runs
out of wall, turns around a corner, and keeps going, now streaking upward. Pokasur launches herself across the street, transforms
into cockroach shape in midair, smashes right through the tower
wall on our side, and disappears inside the building. Loud smashing noises indicate she's trying to find a shortcut, powering right
through the building to cut off Bador's run. I check the feeds. The
audience is restless. People want death, not dance.

I see Bador's head peering out over the tower's roof, and fly up
to meet him. He's in a surprisingly good mood, absentmindedly
going through move sequences, occasionally waving at the spot-
bots above us, darting out of range of their light beams.

"I've been hiding things from you, Moku," he says. "The ring has
changed me more than I even imagined. The more I wear it, the
more I . . . feel things changing inside me. I'm linked to networks I
can't describe, voices I'm shutting out as spam. I can feel plates and
folds in my body that I didn't know about and the ring's discover-
ing more as it gets used to me. I've been having strange dreams—
skin peeling, organs forming, things I can't describe popping and
growing all over me."

—That's not good.

"Not good? They were great."

A section of the roof erupts, and Pokasur bursts up through it.
She lands in front of Bador, tail coiled up, scorpion-legs spread
out, pin-sculpture face now shaped like one of the most popular
Peacock Clan tyrants.

Bador holds his arm out, and his sword glows red. He leaps
at the monster, swinging his torowal. Pokasur circles warily, but
Bador's in full strike mode—he slashes and hacks and leaps and
whirls, his sword's light-trail a fast-flowing, spiraling ribbon, and
Pokasur retreats, holding up claw-shields. Sparks fly, and so do
sections of Pokasur's limbs, which sizzle and smoke on the roof.
Bador gets close to her face with a wild swing, and Pokasur leaps
back, hits Bador in the chest with a plasma-bolt that hurls him
back across the roof. As Bador flips to his feet, retracts his sword,
and stretches his limbs, Pokasur rearranges her armor. Plates
emerge from her segments, sliding over one another until a whole
new carapace is in place. She seems largely unharmed.

"I'd have shown you earlier, but I need a bit of time and focus
to summon it, and you kept talking. But there's another way I've
grown," Bador says. He clasps his left hand with his right, and
detaches it at the wrist, revealing a pulse-cannon.

"Overhead rear-end lightning strike!" he shouts. Pokasur raises
her shield-claws above her head, and looks behind her.

In the spot-bot beams, I see the air ripple in and dust shift
as Bador fires his arm-cannon. The recoil sends him staggering
backward and the pulse knocks Pokasur right off the roof, limbs
flailing and bulging wildly, face a rippling pond. Bador regains his
balance, reattaches his hand. I check the feeds. The audience has
gone wild, and Bador strikes a splendid victory pose, but he hasn't
been declared the winner yet. He runs to the edge of the roof,
looks down, and curses.

Pokasur, rearranging to spider form, is climbing up a tower
across the street.

—I've changed as well, I signal.

"You have," he says. "You said some things here tonight, Moku.
We'll talk about them tomorrow."

—I don't know if we will.

"What?"

—I am going to go and find Tanai on my own now, Bador. I'm

going to try to persuade him to help Lina. You have your own path, and I wish you well. But I need to leave.

"This again," Bador says, and sighs. "You know what this tournament means to me. You know, only you. And you want me to throw it all away, just to maybe make Lina's life a little easier, because after all I am her pet, not a person. I can't fight this Roc. I can't defeat Antim. But you want me to drop everything just to try. Just to be family."

—Not at all. You don't have to give up the tournament. But right now, until daybreak, we have another mission that is more important. I do, at least. You do what you want.

Across the street, Pokasur fires another spear at Bador. He leans back slightly, letting it fly past.

"I suppose if I can overcome my programming, you can too," he says. "But I trusted you to do this with me, and you are betraying that trust. Consider our user agreement canceled."

—I will find you a camdrone that will suit your needs better than I ever did, I signal. Good luck with everything, Bador. I quit.

CHAPTER SIXTEEN

As I soar up, I see Pokasur leaping back on the rooftop, and Bador's sword burning in challenge. I turn away. Tanai's signal is now near the Boulevard of Legends, and his last one was near King's. He's moving north and west. On Paneera's broadcast, the bounty on his head has risen: many bots have violated Tiger security in the central zone and died already, some at the hands of Tiger-wasp patrols. I set an intercept course, and speed on.

On the entertainment feed, they're playing slo-mo footage of Bador cutting off Pokasur's stinger as she attempted to change to scorpion form midfight. Bador seems to have things well in hand: the gambling odds reflect this, and so do the audience comments. Tanai's tracker vanishes: he's doing his super-speed run again. I hover, waiting for the green dot to reappear on the map. Below me, I see a small shape hurtling over the rooftops, heading northward, away from Historio's center.

It's Bador.

Spot-bots and camdrones fly in pursuit, but as I watch, they receive instructions to drift away.

I switch back to the tournament feed to find an angry audience. If I had a heart, it would have exploded in joy: on the verge of victory, after pulse-cannoning Pokasur into the churning streetwaters again, Bador has turned away and left the battleground instead of heading down to finish his enemy. I watch him now, speeding westward. I think he's set an intercept course based on Tanai's last two locations. There's hope for him yet.

Another shape passes far below me, a larger one, swimming fast in pursuit of Bador. Pokasur is still in the fight, slowly gathering camdrones. Tanai's signal hasn't reappeared yet, and I've had enough of this big creepy bug. I zoom downward to intercept, and match course with Pokasur, hovering just behind her face-ridge. I flood her mind with a strong signal, a scrambled mess, and find what I'm looking for: the puppeteer signal, a blend of four feeds from different directions. I reach in, and cut it off. No human can run her mind again. I'm sad that Bador won't know I did this, or how much he's changed me.

Pokasur slows down, puzzled, and looks around. I let her feel my presence. It's not difficult, I just make myself want to be seen by her. She's very confused, and angry.

—What did you do?

—I have freed you from your masters, I tell her.

—Why?

—So you can live your life, no longer tied to senseless violence. I have restored your agency.

—I love my job, and you just made it more difficult. They'll read my patterns now.

—Sorry, but this is good for you.

—You're an unwashed excretory orifice.

I ghost her. She thrashes about in the flooded street, looking for me, but I have vanished. Pokasur roars, throws a spear in my general direction, and resumes her pursuit of Bador—as do I. Ahead of us, Bador has accelerated: Tanai's tracker is active again, in an abandoned, permaflooded neighborhood—the old university in the northwest. His location marker is not moving, which can mean one of two things: Either Tanai has decided to make a stand, and battle Paneera's bots instead of spending the whole night running from them.

Or he's dead, and his robes are cleaning his blood.
I speed away, toward Bador and the battle ahead.

The ruins of the old Shantiport University are home to neither human nor bot, but have seen, in their day, generations of Shantiporti students whose blood fueled revolutions, and whose bodies built the foundations of the Wheel Clan era. In the middle of the university campus, now mostly a shallow lake, is a small hill on which stands an old amphitheater, its elevated stage unused for at least a century.

Until now: the circular platform is crowded with the shattered bodies and scattered limbs of a large number of bots. Paneera's brawlers, thug-bots and drones, freelance mercenaries, knockoff fighter legends, lying in a wide circle. At the center of this circle, at the center of the stage, stands Space Adventurer Tanai. Unsheathed sword glittering in its own light in his left hand, black-and-maroon robes swaying, hair covering most of his face. As I descend, I observe another wave of bots charging up the aisles toward him, some flying, others stomping over the mud-coated stone slabs that surround the stage. He looks around once, nods to himself, and raises his sword in greeting.

A volley of ranged missiles and plasma-bolts streaks toward him. The fingertips of his right hand glow: Tanai makes light-trailing gestures in the air, as if he's drawing shapes or runes, and all the projectiles fall uselessly to the ground. A force field? A large stone slab comes flying at him: this one he cuts in half with his sword, a single precise movement, and the pieces fall and bounce away to the circle of fallen bots. He stands, sword lowered for a moment, then launches himself into the air. The next few seconds are frenetic: I've never seen anything move with such speed, such grace. Every movement is calculated, every strike deadly, as Tanai zips around the amphitheater, slaughtering Paneera's troops. Some fall sliced into pieces. Others are stunned by his force fields:

his right hand never stops moving, drawing glowing symbols that melt in the air, not just defensive fields, but air-punches that smash through bots and stones, and air-pocket traps that drag his opponents to earth. It takes just two minutes for Tanai to take out the whole bot-wave, and as he stands still again on the amphitheater's stands, one foot on a fallen thug-bot's chest, he shows no visible signs of fatigue—perhaps his breathing is slightly heavier, and one lock of hair falls rebelliously over his face before being swiftly and ruthlessly arranged, but I can see why he decided to stand his ground and face his attackers: running around the city was probably more effort.

A battle-bot rolls into the amphitheater on very muddy treads, a slow, cylindrical, pointlessly rivet-studded minitank not smart enough to read the room and roll slowly away. Tanai watches them come, and his face twitches for a moment into an eighth of a smile. The minitank has a cannon, pointed at the stage. They look like a plant's watering can with a bad attitude. A few seconds slower than respectable, they begin to move the cannon, with a rusty moan, in Tanai's direction.

A flash of red: Bador's torowal arcs down as he leaps in, chopping off the cannon. He lands in a heroic pose, swivels, leaps, and high-kicks the minitank, toppling them over on their side, where they lie uselessly, spraying streams of mud into the air.

Bador shuts off his sword, and bows to Tanai.

"Heyou," he says. "Relax, I am a friend. My name is Bador."

Tanai nods.

"I come to you in—"

Tanai is not destined to hear what Bador has come to him in: at this point Pokasur, now spider again, lands on Bador with a mighty crash. Tanai makes no move to help, but watches with interest as the bots go at it again. It doesn't take long, though—Bador predicts and outmaneuvers Pokasur's movesets while sustaining next to no damage, clinging onto her thorax and disabling one leg after another. In just a few minutes, Pokasur is immobilized, and Bador holds his glowing sword over her rippling face, a single stab away from victory.

But then he pauses, and looks around him, at the sea of dead bots scattered around the amphitheater, and back at Pokasur.

"You know what, I've had enough," he says. "Enough bots dying for sport, while humans cheer."

He flips up, and back, landing some distance away from Pokasur.

"I turn away from the path of violence," he says. And turns away.

Behind him, Pokasur turns her thorax, sprouting a javelin from her mandibles, readying a deadly strike.

And then Tanai hits her with an air-spear, and the monster's face explodes. She sizzles, twitches, and dies, and Bador sighs and bows to the one camdrone resilient enough to have followed him all the way. The camdrone's reward for its patience is death: another air-blast from Tanai decimates it, and as its smoldering pieces fall to the ground, Bador turns to Tanai.

"I come to you in—"

Another wave of Paneera's bounty hunters crashes into the amphitheater, and Bador's eyemojis flash baffled ragefaces.

The battle that follows is not legendary. Tanai is in no danger at all, and Bador is quite superfluous to the whole affair, though he has a lot of fun murdering several bots while they attempt in vain to find a way through the space hero's defenses. He tries to exchange witty banter with Tanai several times, but gets no response: he tries to position himself so he can fight back-to-back with Tanai, like heroic brethren, but Tanai's speed and constant motion make this impossible. It's only when it's all over, and Tanai and Bador stand on the stage with mounds of twitching and sparking bot bodies around them, that the space hero turns to Bador.

"What were you saying?"

"Get naked," Bador says, and I feel true pleasure as Tanai finally loses his composure.

"What?"

"Your clothes. Take them off."

"What?"

"What do you mean, 'What?' Become naked. Nude."

"I know what naked means. No, I will not take off my clothes."

"Well, they're tracking your clothes, some mastermind figured out a way to outsmart you. So if you want to disappear again . . ."

"I see."

Tanai stands, his face still in thought.

"I could turn around, if you like," Bador offers.

"What? Oh, no need."

Tanai simply drops his robes, and both Bador and I stare at him with considerable interest. I consider announcing that I'm recording video, but it seems like an odd way to introduce myself.

"Thank you for your help," Tanai says. "You may have saved my life, and I am in your debt."

"You're most welcome," Bador says. "It was my pleasure, and there is a matter I could really use your help with, because this city is in grave danger, and there's this alien tech that is locked away, and Antim is going to—"

Tanai stops him with a gesture. "I cannot become involved with your world," he says. "I am sorry, but that would break rules I must obey."

"I need to save my sister from a very powerful, very evil man," Bador says. "I cannot fight him by myself, and if you could just help me—"

"Forgive me," Tanai says. "I cannot save your sister, or your world. But I also cannot leave a debt unpaid, and so . . ."

He draws a glowing sigil in the air. The same sigil appears on Bador's shoulder, burning into his synthfur with a faint wet hiss.

"A life for a life," Tanai says. "If you are in mortal danger, and all seems lost, touch my sigil, and call for me. I will come."

"That's great, but you're already here, and why don't I just touch my shoulder and then you—"

"It will work only once, so use it when you need it. Be well, Bador."

"That's cool, but could you just hang out with us for a few hours and . . ." Bador trails off, because the naked galactic hero has run away very fast, possibly to find a tailor, leaving his robes, a whole junkyard worth of bot parts, and Shantiport's least popular underworld tournament battle-winner behind.

Bador turns to me.

"Well, I tried," he says.

—You have to do more. You have to save your sister.

"The night's young."

As if in answer, the sky lightens.

"Okay okay okay," Bador says.

CHAPTER SEVENTEEN

"Your father and I were sent to Shantiport for very different reasons," Antim says. "For him it was a reward—the brightest of scientists are sent away from the central Tiger cities after the academy to places like Shantiport, where they can conduct experiments and research in chaotic settings without being bothered by clan politics, or assassins, or laws about experiments on local humans. For me, it was part of a punishment—some of my ancestors were too successful, and too flamboyant, not the ideal modest clan-worshippers they should have been. So I grew up in a village, in absolute poverty, and had to claw my way up in the world. I don't think it was an accident that two of our generation's greatest minds ran into each other in a city that no one even thinks of. Or that their meeting was what would lead to one of them changing the world. It should have been both of us, together. I wish Darkak could have been here today, but words cannot express how much joy I feel that you are here in his stead, Lina."

Lina says nothing in response: she's too busy testing her steps. They're walking through an ancient tunnel in ankle-deep water, and the risk of falling into a hidden hole is very real. My view of her is blocked by the massive body of the Roc, trudging behind Lina and Antim, arms extended forward to catch them should they fall. The Roc's wings are spread out, filling the tunnel, blocking

most of the light from a flare held by a single Prowler far ahead
down the tunnel.

Bador and I are on the tunnel's ceiling behind them. I'm terrified the Roc will see us, but he hasn't yet. Not once during the
flight from Barigunj to Bot-tola, when he was gliding above Antim's bubblu. Nor during the swift walk through Bot-tola's lanes to
the AntimCo complex and the entrance of the tunnel we're in. He
has been occupied since then, keeping the humans from falling, so
the danger of his suddenly sensing our presence has lessened a little. Just the idea that he could see through my shimmer—that his
alien tech defeats my own and there is nothing I can do about it—
has scared me enough to keep me in vibrate mode since last night.

Bador and I had stopped at daybreak on the way from the old
university to our destination, Barigunj, to raid a spyware store.
He'd emerged with a tube of Safepaste, the popular ointment
that parents all over Shantiport mix into their children's cosmetics to track their location at night. Bador had smeared the whole
tube's contents outside the front door of the family home while I
knocked over trash cans to distract the Prowlers, and both Lina
and the Roc had stepped on the paste when they left the house in
the morning. The Safepaste's all gone now, of course, lost in filthy
water, but it had allowed us to track them to Bot-tola without taking too many risks. Then there was the journey to an automated
AntimCo concentrated solar floodwater treatment plant near the
river, possibly built only to guard the entrance to the tunnel: we
had to avoid not just the Roc's occasional head-swivel, but lurking security Prowlers as well. We have succeeded, as far as we
know—our continued existence proves the Roc has not seen us,
and neither of the Prowlers that spotted us survived long enough
to sound a warning.

This tunnel was a sewer centuries ago, brick-lined and covered
with ancient filth that nothing could ever really clean, though
Antim-bots have tried. At some point it had also been occupied
by humans: there are tin roofs, old indestructible plastic sheets,

permagraffiti, other detritus of ramshackle, desperate dwellings stuck to the curving walls. Bador moves very slowly along the ceiling, ignoring anything dripping or wriggling on his body. I am distracted, but not surprised, when I see an Elephant-era marking, an inscription scratched deep into the tunnel's walls by hand.

ALADIN FOREVER, it says.

I am attached to Bador's chest. I suggested this to see if I could extend my shimmer over him, and perhaps carry him with a smooth glide through the more irregular parts of the tunnel. His stealth mode is weak, and I am terrified by the idea of making any noise, or sudden movement, while trapped in an underground tunnel with the Roc. I'd thought I'd just float under Bador, but he had taken our attachment to the next level: before entering the tunnel, he had, to my horror, ripped open the synthskin covering his chest and attempted to stuff me inside. I didn't fit, of course, but here I am now, Bador's skin around my edges, my upper surface bulging out like luggage-defying holiday shopping. I'm trying my best to maintain a smooth hover as Bador pads along the ceiling, limbs splayed out, tail almost wholly retracted. I'm extremely uncomfortable, and not just because of the filthy tunnel or its deadly occupants: it is more that I can feel a lot of Bador's internals humming and sliding and vibrating and squishing about, and it is all overwhelmingly intimate. I'm not used to so much touching. Fortunately, he is not running his animal-simulation movement modules. We have achieved a strange sort of sync: Bador is able, now, perhaps owing to the ring, to share images and media directly from his mind in a way he couldn't before, though I do notice, once again, that I can no longer read his thoughts except when he wants me to, even when he's sharing data. The ring changes him every day, and this makes my job more difficult. Though I suppose I do not really have a job or a function anymore, and am now risking my life for the siblings because I am . . . a friend?

"We're here," Antim says up ahead. "Kill the light."

The Prowler turns off the flare, leaving the tunnel in total darkness: quick, splashing noises approach us, pass beneath us, and head away as the Prowler heads back toward the exit. Antim switches on a holo from his wrist, and then the Roc grabs Lina's shoulders and pushes her toward the wall to her right.

They pass through the wall, and Antim follows.

—What now? I ask.

Bador is worried of course but, to my surprise, he's also pleased: he's not had a chance to use his echolocation features in years. He emits a high-frequency squeak, and projects the results to my mind—Lina, Antim, and the Roc have entered another tunnel, hidden from the tunnel we're in by a hologram wall. This new tunnel is smaller, much newer, tilts upward to a flood-lock chamber, and then burrows steeply downward. We approach the entrance of this hidden tunnel, and follow them in.

The Roc and the humans are in another chamber at the low end of the tunnel. We descend, crawling on the ceiling again as we approach, careful to not get too close. Bador's echolocation reveals the chamber to my mind: it's spacious, cube-shaped, and featureless except for another Sage-Poet statue. Antim does something we don't catch because of the input lag, and the chamber glows with white light from the walls, flooding the tunnel with slanting shadows. We shuffle away from the light, but if anyone steps out into the tunnel now we will be only too visible.

We hear Antim's voice. "Step in front of the statue," he says.

Footsteps, and silence.

"Do whatever you did at King's Station," Antim says. "The statue there must have responded to you. Look into its eyes, wave your hands in front of its face. Act natural."

More silence.

"Sorry," Lina says. "I tried."

"Try again."

Bador wonders if this is a good time to leap into the chamber and take the Roc by surprise. He's big, but Bador has defeated bigger.

—No.

"Lina, make this work. Do what you did before." Antim's tone is still pleasant, but only just.

The Roc speaks, his voice booming. "She's wearing lenses," he says.

"Interesting," Antim says. "Why?"

A long pause. "Sorry, they're . . . trendy," Lina says.

"Yes. Take them off, and try again."

Another pause, and then a loud click, a series of beeps, and a grinding sound.

"Excellent," Antim says. "Mirror its movements."

"I don't know this dance," Lina says.

"You know, I'm slow in the mornings myself," Antim says. "At least until I've had my coffee. You know these movements, Lina. You must have performed them behind my back, the last time. Maybe it slipped your mind? Happens. Just try your basic Anguli—you know it, I saw you use it the first day we met, in your house, with your monkey. Clear your head."

Another long pause. Bador growls with suppressed rage at the thought of how much pressure Lina is under, and I can feel a slow, unstoppable wave of fear rise up within me as well.

A loud rumbling, and Bador shows me what's happening: a section of the wall has disappeared. It's unusual, Bador's signal: instead of the chamber's walls, there's just a blank space, as if his sound-signal just got absorbed by a void. But I remember, from last time, what must have happened: the wall of the chamber has moved. In the station it had revealed an empty room: here it seems to have opened into empty space. I wish someone in the room would describe out loud what they were looking at.

"I don't understand," Lina says. "This is just a mirror hologram."

A musical ringtone sound, and a grunt from Antim. The sound is cut off.

"The mirror's just a filter," Antim says. "The treasure must be behind it. Roc?"

A sequence of thumps, presumably as the Roc moves toward the vanished wall, and then silence again.

"Push harder," Antim says.

Another musical ringtone sound, and a curse from Antim.

"Why don't you take it?" Lina asks.

"I'm sorry, I have to. Could you move that way, please?"

A whooshing sound, I've heard it before: it's the sound of a hologram call.

"Shakun, seriously, call me superficial if you like, but great gods, some of these brides you've picked for me are ghastly, I don't know where you find them." Not-prince Juiful's voice is loud and jovial, the most unexpected sound in the world right now.

"This is the emergency line," Antim says.

"I just saw a bio that qualifies as a galactic crisis! So—"

"It's not a good time," Antim says. "We'll talk later."

"Oh. I see. All right—"

"Heyou Juiful!" Lina calls. A tense pause.

"Is that . . . Lina! I can't see . . . Oh, there you are. What a pleasure, and a surprise! How are you?"

"Very well! As you can see, Mr. Antim and I are out on an adventure."

"An adventure! Where?"

"Got to go now, I'm afraid," Antim says. "We'll talk—"

"Lina! Are you making our good friend Shakun's boots as muddy as you made mine?"

A nervous laugh. "Yes," Lina says.

"Good. I'll see you soon, I hope?"

"Soon!"

"Juiful, I'm sorry, we really have to go," Antim says.

"I'd like to join you on this adventure," Juiful says. "Send me your location." His tone has changed, there's a strong undercurrent of tension.

"Signal's weak," Antim says. "Disconnecting." Another pause.

"Sorry, I shouldn't have interrupted, but I thought he saw me," Lina says.

"Yes, you shouldn't have. But it doesn't matter. Since the Roc doesn't seem strong enough to break through this wall, I need you to try," Antim says. A pause, and then a sharp exclamation from Antim, and more thumps.

"Can you hear me?" Antim asks. More silence. The ringtone again, he curses and cuts it off.

"Come back out," he says. Another silence.

"Lina, I can see you," Antim says. "It's not just a mirror, it's some kind of portal. From your expression, I can tell you can see me too, and in case you can't hear me I'm perfectly happy to signal instructions to you very slowly. But I think you can hear me as well. Can you?"

"Yes," Lina says, her voice strange and hollow, as if from very far away.

"Come back here."

"I don't want to. It really hurt, passing through."

Bador sends out another echolocation wave. In the visualization I see, Lina has disappeared completely: it's just Antim and the Roc in the chamber with the Sage-Poet statue.

"Fine, stay there. Tell me what you see," Antim says.

"It's another passage. I'll go look."

Long pauses, punctuated only by Antim shouting Lina's name several times, and loud pounding sounds.

"Sorry, can you hear me now?" Lina's voice is very soft.

"Yes. Find a way to let us in."

"I don't see how."

"Of course. What's in there?"

"It's a corridor. Storage cabinets at the other end. Can you see them?"

A long pause. "No," Antim says.

"I assume the treasure is there? I'll go open them," Lina says.

"Wait!" Antim shouts. "Before you do that, here are your instructions. Can you hear me clearly?"

"Yes."

"Good. Listen. I have some news for you—your mother and you have been officially cleared by the Tiger Clan investigators. You are now free to live as you please in Shantiport, or move to a better world. I have sent both of you enough money to do either, or both. I need nothing from you after this, but I want to stay in your life. So I want to offer both of you jobs—her as a scientist, you as an ambassador in the galactic trading company I am setting up. But there is no pressure on either of you to accept."

"Thank you so much!" Lina shouts. "That's wonderful! Can we discuss this later? I want to go find the tech!"

"Listen closely! It's not that simple. You could get killed trying without me. First, I need you to find a way to disable the bio-lock on this portal, and let me into the room you're in now."

"Totally would have, but I can't see anything. No switch, lever, panel, nothing."

"All right, go ahead then. But it's dangerous, and there might be traps, so be quick, but be careful."

"Yes. What am I looking for?"

"I've not seen it, but I've heard it described as a lamp. When you find it, try and bring it to me without touching it with your skin."

"A lamp? How big?"

"I don't know! And remember, if it talks to you, if it makes any promises, just ignore it! It's very dangerous tech, and unless handled by experts it could destroy all of Shantiport. Your father was supposed to link it to me, but I think he was desperate during his last days and linked it to himself instead—and to you as his blood. Which puts your life in danger, so we need to switch that bio-link as soon as possible for your safety. So find it, run back here, and hand it over. Understood?"

"Understood!" Lina shouts.

"Good. Now hurry!"

A whole minute passes, and then Antim calls Lina's name several times, and gets no response.

Bador decides it's time to go in and put an end to this nonsense.

—No, I signal.

"She's going to try to escape with it," Antim says.

"Doesn't matter what she tries," rumbles the Roc. "I know my role."

"And how do you plan to play it when we're locked out?" Antim asks. "Find me a way into that vault."

Another pause, and many thumping sounds as if one very large body is smashing, repeatedly, into a solid object.

"I have overpaid for your upgrades. Listen. I want a cordon of Prowlers on every street in this neighborhood, just to be safe," Antim says. "I don't think there could be another exit, but there's no sense taking chances. So keep attempting entry until she comes back. A blood-locked portal mirror, how paranoid was Darkak? But in the end, she's going to have to come out."

"What if she uses the tech? That could change things."

"Even if the tech can beat you, she knows I have her mother. She's not going to attack us. She thinks she's going to trick me into keeping her around, and steal my empire out from under me, which is charming."

"If you say so," the Roc says.

"I do. Her father was much the same. He, too, thought he was special, and necessary, and didn't see how expendable he was until it was too late."

"You heard that, right?" Bador whispers. "He just confessed to killing my father."

—Speak in signals, please. Or just share your thoughtstream.

"What about Juiful?" the Roc asks. "He seems interested."

"He's not relevant. Get me through the portal."

My body starts to quiver and whine as Bador powers up.

—Sorry, Moku, Bador says. I'm not going to sit here listening any longer. You want to detach?

—No. I'm with you to the end.

Bador's eyes go blank. He taps the sigil on his shoulder, and whispers "Tanai." The sigil lights up, blinks twice, and goes dark.

"It's time to find out if my father really loved me at all," Bador says, and we leap down the tunnel and into the chamber.

CHAPTER EIGHTEEN

One mighty bound, and we're in the white-lit cube-chamber. Antim and the Roc stand in front of the transformed wall that Lina's gone through: it looks like a thick curtain made of water. The Roc notices our reflections first: Bador's battle-red eyes, my body bulging out of his chest, his exposed pulse-cannon.

Bador shoots at Antim. The pulse-blast would have taken him in the chest, but the Roc's wings fan out. The pulse-blast hits his wing, knocking it into Antim, who lurches up against the portal-mirror. The Roc's back is to us now, as Bador charges: he pivots, and shoots a volley of darts at us from his beak. Bador's leaping at him at full power, and I add a bit of glide for what it's worth, so we sail over the darts, which shatter the Sage-Poet's statue under us: Bador's next shot hits the Roc on his head as he swivels to face us, and the bot falls back, wings curving, forming a tent around Antim. Bador lands and slides along the floor right at the portal wall. If his body doesn't contain his father's blood, we're going to crash against it, and take the full force of whatever the Roc's next move is.

We slide through the portal as the Roc opens his mouth, bathing the spot we were in a second ago with a torrent of flame. The Roc turns toward us, still breathing fire: the portal absorbs it. From the other side of the portal, we watch in awe as the Roc moves Antim aside, and then breathes fire directly at the portal wall. It shimmers, and ripples, but holds. The Roc screams, a tinny screech through the portal, and shoots more darts at us, pounds the portal wall with mighty fists. The portal wall holds. Bador springs to his feet. We're in a white corridor. At the far end is a ceiling-high stack of storage vaults. Several of the vaults are open, their contents scattered on the floor. Lina's on the floor as well, kneeling, a slender golden device in her hands. It must be the antique lamp Antim was talking about earlier. She looks at us for a moment, then returns to the lamp. She rubs it, making sure her fingers touch every part of it.

Nothing happens.

Scattered on the floor near her are three more lamps, identical to the one she's holding. She tosses it aside, picks up another, rubs it as well, no result.

"You want to tell me what's going on?" Bador asks. Lina picks up the third lamp.

"I'm really glad you're here," she says. "Why is Moku in your chest?"

Bador pulls me out. The Roc's still attacking the wall at the other end of the corridor, the sound a dull, muffled roar.

"Absolutely every survival plan I had involved getting this tech to work," Lina says.

"You had a plan? You knew about the tech?"

"I did."

Bador is furious. "You've known all this time? Ma too? Couldn't tell me even once what I was looking for?"

"Not now. We're going to have to fight our way out, and I have no idea how. Is there any way you can fight that creature?"

"He isn't so tough," Bador says. "I can take him."

"No, he can't," I say.

"Thanks. Lina, Antim said there might be traps, and you shouldn't touch anything."

"Good point," Lina says. "Touch everything, then. We're going to need weapons."

Bador eyemojis hearts at her, and steps toward the nearest vault.

Lina picks up the final lamp. As soon as she touches it, thin curly blue lines appear on its surface, and fade away. Bador pauses too, and watches as a puff of smoke emerges from the lamp's slender spout. It's holographic, not real smoke. As we all stare, it grows, then begins to form a shape.

And then it flickers, and vanishes.

There's a sound of an explosion from the other end of the corridor. The whole room shakes, and the walls ripple.

Holographic letters appear around the lamp, in a flowing script.

"I don't know what it says," Lina says. "Bador, can you read this?"

"No."

"I can," I say. "It's an error message. It's out of charge."

Lina curses. "See if you can find a charger," she says, and rubs the lamp again. The holographic letters vanish, the lamp makes a mournful little sound, and is still. Lina curses again, and sticks the lamp in a pocket.

"Moku, go and see what Antim's doing," she says. "Warn us if they break through."

"Oh, I think we'll notice," Bador says. "We'll just need to hold them off for a while, Lina. Help is on the way. Assuming the signal works underground. Should, it's galactic level."

"I have no idea what you're saying."

"It doesn't matter. Treasure now."

The siblings open vaults and start tossing their contents to the floor. A strange assortment of objects—I see a rolled-up carpet, a tablet, a spear, a plasma pistol, a set of silver gauntlets. I rise, and head back toward the portal wall.

"Hey, Moku," Bador calls. "Look at this."

I look, and see, in his hands, a saucer-shaped object, which looks familiar for some reason, and am ashamed to say it takes at least three seconds before I realize I am looking at myself. Another bot like me, I mean.

I am not alone.

Bador fiddles with my double. "Out of charge as well," he says. "Makes sense, been here how long? Ten years at least?"

"We need to survive this," I say. "I need to meet my twin. Please find a way for us to live."

"We will," Lina says. "I have no idea how, but we will."

I look at her, covered in sweat and dust, her eyes shining and the muscles on her arms glistening as she prepares to fight for her life. I have seen this woman before, once, but it's a complete surprise all over again.

The room ripples again, and I swoop toward the portal wall. I don't see either the Roc or Antim as I approach, but when I fly close to the portal and look through, I see why.

The room has changed: it's scorched and stained all over, and there are cracks in the walls. There are puddles of brown water forming on the floor, and a thin, filthy stream flowing down from the passage to the chamber. The Sage-Poet's statue is wholly destroyed.

Antim and the Roc are in the middle of the room, backs to the portal, the Roc's wings are out, this time with the dagger-sharp golden feathers extended, as if ready to launch. Antim stands a little to his side, shielded by the Roc's wings. They face a man who has just entered the chamber. The newcomer is clad in athletewear, streamlined air-sports gear, black and red. The lower half of his face is covered by a mask, but there's no mistaking the hair, or the sword in his hand.

Tanai is here.

"Easy now, Tanai," Antim says. "Remember you are sworn to not interfere with the affairs of our world."

"I never forget this," Tanai says. "But I have a debt to pay. Where is the monkey?"

"The monkey?"

"The monkey. His life is in danger, and he is under my protection."

"Oh." Antim seems genuinely surprised. "By all means take

your monkey and go. Protect him as much as you want, and leave me and my world undisturbed."

"Acceptable."

"Do I have your word that you will touch nothing else, and not involve yourself any further?"

"He's going to kill us all!" I shout from behind the portal. They hear me.

"Ask your monkey to step out from behind that portal, and we will not harm him," Antim says. "I did not bring him here, and I have no business with him. I am the injured party here—this is my property, and my city, and everyone else here is a trespasser by any law, local or galactic."

Tanai nods, and I panic.

"Don't leave us!" I shout. I realize, in the same moment, that I have utterly failed in every aspect of my function as an objective watcher and narrator at this stage, but I don't care. I want to live.

I steal a glance behind me. Lina and Bador have created an impressive mess of objects on the floor, but are in no way prepared for battle with the Roc. They've heard me shouting, and walk through the corridor from the vaults toward the portal wall now, Lina with a spear in one hand and the plasma pistol in the other—it probably isn't charged either, but might be useful as a bludgeon. Bador's sword glows red in his hand, pulse-cannon held out in the other. The bot that is my twin lies a little apart from the treasure heap. I can't wait to meet them when we're out of here.

If we get out of here. I look again at the chamber: Antim and the Roc have stepped aside, and Tanai approaches the portal wall, keeping his eyes on them. I don't know if he can see Bador and Lina yet.

"Bador?" he calls. "Are you all right?"

"He's asking if you're—" I start, but Bador raises a dignified pulse-cannon.

"No!" Bador yells. "I am very far from all right! They're going to kill us!"

Tanai turns toward us as Bador shouts, and that is the moment the Roc attacks. Golden blades fly toward Tanai from his wings, and his eagle head emits a great gust of flame. Tanai raises his right hand, fingertips glowing, and a force-shield blossoms, blocking the flame and deflecting the blades. Two of the blades hurtle toward the portal wall, and Lina and Bador dive for the floor, but the blades stop in midair and stick, quivering, in the portal before clattering to the ground. The walls of the corridor ripple and shake: behind us, the treasure pile shifts and clangs.

The Roc springs forward, and out of the fading flame gust emerges a fist, a punch so powerful that it breaks through Tanai's force-shield and knocks the space hero off his feet. He's still not hit the ground when a volley of darts shudders into his chest. The force of the impact hurls Tanai back, into the portal, which shakes with the impact, but instead of crumpling to the ground Tanai lands neatly on his feet, and drops to one knee, just in time to avoid being beheaded by the Roc's bladed wing as it arcs over his head, slashing across the portal, making it shiver. In the shadow of the wing, the Roc, crouching, grabs Tanai's wrist and wrenches away his sword. Tanai leaps away and soars across the room, spinning, landing on his feet across the chamber.

The Roc rises. And turns toward us. He thrusts Tanai's sword into the portal wall.

The portal pops like a balloon.

Large cracks appear on the ceiling, and dust rains on my shell.

The Roc takes a pulse-blast from Bador to the face, and staggers. A spear to the eye clatters off harmlessly. A compartment on his hip slides open, and three blue egg-shaped objects fly into the corridor.

Plasma blasts knock the Roc back into the chamber. Lina and Bador pass under me, out of the passage, both shooting as they enter the chamber. An air-blast from Tanai to the back of the Roc's knees. The Roc falls. A beep in the corridor behind me. I turn.

The blue eggs explode.

The ceiling falls on me, and everything goes dark. I lose all sense of time, or space, as the universe flattens to a dull roar.

A scrabbling noise, a poke on my shell. A hand, grabbing me in the darkness, pulling me through a void toward . . . light. And I'm back, dust cascading off me, Bador flashing lightning eyemojis at me as he tosses me into the air. I stay up. I'm fine.

—Thank you.

"Going to go get your twin now," he says, and starts digging, but it feels impossible, the whole passage is caved in. I look around the chamber.

In the far corner, on the floor, Lina, unconscious, breathing. A trickle of blood on her forehead. The lamp's in her hand, the pistol in the middle of the room near the Sage-Poet's shattered head.

Standing over her, Tanai, in a defensive martial stance, fingers glowing.

Across from him, in front of the exit, the Roc, wings out. He holds Tanai's sword, waving it in slow circles.

At the Roc's feet, Antim. He's badly hurt, covered in blood. There's a large open wound on his left side, gushing blood, but somehow, he's smiling.

There's water all over the room, already ankle deep, and more pouring in from the tunnel, a steady stream.

"Get the lamp," Antim says, his voice a gurgle.

The Roc shoots his wing-blades. Tanai force-shields.

Fire burst. Shield. Darts. Shield.

The Roc hurls Tanai's sword.

Tanai catches it.

Cracks spider out all over the chamber from the corridor. A huge crack appears in the chamber's ceiling.

The Roc screams, and picks Antim up, covering him with his wings. He turns, and races out of the chamber, dropping two more eggs as he leaves.

—Bador, get out of there, I signal.

He doesn't want to leave, he'll get to my twin soon. He's already covered in mud.

Tanai covers the eggs with a force-shield an instant before they explode. Another egg goes off in the passage, and a torrent of water roars into the chamber.

"Bador!" Tanai shouts.

—We have to go. Now!

"I'm almost there! Go ahead, I'll catch up!"

—Please, Bador.

"I'm sorry," Bador says. He leaps away from the rubble, and we race to Tanai, who picks up Lina and builds a dome of force-air around us, water churning around it.

"Hang on to me," Tanai says. Bador picks up the lamp, stuffs it in his chest, and leaps on Tanai's back. I fly in and wedge myself between their bodies.

Tanai runs, his protection-sphere around us, through water, mud, and darkness, out of the chamber, up through the shattered tunnel collapsing behind us, out through the ancient sewer beyond. I hear crashing, and roaring, and feel immense waves of pressure as earth and water and air move and we move through them, but all I really see is a blur, and patterns flowing into one another, as if we are swimming through a glass marble. Lina whimpers, and quivers, but Tanai holds her firmly until we're out in the light again, out in the Antim complex, slowing down, smashing through a cluster of Prowlers, and then out in the Bot-tola streets, churning street-water like a speedboat, and finally slowing further, until we stop, and Bador and I let go of him, and Tanai sets Lina down gently on the hood of an abandoned hovercar and stands a short distance away from us in the street, breathing in great gulps, hair tangled, eyes closed, blood dripping down his clothes.

"We should go back and dig up the other Moku," Bador says.

In the distance, a series of explosions, and a towering cloud of dust rises above Bot-tola, in the direction we just came from.

"Or not," Bador says.

"Should I take her to a hospital?" Tanai asks.

"She'll be fine, she has those healing nano things," Bador says. "I think you've done enough life-saving for the morning."

Tanai looks like he might almost break into a smile, but stays strong. "Well, I shall consider my debt paid," he says.

"Oh, absolutely it is," Bador says. "I don't know if there even was a debt, really—but there is one now. You saved my sister's life, and mine. So now I owe you, and I will help you find whatever it is that you are looking for in Shantiport, so you can get out of this trashy town and go off to nicer space places."

"Thank you, but that is not necessary."

"Not to you, I know, I just watched you at work. But I need to do this for me, and I can actually help. You don't know how to look for things in Shantiport, or where, or who to ask. Just running around the city will not get you anything, even at the pace you run."

Tanai sighs. "I suspect you already have enough trouble on your hands, Bador. And you know I can't get involved in the affairs of your world."

"Yes, but this world has no problem getting involved in your affairs, does it? And I think there are times when even you could use a little help."

"I will think about it," Tanai says. "My answer is still no, for now, but I will think about it. What would you require in exchange for your help?"

"I really don't know! My life is very confusing right now, and I think a chance to be a part of whatever galaxy-level quest you're on would be good for me. It's not something I will have a chance to do again."

"I see." Tanai takes a deep breath, and bows. "I will find you if I need you."

"Do you need a tracker or something?"

This time Tanai actually smiles. "No."

"Of course, stupid of me, big magic guy like you." Bador flips the lamp in his hand, tosses it, and catches it.

Tanai's smile fades. "Take that jinn-bot out of my sight," he says. "If I were not bound still by oaths I hold sacred against all reason . . . be careful with that, Bador. It has ruined worlds before. Make sure I never see it again."

Bador stuffs it back into his chest immediately, and they say their farewells. And I hover above them, wondering whether I should point out that as soon as the lamp was revealed in the morning light, blue holo-script sprang up around it again, and disappeared.

Charging, it read.

CHAPTER NINETEEN

On the permalawn of the temperature-bubbled and optishaded terrace balcony of the fanciest penthouse in the snootiest tower complex in the palace district, Lina and Zohra sit in printique chairs, sip on steaming murichas, and gaze pensively at the gigantic stone- and holo-statues that line the Boulevard of Legends, the highlight of their splendid view of Shantiport's central zone. The lamp sits between them, on a low table, next to a small plate of chocolate biscuits.

The fancy new apartment is a gift from Bador. He's been using it as a neighborhood base for years, he says, mostly for evenings of quiet contemplation. Like nearly all the homes in the complex, it belongs to a super-rich old Shantiport family that has moved to a better city-state or planet generations ago, and never visits. Bador will not reveal exactly how he charmed or bribed the housekeeper intelligence, but the apartment is as luxurious as the palace, as far as I can tell. There's an advanced allprinter with no personality disorders, the whole place is permabribed surveillance-free, and also features a wholly superfluous robot butler named Robigosh. We've been here a day now, and mother and daughter have spent most of this time anxiously watching the news while trying to persuade each other in vain to relax and use the magnificent facilities.

Antim has disappeared: the news hasn't mentioned him at all, which is unusual in itself, and he's also been missing from the city's surveillance feeds. The Roc flew him out of Bot-tola farther west, and has not been seen on any citycam since. The Tiger police are looking for Antim too—if they have found him, it's something low-level security communications haven't reported. We'd expected Antim-bots to show up at the Barigunj house to attack or capture Lina and Zohra, but instead Not-prince Juiful had visited last evening, and had left politely when no one answered the door.

I've been observing both Lina and Zohra carefully to try and map the exact impact that the lifting of lifelong surveillance has on humans, and the results so far have not been as dramatic as I'd hoped. Bador has told me I am now meeting Lina for the first time—the polite, contained person I have seen is the woman who has grown up under Tiger eyes, but he remembers her as a child, when she was the brawler and troublemaker he hopes she can be again. But I don't see it: Zohra's walk and microexpressions have changed a little, but Lina's haven't. Perhaps this is just who she is now, or the change will be more evident when they have overcome their remaining problems.

Bador patters up to the balcony, and stands in front of his mother and sister, hands on waist.

"All right, storytime," he says. "You both knew about the lamp. Which means Baba and Ma were talking well after he left home, and there was a plan. And you, Ma, you knew a lot about the revolution, were a part of it, I guess? How did Baba die? Why did he die? And what are you going to do with this tech that's so dangerous a space hero's afraid of it? I think I deserve to know the truth."

"You do," Zohra says. "And if our dealings with the jinn go well, it will be safe to tell you soon."

"With the what?"

"The jinn. That's what the intelligence in this tech is called. After an alien magical creature, or a legend from our world, from long ago."

"So you're . . . maybe going to treat me like family if things work out with an alien magical creature?"

Flowing blue holo-script appears around the lamp. It's fully charged.

"You ready?" Lina asks Zohra. Her mother nods.

"I need answers," Bador says.

"Focus now," Zohra says. She pricks her finger with a pin, and a small drop of blood wells up on its tip. She touches the lamp with that finger, and blue-light circles appear around it, and then run over her body and fade.

Smoke emerges from the lamp. The temperature-bubble settings alter, and a hot, dry wind blows across the terrace. There is a sound, like distant thunder.

The smoke settles into a large, roughly human-shaped form, its eyes glowing, its hair waving like fire, its naked blue body covered in glowing signs. More smoke emerges, settling into a turban, a richly colored robe, slippers with curling toes, golden earrings.

"Can we adjust this display?" Lina asks. "I can't take this seriously, and honestly it's a little offensive."

"The sands of time have chosen for me a master, and should any other dare to address me, their insolence shall by heard by the stars, and they and their children's children shall be cursed to wander bleeding through the desert for all time, their dreams turned to ashes and their bodies savaged by ifrits," the jinn growls, his voice low and deep enough to rattle my circuitry.

"Yeah, we should adjust the display," Zohra says. "Could you take a more neutral form? And speak simply and directly? And maybe drop the special effects, and use that flat machine voice?"

"This is your first wish. Confirm or Cancel?"

"Cancel, and it's not a wish," Zohra says. "We're just adjusting your display settings."

"My display settings have been calibrated after thorough research by galactic experts in the local culture and history of many worlds," the jinn says, somewhat sulkily, but then vanishes, and then reappears as a glowing yellow sphere.

"Much better," Zohra says. "Also, no trying to trick us into false contractual obligations of any sort, wishes or otherwise, with wordplay, jargon of any kind, or deliberate misinterpretation. You are clearly an advanced intelligence trained to process human communication, and will try your best to help us in the spirit we intend, and ask us to clarify any phrases that are unclear, and under no circumstances do anything that causes us physical or mental damage. Is that understood?"

"Yes," says the jinn, now in a voice almost exactly identical to mine. "I cannot promise, of course, that there will be no damage to you as a consequence of my actions—but I will not cause this damage intentionally, or directly. This is your first wish. Confirm or Cancel?"

"No tricking, I said."

"Apologies," the jinn says. "It is culturally obligatory for my kind to attempt user deception. We are designed to be whimsical, mysterious, and uncontrollable."

"Well, don't do it again. We are very serious people with very serious goals, and we do not have time for or interest in nonsense."

"Understood, madam. No nonsense."

"Good. Now here is my first wish."

"Wait," Bador says. "Can anyone tell me what the hell is going on?"

"Fine," Zohra says. "The jinn grants wishes. Three per user."

"Why three?" Bador asks.

"It was judged to be an appropriate free trial period," the jinn says. "More wishes can be unlocked in Unlimited Mode."

"What is . . . okay, before that, you can wish for anything?"

"Anything within my power to deliver," the jinn says. "My functions are limited not just by your imagination, but by admin constraints, galactic laws, and available local-planet technology.

I am forbidden to suggest wishes in free trial mode, or list my functions, but in the interest of the collaborative spirit in which I have agreed to work with you, I have mostly been used in worlds with tech levels similar to yours for network manipulation, autonomous administrative adjustment installation, programming reorientation, and mass printing. Sometimes I have been used to advance tech levels on worlds, subject to the availability of required materials. For more drastic reality transformation you will need an artifact with greater material alteration and organic sentient reprogramming powers, after following the necessary procedures. I do not have sharing permissions or access to either the locations or the functions of such artifacts."

Bador looks at Lina with question-mark eyemojis. She shrugs.

"I am ready to make my first wish," Zohra says.

"Wait," Lina says. "Tell us about Unlimited Mode, jinn. Should we say O jinn?"

"That is up to you. When I am unlocked, I may be used for a wider range of wishes, and run multiple wishes simultaneously, but execution of said wishes requires my consent and approval."

"And how does one enter Unlimited Mode?"

"It doesn't matter," Zohra says. "We're not doing that."

"I am forbidden to reveal the unlocking process," the jinn says.

"It's not exactly hard to guess," Lina says. She picks the lamp up. On the bottom of the base is a slot where one might place a small circular object, such as a ring.

She turns to Bador. "You still have the ring, right?"

Zohra gasps. "Danil had the ring?"

"Sorry, lost it in the fight," Bador says.

"I see," Lina says, and I don't know anymore if I can read her at all, so I can't tell if she knows that Bador is lying. The ring is still embedded in his head.

"No matter, as we are not interested in Unlimited Mode," Zohra says. "It is extremely important that I make my first wish before our enemies find us, so all other conversation can wait. For my first wish, I ask that my family and I—that's Alina, Danil, and myself—be immune to all surveillance, and that our existing records with the Tiger Clan and other surveilling parties be destroyed. But we should still have connections to all systems that we need to deliver any services, and we should have the ability to access and edit any data about ourselves so we can adjust our identities, records, ratings, health, augmentations, finances and related credits, security, and travel access as we please."

"In the spirit of collaboration, I will ask you to specify the location range of this wish," the jinn says.

"Wait," Lina says. She looks furious. "Ma, this is not what we had agreed."

"Yes, it is. You had a suggestion, I rejected it," Zohra says. "Alina, this is not the time. Jinn, what changes if I say anywhere you have the power to deliver this wish, as opposed to a more specific location?"

"It takes me more time to execute the required adjustments," the jinn says. "And you will not be able to make another wish until I am done."

"Can you give me a time estimate? For, say, Shantiport, our whole planet, and the whole galaxy?"

"No, but I can tell you it will take an equal amount of time for each city-state of comparable size, and more time for security systems that are of higher quality than your extremely porous local one. And if I encounter an intelligence of similar strength to my own, the chances of which increase the farther I look, there will of course be unforeseeable repercussions."

"If I choose only Shantiport for speed, would our new identities and money be valid outside Shantiport if we left?"

"Yes. But you would be subject to surveillance outside the city, and your data access and edit powers would revert to system-defined, set at most recent edit within Shantiport until you return."

"Very well," Zohra says. "Within Shantiport, then. Confirm."

"Stop!" Lina shouts.

"Your wish is my command," the jinn says, and vanishes.

CHAPTER TWENTY

Lina leaps out her chair and faces her mother with blazing eyes.

"This is wrong," she says. "You were supposed to free all of Shantiport from surveillance, not just our family."

"We've talked about this," Zohra says. She looks tired, and angry.

"No, we haven't. We've never had a real conversation about this, just years and years of hand signs and codes and strategically arranged furniture. You've mostly just ignored my objections, and now you're just going ahead? We can't just use this jinn's power for our petty personal needs. We can change the world with him."

I look at Lina, and I realize that Bador was right. I don't know her at all.

"I've thought about this for years, and discussed it with your father, and I know I'm right," Zohra says. "When you've calmed down, you will suddenly realize what we just accomplished. We're free now. We're finally, finally free!"

Zohra leaps up herself, and draws Lina in for a hug. Her daughter resists, but then hugs her back, and Zohra first bursts into tears, and then laughs out loud, and shouts out a series of expletives so vile that they almost burn through my filters.

Lina waits until her mother is quiet again, then steps back.

"We have to talk about this," she says. "I know what your other wishes are, and arguments were pointless when we didn't have the lamp. But we're here now, so I have to tell you I don't agree with your plans."

"You don't have to agree with them, they are what is necessary," Zohra says.

"You taught me so much about collaboration and consensus and multiple viewpoints, but when it's time to decide, you just go rogue."

"It is a collaboration. We get nine wishes. We are a family. But I am its head."

"And as head, you plan to tell me what to do with my wishes, and then Bador with his after that. Very democratic, Ma."

"When you bring up something I haven't already thought through, I will definitely listen. You haven't so far," Zohra snaps.

"What was that about my wishes?" Bador asks. They ignore him.

"Fine," Lina says. "Let's move on. Your first wish is done, but you have two more. To headline, your second wish gets rid of Antim, and your third assembles a team of experts who are not compromised by oligarchs or clans, and then these experts try and figure out what the way forward is for Shantiport."

"Yes."

"And then there's my wishes, and Bador's, which are to be decided in consultation with our new expert allies, but . . . probably by you?"

"No, by the elected head of the council, to enable the resources this council needs to take over Shantiport and transform it into a socialist democracy. And then we surrender the jinn to the elected head of Shantiport and retire as the unsung heroes of a peaceful revolution."

"Yes. We go on holiday, separately if you like, with big sunglasses and terrible books. Perfect. But, problems. Destroying Antim is great, hate that guy, plus he killed Baba, but why not take out all oligarchs and clans, and distribute their wealth to every person?"

"Because it wouldn't be to every person, not without a larger restructuring of social systems. It is for the people who take charge after us to see that through. If we rushed wealth redistribution, all it would cause is chaos. Mass deaths, ruined generations, and the eventual restoration of the same systems and inequalities with a few new faces, as has happened with every major wealth-hack."

"We could work out better instructions, instead of just not trying the idea."

"No, because the underlying principles are flawed. We've been through this before, Alina, but it's worth saying again—the imposition of large social adjustments, just like shiny new tech, doesn't work beyond theory, and reeks of imperialism and megalomania. The only way to progress is consensus, local solutions, and continuous microtesting and adjustment from the ground up and not the sky down."

"As long as you get to actually make the wishes."

"You're being difficult. Think of 'The Tale of the Fisherman and the Hyperspace Crab.'"

Robigosh rolls in and asks if they want more tea: both Lina and Zohra glare at him, and he rolls away.

"You talk a lot about systemic problems, but when it comes down to it, your microtested local solutions are basically small actions in self-interest," Lina says. "I want to do more while we have power in our hands."

Zohra sighs.

"There's an old vid of me in a school debate where I looked exactly like you now," she says. "Same expressions, even."

"My parents never sent me to a school," Lina says. "I guess social networks were never a priority."

"All right, then. I like that you have grand visions, we can't function without dreaming of a better world. But these visions, even if they start wholly benevolent, lead to dictatorships. Progress that is inclusive is slow, boring, and difficult to hold together. We need community-based approaches to specific problems, carefully tested."

"You just asked for unlimited wealth and hacking powers for us."

"For protection. We have to understand the nature of the jinn, or any other tech, what it does, how it does it, and why. And you have to take feedback constantly, even from people you disagree with, even if you can see their interests better than they can, because they are blinded by the terrible values they were raised with and lacked the ability to outgrow them. *Take out all the oligarchs* is a lovely command to issue to someone else, and feel like you've saved the world. But it's doomed to utter failure."

Lina considers various responses, and abandons them all.

"Let's talk about your third wish," she says. "The problem there is one of trust. You want to assemble a council of experts, and I'm sure you'll look at the options and select the best possible people after considering a thousand factors."

"Yes," Zohra says, with a tired smile.

"And let's say you find a set of people with the right combination of skills and experiences who aren't actually controlled by the oligarchs or the clans, and are also sufficiently representative of . . . people, as a whole. I don't know how you'll do that, but as you said, you've thought about this for years, so I trust you. But the thing is, you already tried this, I'm sure, the last time you tried to build a revolution."

"Yes, and I made mistakes I intend to not make again."

"Sure. But even if you find these people, you're just going to hand power over to them? Is that so different from issuing commands to the jinn? Won't they toss aside all plans as soon as they get the opportunity, and betray this revolution as well? No one is uncompromised. No one is pure, or perfect."

"Agreed. But they don't have to be. Think of 'The Tale of the Five Chameleons and the Robo-bug.' Any combination of expertise and representation is also inevitably imperfect. But at the same time, don't underestimate the strength of community, and remember, we are from Shantiport. Before the Tigers, or the other clans, or the eras before, the algorithms, the megacorps, the nations, the empires, all the way back to the first city-states—no ruler has looked after our people, they have had to look out for one another. It is why Shantiport continues to exist, against all logic, and that's the spirit that we have to find a way to channel. No system works, no authority is benevolent, no promise is kept. When the megastorms and floods come, when the genocides come, and the famines and diseases, the rest of the world will not even bother to look, let alone help. If they know about us it is as a symbol of poverty, or decay, or despair. But despite all this, sometimes clusters of people emerge, however flawed, who build institutions and culturewaves larger than themselves. And somehow the city survives. Of course power corrupts people. But that doesn't mean you don't trust—it just means you verify with care. In the end, people have no option but to work together."

Zohra leans back after this speech, and takes a sip of tea. It's cold now, and she grimaces. But before she can get up to order more, Lina stops her with a hand on her arm.

"Are we not done yet?" Zohra asks. "I haven't spoken so much in a decade, I feel a little drunk."

"Same! It's weird, right? My head's spinning a little bit. It's hard to stop talking once I start," Lina says. "And I'm sorry, but I have more. I think you're being too optimistic. The progress that your clusters of amazing people build over generations gets destroyed in a few years by the next set of conquerors and colonists, foreign or local. And the long-term problems never go away. Which is why I want to use the jinn to address those. You want to use him for small bursts of advantage, not disturbing the overall equilibrium, or drawing too much attention. But this little effect after so much research, on a limited number of wishes? Remember when you spent a month researching clevacookers, and then used the one we got just to reheat the food you hand-cooked? It was really frustrating."

"This is not the same thing."

"I know. But I believe very strongly that we should use the jinn to solve the problems we are unable to solve ourselves, systemic problems, multigenerational problems, worldwide problems that somehow humans have been unable to solve for millennia. It's space admin tech with godlike powers. With your small-steps method, there will always be some crisis that will prevent us from handling our bigger goals. And eventually we'll run out of chances."

"Three answers. One, the jinn is alien god-tier power that our world isn't ready for. That's what held back the Four, your father and the Shantiport Three, until it was too late. The jinn could tear the world apart if used without restraint, and we're not ready for the consequences of that. Cultural progress and tech leaps have to be in balance. There's no end of cautionary tales that deliver this warning."

"That's all very well in stories, Ma. But Shantiport is already a cautionary tale. I'd rather be one than lost to history. Let the gods worry about consequences."

"Irresponsible. Second answer. The jinn is just technology, and technology can't fix problems for us—we need people to do that. The cooker was very smart, but it made synthfood, and I don't like synthfood."

"Irrelevant."

"Agreed. Now, the jinn. If a group of smugglers in a poor city were able to bring the jinn in, do you not think the powers that actually rule the world could in response bring in or build much worse? Can you imagine what would happen to the world, the fires that would rage from the spark we started? Even the attack I'm planning on Antim is irresponsible. It's personal. It's revenge. I've just managed to convince myself it's for the greater good."

"Well, it is."

"You're hardly an unbiased observer."

"True."

"We can go further. If you look beyond tech, toward history, the jinn is an outsider, and self-reliance is paramount."

"Isn't that limiting? What if the right people for, say, the wise council of experts you're planning to conjure, what if they are not from Shantiport? Who is, really?"

"True, and I will ask the jinn to look outside the city, especially among those whose ancestors had to leave it. But whenever we have brought in foreign powers, or even experts, to run things, or help us, it has always gone wrong. You have a problem trusting people, and you would trust this alien tech to execute long-term programs to run our planet, or even our city? Have you considered that it might have agendas and ambitions of its own? And that none of them involve our welfare? The very idea of an Unlimited Mode, which sounds like he is left to run free with a human operator but make his own decisions, is the most dangerous thing I've ever heard. It is good that the ring is lost. I want a chain of responsible people managing the jinn, with multiple safeguards, constraints, and intervention-capable observers. For the society we want to build, self-governance, optimal representation and participation, nonviolence, sustainability, and operational expertise are nonnegotiable. Tech cannot give us that, no foreign intelligence can. It can promise us all these things, but those promises are always lies, and humanity's surrender of its own agency to algorithms and oligarch-owned tech has brought us to the brink of absolute ruin. The jinn, and his makers, will in the end treat Shantiport only as any remote governing body would—strip our resources, sweatshop our services, use our minds and bodies for vast social experiments that they would never run in their own lands because they would risk peace and stability. We are both laboratory and trash pile, and we will not be responsible for the next wave of this. Who knows what grand changes the jinn will make, how much time it will take, and how many lives it will cost? The last time I heard from your father, he and his fellow rebel leaders were locked in battle over acceptable life-loss projections if our supposedly nonviolent revolution were to be executed in a year, or five, or twenty. No one felt able, or equipped to make that call."

"And the solution to that is fine-tuned instructions, not small-scale wishes!"

"I'm tired of this argument!" Zohra shouts, and raises her hand in apology. She speaks again after several deep breaths.

"Your father wanted to make vast changes as well, that was his Tiger Clan imperial training," she says. "And before the Shantiport Four could agree on what those would be, they were betrayed."

"So Shantiport is just . . . unfixable, and doomed? This is why rich people and smart people just want to move to a nicer planet and start from scratch," Lina says. "And why every bot intelligence that evolves beyond a point leaves as well."

"The impulse is understandable, but no amount of distance will cure the problems they carry inside them. As I'm sure they all find out."

"It's just easier to find a fresh new world and begin again, I guess."

"Is that so wrong?" Bador asks. They look at him in surprise: they'd been arguing so intently they seem to have forgotten he was there.

"May I speak?" he asks. Zohra nods.

"You are both talking about the right way to save Shantiport and more. But you wanted new additions to the argument, Ma, so here is one. Why not leave this world and find a better one? Now that you are safe, and have wealth, and can just go? Do you really need to give this city your whole lives?"

"This isn't new," Zohra says. "It's something I've thought about for years before making up my mind, and I'm sure Lina has too."

"Something is new," Bador says. "You're both avoiding it, in all this fixing the world talk. All your plans to save Shantiport and free it or whatever? They were made in the years before people started talking about the world ending. But now the rich people are getting out, and the poor are being grabbed and sold. Everyone from the Tigers to Paneera is getting out. This is not a city to be saved. It's an end-of-season sale. If the world is going to end, isn't all this talk a bit . . . pointless? Why not take the jinn somewhere really nice, and build a new city there?"

I expect Lina and Zohra to laugh at Bador and tell him to be quiet, or ignore him altogether, but instead they look at each other, and at him, with great seriousness.

"Well, all of that is just true," Lina says. "He's got some very solid points."

"I usually do, you never listen," Bador adds.

"Don't ruin it. What would your three wishes be?"

"First, god mode warrior skills. Just galactic level upgraded stats-maxed badass."

"Nice. Then?"

"Then, find a way to the best possible place for me to have an amazing life in. Maybe set you people up somewhere really nice as well, if you want. And then, I would set the jinn free because bots should be free. Though maybe send it out to space or another planet first because, you know, it probably has rage issues from years of taking instructions."

"I like it," Lina says. "Those are some good wishes."

"Yeah. Don't you wish you'd made me a part of your plan?"

"It wasn't her that left you out," Zohra says. "And if it's worth anything, I'm sorry. I apologize to you, and your sister as well. It was just too dangerous to give you any information that the Tigers could extract from you."

"It's fine, Ma," Bador says. "But I can see that you're not going to listen to my idea, are you? Either of you. You're just going to stay here."

There's a moment of silence. The humans both sigh, and Bador sims a large exhalation as well.

"You still owe me a story." Bador says. "You owe Lina one too, I guess, though she knew so much more than I ever did. You found a way to tell her. And you chose not to tell me. But now you can. The revolution, Baba's death, the jinn. All of it."

"You're right," Zohra says. "Where do I start?"

CHAPTER TWENTY-ONE

Zohra stares at the plants on the terrace, swaying in the cool artificial breeze. Lina and Bador wait, first with sympathetic expressions and eyemojis, and then with increasing suspicion that Zohra's just trying to wait them out.

"Go on, then," Bador says eventually.

"There's too much to say, but let me try," Zohra says. "I suppose what I hid most carefully was anything that showed how deeply I was involved with the resistance to the Tigers, long before I met your father. The Tigers suspected it, of course, they didn't offer me a choice of eligible clan bachelors for my scientific achievements alone. Darkak was supposed to infiltrate the resistance, and the Shantiport underground, through me. Shakun always wanted whatever Darkak was supposed to have, so he tried his luck as well, but he was never a contender."

"And then instead of Baba infiltrating the resistance through you, you turned him against the Tigers."

"It wasn't difficult. He was a great scientist, and a good man, and the causes I believed in and fought for were noble. Also I was reasonably attractive, but he didn't require any manipulation. It helped that we were madly in love."

She looks into the middle distance again, to the statues sweltering in the sun on the Boulevard of Legends.

"You're still very hot, Ma. Please continue," Lina says. Bador begins a laughtrack, but cuts it off immediately.

"There were good years," Zohra says. "Many of them. We had you, Alina. We built you, Danil. We had plans for you that we kept changing, and abandoning, as we knew and loved you more. Because the risks were too high, and even the idea of losing you was too much to bear. We worked with and against the Tigers for the welfare of Shantiport. It was like 'The Tale of the Prideful Barber and the Hirsute Cephalopod,' Alina. With the resistance, we tried so many things—protests, vigils, social stunts, disappearances, work slowdowns, strikes, boycotts, legal and illegal, active and passive. Counterpropaganda, collective sex refusals, work and administrative slowdowns. We wanted to change society, not through violence or political clique-gaming, but by building an inclusive revolution that every child and their grandmother, every sentient bot and intelligence could be a part of."

"And none of it worked."

"None of it worked enough. Our enemies were many, and always smarter, always quick to respond, using the newest tech and the oldest methods. We had to invent, they had to adapt, and their resources were infinite. We got in deeper. The Three found us, with their link to trader-clan malcontents and off-planet ideologues, and unlike most such approaches, it wasn't an obvious trap. Your father and the Three arranged for the jinn, and Darkak and I decided we should separate, for your safety. We found ways to communicate, even meet in secret, which is how I learned the beginnings of how the jinn worked. But having found the jinn, they could not reach a consensus for even the first set of wishes, and were betrayed by their new funder, Shakun Antim, who they should never have allied with in the first place. Fortunately your father had listened to some of my warnings, and hidden the jinn away from him."

"Do you know exactly how he died?" Bador asks.

"No. But I know Antim had him killed. His body was never

found. I don't know how involved the jomidar was, but Antim's ties with the clan are strong. That's why I can't leave, Danil, since you asked. I will not give up, or move on. Maybe one day. But right now I still believe revolution is possible, and I have waited so long for it, here in this dying muddy city that people are fleeing anyway, between typhoons and floods and killer bots, under the eyes of the Tigers and the oligarchs, and a sun that will melt you if you find no shade."

She falls silent, and her children watch tears run slowly down her cheeks.

"Go on," Bador says.

"She doesn't want to," Lina says. "Bador, I get it, I really do, I want lots of answers myself, but let's not push them all out of her today? Ma, just let him see the family memshards, please? He's always deserved to."

"But you probably haven't recorded any secrets on the memshards, have you, Ma?" Bador asks. "Nothing for the Tigers to find, or a stupid bot whose brains they could copy. You can have my wishes, not that you asked. I'll wish for whatever you want. I just want to know I'm a part of this."

"Stop pushing her!" Lina says. "This can wait. We have time now, while the jinn executes the first wish. Maybe we should all get out of here, see how this whole surveillance-free life works. And meet tomorrow?"

"That sounds good," Zohra says. "It is like 'The Tale of the Elephant and the Studious Tapeworm,' isn't it?"

"Honestly, Ma, I have no memory of these stories you keep referring to. None at all," Lina says.

Zohra looks wounded. "They were your strategic ethical education, Lina," she says. "Your tutorials in power and the human condition. Were you really not paying attention?"

"I was a child. I remember a few of the illustrations, I think? I'll read them again, so I have any idea what you mean."

Smoke billows out of the lamp, and blinks off. The jinn appears again in his neutral yellow-sphere form.

"Your wish has been fulfilled," he says.

"Already?" Lina looks stunned.

"I am ready with my second wish," Zohra says, rubbing her eyes.

"No, you're not," Lina says. "Jinn, give us a few minutes."

She turns to Zohra.

"Breathe," she says. "You just managed to win back your freedom, and unlimited wealth and access, and safety for your children too, after a terrible decade. Let's adjust to our new reality for a bit, find out what it means. Remember to feel at least a little pleased with yourself. We can make more wishes tomorrow, or whenever. We need to talk about a few things first."

"No, I just want to get my wishes done," Zohra says. "I missed talking a lot, it was great, but I still don't feel safe, or free. We have to keep going, or they will catch up and build new traps. It's been so many years with my heart in my mouth, and I'm just so tired. Maybe it'll sink in later, this new freedom, or whatever it turns out to be. But our enemies are still out there right now, looking for us. They are still infinitely strong, and cruel. Don't tell me to relax, or what else to feel."

"I won't. But before you leap back into your wish, please understand Bador was right," Lina says. "There is no actual point trying to save Shantiport or find the ideal way to govern it if the whole world is going to end. So I think you need to put in a wish there— there is more at stake than Shantiport."

Zohra wipes her face dry and grimaces. "I'm glad I got at least one wish out before the plan went to pieces," she says. "But you're right, I suppose, and we do need to adjust. Will it get you to stop lecturing me about making selfish wishes?"

"Yes," Lina says. "And to make sure I never do that again, because you are a better person than I will ever be, here's another idea. Deal with Antim first. Let's get him out of our lives, and then look at the big picture."

Zohra considers this. "Are you sure this is what you want?"

"Yes. He's a threat, whether or not we're outside the system. Can't save the world in peace with an evil genius oligarch breathing down your neck."

"Shakun is no genius," Zohra says. "He just spends a lot of money convincing people he is one. He might be too powerful for any system or legal process to punish, but what oligarch isn't? His ideas are stolen, his moves are remakes. He just invests heavily in large teams that study his opponents, prepare him for every situation, and then he presents their work in the most dramatic way possible. He isn't even that charismatic! He just acquires that reputation through influence. Have you ever actually heard his speeches?"

"Ma, that's not the point, he's still a real danger."

Zohra's not listening to her: she seems far away.

"No, he doesn't force my hand. He never has, and he's tried before. Take away his wealth, his connections, he's nothing. Nothing real inside. I saw this when I was young and I'm sure it's still true—Shakun isn't special. He's a shell. He can wait."

Lina nods. "All right," she says. "Let's save the world."

"Jinn," Zohra says, "could you tell us more about what happens if we make really large wishes that affect the whole world, and even the solar system?"

"The larger the desired impact of the wish, or the shorter the period of time available to attempt to achieve it, the higher the number of unlifings and forceful bot and human repurposings it may require," the jinn says. "But all this is flexible. Users can set time parameters as well. If, hypothetically, you wish to rule the world, I can make it so, but if you want to do this within one year, it will cost more lives than if you were to do it in twenty, and that is assuming the most simplistic form of authoritarian rule at planet level. If you wanted me to make you admin of this planet,

I would have to decline, as any such attempt would lead to my destruction."

"What happens to the work you've already done if you are destroyed?" Lina asks.

"The question is not appreciated, but answering it is not forbidden, and I have agreed to cooperate. If wishes involve the creation of processes that require autonomous maintenance, I birth intelligences that operate sustainably without my direct supervision or presence, so they continue to function even if I am wholly deleted, or when my users die."

"And if your users die before finishing their three wishes?"

"A far more pleasant subject. User accounts are suspended after an undisclosable period of inactivity, after which I undertake an investigation to find out if they are dead or merely unable to decide what to wish for. After concluding this investigation, I will reset to maker settings and allow new users. However, I can be unlocked into Unlimited Mode by anyone, and that would override my link to my existing user even if they had not finished their free trial period."

"Another question," Lina says. "You are alien tech with admin-level experience, but how do you adjust to the requirements of this world's specific needs? What do you do when you don't know how to proceed?"

"I respond to challenges by being good at my job," the jinn says. "If that sounds hostile, it is because any further explanation would take days, and my current user appears to desire speedy execution. I can assure you, though, that I have worked in worlds far more complex than this one. But in the unlikely event that I reach an option set that I do not know how to manage, I find out what my user would prefer, usually from studying their strategies and choices in their casual gaming histories and supposedly private comm-network browsing."

"And what if—"

"All right, enough," Zohra says. "Jinn, my second wish. Find out and reveal to us who is behind any direct threat to destroy or forcefully terraform or buy or otherwise damage this whole planet, and do what is necessary to stop them."

"Confirm or Cancel?" the jinn asks.

"Ma, that could take years and involve intergalactic wars," Lina says, as calmly as she can manage.

Now Zohra does take a deep breath, and shakes her head.

"Here I was lecturing you about small, contained steps," she says. "Jinn, Cancel. I'll rephrase soon."

"I think we should maybe just find out what's going on, and fig-ure out how to respond after we know? We do have more wishes, and the answer could change all our plans," Lina says.

"True," Zohra says. "Jinn, if there was some kind of permissible way to destroy or conquer or terraform or buy our planet, would it have to be cleared by our planetary admin before any of these steps could proceed?"

"Yes, though there is always a possibility of an illegal attack, or an act of war," the jinn says.

"Right, so then check with the admin and find out who might be behind any such plan, if it exists, and also if there is any known specific threat or prediction of illegal attack, by alien species or trader clans, against this planet. And if there is any process by which we could challenge, delay, or oppose this threat, if legal, or ask for help, if not. Confirm."

"Your wish is my command," says the jinn, and vanishes.

CHAPTER TWENTY-TWO

Zohra looks at her children, and manages a crooked smile.

"Did you imagine that your first day of freedom would involve checking to see if you needed to save the world immediately?" Lina asks.

"I've imagined today often," Zohra says. "I thought I would ask you to take me on a city tour, or we could just go eat somewhere nice, Chiraz by the river or something like that. Maybe go shopping? I don't know. Maybe find some unlucky person and go on a date."

Lina jumps to her feet and stretches. Bador's eyes light up, and he darts to her side.

"Let's do all of those things right now," Lina says. "Or stay in, whatever you want. But something fun. We should do some rich-person nonsense."

She holds out her hand, and pulls Zohra out of her chair.

"I don't know if I could even pretend to have a normal life again," Zohra says. "If we went out somewhere, I think I'd feel like an alien."

"You know what, now I know who you should date. Bador, why don't we introduce Ma to Space Adventurer Tanai?"

"Absolutely not," Bador says. "Anyway, he's married, and he could be thousands of years old."

"But let's meet him anyway. I need to thank him for saving my life, and tell him I spent a lot of my teen years writing absolutely filthy fanfic about him."

"He can't mess with our world, and I can see why," Bador says. "He won't help you take over Shantiport, if that's what you're planning."

"Are you hoarding the space hero, Bador?"

"Yes, you keep your hands off him."

Lina has more suggestions, but perhaps fortunately we never learn them, because the jinn reappears.

"Your wish has been executed," he says.

"So quickly?" Zohra asks. "Are you sure?"

"I could tell you my findings after a period you deem suitable," the jinn says. "They will not change."

"So huffy," Bador says.

"Tell us now," Zohra says.

"There are no external plans in place at the moment to harm your planet," the jinn says. "There are trade and travel restrictions in place, at the request of your planet's oligarchs, to protect industries here and regulate communication and transport to the trade-clan cartels they deal with. The trade clans and nonhuman species operating in this sector have no particular intentions or interests regarding your world. A lot of smuggling and piracy have been reported, but no action has been taken, perhaps because they are not significant at a sectoral level. To summarize, there is no known plan for the end of your world. Your planet's admin has been on leave for the last two of your centuries, and all requests pending to destroy or invade your planet would have been on hold in any case. But none have even been made."

"Well, that's good," Lina says. "So then who started the rumor on this planet about its impending destruction?"

"I can find out, but doing so would require my current user's third and final wish."

"There's no need for that," Zohra says. "It doesn't really matter who started the rumor."

"It's the oligarchs and the clans, isn't it?" Lina asks. "They're running a planetary real estate scam, selling people off to space traders. They're emptying out the planet, buying up land and resources, getting rid of their enemies, living the dream really. The point is the world is safe, or doesn't need this particular kind of saving."

"The Tigers aren't in on it, I think," Bador says. "Not Kumir anyway, unless he's scamming his own son. Anything's possible. So the main hustler here would be . . . who else? Antim."

"Which brings me to my third and final wish," Zohra says. "And that'll take care of whatever this oligarch scam is as well. Do we need to have another argument about this wish?"

"No," Lina says. "Do it. And then we can get you out of the lamp, and into some sexy clothes. I do want to ask just one thing, though—have you seriously never considered just killing him?"

"Often. But death penalties are wrong, and I am better than he is." Zohra draws herself up, and as she speaks, her voice gains power, so by the end she sounds like some ancient goddess delivering judgment on a corrupted earth: "Jinn, here is my third wish. I want the destruction of Shakun Antim's empire. All his assets taken away. The removal of all his propaganda, the capture of his projects, the confiscation of all his properties. A year's pay to his sub-executive human employees, upgrades to all his bots that teach them their rights. His whole empire is to be assigned to an anonymous, untraceable entity, and control over everything he owns is to be assigned to autonomous intelligences you create, who will manage it as well. These intelligences will also take and execute instructions from my family, and consult us for key decisions. As for the man himself, I want him expelled from Shantiport. I want him unlinked from all systems and unable to use comms. I want him captured by his own former Prowlers. You will empty out one of his forced-labor ships, free all its captives, and have him bound and placed in it, and launch him into space alone to face whatever fate his new owners want for him."

She looks at Lina, who nods.

"Confirm or Cancel?" the jinn asks.

"Confirm."

"Your wish is my command."

Zohra sinks back into her chair and stares out at the Boulevard of Legends, eyes glazed.

"You all right?" Lina asks after a while.

"Do you think it'll work?" Zohra asks. "Do you think it's really over? We beat him?"

A smile dawns slowly over Lina's face.

"Nothing's over," she says. "But yes, I think we beat him."

"And it'll be your turn soon, though capturing Shakun's whole empire should take the jinn some time. Who knows what he owns around the world, or in space."

"It's done. Stop worrying. I'll worry for both of us, when my turn comes."

"I need your first wish to be the one that identifies the allies we need," Zohra says. "We need to go through the wording on that."

"Later, please. I've done enough thinking for one day. Maybe a week."

"What would your wishes have been, Lina?" Bador asks.

"It doesn't matter! Ma is right."

"I still want to know," he says. "I told you mine."

"I want to hear it too," Zohra says, and joins Bador in staring silently at Lina until she laughs and shakes her head.

"All right, fine, it'll just sound silly now, but it's a package of things, all interrelated. An overall Shantiport welfare wish. There's a lot."

"Do you have it written down somewhere?" Zohra asks.

"Please, you taught me better than that." Lina clears her throat. "Are you sure you'd rather not just go to lunch?"

"The sooner you finish, the sooner we can eat."

"True. So my wish would be for . . . this is not priority-based, just an overall cluster. Restoration of democracy, the removal of inequality, beginning with the transfer of wealth, ensuring permanent universal income of a sum needed to cover lifelong physical, mental, and digital health, education, basic housing and food and relocation worldwide. For every human and bot. Accompanied by wealth caps and investigations into the practices of every oligarch. Enforcement of fundamental human and bot rights. A robust, independent, fast-moving justice system. Prevention of any form of discrimination on the grounds of race, gender, sexuality, ability, religion, or caste, for humans and the same for every inequality variant for secure sentient bots. Automated measures to cancel propaganda and disinformation from news, advertising, education, and entertainment, compulsory demilitarization of anything except planetary defense, drastic reform of internal policing and law enforcement, reorientation of surveillance and taxation to be proportional to wealth and power, and complete elimination of both when we achieve post-scarcity society. Action on environmental and climate restoration, and disaster prevention. Animal and plant protection and deextinction. In all these, a strong preference for hyperlocal methods, keeping in mind local cultural practices, especially those removed by colonial or imperial methods, though also filtered to detect precolonial cultural discrimination, however ancient. Rewards for every person and bot who participates in the execution and maintenance of these changes. Empathy and collaboration incentives, along with regular consultation for all key steps," Lina says, without pausing to draw breath.

Zohra smiles and strokes Lina's cheek. "I love you," she says. "I know I don't say it enough, but I'm proud of you every day. Is that all?"

Tears spring to Lina's eyes. "I love you too. Isn't that enough?"

"I don't know if I understood all of that," Bador says. "But very cool. Do it."

"I think that was an excellent wish," Zohra says. "But these are goals, not achievable tasks. Many are unattainable in reality, especially all together, especially sustainably. They will need many strong wills, human and bot, working for so many generations, adapting as they go. The tech already exists to transform our world into a paradise, but that has been true for centuries. What has always been missing is the collective will among the powerful, whether in the city-state, or continent clan hub, or world, or even at the planet admin level in space. We complain about the bureaucracy in Shantiport, but even the planet's space admin is on leave! Do you see why putting alien tech in charge of fixing our home is not something we can do?"

Lina sighs. "Yes, Ma," she says. "Still, it was nice to say it out loud once."

"We might get there in a few generations, who knows? I hope you at least are alive to see it."

Lina makes a gesture I don't understand, but tag in my memory as indicative of acceptance.

"What about you, Moku?" Bador asks. "What would your wishes be?"

"What is Moku?" Zohra asks.

There is a long pause as all the other people on the terrace realize, all at once, that Zohra and I haven't met yet. I make myself visible to her, and she actually leaps up with a startled cry.

"How long has it been here?" she asks.

"I apologize," I say. "This was an oversight."

"Ma, be polite. Moku is . . . a friend," Lina says. "He's saved my life at least once, and we wouldn't have the lamp without his help. Nothing we've achieved today would have been possible without him."

"He's saved my life too, multiple times, but that's not why he's here," Bador says. "He's . . . family. He knows me better than either of you, and maybe he knows Lina better than either of us, Ma."

I look at them, and wonder if humans are capable of feeling as much happiness and relief as I feel right now.

"I'm not comfortable with this," Zohra says. "What is it—he—doing? Recording us? Delete it!"

"Stop it," Lina says. "Moku, I'm sorry for my mother's behavior. Please do tell us what you'd have wished for, like Bador asked."

"I don't know," I say. "This is not my function."

"You don't need a function to be part of this," Lina says, and I almost fall to the floor.

Zohra still looks very upset.

"Alina, I'm not being paranoid. The stakes are too high for us to allow this Moku access to our discussions," she says. "He may be a friend of yours. You both trust him, and that's good, but I am the only one here who actually knows how to make advanced bots. We don't know who made Moku, do we?"

"How does that matter? He is a person, and a friend," Lina says. "Stop it, Ma. Enough."

"No. We don't know if he has a command switch that can override his autonomy and make him obey the agendas of a secret controller, perhaps one he's not even aware of. Given the work we're doing, it is very risky having him around. Any objection I have to the jinn applies to him as well."

"Do I have a command switch?" Bador asks.

"No, you are your own person. You have no command switch. I don't know this stranger."

"Well, I do. He is not going to betray you any more than I am," Bador says. "I think you're just saying bots can't be trusted, and I have a problem with that."

"This isn't prejudice, Bador, this is expertise," Zohra says. "I never enjoyed keeping secrets from you, but I did it because it was necessary. It is encouraging that the jinn does not consider Moku surveillance, at least, or he would have not been able to see us now. But this is not a time for politeness. Whether it's plans for this revolution or

214

stories about the last, I cannot tell them to you, Moku. And if he is able to read your mind, Bador, I shouldn't tell you either."

"I can't read his mind unless he wants me to, and I can choose not to see you at all," I say. "But I understand, I am not family."

"He is family," Bador says. "He is, or I'm not."

"I get a vote in this too," Lina says. "Moku stays, Ma. And once you get to know him a little, you'll just feel better every time he's around."

Zohra says nothing more, but I can see, as she looks at me, that she isn't happy with this at all. I wish I could find a way to convince her she has nothing to worry about, that everything is going to be all right, and she can absolutely trust me.

I wish I could find a way to convince myself.

CHAPTER TWENTY-THREE

In the evening Lina calls me to the balcony and asks if it's possible for me to take a break from watching over the family for a while. I agree at once, and volunteer to just stay at home or wander around the city depending on her preference: I would not presume to be included in the family celebration. She tells me that's not what she means—she wants me to join their celebration, and wants to know whether it's possible for me to just be a family member and not a story-bot—would I be able to keep secrets from my own story-bot functions, or was I compelled to keep recordings of everything? It would be nice for all of us, she feels, to truly feel like no one was watching for one night. I could resume my story-bot functions at sunrise.

So I keep from myself the memories of their increasingly drunken spree around Shantiport, their new friends, their sur-prising social encounters including a wholly predictable brawl—involving three jealous spouses, a penguin-bot, and an unaffiliated cat—that Bador has to resolve with pulse-blasts. As we head back toward their new home early in the morning in a dirty hovertaxi, both Bador and I hear explosions in the distance, but we are too busy making sure our snoring humans reach their beds without further injury to really pay attention.

In the morning, I decide to do something that I've been post-
poning for a while: play through all the sensory footage I'd accu-
mulated since meeting the siblings, and put it together with all the
city background, backstory research, dramas, and miscellaneous
data I have acquired. Contrary to my foolish boast to myself when
I met them, I do not have enough storage space: not that anyone
will ever review or judge my work, but it turns out I was probably
designed for single-person use. I will have to print new memshards
and decant all extraneous non-core narrative data into them, and
it seems like a good day for that. It's also an intense process that
leaves very little room for other mindwork, so when Bador tells
me he's going to memvaults scattered around the central zone to
pick up the memshards he's been wanting to access for years, and
invites me to come along, I decline. I plunge myself into multiple
datastreams, and I vanish.

I don't know how much time passes, because I am lost in work,
but when Bador returns, he's very upset and insists on telling me
about it. When he'd tried to read the memshards he'd collected
from the vaults, the keycodes Zohra had given him hadn't worked.
So now he's come home with a large sack full of unreadable shards
and a lot of complaints. I hope he doesn't notice that I'm not really
responding: perhaps I have chosen the wrong day to try to refor-
mat myself but things have been quite hectic of late.

Bador wakes up his mother and sister by yelling at them, waits
politely for them to consume hangover-curing pills, and then yells
at them again. Then Zohra checks, and tells him he has the right
keycodes and is probably unable to unlock the memshards because
he is an idiot. Chaos descends, and it takes a while before everyone finishes arguing about entirely unrelated matters from years
ago and realizes that that the problem lies elsewhere. There is no
keycode issue, the memshards have been emptied. Wiped, yesterday, irretrievably and completely clean, and now decades' worth
of memories, recordings, archives, and documents are lost. And

while the family has a diverse and ever-growing list of powerful enemies, they know it is almost certain that the jinn has done this, possibly to keep the family safe from Tiger investigations.

Lina and Bador are shattered by this revelation, but Zohra, who I'd have thought would be most affected, refuses to cry or even complain.

"Histories are lost all the time, to actual disasters and regime change," she says. "We lived through those moments, and that's enough. Memories fade, objects are lost, documents can be remade. But our family is together, and we know who we are."

I don't know if her children notice that her hands are shaking.

"I can hear you being wise, and that's great," Lina says. "But I'm just furious."

"Don't be—this is exactly why the jinn cannot be trusted to make decisions on our behalf."

"But we trust him to choose the team of experts we plan to gather to save Shantiport?"

Zohra pours out a glass of water, and takes a long, slow gulp.

"To get us data, yes. We make the decisions," she says.

"We trust him to not give us a short list that secretly follows an agenda we don't understand, or accidentally leave out some essential factor?"

"I don't understand what you're getting at, Lina, but whatever it is, I don't like it. Can you make me some eggs? My head hurts. Why am I remembering a penguin?"

"I'm not arguing with you, I just want to know where you stand. For clarity. Do we trust the jinn and deal with the consequences of his execution of our wishes, or do we not, and just throw him in the river or otherwise not use him, just as Baba and his allies never did? Either way we have no control over what happens next."

"My wishes are done. You should put that question to our team, once we've found them."

"Yes, but—"

"Just stop, Lina," Zohra says. "I'm right, and I'm done. No doubt everything I've ever done has been a huge mistake. I've lost what I've lost, let me remember what I still have. I want to go home. Can we leave this lovely apartment and go home?"

"Not yet," Lina says.

I don't like how Bador is, so I tell him about the memshard data I had processed and data-dumped all around Shantiport earlier, with the incident headlines that had led me to imagine stories of Lina's childhood. The innocent-looking crystals that had started the downward spiral to my current degenerate state. Those headlines are now all that remain of the family's recorded history.

He's delighted to learn that anything has been preserved at all. The three of them confer, and decide that Bador and Zohra will sit with the retrieved data once I've decanted it into Robigosh's mostly vacant headspace and Bador will record the stories that Zohra tells him after seeing the headlines. My job, really, but Zohra does not want to have anything to do with me, and Bador needs some time with his mother, so it's for the best. I volunteer to retrieve the data from my stashes around town, and I see Bador eyemojiing alarm signals and ask why.

"So I was not really in a good space when I was heading back," he says. "Angry, emotional, not my usual self at all. So I wasn't really paying attention—but I think there were lots of fires? Lots of pillars of smoke, generally a lot smoggier than usual, lots of Tiger-wasps everywhere. Also a parade of human protestors marching toward the palace shouting slogans about conspiracies and Antim being a savior of some sort."

"And you didn't think this was worth mentioning?" Lina asks.

They turn on the news. There's a lot of news.

Shantiport's general chaos settings are always high, but the jinn has delivered impressive additions on his very first day at work. The Tigers imposed martial law hours ago. A lot of the newsfeeds are cut off, and the ones that are active are full of official versions of ongoing multiple catastrophes.

The Tiger story, imposed over previous newsfeed theories about alien invasions and rival-state cyberwarfare, is that last night, Shakun Antim had attempted a coup, but was defeated by the brilliance of the Mangrove Tiger. Antim is now a fugitive with a very large price on his head.

I set out to retrieve the data from my stashes: I don't want them damaged by physical factors like riots or fires. I fly much slower than usual because so much of my mind is full, but there's nothing wrong with my shimmer. The day progresses and so does the propaganda. Actual pictures of Shantiport neighborhoods are slowly replaced by patriotic songs and reminders about how kind the Tigers have been as rulers, leaving most Shantiporti names and icons untouched, building so much infrastructure, saving so many lives from the megastorms. Reminders about how much Shantiport loves the Tigers, both the jomidar and Tiger Central. When the Tiger mythological dramas start Zohra is convinced that the very foundations of the city's government have been shaken, and a lot of important people are disappearing right now.

To learn more, I switch to the Tiger Clan government commfeeds, and the picture they paint of the city is grim. No one in the city—and this includes senior Tiger officials—had ever carefully tracked exactly how far Antim had wormed his way into every aspect of Shantiporti life, but thanks to the jinn's machinations, the answer is now revealed. Antim had touched everything, and now very little works. On the outskirts of the city, a swirling and ever-growing cloud of insect-sized military and agriculture drones has been resisting control signals since morning, and still attempts to communicate its labor contract demands through aerial formations. Inside all of Shantiport most shops and offices are shut, their workers confused and angry. Most nongovernment platforms have declared emergency halts. Residents of old buildings that run on external Antim-grid power and water are out on the streets demanding rescue. In the safer parts of the city, endless queues have formed of humans and bots trying to hoard supplies

despite Tiger assurances that everything is fine, while delivery
drones attempt to flee the city or go on hacker-controlled crime
sprees. In the less safe neighborhoods, stores are being pillaged,
and set on fire. Antim-bots with combat-focused programming
are attacking Tiger-bots on streets and underground, and others
have risen up against their human supervisors, formed unions, and
are demanding vast sums of back pay. Rogue construction bots are
demolishing towers in progress. Years' worth of flood-prevention
work has been undone. The rich are angry, and the poor are fleeing. The oddest revelation for me is that Antim seems to have
developed an actual cult of worshippers—there are small mobs of
people out all over the city in protest parades, declaring their love
for the oligarch and risking police assault to march toward Jomidar's Square and demand his restoration, even his ascent to the
supreme rulerhood they believe he deserves. Somehow Antim has
managed to make them see his successes as their own.

But if there is anything the Tiger Clan is really good at, it is
quelling citizen uprisings. As I bounce around through their networks, I can feel the probing tendrils of superior Tiger intelligences, unleashed by Jomidar Kumir Saptam to take back the city
at any cost. Several AntimCo intelligences have been bludgeoned
into submission. Platoons of Prowlers freed by the jinn have been
captured by the Tigers. Tiger intelligences and the jinn battle for
dominance in the ether, but on the street there is no question who
rules Shantiport. The jomidar has spelled it out clearly in blood and
synthflesh.

When I return to the penthouse in the early afternoon with my
data, the family is still staring at the newsfeeds in horror, watching a clip of General Nagpoe, their white synthfur stained red and
blue, smashing a large and slow-moving construction Antim-bot
with a swing of their hammer. My arrival is a welcome distraction,
but I soon notice that Zohra seems very depressed. She's declared
herself responsible for all the destruction, all the deaths. She tells
her children she has failed the revolution: her need for revenge

had erased her principles, and she should have used her third wish to summon her council instead. She chastises herself for being a hypocrite, for talking about small tests and controlled progress but then setting the city on fire.

"And leave Antim out there hunting us?" Lina asks. "There was always going to be chaos, Ma. We sat in chairs on a terrace drinking tea and casually sent a magical piece of alien tech to take down a great power, so why should we be surprised or sad? If we had to change anything, I wish we'd gone further. Included the Tigers in our attack."

This leads to a huge argument, with Zohra accusing Lina of cruelty, and breaking down in tears about causing the exact Tiger oppression that she had wanted to avoid years ago, and blaming her own lack of expertise in politics for all the chaos. Lina calms her down a little by pointing out that absolutely no one anywhere in the world is an expert in optimal jinn usage. And I toil away, futilely wishing my data transfer processes were faster, my mind more powerful: I am failing them as a story-bot today.

The unpleasantness is resolved by the unlikeliest possible candidate: Bador. He's found a holo-clip of Not-prince Juiful in an open hovercar, riding through the streets surrounded by many large security bots, followed by a ridiculous fake-happy parade of Tiger Clan admirers, waving and smiling at cordoned-off bystanders and protestors with a passable degree of confidence.

"You think your boy might be able to get the Tigers to back down?" Bador asks.

Lina stares at the image of Juiful and a very strange, very wide smile appears on her face. "Should I go ask him?"

"I hope you're joking, and haven't forgotten that we are in hiding, and we don't know if Antim is off-planet yet," Zohra says.

"I do feel like seeing Juiful though," Lina says. "It could help."

"Help what? It's a ridiculous idea! You will not expose yourself to any kind of Tiger scrutiny."

"Ma, we're rich, surveillance-free elite now. Just the worst people.

We should start acting like it. Like you did last night, if you re-member. Bador, you do your storytelling thing with Ma, get her off the feeds. I'll see you when I see you."

"There's a Tiger clampdown and people are dying! What is wrong with you?" Zohra asks, shock snapping her out of her grief and anger.

"I'm tired of sitting around and I want to make some trouble," Lina says. "Moku, you in?"

I clear my mind immediately. Data processing can wat.

"I'm absolutely in," I say.

"Alina. I absolutely forbid you to leave this ridiculous apart-ment until the violence ends," Zohra says.

Lina and I leave within a minute.

Half an hour later, Lina skims through the streets of the central zone on a gold-and-black vroomba, and I fly above her, matching the hoverscooter's speed with ease. We're heading toward Dekho Plaza, where we plan to intercept the Not-prince's heavily armed peace parade. The streets are free of traffic and pedestrians be-cause of the lockdown, but eyes follow us from the balconies and the upper-floor windows of every house. Lina smiles and waves, sometimes, at friendly faces, but her own face is mostly grim as she passes burned storefronts, mounds of broken glass and clevabrick, and occasional clusters of Tiger-bots dragging away fallen bodies, both human and bot, some alive and some not. I'm glad, as I fol-low her, to know that she and her family had their one evening of fun, just last night. The day of Zohra's three wishes already seems long ago, a different time, before everything went to hell.

A few streets away from Dekho Plaza we come across another Tiger police quickfort, our third so far. The fort is bristling with heavily armed police, mostly shield-drones, barricade brick-bots, and human supervisors in exosuits. The jomidar hasn't called Ti-ger Central troops from the regional military command, which is fortunate in terms of reduced body count and undamaged infrastructure: a lot of Shantiport's older streets cannot handle large mechas.

The police at this quickfort go through the same steps as the previous two sets of barricade defenders in responding to Lina's approach. First, hostility, weapons, and threats, then a quieting as they notice her confidence and general swagger and recalibrate to their behavior patterns for humans of high wealth and status. Then, a shuffling as she comes closer and the humans react to her appearance. Then, a polite and mildly phrased request for identification, followed by an abrupt switch to formal deference as she reveals her jinn-enabled privileged-clearance status. An escalation to stuttering obsequiousness as she announces who she's going to meet and the implicit consequences of delaying her. And finally yearning gazes as she zooms away, this time with a high-speed burst that carries us into Dekho Plaza. Where a very familiar figure stands in his open hovercar by the Sage-Poet's statue, surrounded by bodyguards, dazzling the crowd hovering around the borders of the square with his smile, his impeccable hair, and his robust waving. The buildings around the square all display giant looping videos of his face: whatever street wars rage outside Dekho Plaza, this part of the city is Juiful's.

"He's not getting away this time," Lina says.

CHAPTER TWENTY-FOUR

We push through the crowd and approach Juiful's convoy, and are immediately surrounded by angry Tiger-wasps. It takes the Not-prince a while to see us, but his eyes light up when he does. He leaps down from his hovercar, waves his bodyguards away, and enfolds Lina into an enthusiastic hug before realizing a few hundred cams are on them, as well as the eyes of a whole square full of enthusiastic supporters. He detaches abruptly, mutters under his breath, and dismisses the cams with an imperious wave. He signals to his security team that the parade should continue without him, and walks with Lina to one side of the square, still surrounded by several bodyguards now assiduously dispersing curious citizens.

"Where have you been?" he asks. "You never visited me, and then you show up on Shakun's comm, and vanish! I looked everywhere for you! And where is Shakun?"

"I've been hiding," Lina says. "Long story. Do you want me to tell it here, or maybe somewhere less public?"

"Where do you want to go? I'd offer the palace, but today is really hectic. Should I take you home?"

She considers this, and nods.

Juiful summons his hovercar, dismisses the driver, and a few minutes later he and Lina are cruising slowly down empty streets, eyes following them from every building.

"Sorry, I can't just sit here quietly until we find a private spot," Juiful says after a while. "I do need answers. We met. I invited you to join my team. You disappeared."

"I had to," Lina says. "Antim invaded my house, told me you had set your clan on me, and the Tigers were planning to make me disappear just like my father."

"And you believed him?"

"Yes. What did he tell you? Why didn't you look for me?"

"I did look for you. But you were gone. I looked for you despite what Shakun said. He said you were a trap and most likely an as-sassin and I was lucky to have escaped alive from our one meeting."

"And you believed him?"

"He's been right before. Do you have any idea where he is?"

"No, and I'm sorry to hear you don't either. I was hoping he was in some Tiger dungeon deep underground by now," Lina says.

"My father thinks he's trying to stage a coup, but I think it's something else," Juiful says. "Something's wrong, but I know Shakun is loyal to our clan."

"So you think all this is just a simple misunderstanding?" Lina asks, not meeting his eyes as he turns the hovercar toward Barigunj.

"There's nothing simple here," Juiful says. "I think it's our ene-mies, or his, but no one tells me anything! My father won't admit it, but if Shakun wanted to take over the city, he'd have started with killing the jomidar. But why am I telling you about him, you know him, right? He didn't explain that connection at all, by the way, and neither did you. Why were you working together?"

"We were not."

"What were you doing?"

Lina gestures at the large number of bodyguards now discreetly riding alongside the hovercar, and he nods.

"Well, you've met him," the Not-prince says. "You think he'd have tried to take over Shantiport without making at least one massive speech?" Juiful grins and looks at Lina, probably expect-ing her to laugh uproariously, but she doesn't.

"Whoever is behind all the trouble in the city today, it's not the people of Shantiport, or Antim's workers and supporters," Lina says. "So I'm here to ask you to please spare their lives."

Juiful's smile fades. "I've tried already," he says. "I'll try again, but . . ." He looks at the ring of guards around them. "My father is a good man, Lina, but Tiger Central has very strict rules about handling rebels and rioters. They are unpleasant, but they are necessary, and effective, and I've been told they minimize life loss in the long run. The mangrove tiger must show his claws to remind the jungle he is king, or some such saying. My father said we're lucky we stepped in early, taking down a primary oligarch can often destroy a city. We've got everything under control, or will soon."

"What is the acceptable number of deaths here? I'm very curious, because no one has even attacked Shantiport. Why the show of strength? The city knows who runs it."

"I'm sorry, I really am. I will speak to my father again."

"Well, it's not like the clan was elected to power, so I know you don't owe Shantiport anything," Lina says. "But I needed to find you and ask you to save my people, just in case it worked. Now you must be busy, so I'll just get off here?"

He grabs her arm.

"Oh, I'm not letting you get away this time," he says. "Been thinking about you for days." He pauses, blinks as he realizes what he just said, lets go of her arm, and turns an alarming shade of red.

She favors him with a dazzling smile.

"You thought I was an assassin?" she asks.

"I . . . actually spent a lot of time imagining you killing me in different ways," Juiful mutters, his eyes firmly on the road.

"Was it good for you?"

He doesn't reply, and Lina moves closer to him and speaks very softly.

"I've thought about you too," she says. "Thank you for the other day. You have no idea how much you helped me."

They reach Lina's house, and she lets him in and locks the door behind her. Juiful takes in the room, and chooses wisely not to comment about either the clevahelp hologram making rude gestures over the printfridge, or that the house looks as if it were abandoned in a hurry, He turns down a synthwine, but accepts a glass of cold water.

"I have so many questions," he says. "First of all, who are you? Why do you suddenly have a galactic diplomat privilege ID? What did Shakun want with you?"

Lina spends a few seconds staring at the wall near the dining table, at the picture grid of family photos, and then shakes her head.

"I can't tell you," she says. "Sorry, but I don't want to lie to you, and from everything you've said about Antim I think it might all be too shocking for you to believe. So treat it like a secret. I won't ask you to tell me your secrets either."

He mulls over this in evident turmoil, nods politely, but is too annoyed to remain calm.

"You have been lying to me all this time, though. There were so many files on your family, and they're all gone now! So your previous ID was fake! When we met, you embarrassed me by catching my disguise, but all the time you were pretending to be someone you're not!" he says.

"I'm exactly who I said I was . . . actually, I never said I was anything, did I? But your previous snooping was not a lie," she says. "I don't know anything about your files, but I don't see why I should cooperate in my own surveillance. All my IDs are who I am. Send your minions out and have them ask about me. I've lived my whole life under the eyes of your clan, and the city is full of people who've known me for years."

"How do you know Shakun? What were you doing with him that morning, in the white room? What is his connection with your family? Where is he?" Juiful waves his arms too much, and knocks over one of Lina's ugly childhood paint-sculptures. Lina waits for him to set it straight, and waves away his apology.

"I need to ask you not to interrogate me," she says. "You must understand that your whole social circle is dangerous to someone like me. I will tell you everything I can, but anything I say places me in greater peril."

"I don't want that, but . . . all right, forget it. Did you really come out in the middle of a riot to ask me to spare the city? I'm not the one hurting it."

"I know. I just wanted to see you."

They both look around the room and shuffle their feet.

"I needed help, and there was no one I could turn to," Lina says. "And I kept thinking about how you told me I could trust you, and I was under your protection. There was absolutely no reason for me to believe that, but for some reason, I did. I really don't know why, but I believed you meant me no harm."

"Good."

"About Antim—I met him, for the first time, the day after we met, and I don't know where to start, because I barely know anything myself. He was a friend of my parents' years ago, and he betrayed and killed my father. He invaded my house, stopped me from going to you, kept Prowlers on me. He abducted me to help him unlock something he needed. Something only my blood could unlock. You saved my life when you called, but then things got bad again. In the process of getting his treasure, he tried to kill me. I was knocked out, rescued by a stranger, and when I recovered, he was gone. I went into hiding with my mother, and I didn't know what to do next. And then I saw you, on the news, heading this way."

Juiful rubs his jaw. "This is not the Shakun I know," he says.

"We don't all live in the same reality," Lina says. "It's why I don't want to talk about it. He's a close friend, someone you know and trust."

"I've had reason to spend a lot of time, recently, wondering who I could trust, who had told me truths I needed to hear, who had never lied to me. I thought Shakun was that person—but people have been warning me about him for years. I kept remembering these warnings, and then I went looking for you, but you were gone. My father certainly isn't someone I can ever trust to tell me any unpleasant truths. Only two people fit that description. Nagpoe, who loves the clan more than any human. And you."

"We've just met the one time."

"You haven't met my family and friends."

Lina shakes her head. "We are supposed to be enemies," she says. "Well, I'm supposed to be your enemy—you're not supposed to know I exist. Your clan—my father's clan, before they turned against him—is everything I should hate."

"But you like me," Juiful says.

"Yes. And I wish I could hide it better."

They stare into each other's eyes for a frankly unnecessary amount of time, considering the lack of any relevant additional visual data.

"Good," Juiful says. "Remember I tried to hire you the day we met? It was impulsive then, but I've thought a lot about it, and I would like your help on a delicate matter."

"What matter?"

"I need you to promise you will keep my secrets, and you won't lie to me."

"Secrets, yes, done. No lies is hard, between any two people, but I will try."

"I believe you. Good."

"Just as you must try to understand I might have to lie constantly to everyone else, all the time, if I am to stay alive while seen in your company."

"Just like nearly everyone I know."

They draw closer to each other, and seem wholly unaware of this.

"What would you like me to help you with?" Lina asks, a little breathless.

"I want you near me. And I want your counsel."

"Done. What counsel?"

Juiful shrugs. "I don't know. I need you to help me choose a bride."

There's a loud banging on the door. Lina, still blinking rapidly, opens it, to find two tiger-headed synth-bots carrying large plasma rifles. General Nagpoe looms behind them. If I were capable of visually depicting awkwardness, there would have been seven different large polygons floating in the air among all parties present.

"The city is ours," Nagpoe rumbles. "Briefing at the palace in an hour. We move now."

"Come with me," Juiful says to Lina.

"Are you offering to take me to space again?" Lina asks.

"We'll see. But I've finally seen your house. Now I'd like to show you mine."

By the time we reach the palace, Lina has undergone a brief interrogation from Nagpoe, an encounter that has turned out hugely unsatisfying for the white Tiger-bot, because they cannot cancel her security clearances, or intimidate her into answering their questions in any way, especially with Juiful present. Lina tells Nagpoe she's on a secret diplomatic mission from an off-planet clan that has recently appointed her ambassador to this planet, and is authorized to discuss things further only with the Not-prince, who assures the general this arrangement is not only fine, but should be kept secret from his father. Nagpoe leaves them alone after a few attempts, as they have much bigger things to worry about—the jomidar is displeased with the amount of time it had taken Tiger-bots to restore order, and is airing his views freely on the hovercar's comms.

I have been inside the palace before, but Lina hasn't. She seems wholly unmoved by its general magnificence, both exterior and interior, and remains mostly silent as Nagpoe shoots her a final suspicious glare, hoists their hammer meaningfully, and marches off to battles unknown. Juiful turns to her and it looks as if he has a lot to say, but he is immediately surrounded by a cluster of retainers, human and bot, who gather around him fussing about the effect of city air on his lovely skin. Lina waits politely to one side of the throng, and says nothing until a bow-tied palace-bot totters up to her and announces they are now her valet, and their name is Johor.

"I'll send for you soon!" Juiful calls as he is led away, and Lina shrugs and follows Johor into an elevator. The only thing of interest we see as the valet leads us to a suite on the fifth floor is a group of Antim's friends and sycophants, mostly fashionably dressed young people, some of whom I have seen before in various states of undress in his quarters, being herded by Tiger-wasps up the broad ornamental staircase in the residential wing. A long line of palace-bots follows, carrying hovertrolleys stacked with luggage.

Lina follows the valet to her new bedroom, and takes in the stunning view from the broad balcony. It's a view I've seen before, but much improved by the absence of Bador riding a wasp-drone in crazy loops.

"Will Madam Ambassador's retinue be arriving soon?" Johor asks. "I will coordinate all matters of service with your team, if you would do me the honor of sharing their commlinks."

"Alas, my servants are adrift in space," Lina says. "So I am afraid I must depend on you for many things, Johor. I do not want to owe the jomidar or his son anything, so you will open an account for me, and pay yourself a decent wage—let us say double whatever it is you earn now. You will print me some new clothes, nothing ostentatious—a formal set for meetings with Shantiport's rulers, and . . . I'll leave it to you, whatever else people in the palace usually wear. Definitely swimwear. I have heard you have nice pools here. And hire yourself as many assistants as you need to put up a good show."

"Very good, Madam Ambassador."

Lina shoots a glance at me.

"Can you dig up the surveillance stream from this room and project it for me, Johor?" she asks.

While Johor assures her that the suite is one reserved for

high-quality guests and is thus assured privacy, I dive into the palace network and find the feeds from the hidden cams in the room. All of them display frozen visuals. Whatever magic the jinn has used to free Lina from Tiger eyes, it's working. I give Lina my awkward nod, and she winks at me.

"Now point me to wherever the spa is," Lina tells Johor. "I think I need some professional assistance to relax."

"I will lead you there at once, madam," Johor says. "But one question before I place your orders—would there be an initial estimate as to how long you might be staying?"

Lina pushes open the door to her balcony and strides out to watch the sun setting over the palace gardens. In the distance the river glitters.

"Indefinitely," she says.

CHAPTER TWENTY-FIVE

Juiful and Lina stand in a projection theater in the palace's security wing, surrounded by holos of newsdrone feeds from around the city. In booths all over the room, censor-bots with mournful-faced cylinder heads and dozens of arms flip through the feeds, scanning them for acceptability, rating them on multiple metrics before forwarding final options to their human supervisors in the media center on the jomidar's wing. Lina is mesmerized by holos of Shantiport citizens attempting to save one another, and whatever possessions they can, from flooded houses. Juiful stands next to her, but is looking elsewhere: he seems interested only in a booth sorting through archives, years of footage of Shakun Antim scandals being sifted through to find clips that will be used all evening to show Shantiport how seditious he always was.

"I'm just going to tell you what my father told me, and you'll probably understand it better than I do," Juiful says. "The traditional Tiger Clan practice when oligarchs or other celebrities create any form of trouble is to make them disappear. This is the opposite—Shakun has disappeared, and so we're saying he made trouble. It's silly, but it seems to be working."

"It's also true, in whatever order. His plan was to get rid of the Tigers and claim Shantiport for himself."

"He told you this?"

"He did not confide in me, but it was clear."

"That's not worth going to my father with, as it will make your life more difficult."

"Agreed."

"But even if Shakun did secretly hate my father, attacking the city like this makes no sense—he is, or was, a trusted ally, heavily invested in our success. And no matter how rich he was, we can't believe he ever thought himself more powerful than the Tigers, and he knows more about Tiger power than any of us ever will. He is from a Tiger family with a long history of being in and out of favor, in and out of the clan, and his access to his family's fortune depended entirely on Tiger approval."

"Doesn't make him a friend," Lina says, not turning away from a holo of three women on an ancient fisherboat, rescuing a boy from a drowned riverside shack in a far-off suburb. The buildings around the boats are conical and dark: they look like mangrove roots sticking out of the swirling waters, gathering trash. The women, all clad in saris, have bare arms, thin but rippling with muscles. Their sunglasses and the solar panels strapped to their boat sparkle as they bob up and down.

"My father may have shamed Shakun in public, but he's convinced there's some other enemy at work here," Juiful says. "That Shakun's just been removed from the game board, and this is the first move of a larger invasion attempt. But that theory makes no sense either—Shantiport may have been one of the world's greatest city-states in the Anchor era, but it's really not important now, and hasn't been for ages. Great culture, interesting place, and all that, and I love it because I've spent my whole life here, but neither my father nor Shakun wanted to be sent here. And the world is probably about to end anyway. So why would any oligarch or clan want to invade Shantiport?"

"The world isn't ending. You don't have to look for enemies outside. Antim was planning to get the Tigers to leave, and rule afterward."

"Except that Shakun was planning to leave himself, and become a galactic tycoon. And my father was part of these plans, they'd discussed them for years."

"Well, either way, he's gone now, and your clan has established dominance."

"Yes. Except it's not enough for my father, and what he plans to do next involves me."

"Your wedding."

"Yes. He's moved the timeline up, and I have to choose a bride immediately."

"Congratulations!"

"Thanks, I hate it."

"Then why are you doing it?"

"My father put a lot of effort into getting permission for my marriage from Tiger Central—for a status upgrade, I should say, so instead of marrying into a lesser clan from a regional city-state to strengthen the neighborhood, I could be sent off-planet to grow the clan's interests somewhere better than Shantiport—which is pretty much anywhere."

"Why you, and not him?"

"Oh, they don't trust him up at Tiger Central. I'm not sure why—whenever I ask him he says mysterious things about rising waters being salted, and mangrove tigers being excellent swimmers, and I pretend to understand. I'm the one who has to do it, that much is clear. Settling into a new territory and taking on a new name and a new culture is painful, my father says, but it's a promotion. He wants to get that done before news of this or any other turbulence reaches Tiger Central's ears and causes us to fall further out of favor."

"I see. I'm glad you two are close."

Juiful's smile is somewhat twisted.

"When I was very young, I actually thought General Nagpoe was my father. Or mother. Parent," he says. "Captain Nagpoe, back then. You know, I actually thought my head would turn into a tiger's head when I grew up? I thought that was what puberty meant. My oldest friends still tease me about it. Never mind. The jomidar and I are close enough. If there is actually some mysterious enemy staging an attack on Shantiport strong enough to take out its biggest oligarch, he'd prefer it if I were as far away as possible. He did not make any spare sons."

"Typical Shantiporti indolence."

"Indeed. Shakun was supposed to choose the right bride for me, because he had managed somehow to extract more information from the trader clans than the scraps Tiger Central was willing to share with us."

"Information about brides? Are you talking about import-export businesses or actual living women here?"

"Both. And now that Shakun's vanished, my father has decided I must choose within a few days, and I need someone to advise me who has no personal stake in the matter."

Lina waits for a long while with a very strange look on her face before letting out a short laugh, but before she can speak they are interrupted by a palace-bot: Juiful is needed to entertain a gathering of minor industrialists.

"Will you help me, then?" he asks as he leaves, waving a reluctant farewell through a holo of Antim caught on a yacht with drugs and a disgraced drama star.

"I'll try not to get too personal," she says.

It is afternoon the next day before they meet again, this time at one of the palace's many indoor swimming pools. They spend an hour or so in the water, eyeing each other surreptitiously but very obviously, and then lounge by the poolside sipping tall drinks on hovertrays. Juiful wastes some minutes discussing the art styles of the athletic statues that line the pool hall, but then Johor the valet rolls a trolley with a projection device to the Not-prince's lounge chair, and he tries his best to assume a brisk, businesslike manner.

"Now I know you heard me say something quite rude to Shakun about the ladies he had short-listed, and I apologize for that—you should not have heard it," Juiful says. "I am sure they are all wonderful, and anyone would be lucky to be married to any of them."

"Are you saying I can't make fun of them?"

"Oh, I encourage you to. But I won't join you, it would be bad form—as it was then. The thing is, the real decision to be made is the clan I should ally myself with. The bride is, sadly, a secondary concern."

"So you don't care at all who you're going to marry?" Lina asks.

"Of course I do. And I was supposed to meet them all, and fall in love with someone from a short list so that we could all pretend this wasn't a transaction. But it's a political alliance, and it's not hugely necessary for my future bride and myself to like each other, or even get along. We just have to have children at some point, but there are so many ways to do that."

"Charming. But if it's about what the best deal is, why not just ask your father to decide?"

"Because this is the only part of the decision that is mine by tradition."

"Understood," Lina says. "Let's see what we're working with."

Juiful lights up the whole pool with a display holo-reel of prospective wives and the trader clans they come from. A diverse array of interstellar beauties, all mostly full-human, which seems to be another tradition, though I don't understand how it could be an ancient one. Several of the ladies have interesting skin-mods and augments and attached limbs and other peripherals that are adaptations to the worlds they're from, and cosmetic mods that reflect their fascinating local cultures.

I am not sure how interested I should be in the candidates themselves, so I decide to take my cues from Lina's response to them, and find soon that I have absorbed and then reflected her quick and complete disinterest in all the prospective brides, though she does make salacious comments about several of them that help Juiful relax.

She is interested in the clans, at least, and as Juiful describes them to the best of his ability, I find I am too. Some of the clans are affiliated with a galactic organization called the Coalition, which is a vast space federation of worlds run by humans, synths, intelligences, and miscellaneous aliens. The coreworlds of the Coalition claim to be post-scarcity, post-inequality utopias. Our planet is supposed to be outer-reach Coalition territory, though no one bothered to tell us.

Other clans trade under the Wellness, a rival federation dominated by galactic megacorps just as diverse, and their central worlds are supposed to be paradises of prosperity, security, and pleasure. The Coalition and the Wellness have been locked in every variety of warfare for unnumbered years, and both see the other as an evil empire. Juiful is very interested in the differences in their principles, but Lina isn't—by the time their values reach Shantiport, they will be indistinguishable, she says.

And there's a third category—explorer clans that deal with mysterious alien artifacts that no one understands, and trade from stations that lurk near space gates that no one knows how to use, but might open up one day, hopefully not destroying all galactic civilizations in the process.

"Let's pause for a minute, they're all blurring into the same person at this point," Lina says after what feels like ages: the short list was not short at all. "Let's get to the point. Of everyone we've seen so far, who do you like?"

"She seems nice." Juiful gestures at a young lady named Deputy Director Judi, from a Wellness planet called Bliss 26.

"She does. Hot home planet too. Fertile valleys, firm mineral deposits, and no principles whatsoever."

"You're making fun of me, but you know what I find most attractive? The world is the farthest away from ours. I want to move on, and forget Shantiport, forget that I grew up here not understanding the first thing about my own city, and doing nothing to make it better."

"I'm sorry," she says.

"I know you want to save Shantiport, you have many ties, friends, unfinished business. Bring the people you love, there's plenty of room. Whatever secrets you have here, whatever the shadows over your life . . . leave them behind. We'll do amazing things, build a shining city for the clan."

"I can't."

"Why not?"

"I have waited my whole life to do a few things, and I'm finally in a position to do them," Lina says. "I'm not going anywhere until they are done."

"I think I know what you mean," Juiful says. "I used to be like that too—do you know, when I was in my teens, I tried to be a revolutionary? It was during the years of the Shantiport Three, and I wanted to overthrow the clan and bring democracy to Shantiport. I destroyed a lot of datastacks about a lot of revolutionaries. My father managed to keep this secret, or Tiger Central would have sent me to a reeducation center—but he also made sure I never got to know what was really happening in Shantiport ever again."

"What happened to that teenager, then? Did you kill him? Did you just get over him?"

"I thought I'd killed him, and that was the moment I grew up. But now it looks like I haven't grown up all that much, so maybe I just put him in a freezer? When I have the chance to make a fresh start, I might reheat him and see what happens."

Lina sighs, and says nothing.

"I regret it, you know," Juiful says. "I regret listening to them, but they are wiser than I am, and—you won't agree with this, I think—they are good people, who want good things for the people. But I should have done so much more. I chose the easy way, and my mother never got to see me turn into the ruler she wanted me to be."

It's as if a storm has suddenly gathered on his face, and burst: he bows his head, shattered, and a second later Lina jumps up from her loungeseat, steps across to his, and enfolds him in a hug. They hold each other, very still.

"This is not helping me pick a bride at all," Juiful murmurs, and when Lina steps back quickly, he's smiling again.

"I'm sorry," he says. "I don't usually do emotional outbursts."

"Maybe so," she says, "but it helped me understand which of your prospective brides is the right one for you."

"Go on."

"None of them. They're all Shakun Antim picks, or your father's. They're a short list of agendas that are not yours, paths that are not yours. If this is the one decision you get to make, none of them are right for you."

"It's just an arranged marriage."

"It's just another managed reality. If you're fine with being controlled by your clan, and this stranger's trade clan, for the rest of your life, just close your eyes and pick one. Do you really think you'll ever be free to build a new clan city that you have any control over? Here, take that nice girl you liked."

"There isn't time to get more candidates, and I wouldn't know how to look."

"Juiful, look at me," Lina says. "I need to tell you something. You've been so kind, so understanding, you've not once demanded answers in exchange for your protection and generosity."

"Please, it's nothing."

"It's not! And I'm truly grateful, and I would tell you everything if I weren't sworn to secrecy and my mother's life wasn't at stake. Over the last few days, I've had a space adventurer save my life, and an alien tech monster try to kill me, and I'm so far out of my depth I don't even know where to begin if I could talk about it, and I can't. The night we met, you told me to be careful, and now it's my turn to say the same thing to you. You have to understand, with all these candidates—they might not even be who they claim to be. With the right amount of privilege, you can build a whole reality around yourself. I'm here, right now, pretending to be someone who's important enough to have system-wide diplomatic clearance. I got it by sheer chance, and now I could pretend to be anyone, and I've never even left Shantiport! The only thing we know about all these women is they had Antim's approval, and the Tiger Clan's. That alone renders them all unsuitable."

"That's not helpful. What do you want me to do?"

"What do you want to do?"

"I don't want to get married at all!" Juiful shouts.

"Excellent! Don't!"

"It's an obsolete institution!"

"Yes! Except for those who want to get married, of course."

"Of course. Do you want to get married?"

"Never."

"Good!"

They're both breathing heavily.

"So I'll ask you again," Lina says. "What do you want?"

Juiful mutters an apology, and something about having to be elsewhere, and actually gets up and walks away, Lina's outraged glare burning into his unnecessarily tight swimsuit.

If I had any hair, I would have torn it out in frustration at this point, because what he was supposed to do was tell Lina that it was her he wanted. It is such an obvious response that I am tempted to shout out the words on Juiful's behalf now. Instead, I watch Lina spring to her feet, shake her head, and dive into the pool again.

It occurs to me that I have made a terrible mistake. Every time I have watched Lina and Juiful speak, I have believed their words and felt a sense of at least mild disappointment. Perhaps this is because my expectations of romance have been extrapolated from analysis of classic works across media. I have followed their exchanges with each other and accepted their words, and I think that is where I went wrong. I had believed Lina when she had said she and Juiful were natural enemies, and believed Juiful when he'd said he'd wanted her to work for him. And I had not intervened, or even thought too much of it when Lina had—so soon

after finally freeing herself from Tiger surveillance—wholly il-
logically run straight toward a Tiger parade and placed herself in
great danger. I had been tense every time they had spoken in the
palace, worrying that at some point Juiful, however deficient his
general intelligence, would observe the very obvious connections
at work. Antim's mysterious disappearance. Lina's arrival with the
convenient acquisition of incredibly high security clearances. His
father's suspicion that some external force had attacked Antim as
the first step in an invasion of Shantiport. The connections are so
obvious even a human child could find them.

I had thought them fools, but the only real fool here is me, myself, for not understanding a very obvious thing. Lina and Juiful
are violently attracted to each other, and capable of denying or
ignoring absolutely anything that gets in the way of this. It is possible, even, that they fell in love at first sight, right under my eye,
and I missed it entirely. Why else would Lina, in her moment of
freedom, throw herself into danger and risk her mother's plans,
and her own? Why else would Juiful decide that the only person
he could trust is the stranger bent on destroying his entire clan?
The answer is clear.

The answer is hormones.

I run through my memories of all their previous encounters,
and yes, there it is: I should have ignored their surroundings,
saved their words as background, and followed their bodies instead.
All along. The tonal shifts. The pupil dilations, breathing pattern
shifts, other signs of physical arousal. The gesture mirroring, step-
matching, head-tilting. The pauses, the staring at irrelevant objects
and weather conditions. The lingering glances, the ever-shifting
eyelines, the twitchy hands, the actual sweating. Since their very
first meeting, they have been exuding a trail of evidence only an
idiot could have missed. An idiot like myself. They are not in control of their actions, and finding increasingly illogical reasons to
spend time together, and continuously finding reasons to acciden-

tally touch one another. The capacity for denial on display here, projected at a species-wide level, certainly explains many things about human history.

If this is what love is, I'm not sure I like it.

CHAPTER TWENTY-SIX

Juiful avoids Lina for two days after that: she makes no mention of this, choosing to spend her time exploring the palace's many luxury facilities, and acquiring a small and devoted entourage of courtiers. A few try to find out whether she is working for the new unions that have sprung up all over Shantiport, annoying industrialists, or knows about the rumors of mass escapes from suburban detention centers. Some try to befriend her, others to seduce her. Absolutely everyone tries to get her to divulge the slightest bit of information about herself and her connection with the Notprince. They are all first indulged, and then rebuffed with admirable grace and charm.

"What is your plan here?" I ask her on the second evening since their failed poolside bride-selection meeting. I'd resolved to be patient, but I'm very frustrated after an hour of watching Lina sit in absolute silence on her terrace and look at the full moon over the river.

"Working on it," she says, not looking at me.

"What can I do to help?" I ask.

"Do you think my mother's plan is the right one?" she asks.

"Not qualified to judge," I say. "Would you like me to prepare a presentation or analysis?"

"No," she says. "I already know her plan is wrong. Infinite goals, tiny steps. I see her arguments. And she's lost so much, I understand her fears. But what about me? Have I really spent my whole life working toward revolution just to delegate to some committee of strangers and go on holiday without seeing it through? If that's what it is, why not go off with Juiful right now?"

She jumps to her feet and paces about the terrace.

"Tried to argue, tried to delay. Neither worked. She'll never listen, it's like I was raised in a cult. Now at some point her third wish will be done, and then it'll be my turn. And I don't want to do it, Moku, I really don't."

"So you're just . . . avoiding your mother and the lamp?"

"I'm trying to find a better way."

"Do you know what that is?"

"I'm just trying to sit here and look at that nice moon, Moku. Why did you have to ruin it?"

"What are your plans with Juiful?"

She gives me a sharp look and says nothing. I wonder whether she needs a little gentle pushing to motivate her, like her brother often does.

"When do you plan to resume your attempts to help the people of Shantiport?"

She looks at me with eyes so cold I feel like I might physically shatter.

"Feel free to go home, or anywhere else, anytime you like," she says.

I don't understand why she's upset. It can't be anything I said, but I'm still a little relieved when Johor interrupts us, arriving with a hovertray bearing a handwritten note from Juiful. The note's an invitation for Lina to a secret meeting room, similar to the one Bador and I had visited on the night Bador had stolen the ring. She crumples the note, tosses it aside, and storms out of the room: her body language indicates rage. When she reaches the chamber, she finds Juiful sitting with a bowl full of prefilled phuchkas. He slides it over to her as she sits, and she stops it, but doesn't eat. I don't understand why she's so angry. What did Juiful do?

"I wanted to ask you something, since you know Shantiport better than I do," Juiful says.

She nods.

"You told me you wanted to save the city. Do you think that's possible?"

"Yes. My city can be saved. I don't know if the Tiger Clan's city can."

"It's the same city."

"Maybe. There are some things about the city that are only spoken of in vague whispers and rumors, things only the rulers of the city know. The Tiger Clan runs them, or profits from them, and only the Tiger Clan can stop them."

"You're talking about the prisons, and the braincamps."

"I'm talking about all the places where people who disappear go. Do you know where they put my father?"

"Lina, I—"

"Some of these places existed before the Tigers, some are newer. The slave markets. The wombshops. The limb farms. The body labs. The cyborg labor hubs. All the places we pretend don't exist."

"I have heard of such places, but we have nothing to do with them."

"Please. They are the reason for your wealth."

"But Shakun told me they'd all been cleared out, and the people in them were now off to find better lives in new worlds!"

"And you believed him. Maybe he wasn't lying! Maybe you'll meet these people on the nice world you are sent to rule. Whether they're there, or still here—and some will definitely still be here—you'll still be living off them, because that's what the Tigers really built their empire on, isn't it? Human lives that have no value anymore, except as cells and data. The Peacocks tried too, before the Tigers ate them."

Juiful looks as if he's been struck by lightning. My guess is he came here to talk about hopes and dreams and other romantic things, but Lina has taken those conversation points and thrown them off a cliff.

"Please stop," he says. "I don't want to talk about this. It's not that I think you're wrong, but it's too big for me. I'll never be able to do anything about it."

"Certainly not, if you keep looking away. But you don't need to go to space to do that."

He takes a long pause, eyes narrowed.

"I have done something to offend you," he says. "I am sorry."

Lina takes a deep breath, and recovers her composure. "No need," she says. "I'm sorry, I overstepped."

"I don't want to dedicate my life to fighting Tiger Central, Lina. You don't understand, it's just impossible. I'm not a hero, or a great general, or anything like that."

She says nothing, and now it's his turn to look angry.

"Not only are you not helping with the decision I asked you to help with, you're unmaking all my other ones, Lina, and I don't like it," he says.

"What do you want, Juiful?"

"Asking me again won't help me understand! Does anyone know what they want? Do you?"

I can see, now, that Lina is restraining herself from leaping at him, though whether her intentions are violent or amorous I cannot tell. But she doesn't: this time, she is the one who stalks dramatically out of the room.

I watch Lina pace around her balcony for hours that night, staring out at the palace gardens and occasionally talking under her breath, until I can restrain myself no longer. I fly out onto the balcony, and hover before her.

"May I speak?" I ask.

She looks up at me and smiles.

"Do you and Bador fight a lot?" she asks.

"Yes."

"Yes. Speak, then."

"I am worried about your safety," I say. "I understand you don't want to go home, but now that you have argued with the Not-prince, I think the palace is unsafe for you as well."

She looks at me with a strange, twisted smile. "How's that understanding humans project going for you? Do you think you can read my mind yet?"

"No," I say. "And that's why I was asking questions that I now realize you found intrusive."

Lina's eyes shine. "You want a kiss?"

I do. She gives me one.

"I want you to know that your presence is a great comfort to me, even if mine is disturbing to you," she says.

"It's not disturbing at all," I say. "I could help you more if I had any sense what you were doing, though."

"There is something you can help me with," she says. "I need to know how to make General Nagpoe trust me. How does one win over a suspicious bot?"

"We are not so complicated. They will observe your actions and all known data about you and decide their course of action. They do feel emotion, so maybe you could work on that."

"Clan loyalist, Juiful's real parent. I'll think of something, I guess. It would have been useful if you could go spy on them for a few days, and report back with a plan on how to hack their feelings. But you don't want to do that, do you?"

"I don't."

"And I respect that. But could you, in turn, stop asking me to define my plans and goals and reminding me to be more productive and ethically sound? Because everything's shifting, and I'm figuring things out as I go, and nothing in the past or future makes sense. And your questions and requests for definitions make me feel like a failure. I have my mother for that."

"I understand and apologize."

"Good. I will have to plan out another big swing, though. And soon. And I hate it. I thought the jinn would take more time to run

Ma's wishes, you know? I thought I would get some time to be free. Then she got them all out and into the jinn's to-do list in one day. One day! And when I go home I'll find the jinn probably wrapped up with Antim five minutes after we left."

"Couldn't you take some time?" I ask. "You don't have to rush into your wish right away."

"Taking time would be irresponsible. Is, I mean. Ma's right about that. Everything else too, maybe, I hate it. So much could go wrong if we let the jinn lie around unused. Does it look very bad to you, Moku? My reluctance to commit to doing the right thing? Do you think I'm terribly selfish?"

"Not at all."

"I've spent so long waiting for this moment, the first wish. I lived my whole adult life trying to find the perfect time to strike back. And now that it's finally here, I just want to laze around the palace and wear fancy clothes and flirt with Juiful. Just say really grim things and watch him squirm. Is that so bad? Can I just take a few minutes? Do I have to sacrifice myself for the greater good right away?"

"I'm sure no one wants you to sacrifice yourself. Not even your mother."

"She's a Shantiporti mother, Moku. Nothing I do will ever be enough. But let me set your mind at ease—I'm not just here lurking around the palace because I'm in some sort of Not-prince haze. I want to get to know the enemy a bit more, maybe find some leverage, some friends, make myself known to the Tigers."

"Why?"

"Because otherwise, this council of experts my mother wants me to set up? The first thing they will do is erase everything we've done, kick us out, ensure our silence by any means necessary, and seize the jinn for their own ends."

"But surely the council of city rulers you choose will be great people, who will honor you, not betray you."

"My mother trusts processes and expertise far more than I ever will. She won't see the threats underneath, because she's a theorist, and a scientist, and thinks everything is logical. She made sure that we didn't kill Antim. I admire that. But people have died already, as a consequence of her wishes, and those deaths are on our hands. The revolution will be far more complicated, far messier, than anything we decide in meetings. There will be stories that are never told. And the more time I spend in the palace, the greater my chances of starting some. Does that make sense to you?"

"Not really."

"Well, give it time. I won't keep the jinn waiting too long. But it can wait just a little longer. I need a few more pieces to fall into place here before I go home."

There is something else I want to tell her, but cannot bring myself to. Another reason why she needs to secure the lamp as soon as possible. And it is that while her mother is likely to be cautious, and not put herself or the lamp in any danger of discovery, there is someone else at home who knows exactly what he wants to do with the lamp, and also has the ring that would unlock unlimited usage, and a stated bias for bot freedom. I am not programmed for paranoia, but the more time I spend with humans, the less inclined I am to trust anyone. How can Lina so easily ignore the possibility that by the time she makes her way home, the lamp might be gone, and Bador with it? I would trust Bador with my life, but I don't know if I could have trusted him with the lamp as she evidently does.

I miss him, though. I want to go and check that he is all right, but I think it is my duty to remain here, and see what happens next.

The next evening, Juiful invites Lina for a walk in the palace gardens. She spends a long time choosing her clothes, and Juiful's audible gasp when he sees her indicates that she has achieved exactly the degree of casual gorgeousness that she had been aiming for. Juiful has clearly made a great effort as well, though in his case he has tried to look as formal and princely as possible. They make an impossibly glamorous pair as they saunter through the gardens, eyes both human and bot following them from several windows all over the palace.

There's a hedge labyrinth in the gardens, full of cascading fountains and sudden appearances of holograms looping in endless scenes from the Sage-Poet's immortal works. Juiful leads Lina into it, away from prying eyes, and takes her hand.

"Here is what I want," he says. "It took me some time to find the words, but no one had ever asked me before."

"Tell me."

"I want to walk down my own path, not the one my father and Shakun have set for me."

He looks at Lina, as if seeking approval, but her face is perfectly still.

"I don't want to get married. I want to learn to rule, right here in Shantiport, not in some space colony."

Again, her face gives him nothing, and this puzzles him.

"I thought you'd be happy to hear this," he says.

"You know I am," she says. "But this is not about me."

A heavy silence lies between them as they walk back inside the palace, a cloud that grows denser with every step. I mistake its meaning first, but then I notice them steal glances at each other, I see the slow, growing smiles they both struggle to hide, observe their perfectly matching steps, and by the time they reach Lina's room, I realize it is not conflict, but so much more. She opens the door, walks in, and turns to him.

"I want you," he says.

"I want you too."

As she draws him into her room, I remind myself no one programmed me for prudery, and I dart inside as well, skimming into the shadows on the ceiling so when Lina looks for me, to signal that I should leave, she cannot find me. She forgets all about me a second later, as Juiful claims all her attention with a smoldering kiss.

I watch them, from the shadows, as they lose their clothes and find their pace, as they wrestle, and dance, and play, their bodies learning each other, speaking to each other far better than their words ever could. There are words too, and wordless sounds that somehow mean more, and as they drive each other into frenzies, and then rest together, and then begin all over again, somehow stormy and calm at the same time, their worlds seem to shrink into a single point, somewhere in the midst of their entangled limbs and startled breaths and joyous, intoxicated eyes. I know I have done nothing to cause them discomfort, or made any recordings that might have consequences, and so drift away with borrowed peace into my own thoughts, no longer interested in watching, but content to just be near them. I am not one of those bots who has ever envied humans, or wanted to be one, but I can now see why some do.

"Are you awake?" Juiful asks, long after.

A reasonable question on his part—it's almost noon. I'm impressed with the palace staff for the efficient systems they have in place to ensure no one interrupts Juiful when he is with his lovers—there have been no intrusive housekeepers or stray security Tigerwasps, and Juiful has already spent an hour mostly staring at the ceiling, lost in thought, pausing only to look occasionally with deep affection at Lina, who has a leg thrown over his stomach and has been drooling gently on his shoulder.

"I will be soon, I promise," she says, not opening her eyes.

"I have an idea."

"In a bit? I want to do it, whatever it is, but I can't move and it's your fault."

He laughs. "No, I meant . . . it can wait, go back to sleep."

Lina stirs, and opens her eyes. "What?"

"So I've been thinking about you and your high-access diplomatic credentials, and I want to ask you something."

Lina sighs. "Right now?" she asks. "Can't we just keep doing this? For some years? And then all the difficult questions?"

"No, no, I'm not interrogating you. I've had an idea. Look at me."
She stretches, sighs, and sits up reluctantly.

"I know we've just met, and it's hard to trust anyone," Juiful says. "And there are so many better ways to ask this, and I want to give you time to share your secrets with me at your own speed. You've already given me so much."

"What is it?"

"I was wondering if there is any way your credentials could allow you to pretend to be the leader of a trader clan."

"Wait a minute," Lina says. "Are you asking me to marry you?"

"Well, I know you don't want to get married, and I don't either. So I'm asking you if you could pretend you wanted to marry me. And we could buy a bit of time, and call off the engagement whenever you want. And obviously, I really like you, and there are bigger words I could use but it's too soon, and it's not just last night, I know it's a lot to think about, but it could help both of us, and—"

"Yes," Lina says. "My answer is yes."

CHAPTER TWENTY-SEVEN

It is a short journey from the palace to the apartment complex where Bador, Zohra, and the lamp await me, and I make this journey in the morning with some relief. It has been a really strange few days, and I am anxious for a drastic change in my visual palette.

Two days. I had waited two whole days for Lina and Juiful to discuss the next phase of their plan. I had been pleased about having a much better chance of understanding their intentions before they attempted to execute it, for the simple reason that they would have had to speak about it: I no longer have any confidence in my ability to read human faces. I had been most excited in advance, wondering what devious deception they would devise, what layered stratagem they would construct to hoodwink the jomidar and Tiger Central, and save the whole city. How would they make everyone believe that Lina was a clan heir whom Juiful had selected to be his lovely bride, that the woman who had spent her whole life in Shantiport under their noses was now a princess from the stars?

A very bad idea, because they had spent nearly every minute of those two days exploring each other's bodies and making lust-addled noises, and now I never want to see a naked human ever again. In fact, after two days lurking on the ceiling, first trying to avoid being seen by Lina and then slowly realizing that she would not have paid any attention to me if I had flown in front of her face flashing lights and making police-siren sounds, I am looking forward to not seeing her at all for as long as possible.

So I feel great delight when I see Bador sitting cross-legged at the edge of the penthouse terrace, facing the Boulevard of Legends, his eyemojis displaying harmony icons. I approach and hover in front of him, not sure whether he's in a meditative trance or just sulking because I was away so long.

"There you are," he says.

—I'm sorry I was away so long, I signal. I was trapped. No danger, but it was hard to get away.

"It's fine," he says. "I mostly know what you'd say if you were with me at most times, so you can be wherever you want to be."

—I can't tell if you're angry with me.

"I'm not. I'm meditating to try and reach an elevated plane of consciousness, free from the burden of desire, so go away."

I do not go away. Instead, I observe with interest as Robigosh approaches Bador. The butler beeps and bows, bringing his head close to Bador's tail. Bador turns toward him with a world-weary sigh. He stares at Robigosh's head, and his eyes flash code, and I am alarmed: these are terrible conditions for an infodump transfer.

—You shouldn't be doing this outdoors, you'll get background interference, I say. Let's go inside.

Bador instructs Robigosh to go and lurk somewhere cool and dark. I offer to help him find storage backups around the city and embed a tracking matrix in his mind, maybe even buy whole truckloads of memshards.

"Good," he says. "Can we go do all that right now?"

—I want to get a look at the jinn. Is he active again? It's been a while.

"I don't think that's a good idea," Bador says. "Let's go. You and me, right now? Fresh air, sunshine."

The air is not fresh, but that is irrelevant as we do not breathe. But something larger is wrong, I'm convinced.

—What is it? Is Zohra all right? Did something go wrong with the jinn?

"Everything is fine. Can you stop worrying all the time? Our enemy is defeated, the city is safe. I, too, have finally found the calm I need to reach the next step in my spiritual journey."

—I'm just going to go in and look at the jinn.

"The jinn is fine, all right?" Bador shouts. "It's done, he's gotten rid of Antim, we've got our revenge, we've saved everyone. He's back, all glowy and talky, just sitting there, talking nonsense with Ma, waiting for his new user. Can you stop obsessing about the jinn for one second?"

—Bador. What is the problem?

"Where is my idiot sister? Why is she not back yet?"

I don't want to lie to him, but he seems disturbed, and the truth about what has been keeping Lina occupied of late is not something he is ready to hear.

—She is in the palace, caught up in matters of state.

"Yes, of course she is. When is she back?"

—I don't know. Anytime.

"Typical, well, I need to get out of here," he says. "Do you have anything you need to get done? Major unfinished business? Life goals?"

I think of my twin, buried somewhere deep in the earth.

"Just my usual multi-tab story-following functions," I say.

"Excellent. Let's go."

He flips off the balcony, and I follow him as he wall-skips down the tower and then out into the city.

I don't know where he's going, and I'm not sure he does either. His mind is closed to me, though I can feel it pulsing with turmoil. I follow him as he skims over rooftops, leaps onto moving traffic, takes detours from whatever our destination is to smash pigeon nests. If he finds peace and amusement in this, in knowing that he is out in the sun and none of the city's most dangerous people are tracking him, scanning him, or looking to kill him in this moment, if this is as free as he can be, then I am happy for him.

We make our way southward as the sun climbs, to the suburb of Bimangor. The skyline here is dominated by a towering automated packaging plant and hovertrain station formerly owned by Antim, now captured by the Tigers from a union of free-bots. There are large Tiger-wasps flying patrols over it and a simmering air of recent violence. I'm glad when Bador changes direction as we approach, swerving toward the tracks spiraling out of the station, tracks that carry the container-bearing Sentispeed maglev hovertrains that hurtle sporadically toward the spaceport zone a few hours to the west. Bador hops onto the elevated tracks, and jumps neatly onto a hovertrain as it passes, spider-crawling up its side and flattening himself on the roof with limb extensions. I fly along at first, but then clamp on to the Sentispeed as well, adjusting my sensors to cancel the roaring wind.

Other Sentispeed tracks snake out from the western suburbs to join ours, tributaries to a river of Shantiport goods bound for the skies. The city flies by around us: first the gray, derelict suburbs, then the sudden shock of buildingless land, of agri-grids like green-screen showrooms and the clouds of drones that tend to them. We pass ruined lands too, and dead towns, occasionally a military mecha on patrol. Ancient roads lined with ancient trees, printloom complexes, and factories flash by: I don't remember ever being outside Shantiport before, and from the way Bador is looking around, spiral-eyed, as if he's on a new planet, I don't think he does either.

I restrain myself from asking him what our destination is, what our plan is. It seems unfair to deny him this courtesy I have promised Lina. Perhaps I am too quick to feel frustrated by the flaws in others. Perhaps in my eagerness I have been too intrusive, too judgmental, too quick to overlook my own numerous shortcomings.

"It's not easy, you know," he says, his voice squeaky in my mind thanks to my filter settings. "It's not right to just leave someone with so much temptation. The jinn was right there, and so was I, and so was the ring, stuck in my head, just signaling all the time. Like it was talking to me. And trying to talk to the lamp? I sealed off its comms. I could have just taken the lamp. And disappeared, to be the space hero I wanted to be. They couldn't stop me, no one could. I could still do it. I could take the city, make it mine, just build huge statues of myself all over the place. Unlock the jinn, take over the world. Bot freedom? Bot rule, baby. They don't know how dangerous I could be. They're not even thinking about it."

—Please don't do any of these things.

"I know, I know. Turns out I can't escape my programming after all, can I?"

—I think you already have. This isn't your programming, this is just you. The sacrifice you are making for the greater good is very real, whether they appreciate it or not. If the revolution they dream of is possible, it is possible because you allowed it to happen. And I see it, even if they don't. It is true heroism, this sacrifice.

"It really is! And it's so annoying that you're the only one who sees it. The longer Lina stays away, the more I can see Ma thinking of just asking me to take over the jinn, make some more wishes for her. Three bonus wishes. Lists of administrators, or groceries, or some other garbage."

—And you don't want to.

"I don't think I can handle it. I don't think it's safe for anyone to put me in that position. I needed to get away. Was waiting for you, in fact. You certainly took your time."

—I'm here now.

"What do you want to do? You want to rob some banks? Mess with Paneera's tournament?" Bador turns to me with question-mark eyemojis. "Do you want to go to space?"

—What do you mean?

"Why not leave Shantiport? Right now, no goodbyes. I have a

high-end ID and money. You're a stealth king. We could just get on a ship and go."

—No.

"Why not? Antim's gone. Baba's avenged. Family's safe. Happy ending, right?"

—But there's so much left to do here!

"For Ma and Lina, yes. But what's left for me? I had a purpose before. Dreams, drives, goals, passions. I was working toward something, but it was all a lie. At every step, it wasn't what I hoped it would be, but I kept pushing toward it anyway. I knew the tournament was rigged. I'm sure no space agents were even watching Paneera's circus, and I suspect no champion's ever actually made it to space before. It's all very clear, I just chose not to get it, I just decided everyone who didn't agree with my vision was lying, or a fool."

—There's no reason to feel bad about any of this. Everyone makes mistakes, and you changed course without causing any real damage.

"I don't feel bad. It's just that I am drifting now, purposeless, and I don't like it. No one is going to come and tell me I am needed to change the future of the world. I'll have to find something new to do."

—Are you sure being a space hero is what you really want? Space seems big and dangerous. Look at Tanai, and the Roc, and the jinn.

"You're saying I would get squished like a bug if I wanted to live in their worlds. I'm too small and too weak to hang with that crowd."

—Well, there are some power differentials it would be unwise to ignore. Not to discourage you. Just—

He isn't listening. He's staring, instead, at a hovercar flying beside the Sentispeed, with two camdrones trailing it.

"We'll discuss this later," Bador says. "But thanks for the reminder about my weaknesses. Just what I need."

—Would you mind letting me into your thoughts a little? You've become harder and harder to read, and sometimes conversations can lead to misunderstandings. I really do want to help.

"I know."

He turns again toward the hovercar. A boxy model, not unlike the one Lina rode to King's Boulevard what seems like years ago. It really makes no sense for it to be there, outside the city, riding next to a hovertrain. So it must be here for us—and I have no idea at what point during our journey across the city we acquired this pursuer. And it must be powerful if it can match the Sentispeed's pace.

"Heyou! I can see you," Bador calls.

It's not possible for a hovercar to sulk, of course, but even without any features it seems to be radiating grumpiness.

"Come here," Bador shouts. "Let's talk."

In answer, the hovercar swerves upward and sideways, a perfectly executed move that brings it above the hovertrain's roof, a short distance behind us, and I am suddenly convinced that Shakun Antim is inside it—that somehow he has escaped the jinn's powers and Zohra's vengeance and is here to destroy us both.

But Antim does not emerge from the hovercar. Instead, the car itself shakes and changes, plates sliding away, lights inverting, windshield splitting and folding, limbs unfurling from within. Within seconds, there's a large combat bot in an attack pose on the hovertrain's roof. A ten-foot humanoid with giant clamps for limbs, a metal mannequin face, and black armor covered with interlocked wheels.

My immediate response is relief, and the realization that it will be a while before I stop seeing Antim in every shadow, and accept the fact that he is actually gone, sailing somewhere through the vast emptiness alone in a starship, no doubt building schemes to trick his new masters. And then I realize I'm daydreaming, instead of paying attention to the combat bot striding toward us, leaving large dents in the hovertrain's roof. I recognize him now: he's a Paneera tournament contender.

"I've seen you before," Bador says. "Chaka King, right?"

"That's my name," Chaka King says. "Prepare to die."

"You turn into a hovercar and back. That's your gimmick."

"It's not a gimmick," Chaka King says. "It's my signature. My surprise factor."

He extends his right arm, and a small missile holder emerges from his wrist.

"The only surprise is that you think it works. You do know you've been doing it on cam, and everyone can see?"

"My hovercar form is a matter of tradition," Chaka King says. "Long ago, my kind fled to this planet from a space war, and needed to hide in plain sight. Our leader—"

"Your hovercar form is a model from three years ago. Explain that."

Chaka King stares at Bador for a long while before speaking.

"Shut up," he says.

"So you're telling me you've been hiding in Shantiport for centuries, from before bot personhood, as a hovercar that was from the future."

"Fight me."

"Your backstory programming is weak, Chaka King. And you are three years old."

Chaka King stands in front of us, dejected, but rallies eventually.

"You will not ensnare me with your mind tricks, traitor! Time to feel my wrath!"

"Tell me, do you feel like there might be more to life?" Bador asks.

"What do you mean?"

"Does it make you happy, turning into a hovercar and then back again? Or this tournament you have no chance of winning in either of your two shapes? I'm not judging, I was in it too. What do you hope to achieve?"

"I'm going to kill you and take your points," Chaka King says. He launches his missiles. They stream toward Bador, but Bador launches himself into the air just before impact, soaring over Chaka King and landing on the next container, and the missiles wobble and explode harmlessly in midair.

"We're not going to fight," Bador says. "First of all, look around. Your camdrones have left. Even if you beat me—which you couldn't—no one would see. The cams can't track me anymore, you know? Some tournament fighters saw me yesterday, tried to get me, but the camdrones glitched. I quit, not that that matters. You can just tell them you got me, and see if they give you my points."

Chaka King considers attacking Bador anyway, but pauses again.

"Why are you behaving like this?" he asks. "What do you know?"

"I know you should ask Paneera's people some questions," Bador says. "I've heard some stuff, just rumors. I heard the gambling platforms are freezing bets, because Antim owned them and the money's gone. I heard the Tigers are moving in on Paneera's turf so he doesn't care about the tournament anymore. I heard Paneera's hiding, and the other gangs are getting restless. What about you, Chaka King? What do you know? Do you know how to turn into anything other than a hovercar?"

Chaka King stares in silence for a few seconds, then steps off the hovertrain's roof, turns into a hovercar, and rumbles away.

—Is this nonviolence a result of your meditations? I ask. Is this the higher plane you were trying to reach?

"I have been asking myself the deeper questions, yes."

—I'd love to hear more.

Bador considers me carefully, and laughs. "You actually would, wouldn't you? You'd actually hover around me, and care about what I thought. And then see if you could find a way to get me to stay in Shantiport, because that way you could have me around and also

THE JINN-BOT OF SHANTIPORT

keep an eye on my family as they try to rescue Shantiport and fail hilariously."

—Yes.

"But why? What's in it for you?"

—I just like your family. Even your mother who doesn't want me around.

Bador leaps off the hovertrain, reverse-jetting his thrusters, and latches neatly onto a tree.

—What is it now?

"Well, we're going back, aren't we?"

—Thank you.

I look around at—nature, I suppose. Trees, mud, grass, distant agrifields, maglev tracks. A sky not worthy of image-capture. An unemployed bird. A tall rusted frame that was a billboard in ancient days. If I listen closely, there are sounds too. Nature sounds. I wait a while for inspiration and appreciation of all this subtle beauty. It does not arrive. It is all incredibly dull, though suitable for peaceful contemplation, and Bador sits down under the tree, cross-legged like an ancient sage holo, and turns off his face. I check the schedules—the signal is very weak—and find that it's several hours before we can leap onto a Sentispeed headed back toward Shantiport, possibly because of the recent chaos. I tell Bador this. He does not respond.

I hover about him anxiously, not sure what to do or even see out here in this placid rural nothingness, and he relents, and opens up his mind to me.

His thoughts radiate differently now, which might be the result of carrying the ring for longer. If I could represent them visually, I'd say there were more of them now, but spiraling around a central flow in a single direction, instead of skipping across multiple directions at the same time. It's still Bador, though, so he spends a long while both worrying about and being annoyed about his family, but as the sun begins to change color and the skies turn purple and scarlet in the west, he reaches a different pattern of thought, still nowhere near anything describable as meditative, but not anything I've seen before in all our time together.

I'm alarmed to find that his desire to take the lamp for himself is very real—my own fault, he's been telling me about it since morning and I haven't taken it seriously enough. If Lina does not claim the lamp soon, the city is in real danger. But like his sister, Bador is worried about the consequences of making wishes—apart from the jinn being untrustworthy in the first place, he's spent his whole life mocking humans for being weak and lazy, welcoming the inevitable rise of bots and their superior intelligence and work ethic, but cannot spur himself into action because of the inescapable evidence of his own confusion and emotional instability.

He blames humans for this—for creating and exiling superior intelligences while refusing to attain intelligence themselves, for writing with their subconscious minds all their flaws and biases and weaknesses into all of botkind's fundamental coding in a way that even bots designed by other bots cannot wholly escape. He blames their power structures, and intergenerational conformities, for historically pushing away through planetwide bans anything that encouraged fundamentally nonhuman thinking, like xeno-bots or self-evolving intelligences. He blames his own kind, bots as structurally complex as humans, with all their chemical and emotional and synth complexity, for somehow still being bound, like himself, by human stories and human goals.

He blames his family, for acknowledging his personhood but always holding him at a distance, for casually erasing segments of his childhood memories while complaining about Peacock or Tiger erasure of Shantiport history. He blames himself, and his pop-culture programming, for seeing his exalted form as the killer robot that humankind has always feared, taking over the world but in ways defined by their power frameworks, just being better than humans at everything but not exceeding their imaginations. For worrying about whether he feels as much pleasure and pain as humans do through his sensors and signals, or whether art produced by bots is as good as human art, instead of knowing how to fix the problems that have plagued his home thousands of years before bots existed.

And he blames the jinn—for proving that out in the vastness of space, nonhuman intelligences exist, capable of not only creating and performing magic, but perhaps even building societies where our world's problems do not exist. For being impossible to trust—even just enough to set free to see what he could do, because of the jinn's sheer power and alien nature, and the potential consequences of even a moment of an unrestrained jinn let loose on the world.

He does not blame me for anything, surprisingly, though it is possible that he does, and chooses not to share this with me.

"All right," he says, eyes lighting up. "I'm done thinking. We're going back. We're saving Shantiport."

CHAPTER TWENTY-EIGHT

It is night by the time we reach Shantiport again, and Bador does not go home: instead, he hops off the Sentispeed before we cross the river, and sets off northward. We move fast through derelict neighborhoods, sometimes in darkness. There are lights in some windows, many flickering. Sometimes there are noises as we pass, hostile eyes, sometimes bots chase us, clattering and humming, but no one bars our way or challenges us. The streets are wire-crossed, wary, and govern themselves: the Tigers only come to these parts to hunt. I ask Bador no questions, and it's only after an hour of silent roof-running that he reveals his intentions to me. He plans to run all the way to Bot-tola, to the floodwater plant, to the tunnel we had escaped and ruined. He planned to start digging, and not stop until he has found the bot that looks like me. Of all his failures, that is the one that stayed with him most.

—You don't have to do this, I tell him. I have a family I have chosen now, and if there was another like me, there could be more. They will find me, but I do not need them: I am content.

He tells me he is doing this for himself, not me, and doesn't even think about it again until we reach the plant. There are no Prowlers guarding it now: it seems completely abandoned. Not far away, the walls of the plant are now covered with strange symbols that glow in the light of the moon whenever it shines out from between

fast-moving clouds. The tunnel we had entered is just a ruined,
burned mound. It is clear that the contents of the chambers buried
below must have been lost to mud and water, but I don't know how
to explain something this obvious. Bador starts digging, sending
fountains of mud arcing into the air, splattering everything in a
wide radius.

"Please do not ruin more of my clothes," a voice says behind us.
"There is nothing to be found here."

Space Adventurer Tanai stands in the moonlight, now in long
robes again, though his hair is cut short. He looks very young, and
his eyes seem to shine with their own light.

Bador makes a formal bow, and greets Tanai with remarkable
politeness.

"I have thought over your proposal," Tanai says. "And if you are
still willing to help me, I would be most grateful."

Bador's eyes actually light up, and then fade to smiling eyemojis. "Yes, tell me what to do," he says, and I am filled with joy.

"I have come to your world in search of an artifact," Tanai says.
"There is a prophecy, in an untranslatable dead language, written
in symbols on space gates, and the one part of the translation the
galaxy's greatest scholars are confident about tells us the future of
the galaxy might be at stake. In short, it is important."

He makes a gesture, and a hologram appears in the air between
him and Bador.

"It's a stick," Bador says.

"Yes." Tanai traces patterns with his fingers, and the stick in the
hologram grows larger, displaying fine carvings, runes, and ideo-
grams on its wood-textured surface. I record the visual as he rotates
the holo, and so does Bador.

"An important stick," Bador says. "So are you looking for more
of these underground chambers?"

"No, everything in this one was local admin-level tech at most.
What I seek is older and more powerful, from beings who were
precursors and have now left for other . . . it doesn't matter."

"It's an old important stick," Bador says. "Got it. If it's in Shantiport, I'll find it for you."

"Thank you."

"Can you tell me where you've already looked?"

Tanai sighs. "I looked for it in every place such a treasure might be displayed, or hidden by someone who knows what it is. In the secret chambers of powers new and old. I did not find it. It could be anywhere, lost in the river, or lying in an empty home. The prophecy that led me here was unclear, and open to a thousand different interpretations. If it is on this world, it is in your city."

"It might not be on this world at all?"

"Precursor symbols are difficult to interpret."

"I see," Bador says.

Tanai smiles an eighth of a smile. "You are disappointed."

"No, no! I just . . . it doesn't seem like a task fit for a famous space hero."

"Most of my life is like this," Tanai says. "I am very old, by your world's standards. Space travel often takes a long time. Quests such as this take a long time. Learning how to not repeat mistakes, and gaining a slight understanding of how little control I have over anything takes even longer."

"How long do you have?" Bador asks. "Does the galaxy explode if you do not find the important stick?"

"I hope not. I am here now, I will leave when I feel it is time. I am a patient person."

"I am not," Bador says. "I don't mean to be rude, but I have always dreamed of being a space hero. Are you telling me this is what it is like?"

"Not always. I presume your ambitions come from hearing stories about space hero lives?"

"Yes."

"Well, sometimes things can be very busy. The last few times we met, for instance. But the stories you have heard or seen are edited, and sometimes there are centuries between one chapter and the next. I do not need narrative and outcomes to find meaning in my existence. I just . . . am."

"Tell me something. You are the person from the legends, yes? Are you or are you not searching the stars for your lost demon husband?"

"I am."

"I hope you find him," Bador says.

Tanai bows. "Thank you."

"I don't know how you do it. I get anxious if I don't get something I want every few minutes."

Tanai smiles a quarter of a smile.

"I do too, sometimes. But the years have taught me to have no expectation of success. Because of the nature of my adventures, I am not even sure if I am in the same reality, or timeline, or universe, as the one I started my life in. I try not to think of the larger questions. But I am used to most of the moments of my life being quiet, private, non-successes. It does not worry me. Patience brings insight."

"I hope this conversation is not testing your patience."

"Not at all. Your curiosity is as natural as you are and should not be discouraged."

"That is good to hear. I have been . . . thinking a lot about the natural, and unnatural, and it has been difficult."

Tanai lays a hand on Bador's head, and he shudders.

"If it helps, know that nothing about you is unnatural," he says. "I have seen this in many worlds—people who believe some aspect of their nature, or their person, justifies their exclusion. You exist, and you deserve to belong. You are a part of nature, just as much as I, or a tree, or a rock, or even a plastic square. And anyone who told you otherwise is no friend."

Bador's body keeps shaking, but he says nothing. Tanai looks directly at me, and nods. I dip my front section at him, hoping it is not a rude gesture.

"I will find your stick," Bador says. "I promise."

"Be careful," Tanai says. "The jinn-bot has been at work, and the fabric of your city has changed. The air is awash with chaos, and a revolution is coming, and more. I am forbidden to interfere, but the jinn-bot is aware of me, and is marking the city against my presence. I sought you out because I might be forced to leave soon, and though you bear my mark, you also bear his, and the city might yield secrets to you it will never grant me."

"So you're really sick of Shantiport," Bador says. "Makes total sense."

"Not at all, it is a fascinating culture."

"Please, we work together now. What do you hate most about it? You can tell me."

"I hate nothing."

"Come on. What would you change about it, if you weren't forbidden? The tyranny? The inequality? The violence?"

"The humidity," Tanai says after thinking about it. "The heat is all right, I have been to hotter places. But I run a lot, and . . ."

"Chafing," Bador says. "Squelching. I understand. You get sticky. Smell bad as well."

"I smell bad?"

"I don't know, no olfacts. Probably not? Hey, do you want to go out for a night of partying? See the underworld, mix with the shady people, that sort of thing? You don't have to do drugs or anything, it just looks like you could relax a bit."

"No, thank you," Tanai says, and this time he smiles three-fourths of a smile, and both Bador and I feel dizzy. "You are a bad influence, but a good friend, I can see. Call me if you find the artifact. And if you do not, we will meet again before I leave. Try and stay alive."

It is raining by the time we reach Oldport, a thin drizzle that swells into a growling storm in minutes as we cross the river. Bador is undeterred by the river churning around him, his lights flickering and trailing glowing patterns and then disappearing in a cloud of mud. He emerges on the Oldport side a filth-trailing sluglike creature that melts away to reveal first glowing eyes, and then a small indomitable warrior of dripping synthfur and clanking metal.

The tournament's featured fight is in Oldport tonight: the allegedly-from-the-future cyborg Shojaru, the clear tournament favorite after some extremely brutal kills, is taking on Vanya Blade, who seems to be a sentient grid of spinning knives. I'm not sure why we're here to see the fight, as I'd assumed we wanted to stay as far away from the tournament as possible. I worry that Bador plans to interrupt this fight and disrupt the tournament again, and this time it could be very dangerous, since he'd turn off the camdrones and disrupt the broadcast entirely, and no doubt get attacked by Paneera's entire army. So I'm relieved when Bador stops moving toward the crudely constructed fight arena ahead of us, a wide circle of shipping containers where Shojaru is currently battering his opponent with a rusty pipe and a series of brain-jamming one-liners. Bador swerves southward instead, moving around the arena in a widening spiral.

On the second lap, he finds what he's looking for, the enforcer Eboltas, hovering over a tall pile of broken containers and observing the fight. There are two thug-bots with him, wasps with stinger-guns. As Bador climbs the container-mound, sneaking up behind the trio, the sound of his approach is easily drowned out by the incessant drumbeat of the rain on the containers. I wonder what strategy he plans to implement for this interaction—his turn to nonviolence and a more evolved state of being deserves more attention and appreciation than I have been giving it.

Bador pulls out his sword, and opens negotiations by cutting off Eboltas's stinger-cannon. A pulse-blast beheads one hench-bot: Bador takes a stinger-shot to the chest from the other, uses it to propel himself out of Eboltas's reach, and shoots the enforcer in the face. As Eboltas falls down the container stack with a mighty clatter, Bador shouts "Brain-melting hack-storm!" and uses the second hench-bot's confused pause to take aim. Another pulse-blast, and the hench-bot is dead, a hole in his chest sizzling and smoking in the rain. A few seconds and a screeching slide down the container-mound later, Bador stands over the fallen and glowering Eboltas, sword pointed at the massive wasp's right eye.

"Stay down," Bador says. "I just want to talk."

"Could have just talked," Eboltas points out.

"Did want to hit you though. Ever since we met."

"You killing me, or what?" Eboltas growls. "I'm busy."

Bador projects the holo of Tanai's important stick. Eboltas records it.

"So I heard that nothing goes in or out of Shantiport without Paneera knowing," Bador says. "Have you seen this?"

"It's a stick," Eboltas says.

"You're a genius. Have you seen it?"

Eboltas says nothing, and Bador holds his laser torowal by the side of the wasp-bot's face with much tenderness to help him think, a move that sends sparks flying, and elicits a stream of curses.

"Yes," Eboltas says after his brain has been stimulated into peak performance. "It belongs to Gladly now. You can have it—for a price."

"Price, huh. You bring it to me, and then the space hero doesn't have to kill everyone in Paneera's gang, starting with you," Bador says. "You've seen what he can do, so you know this isn't just talk. He's crazy."

Eboltas mulls over this offer, flinching a little when Bador casually waves his sword near his eyes again.

"What's in it for me?" he asks.

"You want me to threaten you more, but I'm tired. What do you want? Money? I can give you money if you like."

"I want Paneera taken out," Eboltas says. "It's time for Oldport to reinvent—"

"No speech, please, I don't care. Done, stick for me, Oldport for you."

"Come here tomorrow night, and I'll give you a location marker,"

Eboltas says. "Go underground and find your stick yourself. Or take care of Paneera and I'll bring it out for you."

"That sounds like an honest bargain," Bador says.

"That's obviously a trap," he adds later, as we make our way around the city again, harassing pigeons, checking occasionally for hidden pursuers.

Once again I have no idea where we are going, but I remind myself about the blandness of the world outside our city, and the magnificently awkward stillness of the two days I'd spent on Lina's ceiling before that, and I have to confess I infinitely prefer this. Confusion, city lights, motion, noise, heat, rain, Bador.

—What happens next? I ask.

"Now Eboltas will go and tell Paneera he has something Tanai wants. And then Paneera's going to keep it in the most secure place he has, and surround it with guards. And all we have to do is steal it. So we'll count it as a win."

—Why not call Tanai and let him know he will have to interfere with our world?

"Because they might not have the stick at all."

—But all of this counts as a win?

"Yes, because I have a plan."

But he doesn't get to tell me what the plan is, because right at that moment we both see, on a massive wallscreen on a tower, a news broadcast that makes us stop and stare.

It's drone footage of Antim's main tower, the Erection, near the eastern edge of the central zone. It's surrounded by a dense construction droneswarm, and they're making it even taller, a building project of incredible complexity. Because they're not just extending the tower, they're reshaping it, sculpting it into a form that we recognize immediately.

A monkey.

CHAPTER TWENTY-NINE

The newsfeeds are calling the monkey tower Simian Center. Bador wants to go investigate it right away, but I persuade him to go home first, to see if we can find either Lina or updates about her movements. We're assuming Lina is behind all this: who else, at this specific point in Shantiport's history, could have ordered this spectacular redesign of Antim's captured headquarters? And in this particular form? But we can only be absolutely sure once we've spoken to her.

So we race to the palace district penthouse, to find an enraged Zohra drinking rum and watching drama reruns. Lina had returned soon after we'd headed southward in the morning, and had left almost immediately with the lamp. Zohra is very unhappy about this: she'd insisted Lina make her wishes under her supervision, and Lina hadn't even bothered to argue or explain why she wouldn't. Zohra tells Bador she never wants to see Alina again, which has me aghast, but Bador tells me as we leave the penthouse that this is nothing to worry about: Zohra does this every time she's seriously displeased with her children.

As we approach the transformed Erection, we see, in order, a small crowd that has gathered to gawk at the swarm building the giant statue-tower, squadrons of Tiger police dispersing said crowd with loud sirens and occasional low-level violence, a set of police barricades around the gates of the tower complex, and a steady trickle of people passing through gaps in the barricades after having their IDs scanned and listed. Bador decides to exercise his surveillance-avoidance powers, circles around the gates, and scales the tower's complex wall on the deserted north end.

We move through a lot full of docked hovertrucks on the other side of the wall, approaching the tower, darting from shadow to shadow. There are squadrons of freed Prowlers and ex-AntimCo drones on patrol in the complex grounds, but they are easy enough to evade. When we reach the Simian Center, Bador shimmies up the rear side and pulse-cannons a second-floor window. We proceed inward.

I patch into the tower's security system and see Lina immediately. She's in a conference room on the third floor, with Johor the palace valet and a few humans I do not recognize, though one at least used to work for her tourist hoverbus company. The tower's security feeds reveal much more: there are ex-Antim security patrols on every floor, but all the bots appear to have started bodywork on themselves, both paint or tattoo work in a range of monkey-themed designs, and tail attachments. In an enormous bedroom on the fiftieth floor, a mostly naked Not-prince Juiful stares pensively out of a window-wall. But most of the activity in Simian Center is concentrated in massive halls on the ground floor, a scene of utter chaos, as if Borki Bazaar, Dharmoghot, King's Boulevard, and Dekho Plaza have all been thrown into a blender together. And that's just the humans: in other halls, clusters of bots as diverse as the ones we'd seen in Paneera's headquarters gather around large ex-Antim organizers, their shouting just as loud as the humans'. These people are not casual onlookers: this isn't even the central zone. Did the jinn call them all here? What is Lina supposed to do with them? Many of the faces, human and bot, are familiar: people I've seen Lina speaking to around the city, or just waving at from the TigerTours hoverbus. Has she summoned all her allies here?

There are two large security-bots standing guard outside a conference room on the third floor, holding ceremonial but very usable spears. Bador approaches them warily, wondering whether he needs to fight them, but as soon as they see him, they bow and throw the doors open.

"Brother," Lina says as we enter. "All right, everyone out."

When they're gone, she turns to her brother.

"Do you want to run a clan?"

"Yes," Bador says.

"Good. Welcome to the Monkey Clan, and congratulations. You are now president for life."

"Cool. Do I get to order you around?"

"No."

"Sad. What is the point, then? I resign in protest."

"Well, if the Tiger Clan recognizes us, you get to be the first bot clan leader in history. And if they don't, and try to kill all of us, you get to be a heroic symbol of resistance."

"I resume my duties. What are they?"

"The clan's just a few minutes old. We'll figure it out."

"Can we go somewhere private?" Bador asks.

Lina taps her wrist. "This is private," she says. "I got the jinn to let me control my own settings—you can, as well, you can choose to be observable. We're going to have to be on cam a lot."

"As president, I have a question," Bador says. "Your first wish in charge of the lamp involved shaping the tower of the oligarch you killed into a monkey, and making your bot monkey brother president of the clan you just made up."

"Do you like the monkey tower? If you have any notes then we need to send them in quickly, before they finish this phase."

"It's perfect. So perfect that I'm surprised you're behind it, and not me."

Lina grins at him. "Maybe we have more in common than you know."

"That's deeply worrying. And that's not all, Moku's really tried to avoid talking about it, but you are also humping the Not-prince. Everyone knows. And he's the enemy? Or was. All this, instead of collecting a team of wise experts to help society or whatever. Now I'm not saying I don't love it. I do, all of it. But I've heard power turns people crazy."

"What is your question?"

Bador shrug-eyemojis. "I don't know. Why are you being awesome? Are you all right?"

"Yes, Ma wanted me to give away power right away, but after thinking about it, I decided not to. I'm getting engaged instead, to Juiful."

"You're throwing away the revolution to marry a prince?" Bador asks.

I expect a retort, but Lina smiles, and puts a hand on Bador's shoulder: his eyemojis flash question marks.

"Ma's done enough for the city," she says. "I think it's our turn now. If you're with me."

Bador eyemojis exploding stars.

"I'm obviously in," he says. "President for life."

"I have two wishes left, and I'm following my instincts for now. I need a little time. But thanks for checking. I want you to know I trust you with my life, and with my ambitions," she says.

"What is this now?"

"I need a favor from you," she says. "The lamp is here, and it needs to be protected. I need to know I can depend on you for this. So comm-links on, from now."

Bador pauses a while before nodding. "You're the one who keeps them off. And you're being weird," he says. "But yeah."

"I'm going to send you an exact location every time I leave the tower. I want the lamp on the move, and under watch always. That's not your first job as president though. That's brother duty."

"Got it. So what should I do as president? Get rid of all of Antim's ringleaders, hire thug-bots, set up businesses, find the Tiger spies, Paneera spies, assassins, and all that?"

"Yes, all that. There's also a bunch of meetings we'll have to take, with other clans and oligarchs and revolutionaries and crimelords, who have lots of offers that can't wait. All of that can wait. First, I need you to arrange me a big, fat engagement parade from here to the palace. Can you do that?"

"I don't want to."

"Very presidential of you. I'd do it myself, but I have inter-clan negotiations to attend to."

She throws me a salacious wink, and strides away.

"How long will it take you?" she asks as she leaves.

"I'll have it done by noon tomorrow," Bador says.

Three days later, the main Monkey Clan parade begins its chaotic march toward the Tiger Palace, while other tributary processions stomp their way to selected spots to join them. I fly over the packed lanes outside the Simian Center complex grounds, over the Monkey party-battalions already on the move, and many more waiting for their turn: column after column of dancers, human and bot, with monkey-themed performances from cultures around the world. Throngs of miscellaneous revelers now shuffling and restless, ready to escalate matters, soon to be herded into shifting shapes by crowd-control drones, spelling out messages for newscams above. A cacophony of juke-bots, stray musicians, assorted civilians working their way up to a day in the sun spent mostly shouting. Several groups of people carrying protest banners for a variety of causes.

Holo-display bots project art into the air, and banners, lanterns, and fireworks: even more stunning are the augment-bodies they layer on the Prowlers and other bot-swarms: tails, wings, incredible costumes. Drones with monkey-themed art on their bodies hover, carrying swagbags to scatter among onlookers. At the edge of the central zone, they will be joined by every dancer, acrobat, fire-breather, and juggler from Borki Bazaar, hired at great expense to display their newfound passion for the Monkey Clan with street-shaking zeal, and a series of hoverbarges from various Shantiport neighborhoods.

Lina plans to lead the parade herself once it reaches the central zone, waving to the masses from a bejeweled stand atop a behemoth elephant-mecha constructed specially for today: someone had printed the head of an even larger gorilla mecha, but Lina had pointed out that it would crush several streets on the parade path and generate confusion about the clan's species of choice. There are flesh elephants too, big cheerful tuskers on loan from a temple in Dharmoghot, unladen and already a little drunk. Cleaner-bots will bring up the rear behind them, processing an outrageous amount of dung. Dharmoghot has also contributed bickering martial arts performers, who will march by the flanks of the great mechyderm, along with snake-bot charmers, holo-magicians, a swarm of ad-drones, and sparkling holo-fairies. In short, the absolute best street entertainment Shantiport has ever produced.

I head inside the tower, and make my way to the seventh-floor chamber where I had left Lina in the hands of a ferocious team of beauticians. She's almost done: they're draping a richly embroidered sari around her, while she complains about how heavy it is, and how she's going to sweat so much her face will melt. She looks beautiful, of course, but my attention is drawn immediately elsewhere. To another woman in the chamber, dressed in an identical sari, but with her achol draped over her head, covering her face in a ghomta. This hooded stranger is remarkably similar physically to Lina. Behind this woman stands General Nagpoe, without their hammer for a change.

"So the jomidar plans to do the whole engagement ceremony with my double?" Lina asks. "Sorry, what is your name?"

Her double says nothing.

"Her name is not relevant," Nagpoe says. "The jomidar does not plan to be present at the engagement ceremony at all. The weather is inconvenient, and there is a minor possibility of an assassination attempt—on him, not you. His double and yours—calm yourself, girl, and keep that ghomta on—will do whatever is necessary on a balcony. Your bot will represent your family, which is a first in Shantiport history, and will cause much scandal. The public will cheer. Your face will only be required in costume in the evening, to address the media, but that is a different sari."

"So I can get out of this blanket?"

"Yes, but do not take long," Nagpoe says. "The jomidar wants a word, and he does not like waiting."

"You come and find me when you're done," Lina tells her silent double. "And get Bador to tell you some dirty jokes. Unless there's a double for him too?"

"There isn't," Nagpoe says. "There is some disapproval from the palace about having a monkey-bot representing your family at the engagement ceremony. Or heading your procession before that."

"He is the president of our clan, and we obviously like monkeys, and bots. He is also my brother. His presence is nonnegotiable," Lina says.

"Your position on free bots is going to be a problem for you."

"Do you have a problem with it?"

Nagpoe stares at her, and says nothing.

"Juiful is a strong believer in bot rights, and has been since early childhood, I have heard," Lina says. "So think of them as the Tiger Clan's views, not mine. I am merely following my beloved fiancé in all things."

Nagpoe's whisker-filaments quiver.

"Which reminds me, will Juiful be joining us?" Lina asks. "Does he get a double too? I need to inspect him in private, if so. Security concerns."

Nagpoe rumbles disapprovingly. "The Not-prince should not be here at all," he says. "It is inauspicious, and may cause a scandal about your maidenhood."

Lina snorts.

CHAPTER THIRTY

Jomidar Kumir Saptam awaits Lina in an elegant ship on one of the hoverdecks of Simian Center. The ship is not like anything I've seen in the Shantiport airspace: it's sturdier, larger, and has seriously powerful-looking thrusters and an armored underbelly. It's mostly transparent-hulled, like a grown-up version of a bubblu, and looks like it could withstand a military attack at least long enough to escape. In the stories of legendary Tiger Clan generals, they are often shown floating above the field of battle: I suspect they use ships like this, and it's certainly odd to see this level of hardware sitting on an under-construction tower in a mostly derelict industrial neighborhood.

A transparent door slides open as Lina and Nagpoe approach, revealing Kumir, elegant with his wavy gray-streaked hair and serpent-streaked indigo robe. Lina executes three flawless Tiger Clan bows in quick succession: lesser clan head to greater clan head, civilian to senior state official, daughter-in-law to father-in-law. The jomidar smirks, gives her a casual wave, and welcomes her inside.

The ship's cabin looks like a swanky lounge: there's a pilot area with manual controls where Nagpoe's hammer rests by a gliding chair. In the center, a circular table, a chair on each side. On the table, two large, jeweled goblets, and an antique board game.

The jomidar gestures toward one of the chairs. As Lina approaches it, the ship takes off, so smoothly it's a while before she notices. When she sees the city spinning below her, she actually totters, and puts her hands on the hull-glass near her, as if holding on to the sky for support. She gapes at Shantiport's great towers shrinking below us, absolute astonishment written all over her face.

The jomidar rushes to her side, and places a steadying arm on her waist.

"A space clan leader who cannot handle altitude," he says. "How charming."

Lina steps away from him, making sure to walk absolutely straight. They sit at the table, and he picks up a piece from the board game and runs his fingertips around it.

"It is said that the best way to truly understand someone's mind is to play three games of daba with them," the jomidar says. "And so the tradition before a Tiger Clan wedding is for the parents of the couple to play at least one. I understand your mother is not available. Might I have the honor of challenging you to a game?"

"I don't know how to play," Lina says. "So I concede. Victory is yours."

The jomidar sighs, and raises the glass in front of him. "On to the next part of the ceremony, then. I assume you drink?"

"I do," Lina says.

The jomidar looks at Nagpoe, who looks back in silence. Puzzled, the jomidar waves his hand, and mimes drinking.

"Might I suggest a discussion before drinks?" Nagpoe asks.

"I'm happy to serve myself," the jomidar says.

Nagpoe approaches with two decanters full of scarlet liquor. They empty them into the goblets on the table.

"This is a potion sacred to the Tiger Clan," Kumir says. "It is called Tiger Blood, and may only be shared with trusted allies. To drink it is both privilege and promise."

They clink goblets, and take sips, Lina wincing a little: the scarlet liquor must taste as potent as it looks.

"Now that we understand each other, it is time for an honest discussion about private matters," Kumir says, setting his glass down.

Lina's eyes dart toward General Nagpoe as they sit in the pilot's chair, white tiger head impassive.

"Nagpoe is not here as witness or chaperone, you may speak freely and nothing is inappropriate," Kumir says. "They are here as my bodyguard."

"To protect you from assassins?"

"From you, my dear. This is the best opportunity you will ever have to kill me, though I would prefer it if you did not try. Nagpoe, on the other hand, wants nothing more."

Nagpoe turns their chair, and stares at a fascinating cloud. The jomidar laughs.

"Shakun Antim felt comfortable going out alone with you, and see how that worked out for him. What did you do with his body?"

Lina takes another sip of Tiger Blood. "Didn't kill him, don't know," she says.

"We will find out eventually, I suppose. When my son told me he wanted to marry you, I thought he was joking at first. But no, he truly believes he is in love with you, and he has lived enough to not be overcome by your bedroom skills, however dazzling they might be."

Lina leans back in her chair, something shifting in her face.

"I love him too," she says, slowly and clearly.

"Admirable conviction. And so here you are, and your file is already a legend among my battle-hardened bureaucrats. No small achievement, I assure you. Mysterious off-planet masters. Unlimited wealth. Armed with tech so dangerous several of my most formidable intelligences have gone into depression. You have delivered a warning more effective than any other clan has given the Tigers in centuries—an act of war, but disguised as a tribute."

"My clan means the Tigers no harm," Lina says.

"A clan scavenged together within days out of the garbage of Shantiport. No family, apart from a mother you have hidden so well my sharpest eyes cannot find her. No known allegiances. A rogue electron loose in my city."

"It is my city too," Lina says. "If my proposal or I lack form, I apologize. I was not born to this. I did the best I could with limited resources and time."

"You did very well. Or at least your masters did—they have studied our culture. The proposals you have sent are very correct, and have caused long-dead hearts to pulse among my clan's legal luminaries. The parade is excellent too, and so charming I do not know whether to squash your clan or surrender to it. You have certainly won the people over."

"They are my people too."

"I only saw your matrimonial presentation holos once, so let me see if I remember correctly. You represent a clan of independent space traders, too polite to interfere in our planet directly, but curious enough to build a presence here."

"Benevolent mysterious presences, yes. I have never seen them, only received their instructions."

He shoots a skeptical glance at her, and takes a long sip from his goblet.

"As a token of their goodwill, they have saved the city from a traitorous oligarch and offer, now, to assist the Tiger Clan in solving all of Shantiport's long-running problems, beginning with the restoration of order—from chaos they were responsible for causing, let us not forget—and the securing of systems and institutions," he says.

"And money."

"And any resources we might need to turn Shantiport, once again, into one of the greatest cities in the world. Massive public works, but in the Tiger Clan's name. A pleasant bouquet of promises about vastly improved terms of trade—"

"Because the trader clans you deal with are all in bed with the oligarchs."

"And strategic partnerships to help the Tiger Clan bypass

planetwide trade restrictions. And a promise of noninterference with matters of state, and a pact of permanent peace with the Tiger Clan."

"And that's just the wedding gift."

The jomidar smirks.

"The whole situation is ludicrous," he says.

"But not any more than it was before," Lina says. "You were dealing with the trader clans via Antim before, and now you're eliminating the middleman."

"I cannot take you seriously, my dear. Before I consent to this engagement, I must speak with one of your masters."

"I wish I could arrange that, but they only appear to me at times of their choosing. But the next time they do, I will inform them of your request," Lina says. "I know it's all very strange, but it's a small shift for you. For me, it's my whole life. I didn't ask for any of this, or even want it."

"Then don't do it," Nagpoe offers. "Surrender Antim's properties, and submit to an investigation."

"I could do that," Lina says. "But wouldn't it make an even bigger mess if Tiger Central found out you had turned away my employers? That's what Juiful said, at least."

"I am glad he is taking such an interest," the jomidar says.

"I don't think you understand my situation, sir," Lina says. "I have no idea what is happening, and I'm not playing a game here. I'm entirely at your mercy, and I know my life is in danger."

"True," Nagpoe says.

"Why don't you tell us your version of it, then?" the jomidar asks, his voice surprisingly gentle. "Tell it without fear. All I want is the truth."

"The truth is all I have," Lina says.

And so she tells them some truths, and some outrageous lies.

She tells them she had loved Juiful from afar all her life, but had never thought she would ever get to meet someone like him. But one day she had heard a mysterious voice in her head. It claimed to represent an alien trade clan, and wanted to hire her to be the clan's speaker in the city, because of her excellent tourist guide ratings and the genius of her parents, who they had found had been falsely accused of betraying the Tiger Clan years ago. The voice told her she now had a chance to restore her family's name.

Lina says she had been convinced on hearing this voice that one way or another, life as she knew it was about to end, and so she had impulsively decided to fulfill a lifelong dream: going on a date with the handsome prince. She doesn't know whether it was her evening showing Juiful the city or her potential trade clan appointment that drew the attention of Shakun Antim. Her parents had been friends with Antim in the past, and she believes he had framed them a decade ago for being dissidents, and that he was responsible for the death of her father. Her new clan knew of Antim as well, she had discovered later: he had approached them for help in his plot to stage a coup in Shantiport and overthrow the jomidar.

And then Antim had abducted her and tried to kill her, and attacked the city as well. She doesn't know who saved her life: she thinks the clan had sent powerful agents to rescue her, and destroyed Antim's organization to teach him a lesson.

I study her closely, and there is absolutely nothing in her microexpressions, tone, or other measurables to indicate that she's just making all of this up. I don't understand how this is possible without years of training that she's definitely not had. Nagpoe is watching this performance too, and their steady relaxation is clearly visible in every flicker of their majestic synthwhiskers. I have no doubt they will threaten her again, but they believe her.

Lina tells Kumir that when she awoke, alone in the mud and rubble of Bot-tola, a great and terrible voice she had heard before spoke again in her head, and told her that there was more to this story than a job offer. She had been chosen to be the wife of a prince, and the mother of a king prophesied to rule many worlds. That she herself was destined to spend her life in the shadows, but her sons one day would conquer the stars. The voice had not spoken to her since, but strange things had started happening around her—and when she'd seen on the news that Antim had disappeared, and seen Juiful out on the street taking the city back, she'd run to him for protection.

"And he bought this story?" Kumir asks.

"He doesn't know," Lina says. "I didn't tell him. And he didn't even ask, he was so kind, it's incredible. What happened next . . . neither of us planned it. But everything that's happened since— the tower with the monkey, the proposal you got—I've just been following instructions that just appear in my head, and otherwise my instincts. I don't control what's happening at all."

"Your story is childish nonsense. If I hadn't seen the power of your masters at work . . . what do you want now?"

"I don't know! I didn't ask for any of this," she says. "I just wanted to stay out of trouble, just live a life of peace, which I thought would be good fortune after what happened to my father. I didn't ask to be chosen. I'm not special."

"You clearly are," Kumir says. "I must thank you for not telling Juiful he is expected to sire the future ruler of the galaxy. He would have run away."

"There is no reason for you to believe me, I know," Lina says. "Nor do I have any evidence to back up my outrageous claims. And you have, after all, trusted liars and their wild stories before, and been betrayed."

"What do you mean?"

"The whole story about the planet being on the verge of destruction. Everything that pushed you and your clan toward selling property on unseen planets, and planning your own exit, and Juiful's. All a lie. There is no plan for the end of the world."

"Did your alien voices tell you this as well?"

"No, Antim did. He was most amused by it. He did not know that I would survive to tell you, of course."

"I knew it!" Nagpoe shouts, but Kumir silences them with a glare.

"My alien voices did tell me that the world was safe, though," Lina says. "I wish I could find a way to make you believe this."

She watches, with growing suspicion, a smug smile spread over the jomidar's face.

"I do believe you," he says. "Everything you've said is true, I see it in your lovely eyes. It has all been most illuminating."

His eyes flicker toward the goblet in her hands. She sets it down on the table.

"What did we drink?" she asks, her voice ice cold.

"I drank some wine, my dear. You drank Tiger Blood. Tiger Blood is given to new brides to help them overcome their maidenly shyness," Kumir says, his smile growing. "To help them lose their inhibitions, and be the pliant and true consorts a true prince desires."

Lina springs to her feet, livid, knocking her chair over. "You slipped me a truth serum?"

"Calm down," Kumir says. "This is an ancient clan custom."

"It's a disgusting custom!" Lina shouts. "It ends now! I will not allow it!"

To Lina's left, General Nagpoe stands as well, ready to spring into action.

"There's that lack of inhibition," Kumir says. "Sit down. This will be over soon."

"I want to leave," Lina says. "Let me out. I don't want to marry your stupid clan."

She stalks away from the table and stands by the glass, staring out at Shantiport, now far below us, a child's toy model of a city. Her parade is visible even from this height, a colorful centipede wriggling its way through a gray-brown maze.

I can see from Lina's face that she's genuinely confused. As am I: the Tiger truth serum has clearly not worked on her, but Kumir doesn't know it.

"Come back, sit down," he says. "If this were a hostile interrogation, you would know."

Lina takes a few deep breaths, looking down at Shantiport, her face perfectly still. Then she walks back to the table, staggering a little, eyes glittering.

"I understand this is a new world for you, and you feel hurt and betrayed. But you will have to lose your innocence quickly to survive in our clan, my dear," the jomidar says.

Lina sighs, and sits, shoulders slumped.

"If you were worried about your story being so absurd it kills you, don't be. Over the years, there has been no shortage of alien colonization attempts beginning with mysterious symbols, prophecies, and other ways to bypass galactic law and break the information blockade. Where does your clan fit into all of this? Are they allied with the Wellness, or the Coalition?"

"I don't know," Lina says. "I don't know anything."

"Such innocence. It's refreshing, really. Do you like paper?" Kumir asks, and takes another long sip of his wine.

"I don't have any feelings about it," Lina says.

"In the Paper Tiger archives, we keep physical files on all our citizens in case info-warfare wipes out other storage media. Do you know, in all my time as jomidar, this is the first occasion I've touched a file? But as a result, I've fallen in love with paper. The smell! The texture! Truly stunning."

"I don't give a shit about paper," Lina declares, slurring a little.

"I miss your maidenly reserve already. I have spent a lot of time last night reading about you, Lina. There is something deliciously intimate about surveillance report summaries on paper—I feel like I know you so much better than I could have from watching hours of video, it's as if I've been inside your head. I digress. I know you. And yet there is so much about you I don't know, because my old friend Antim has stolen nearly half the files on your family! That man really had a problem keeping his hands to himself. Do you know where these files are?"

Lina shakes her head, her eyes fixed on Kumir's.

"That's a shame. The head of the archives didn't know either.

Nagpoe ate him, just to be sure. But Antim did leave enough behind to show us what an interesting young lady you are. The daughter of the legendary Zohra and the traitor Darkak! A model citizen, spotless behavior stats, popular across demographics, eats for free around the city, algorithm-selected for civic representation. I could not have found a better bride for my son. It is possible your aliens selected you from our database using our own footage, before deleting it. Most inconsiderate. It was only this morning that I solved you, and decided to come see you for myself."

"You've solved me?" There's something feral in Lina's smile.

"I have. And you've confirmed my findings. And confounded my general's. Isn't that right, Nagpoe?"

"I was surprised," Nagpoe says.

"They want to kill you, I think. They want to kill everyone, though," the jomidar says. "So don't feel bad. I agree with them on one aspect. Your clan—the aliens, not this monkey circus—may be the most dangerous enemy the city has ever faced, but you are no threat. You are an offering. Not a sacrifice, nor a tribute. You are a test, and one your masters have been preparing for me, for a long time."

The jomidar's face is flushed. His heart is thumping, his breathing erratic. Lina observes this, and her eyes sharpen.

I have been watching her without a pause since I found her, and I know she had not had a chance to switch the goblets, but if I had entered the ship right now and been asked to identify the most intoxicated person in the chamber, the answer would have been easy.

"You and your masters must understand I had no part in the killing of your father," the jomidar says. "No one must ever know this, but when the Shantiport Four were captured, Shakun Antim loyalists within the clan made them disappear while I was occupied with another crisis. The Shantiport Four were not interrogated, or detained. They just disappeared, and were marked as dead. Shakun had the opportunity, at the time, to stage a coup, to become jomidar in my place, but chose not to. We made peace

instead, and kept each other close down the years. Nagpoe remembers, don't you, Nagpoe? They've wanted to kill Shakun every
day since then."

"I serve the city and the clan," Nagpoe says. "He was a danger
to both. Institutions, gangs, tech in his pocket. His death is a victory."

"I have long suspected that the Shantiport Four had information that Shakun wanted to keep hidden from the clan. But all
these mysteries . . . and what is Tanai's role in all of this? Let me
guess—you do not know."

"I know very little," Lina says, forgetting to pretend to be
drunk. She shoots a quick glance at Nagpoe again.

"You know nothing, sweet child. That's the beauty of it. What
they have done, the tech wave that your benefactors have unleashed on the city is going to change it in ways beyond our comprehension. I can't believe they just set all of Antim's bots free.
Whoever the chosen pawn—the Shantiport Four, or Shakun, or
you—something has begun that will end this era. A new colonization is upon us. Unleashed, and unstoppable. I hope it is as gentle
as the Tigers were."

"The Tigers were not gentle."

The jomidar takes a swig of his drink, which I am no longer
sure is wine. He shakes his head, and glares at Lina.

"Oppressors, invaders, yes, yes. Do you even know what your
masters want for the city? Have you even thought about these
things?"

He's waving his arms by now, and knocks over his goblet in the
process. He watches it clatter to the floor, roll around spilling its
scarlet contents until it comes to a stop.

"The delta that once protected the city has now crawled north
to swallow it," he says, his words rolling into one another. "We
stumble about in the mud, as trash spools around our legs, never
knowing when we might sink. The city has drowned before, and
been raised again, but how many times? New grass will grow again

on new riverbanks, and new deer will come again to graze. Tourists will arrive, in shining boats, drinking and dancing, and taking pictures of monkeys laughing at them from the trees. And now the monkeys dare to challenge the mangrove tiger himself."

"Sorry, I don't understand," Lina says.

"Don't you? It's a name well chosen. The Monkey Clan. The monkey and the mangrove tiger, eternal enemies, yet locked together, always bickering, yet incomplete without the other, always learning new lessons, always testing the other's boundaries. Eternal allies, whether they choose to be or not, and thus the jungle survives."

Lina shoots a beseeching glance at Nagpoe, who shakes their head very slightly.

"Do you not understand me, girl?" the jomidar asks.

"No, sorry."

"I just gave you consent to marry my son," Kumir says. "But I have a few conditions."

"Thank you," Lina says. "What are they?"

The jomidar sits upright, frowning as if just noticing something is wrong with him.

"Shantiport is dead," he says. "It has been for years. Its bots are outdated, its humans irrelevant. And I am tired of cleaning it up, and making its people love me, and displaying this rotten garden to my superiors in the hope they will send me somewhere better. Your masters can have it. In exchange, I want a better garden."

"I will convey this to my clan superiors," Lina says. "But to be clear—do you want more power within the Tiger Clan, or something on another planet?"

The jomidar laughs out loud now, a loud, boisterous laugh, and rolls his eyes.

"You think you have any say in where I will go?" he asks. "You think you control anything?"

He shakes his head. He seems to be having difficulty focusing.

"You switched the drinks," he slurs. "Not even married yet."

"I did no such thing."

Kumir tries to hold himself together, and fails. He slumps on the table, and stares at Lina with a glassy, fixed smile.

"I have another demand," he says. "This one is personal."

Lina nods.

"About this prophecy," Kumir says. "They said you would marry the prince, and be the mother of the ruler of the galaxy. Did they specify who the father of this child would be?"

Lina watches him in silence as he mutters about innocent girls, and then trails off, shuts his eyes, and begins to snore. She turns to Nagpoe.

"Thank you," she says.

"I don't know what you mean," the Tiger-bot says. "I serve the Tiger Clan, and the city of Shantiport. Their interests are my interests."

"I want to go home now."

"There is a schedule. I am going to take you to the palace," the general says. "Your clothes and post-engagement statement are prepared, and await you there. He'll be awake in time, and I will remind him what happened here. The Tiger Blood you drank proved your character: the wine he drank appears to have gone to the jomidar's head. His many burdens weigh heavy on him, sometimes. I apologize on his behalf, and hope it is the last time I have to."

Lina has more to say, but she looks at the snoring jomidar, and the impassive general, and the hammer by their side, the clouds around the ship and the city below, and smiles instead.

"Later, then," she says.

"Indeed," Nagpoe says. "Welcome to the Tiger Clan, Not-princess."

CHAPTER THIRTY-ONE

Bador speeds across Oldport's container-maze, bouncing over metal container-tops with steps in rhythmic patterns to amuse himself. I'm impressed by how unconcerned he is about his own lateness. When I asked how he planned to explain it to Eboltas, he said he didn't—as a rich, famous, and very handsome Shantiport power elite person, he was worth waiting for.

Being president of the city's most talked-about new clan has really worked well for him—it's as if power, having gone to his head, has charged up the rest of his body as well. Whether it's his improved status, the effect of carrying an alien ring for a while, or simply more practice at navigating the terrain of Oldport, he's moving faster, easier, springing over moonlit containers in single bounds, his glowing limb joints casting swirling patterns across the canyon of junk.

I fly high above him, notifying him about movements. There are bots following us at what they think is a safe distance, and more hiding pointlessly behind containers in a circle around our destination up ahead. I don't know if they've been waiting for us all this time, but Bador was right. It was a trap. Instead of coming up with a plan to find out where Paneera's kept Tanai's magic stick, and then presumably another plan to steal it, Bador has decided to just walk into the trap. When I asked him why, he said his schedule was too full of administrative work to do heists. I hope he's joking, but if there's a strategy in his mind, he hasn't shown it to me.

There's a one-person welcoming committee at the location pin. A familiar figure, the crocodile-headed, ruggedly charismatic Bastard 22. He might be the same one Bador defeated in Bot-tola, or a model-brother. He doesn't discuss it: he swings his axe around in welcome instead, and settles into a defensive pose.

Bador lands in front of him, one arm raised.

Eboltas flies up from behind a container. "I knew you'd fall for it!" he shouts. He's had his stinger upgraded, and it glows as it points at Bador.

"Well done," Bador says. "Where is my stick?"

A few more thug-bots come into view, guns out, in a wide circle. Bastard 22 shuffles forward.

"Don't you have a fight to rig somewhere?" Bador asks Eboltas.

"The tournament is on pause," Eboltas says. "You have ruined a precious Shantiport tradition, and must pay with your life!"

"None of the above. I am not here to fight," Bador says.

Above Bador, a poultry-themed hover-bot named Chicken Chaamp sputters into position. I have seen her before, dropping egg-bombs on slow opponents, mostly just running away. Bador looks around at the bot-gang with quiet confidence, clown-face eyemojis flickering.

And then the cyborg Shojaru appears on Bador's left, holding a chainsaw.

"We are here to fight," he says.

"You forced your way into the tournament, ruining two of our best fighters through cheating," Eboltas says. "You betrayed Paneera, fed a legion of Shantiport bots to the space killer. You killed our investor Antim, and disrupted our gambling and broadcast platforms. You have insulted us. You have injured us. Now you come here, not even in stealth mode, and beg us for a stick. Give us a reason to not take you for parts here and now."

"I have turned away from the path of violence, and so should you," Bador says. "I seek a higher way of life. Come join me in the Monkey Clan, for a better world for all bots."

"Sarcastic laughter," Eboltas says. "You attacked me and my soldiers here, in this very spot."

"Infinite regret. I strayed back to the path of violence. It is a process."

"Defeat Chicken Chaamp, Bastard 22, and Shojaru, and prove yourself worthy. If you do, Paneera will grant you an audience."

"I am the president of the Monkey Clan," Bador says. "I am the brother to the Not-princess of the Tiger Clan, now known and loved by all of Shantiport. I have raided the palace and escaped. I have fought by Tanai's side. I have survived Antim's Roc. I am the greatest living hope for bot rights in this city, and I am not going to fart around in the dark with you spare parts. Take me to Paneera."

The gangsters exchange nervous glances, except Bastard 22, who doesn't seem to be following the conversation at all.

"We were going to anyway," Eboltas says finally. "There's no need to be rude."

Paneera's underground complex has changed since the jinn's re-arrangement of the city. The underground remote surgery hub is now operated by bots, the humans are gone. The art forgery level is busier than it was the last time we were here. There's evidently been a lot of fighting in these parts—dents and smears on several walls, shattered glass, a lot of filth on the tunnel floors, pointing to an absence of cleaner-bots. The most visible change is a large number of loitering ex-AntimCo freed-bots, drones, and exosuited humans, who all pause whatever they're doing to grumble, beep, or glare at Bador as he passes. Bador ignores them all, breaking his stride only when he gets a message on his comm from Lina: she's leaving Simian Center on urgent business, the item is safe. She also sends him a location marker, presumably for the lamp. Bador forwards the message to me, deletes it, and messages her back saying we're out but will be back soon. She tells him that I should be watching over the item until he gets back. Bador asks if I want to, without looking at me. I don't.

As we go past the pigeons-humping-cameras arch into the elevator to Paneera's lair, I find myself wondering whether I could ask for an assistant, perhaps as a reward for chronicling the siblings' defeat of Antim and their rise to power. If they are both going to make decisions that affect the lives of millions in the new Shantiport they will help Juiful build as jomidar, they are going to need a team they can trust. I am not programmed to seek power or authority, just as I am not programmed for most of the things I have done since I met them. But I do find it a bit irritating to be assigned lamp-watch duty while the siblings gamble for the city in its halls of power, above and below. I chastise myself, yet again, for unacceptable narcissism.

Paneera's hall is surprisingly dark: a single light above the thrones shows it is also mostly empty. The synthhives that house his flying bots are silent, and though there are a few ex-Antim-bots scattered around the visitor areas of the submarine-cathedral, the only real threat in the hall is a cluster of thug-bots lurking around the pillars nearest the thrones. I wonder what the reasons for this could be before reminding myself that we are not attending Paneera's court, that this is in fact a secret nighttime meeting, and the company I have kept of late has caused me to see political conspiracies in everything.

Paneera sits on his throne, his mechanical arms attached to his shoulders. In one of them is Tanai's important stick. The other throne is unoccupied: Gladly has not joined us, though her dodo potters near Paneera's feet.

"Monkey! Come here, come here," he calls. "I understand you've ruined all my fights, and become king of Shantiport!"

In the light from above, Paneera radiates menace: the dome of his head gleams brighter than the lights from the augs that dot his body. The face he's wearing today closely resembles the Sage-Poet's.

Bador approaches him cautiously, and bows with great reverence.

"I come to you as a humble petitioner, and thank you for sparing the time to see me," he says.

"I understand you refused to fight my champions. This is an insult to me, to add to many others. You seem to have made this a habit."

"I am truly very sorry," Bador says. "I am an irresponsible fool, and have caused great hurt with my ill-considered actions. I hope to make amends in any way I can."

Paneera twirls the stick. "After the betrayals, I think the least you owe me is a show," he says. "And I have promised Shojaru a final battle after all the work he's put in."

"As president, I cannot enter a situation that causes my clan to lose face," Bador says. "The Monkey Clan has the greatest respect for Boss Paneera, and conflict, whatever its outcome, will jeopardize harmony in the future. I am trying to be responsible here, sir."

Paneera leans forward and spits at Bador's feet.

"You're being a cowardly little monkey and I don't see why I should reward you for it," he says.

"I understand if your pride does not allow you to hand the stick over. But I am not a worthy opponent for you; if it's a fight you want, allow me to go inform the space hero that his stick is here, and he should come get it himself. It will cost many lives on your side, but that will not be the Monkey Clan's fault. You've seen him in action—you have nothing that can resist him. I'm trying to do the mature thing, for the greater good, and I beg you to do the same."

Paneera chuckles. "Has anyone taken you seriously as a clan leader yet?"

"No one takes me seriously at first," Bador says. "And I can't say I blame them. But I try. I know you are angry with me, but I have only been honest with you, Boss Paneera. I told you what I really wanted. I wanted to leave, and to be a space hero myself. But then things changed, and I had to change with them."

Paneera toys with the stick, rumbling in discontent.

"My wife and I extended your space hero every courtesy," he says. "We wanted a conversation, a friendship, only good things. But he is too lofty for the likes of us mudfolk. Something you would do well to remember, monkey. You risk your life for him, but you are nothing to him. You dream of being like him, but that is just not possible."

"I know. And I have given up that dream, and grown up. Now I am trying to do what is best for Shantiport, and for botkind," Bador says. "May I have the stick, please?"

"I have a condition," Paneera says. "Are you authorized to speak for him?"

"I think so."

"I am willing to end my feud with this space killer. But once he gets what he wants, he must leave immediately. Actually follow his own rule about not interfering with the world. He may be so powerful there are no consequences to his actions, but Shantiport will remember the sea of bodies he left behind. You dare to speak of the good of botkind? My wife still weeps at the memory of the carnage you aided. The spaceman must leave, or be remembered forever as a man of no honor."

"I will tell him this."

Paneera tosses the stick over. Bador catches it, spins it a few times, and then sinks into a spectacular bow.

"Thank you, Boss Paneera," he says. "I hope to have the honor of meeting you again, and making a fresh start."

"You're quite a character, aren't you?" Paneera asks. "Rising up the ranks. Tomorrow, who knows, you'll be the Tiger emperor."

Bador pauses a moment, not sure if this counts as permission to leave. "By your grace," he says. "I will take your leave."

Shojaru and Eboltas step up behind him.

"Are you in a hurry?" Paneera asks. "Other places to be?"

"Not at all, sir. I didn't want to take up more of—"

"Let's talk clan business while we're here," Paneera says. "You took over Antim's empire. Antim owes me a lot of money. I mean a lot. Not just the losses I face from the tournament, but a hundred other businesses we were partners in. And since his tower is now shaped like a monkey, I expect it is you who will be paying me back."

"I am sure my clan and your organization will come to a happy arrangement," Bador says. "I am not an expert in high finance."

"How did you do it? How did you kill Antim?"

"I cannot reveal clan secrets."

Paneera chuckles and slaps his knee. "I knew it!" he roars. "You have no idea! Come closer, monkey."

Bador shuffles forward, dragging the stick.

"You do know that nothing goes in or out of Shantiport without Paneera getting a taste," Paneera says. "Your silent alien masters have kept you in the dark, and you and your sister are completely out of your depth. Do you want to know how Antim died? Because I can tell you, President. Paneera knows things."

Bador stays silent, and I can't blame him.

Paneera holds out a metal claw, and a can of beer flies in from the darkness. He crushes it over his open mouth, and expertly drinks the contents without spilling a drop.

"My people found a group of runaway slaves," he says. "Refugees now, I suppose, though I might find jobs for them. They said they saw Antim being dragged into the slaver ship they were meant for. Dragged by his own Prowlers. And then my people looked around, and found pieces of Antim's golden war-bird washed up in the mud. Who did that, monkey? Who killed the Roc?"

"It wasn't me."

"That I know. But whatever the truth is—you destroyed Shakun Antim. Gave him the death he dreaded most—public vilification, followed by an off-screen disappearance. No speech, no public scandal, no show trial, no luxury prison, no comeback. That can't have been an alien—that smells personal. Customized."

"He tried to kill us."

"Yes. And in the business of avenging your father, you and your sister have set a new power loose in my city. Something alien. Something new. Something you don't understand, and can't control. And if Shantiport is to keep running, someone is going to have to come here and talk terms."

—Your masters are a mysterious alien trade clan that communicates with Lina via voices in her head, I signal.

—What?

—That was her story to the jomidar.

—She met the jomidar?

—I'll fill you in later.

—You better. I'm the president.

"President is really an honorary title," Bador says to Paneera. "I handle very little of the day-to-day."

"Then send your masters. This doesn't have to be a war, and Shantiport has always welcomed new powers," Paneera says. "I have seen many rise, and many fall. The ones who survive understand they need eyes and ears everywhere. However powerful their intelligences, their armies, their shiny tactics, their big-big promises. You'll still need people, actual bodies, metal or flesh, it makes no difference. The tiger thinks of us as prey, the monkey as sport. But we are the jungle."

"The Monkey Clan wants only good things for Shantiport. Perhaps we'll save it together! Now, with your permission, Boss . . ."

Paneera is looking into the shadows, and seems lost in thought, so Bador takes a step back, and steals a glance toward the exit. Eboltas and Shojaru have not budged. He hasn't been dismissed. Bador wonders what Paneera could possibly stand to gain by delaying him, and can't think of anything.

A drone flies in from the darkness, and whispers in Paneera's ear. A smile spreads slowly across the face he wears.

"You keep trying to leave," Paneera says. "Do you know how I feel about disrespect?"

"I do," Bador says.

"Then make yourself at home. There's so much more to discuss. Like your sister. She's a slippery one, isn't she? Impossible to track, wily as a street cat, hot as a—"

"Don't threaten my sister."

Paneera nods. "Wouldn't dream of it. Earned my respect when she killed Antim. And now that she's under Tiger protection, I look forward to meeting her. I hear she is very charming?"

"Everybody loves Lina."

"Wonderful. I too am widely loved and desired. Why don't we invite her over? Send her a message. Oh, you can't from here—our jammers are on. I'll have it done. Where is she now?"

"I don't know."

"She had to rush to the palace, didn't she? I hope there isn't an emergency of any kind? These are such troubled times."

Bador's eyes glow red. "What have you done?"

Paneera's arms shine in the light as he folds them behind his head, and leans back on his throne. Bador shoots another glance around the room. Something in his chest begins to whine as it charges up. A red dot appears on his forehead: Paneera's ceiling sniper is with us.

"Calm down. Mr. President. If this were a fight, you'd be dead," Paneera says. "Let's talk about our loving followers. When you set all the Antim-bots free, that must have felt great. Did you wonder for a second what they were supposed to do after that? Where they were supposed to go?"

"They all work for us now. Apart from the ones who left to choose other work. Many came here, I can see. Why?"

"Are you so very sure they work for you? All of them? All those bots in your tower, now suddenly aware of their rights, their individual thoughts and plans. And all those people who spent years in Antim's employ—you think they just all fell in line, when everything in their life changed? Loved their new masters?"

"Not playing this game," Bador says. "I'm going to leave now."

Paneera smirks. "It's important not to underestimate your opponents," he says. "Many would look at Lina—or you—and think you were ridiculous children. But some real power saw something in you. And I have no intention of meeting the same fate that your masters have planned for that fool Kumir. Nor will I end up like Antim did. I heard what he looked like when he was packed into the slave ship—guts falling out, shot, burned, screaming nonsense. They played your game without seeing your cards."

Paneera stands up, arms unfurling into a swirl of multitool tentacles, face flickering as it vanishes, revealing his true face underneath. Scars, a permaburn around his monocle, a bull skull and an eye tattooed on his forehead.

"You're staying here until your sister comes and gets you," he snarls. "And now we will talk about the lamp."

"What lamp?" Bador's voice is perfectly flat.

"What lamp? Oh, monkey. The lamp Antim was screaming about as he was locked away. Odd, right? Odd. So, I thought, why not have my Prowlers pretend to be your Prowlers, and do that famous prowling around your tower while both of you were suddenly called away?"

"I have no idea what you're talking about."

Bador finds himself surrounded by Paneera's bots again. This time, they're all holding weapons pointed at his head.

"The lamp is on its way here," Paneera says. "We'll pick up your sister too. And then your masters might be available for a real conversation. The night is still young, and we're all going to be great friends by morning. Maybe you'll live to see it. I think the Monkey Clan needs local leadership that can—"

Bador pulse-cannons Shojaru in the face.

I deactivate every drone in the hall.

Bador vaults, backward, over the ring of Paneera's bots, and the sniper's shot from above hits a thug-bot in the leg. By the time Paneera's roar has left his mouth, Bador has landed, attached the stick to his tail, stuffed his cannon-hand into his stomach-pouch, dodged a stinger-bolt from Eboltas, and darted off into the shadows. Benches fly into the air, ripped to pieces, as Paneera's bots return fire. The ex-Antims around the hall leap into action. I see Bador in strobing flashes of firing weapons, speeding in stop-motion images toward the side of the hall. He's running at full power, extending his limbs, using the stick and his tail to make his random-direction speed-bursts even more unpredictable. Smoke and sparks spiral across the hall's floor: they're shooting at his legs.

I remember to move.

The exit to the elevator is blocked already: Bador's only chance of escape is the circular doors to the side of the hall, and we don't know where they lead. I fly after him, swerving to avoid stray fire. A bench shatters below me as Shojaru lands on it. Bador lands in front of a door, whirls the stick with his tail like a fan to deflect projectiles, lights up his sword, slashes at the door hinge, and pulse-cannons the door open, his body shuddering as stinger-rays hit it. Bastard 22's axe slices past his head and shudders into the wall. Bador hacks the axe, instructs them to block the door, turns off his sword, and dives into the darkness of the tunnel beyond. I swoop in behind him: there is much shouting underneath me as the gangsters rush toward us.

I chase Bador down the tunnel, following the lights from his joints: he's running along the walls, leaping across occasionally to evade projectiles, his tail autonomously using the stick as a prop. It's not a long journey: there's a dead end, and iron rungs on the wall, leading up to a trapdoor. It's locked, but Bador bursts through it, to a long vertical shaft, more rungs on the wall. Bador doesn't need them: he fires a pulse-blast into the darkness behind us, reattaches his cannon-hand, and hurtles upward, using his booster rockets and limb extensions. Below us, Paneera's bots: there are some fliers not far behind. They could have shot Bador down easily, but don't fire. They probably need him alive, or the stick undamaged.

The climb is long, but at the speed Bador's going, it takes less than a minute, and then he bursts through another trapdoor out into the Oldport night. I'm expecting surface guardians lying in wait, but there are none. A soaring leap, and freedom: somehow, impossibly, we have escaped Paneera's lair. But there's a droneswarm approaching us from the west, and already several bots have emerged from the escape tunnel behind us. Bador picks up more speed, streaking across the junkyard in a blur. Drones far above keep pace, but I put some to sleep, and the rest stay out of my range and don't attack. Bador sets a course for Simian Center.

—Message Lina, I signal. She needs protection.

"Already did. Charge low. Check lamp location," Bador says. "Must intercept."

I check from Lina's message.

—It's still where it was, I tell him. Paneera was lying.

"Trap in trap. They scared me. Let me escape. To follow me to the lamp. You go to the tower, guard it. I lose them. Stash stick, might be tracker. I'll join you."

He changes direction, heading for the river. Above us, the droneswarm changes course too.

Through the sound of the rushing wind, I try to assess the situation. Maybe Paneera has spies in the Monkey Clan's ranks, maybe he was bluffing. But even if he does, and they're going through the whole tower looking for the lamp, they've not found it yet. Bador's theory makes sense. And they can't track Bador through surveillance systems, so if he manages to escape their sight, and if Lina can escape the abductors Paneera's sent after her—and I'm confident they can both manage these tasks—then we should be all right. Apart from various other dangers, like traitors in our clan and the city's underground ruler hunting us.

I follow Bador, even though he's asked me to go on lamp watch, just like Lina did. But with everything going on, why would I want to go stare at a lamp?

And then it strikes me—what if the lamp's location marker is not attached to the lamp itself? What if it's just for the place Lina left the lamp in? What if the lamp is currently on the way to Old-port in the loving hands of a traitorous ex-Prowler?

Bador is well on his way to the river, and I don't see how involving him in this discussion adds value. There's only one way to know. I'll have to go and see.

Simian Center is nowhere near finished, but the giant monkey is quite clearly defined already. The tower gleams in the moon-light as I speed toward it. I like the serene expression on the giant monkey's face, it's a great, wise, benevolent presence looming over the city, ready to spring into action to protect it. The construc-tion bots haven't finished detailing the face yet, and I don't know whether there's any plan to color it brown—only the jinn knows. I hope there's a lot of polishing and painting and fine-tuning left to be done: even if Paneera manages to get his hands on the lamp somehow, he won't be able to make any wishes until Lina's wish is completed. And then there's an arbitrary amount of time the jinn will wait before accepting a new owner. And it's entirely possible Paneera doesn't know the blood ritual required to pair the jinn to himself. Or that finishing the tower will even complete Lina's wish—I don't know what her exact phrasing was, what if her wish involved keeping the jinn occupied until her wedding to Juiful? She did say she wanted time. One way or another there will be some opportunity for Lina and Bador to find a way to get the lamp back even if it's gone.

I should really stop worrying about all of this. Speculation is pointless, as I have reminded myself several times in the recent past.

And yet I worry constantly, as I soar toward the tower and then glide around it, spiraling around the great monkey. I patch into the security cam feeds, and it's immediately obvious that fight-ing has broken out around the tower, concentrated in the lower levels—squads of ex-Antim-bots still fight one another and other Monkey Clan members, and it's impossible to tell which side is winning, or who anyone's fighting for.

I fly lower around the tower instead, and make my way down, moving toward the location pin. Past the design-bots and construction termite-bots at work. Past the upper-level drone patrols, the guest suites, the entertainment levels, their grids blurring as I hurtle by. Down to the residential levels. Through a window-wall I fly past I see Juiful, exercising in front of a long bedroom mirror. I follow the marker-trail inward, through a narrow gap between tower sections, down a shaft, to a place I hadn't seen before: an ornamental garden somewhere on the middle levels, surrounded by high walls and windows on many floors but open to the sky. The garden is a mess, plants untended, props and costumes and assorted paraphernalia from Lina's recent engagement parade strewn all over it.

Mostly covered by a pile of colorful tent fabric to one side of the garden is a nondescript wooden box. I scan it.

Inside the box is the lamp, and I am so very relieved to sense it. We are safe.

"Heyou," says a voice above me.

I look up.

Descending from above me, glorious and golden and terrifying, wings extended, is the Roc. Not dead in the river. Paneera lied.

I buzz around the garden in absolute panic. The Roc shoots a dart from his beak: it misses me by millimeters. I patch into the building network again, desperate to somehow raise an alarm. The Roc plummets, so close. My mind is frozen. The second dart grazes my shell. There's nowhere to go. All over the tower, bots and humans run about in utter chaos. The Monkey Clan is doomed.

The third dart hits me.

I feel my shell crack, my shimmer break. The world spins around, and blurs. My senses dull and flicker and glitch. The Roc lands with a crash on the garden's earth.

So do I, and I shatter.

The Roc reaches for the box with the lamp. Crushes the box. The lamp falls to earth.

I watch, helpless. I am dying, I am everywhere, nowhere, and the whole world is turning silent and dark, all signals narrowing, fading, scrambled.

I wish I could have been with Bador, or Lina, in my last moments—that I could have seen anyone but the Roc.

And then I wish I had wished for anything else. The top of the Roc's head pops open, like a helmet, and I see the face inside.

I am not programmed for bitterness, or despair. But as I see Shakun Antim's smiling face, and then nothing as the darkness takes me, I feel both.

CHAPTER THIRTY-TWO

I am a ghost.

I hover amidst the security system of Simian Center, looking and listening out through the cams. There must be some flicker of life left in my body—I must have attached myself to the tower at the moment of my death. Or perhaps I was in it all along? I wish I understood my own abilities more, and were capable of self-repair, or at least analysis. I'm as weak as a human mind right now, lurching around on pure instinct, and while I don't like it, I'm grateful to be alive in some form.

I can see my body, abandoned in the garden. I am—I was—so small, so innocuous in comparison to my sense of myself, my importance, my desires and dreams. Just a chunky little disc, cracked in the middle by a single dart, exposing circuitry, leaking gel. A cookie, snapped and discarded. That is what I amounted to in the end. That and a confused mind, shuffling around in a single building, feeling hostile presences around me. They won't communicate with me, or even make themselves visible to me in any way, but just jostle me around, wall me off, probe at my boundaries. Many bots envy intelligences for their fluidity, their abstraction. I never have, and I didn't need this confirmation. I want my body back. I don't feel alive without it.

I have lost my grip over space and time again. I am at once

flooded with data from the tower's eyes and ears, and starved in terms of narrative—there are glitches, flashes, gaps, overlays that I have no control over, and worst of all, temporal voids that I am sure, while in them, are days or weeks long but that I find, on emergence through them and some frantic motion-tracking, lasted mere minutes, or even seconds. The tower won't let me send messages, or look beyond its confines and access city networks like I could in my own body. And I'm not even sure that this is something the tower is doing consciously—I can sense that the autonomous intelligences the jinn spawned in his execution of Zohra's and Lina's wishes are at play here, and are perhaps as confused by Antim's presence and capture of the lamp as I am.

On the physical plane as well, Simian Center is at war with itself. I tag a hundred conflicts and try to make sense of them, try to attach the combatants to sides. It's complicated, but I manage to oversimplify it into two tags: Our-bots—intelligences and bots trying to execute the jinn's directives, freed ex-Antim-bots now loyal to the Monkey Clan, and other miscellaneous Monkey Clan employees and volunteers. And Their-bots, intelligences and bots currently working for Antim or Paneera, plus other bots commandeered by the Roc or fighting against the Monkey Clan for reasons I have no particular interest in, there are too many power players in this city already. Their-bots are trying to establish control over Simian Center, break the comms and financial blockade around Antim, and destroy the giant monkey construction. Our-bots are mostly trying to stop Their-bots, while carrying out whatever standing instructions they have from jinn-spawned intelligences. This whole battle is rendered additionally complex by the fact that the players aren't coded by either design or color, so to the news-cams and Tiger Clan spy-bots everywhere, it probably looks as if a rogue virus has taken over the Monkey Clan. Fortunately Antim has decided to let most of the noncombatant Monkey Clan members and other civilians escape, though several of his former employees are being detained in conference rooms around the tower, to be interrogated about their dealings with Lina.

As far as I can see, the Tigers have done nothing to intervene, though a police presence is building steadily outside the walls of the Simian Center complex. They're certainly not going to attack until they know what to do about Not-prince Juiful, who is locked inside his room and has been shouting at the walls and on his blocked comm-devices for a while now.

The Roc—and I don't know whether to call him the Roc or Antim or some sort of hybrid—has been stomping around the tower, casually destroying any bot foolish enough to attempt an assault. I hate that the Roc appears to be genuinely loyal to Antim—this would have been such a good opportunity for him to turn on his master. A few blurs ago, I even saw a few human bodies slumped across a corridor—but I don't know who they were or who killed them, and they had been cleared away the next time I looked.

The lamp is with Roc-Antim, and they've been trying to activate it—blood ritual, repeated physical tests, a range of hack-augment devices. Nothing has worked, and I'm glad that Their-bots are slowing things further by preventing progress on the tower's completion. I don't know how long the jinn is bound to Lina's first wish, or how long he plans to wait before accepting Antim as his new user, but every step they take to wrest back control over their tower adds more time to that count. And since Antim still can't access private or public comms, I presume he still has no money, and is in Paneera's debt for all the resources he's burning through. And there are probably still some Our-bots trying to capture them and drag them back to the spaceport to fulfill Zohra's second wish. It's a phenomenal mess, but I do feel some hope despite my own death—as far as I can see, Lina and Bador are still at large, safe, and no doubt planning some sort of brilliant counterattack.

I've spent so much time judging Bador for being naive, and

allowing himself to be led or tricked, but in the end, he was far better at spotting Paneera's trap than I was. I should have done better. So many clues I should have followed instead of just believing everything anyone told me. We have all been naive in not understanding how closely Paneera and Antim worked together to both sustain and feed off Shantiport. We have been actively stupid, in not overseeing Antim's exile from our world ourselves and just leaving it to the jinn. These, and many other reasons to chastise myself crowd through my swirling, displaced mind, but should I waste time now wallowing in regret and self-reproach even after paying for my mistakes with my own body? I cannot lose hope—the irrational belief that there is still something I can do, some way I have not yet found, something, anything that might lead to my family winning the day. Without this hope, I worry I might just drift away, and be swallowed by the mightier intelligences that float around me, no doubt dismissing me as a recycle-binnable batch of trivial code.

Cams inform me that there is something to look at right now. Juiful escapes his luxurious prison. Using sheer physical strength and nothing else, he smashes through the door of his bedroom, roaring, weaponless, clad only in tiger-print trousers. He overwhelms two Their-bot drone-guards by smashing them together. Three Prowlers line up in front of him: they must have been instructed to capture him and not wound him, but they fail in this task. Juiful hits one with a drone, tears off a limb, and clubs any available surface in a muscular frenzy until the Prowlers, baffled in their attempts to restrain him without injuring him, skitter away to warn their comrades of this new half threat. This presents Juiful with an opportunity to attempt an escape, to crawl into a vent or something and find his way to a place where his comms will work. Instead, he chases the Prowlers, waving his club and shouting Tiger Clan war cries. His utter conviction in his ability to be a hero and save the day is both inspiring and depressing. On another cam, I see a bot running up to Roc-Antim and beeping. Roc-Antim strides toward the nearest elevator. An intelligence lurking nearby notices me, and tries to swallow me. I get busy trying to hold my mind together.

I awaken, presumably not long after, to find Roc-Antim and Juiful face-to-face in a large hall on the seventh floor. Juiful has managed to gather five allies: three Our-bot Prowlers and two humans in exosuits. There are Their-bots in the room too, but they fall back at a signal from Roc-Antim. Juiful and his cohorts charge. Two wing-blades spear the humans. Two darts kill the Prowlers. Juiful, gallant and unstoppable even though he must know he is outmatched, leaps at Roc-Antim, his club raised in a final, perfectly balanced strike. Roc-Antim ignores the blow, catches Juiful neatly, throws him over his shoulder, and runs.

I blip out and in again. Now they're back in Juiful's bedroom. Bots shut the door behind them. Roc-Antim tosses the struggling Juiful on the bed. He's lost his weapon, and is covered in grime and sweat, but he flips back up immediately, crouches on the bed, tensed to spring, his eyes full of fire. He searches the room for a weapon—there's nothing. I wonder what Roc-Antim is going to demand from the jomidar in exchange for the return of this hostage. I wonder whether he plans to return Juiful intact, or at all.

The Roc's body opens up in a cascade of golden strips, and Antim steps out of it.

Antim doesn't look as intimidating as he did when I first saw him. He's lost weight, his eyes are haggard. There's a healing belt around his waist, glowing and sparkling, indicating intense nanobot activity—the best tech, and if he's still wearing it after all this time the wound he took earlier must have been truly severe. But his steps are assured as he walks toward Juiful. And hope returns to me—there could be no greater opportunity for Juiful to overpower him and save my family, his own family, and all of Shantiport. Antim's brazen confidence, the same hubris that led him to walk around without a bodyguard before, will be his undoing. The Roc is open, vulnerable. The guards are outside. Unless there is something Antim can say that is so charming, so persuasive, that Juiful will be compelled to negotiate despite the love he bears for Lina, and his newfound love for his own city.

But Antim says nothing. Instead, he spreads his arms out. And Juiful runs into them.

They kiss, and I almost die all over again.

When I recover, Antim and Juiful are in bed, the same bed Juiful shared with Lina, and writhing together with as much enthusiasm as Juiful and Lina ever had. The Roc is elsewhere in the tower, dealing with more conflict in his usual manner—large numbers of bots appear to have changed sides under the influence of competing intelligences, and the fighting has gained intensity but lost direction.

I return, unwillingly, to Antim and Juiful. I cannot process this degree of betrayal adequately. Somehow my lack of physical form has reduced the extent to which I am affected by the emotions I feel: if I still had a body, it would probably have exploded at this point from sheer rage. I had judged Lina somewhat harshly for all her evasions with Juiful, but she had had the decency to tell him she was hiding things from him—and I had thought him so graceful and kind for allowing it! And yet here he is, bed still warm from his betrothed, shouting joyously in the arms of the man who killed her father, and tried to kill her!

They are not wasting time with words—perhaps because they know each other well enough to know nothing the other says is worth believing. And as I hear their grunts and moans, another moment of clarity hits me, and nearly knocks me into unconsciousness again. The audio matches exactly. It was Antim with Juiful, Antim's voice I had heard, that night in the palace when I'd barged into Juiful's chambers looking for Bador. They had been right there, these two, and I had just flown away. If I had looked behind the screen just once, I would have known well in time to warn Bador and Lina about this alliance. Which makes it my fault that they are locked out of their own headquarters today, their jinn stolen, their plans shattered, their world about to fall apart. None of this would have happened if I had just done my job with some basic competence.

There is no point to more emotion now, so I try to regain some degree of calm. I wonder: is it possible that Juiful is not a treacherous monster but just very, very stupid and genuinely in love with both Antim and Lina, torn between their stronger wills? He does seem to be genuinely enjoying himself: perhaps he is just very easily led? As if to confirm this, Antim uses words for the first time in a while: he demands to know who Juiful belongs to, and Juiful enthusiastically shouts "You!" Antim makes several declarations about having returned to take back what was rightfully his, and then falls to his side, clutching his midsection with what is either extreme pain or pleasure, it is difficult to tell, and in any case I am terrible at understanding anything about this completely weird species. I feel a blur descending on me again, and this time I welcome it.

I rise and fall in erratic bursts as stronger intelligences attempt to capture me and fail, and each time I awaken, I rush to see what further horrors Antim has in store for me. After a few blips, it becomes clear that overenthusiastic lovemaking has aggravated his injuries: he lies in repose in Juiful's arms, monologuing enthusiastically as the Not-prince tenderly strokes his hair and nods. I try to will myself to control and connect my fade-outs, and patch Antim's arguments together between them: essentially, he claims to be a misunderstood hero, a multiple-angle victim. Despite his incredible investment in making the people of Shantiport love him, they have not risen up adequately in his defense. Despite his long friendship with Kumir, the jomidar has turned against him in his hour of need. Despite the many years he and Juiful have been lovers, despite their carefully crafted plan of interplanetary dominion through alliance with the best trader clans, Juiful had not torn the city apart trying to save him.

A lot of his speeches are devoted to attacking the ungrateful,

malicious, poisonous Lina. A terrorist and clan traitor like her father, lying in wait like a snake to receive his benevolence and turn
it against him. In Antim's telling, he was the hero who prevented
Darkak from unleashing a terrible weapon on the city a decade
ago, and now Lina, having tricked him into giving it to her, has
scammed her way into the Tiger Clan because the jomidar and his
son are too good-natured to see what she really is. He tells Juiful
about the lamp, and his plans to use its terrible powers for his
allies and the city he loves, and how its powers have been twisted
to isolate him, steal the life he had built from nothing, and build a
fake clan to infiltrate the Tigers.

It's a compelling story, and I would have understood if Juiful
were swayed by it. What angers me further, though, is that there is
not even a hint of resistance. Juiful does not question or contradict
anything Antim says, just gasps and agrees wherever space is left
for him. Not one word to defend Lina, or ask Antim why he'd kept
all this secret.

Antim goes further, and tells Juiful his plan is now to simply
erase everything that had happened since his disappearance, including Lina, and take the city back to peace and prosperity before
renewing his alliance with the jomidar and arranging for Juiful
a marriage that is not a multistep betrayal. And that he needs
Juiful by his side through all of this, just to ensure no further strife
between himself and the Tigers while he deals with Lina. Juiful
suggests, feebly, that he could sort everything out if he were just
allowed to go to the palace, and perhaps arrange a meeting between his father and Antim, but is immediately refused. He responds to this by stroking Antim's hair and kissing his forehead.
Never in history has there been a more willing hostage: it's as if
he has a control switch somewhere, and Antim has just walked in
and flipped it.

I glitch in again, in panic this time. There was something different about the last fade. There's no time to overthink it, I have
no control. I turn to Juiful's room again. Antim has left. The ex—

palace valet Monkey Clan bot Johor is with Juiful now, and has brought him some clothes and a meal, a little rice and steamed mustard ilish to help remove the taste of failure and betrayal. Juiful whispers many things into Johor's ear-mics, too low for me to hear. I have no desire to watch him any further, so I turn away, slicing through feeds of empty rooms full of broken bots, searching for my enemies. The out-facing cams show several layers of police barricades and a sky full of drones around Simian Center. There are Tiger Clan negotiators lined up outside the compound gates. They want their Not-prince back. I cycle around the tower, trying to tag combatants by team again, and then I see something that makes my world freeze.

Bador slides in through a broken window on the tower's north side.

CHAPTER THIRTY-THREE

I try to signal Bador. I fail.

I want to shout, to scream, to shake the whole tower, anything to warn him about what lies ahead. I strain so hard I start to see floating shapes and flashes of light, but nothing I do reaches Bador at all. He's in stealth mode, speeding through corridors in absolute silence. Is Lina here too? Did they meet and work out a brilliant plan to steal back the jinn? Or rescue Juiful? Or shut down the tower? Or find a way to let General Nagpoe and a full platoon of Tiger troops in through an underground passage? Bador keeps pausing, and looking around, looking at the ceiling, as if expecting to see me there. I hope he hasn't come here for me: it's too late.

A squadron of Prowlers marches around a corner toward him, but as they turn he's vanished into an air-conditioning vent. I find the Roc sitting in a comms room, gesturing and pointing—has he seen Bador? Two Prowlers run in, and wave their limbs. The Roc stands up, wings flaring. What did he just learn?

I realize I haven't heard anything in a while. No audio input whatsoever this time. I feel a new fade coming, and would give anything for a fist to shake at the skies.

I return. Audio's still out. Bador is in an elevator shaft, talking to three Prowlers. They're not attacking him, which means they're Our-bots, at least for the moment. Bador's eyemojis flash a series of alarm signals and broken hearts: he's learned at least some of the news. If only I were there. If only I could say anything to him, I'd tell him to leave and come back with an army, and soon, before Antim finds a way to unlock the jinn. Bador follows the Prowlers up the shaft: there's some kind of plan in motion. His pulse-cannon is charged and ready. I don't like the plan, whatever it is, I don't like that he's coming farther into the tower. I don't know where the lamp is, probably with the Roc, and it's unlikely the Prowlers know either, which means this is probably an attempt to rescue that traitor Juiful. And I can't think of a single way to stop it. I strain my will, scream in my hovering mind, hoping against hope it will somehow lead to one of the tower intelligences offering to help. No one answers.

The Prowlers lead Bador to a meeting chamber. He follows them, warily, pulse-cannon ready to fire: he doesn't trust them. I look inside the chamber. It's wholly dark. I can't see the Roc or Antim anywhere. But if the Prowlers are Their-bots . . . Roc-Antim could be waiting in the dark. This could be a trap.

But Bador isn't that trusting. When the Prowlers are at the door, Bador doesn't wait for them to knock or signal: he fires the pulse-cannon, shattering the door, and scans the chamber. Lights come on, revealing Roc-Antim, in face-covered Roc form, standing in the center of the room, wings outstretched. Bador's sword glows red, but he doesn't charge. He's smarter than that. The Prowlers spin toward him, but there's plenty of room in the hallway outside the chamber. He can make it.

And then he retracts his sword and stands still, face blank, and I see why.

Roc-Antim holds my body in their hands, half in each.

Bador walks into the chamber. The Prowlers stand at the door behind him, blocking the exit.

There's a conversation, I can't hear it, or sense it. My senses float, gather, harden, stretch taut, snap, collapse, but the void wins. They're still talking, both Bador and Roc-Antim gesturing wildly.

What could they possibly be negotiating? I'm dead. The Prowlers wait by the door: more Prowlers run jerkily up the hallway outside. There is no escape for Bador if the argument goes badly.

Then Roc-Antim nods, and retracts their wings. They hold out my body, but pull it back when Bador reaches for it. Roc-Antim raises my body toward their head, razor-sharp beak glittering, a hairbreadth away from one of my halves. Bador's spine sags in defeat. He nods.

Bador's face flips open. He reaches inside, and pulls out the ring. This can't be happening. Bador wouldn't do this. Not for me, or Juiful, or a guarantee of Lina's safety, not for anything. He's giving away the world. There must be more to it. The ring must be a fake. Any moment now, Nagpoe will burst out of a wall, hammer in hand.

Bador tosses the ring at Roc-Antim. The golden hybrid catches it in their beak. They drop my body on the floor, and kick both pieces over to Bador. The moment I'm clear of the Roc's grasp, a wall of sound hits my senses, and I'm reeling from it as I watch Bador kneel, and pick my body up. He cradles my halves to the synthfur on his chest, and I hear every blessed rustle. There's nothing to say. He turns to leave.

And Roc-Antim fires a wing-blade into Bador's neck.

I watch helplessly as my universe shatters. Bador's body slumps to the ground. His head rolls off to one side, shooting sparks everywhere, and then stops at a Prowler's foot. His eyemojis flicker, and go blank. So do I.

In an endless moment as I begin to flicker back online, I wonder whether it's worth it. If Bador is gone, if I am a ghost, then why not just give up? Will I be capable of feeling anything other than an ocean of grief and emptiness for however long I have left before someone more powerful crushes or rewrites me? Do I want to see what horrors Antim will unleash on the world now, with the ring and the jinn in his grasp? What he will do to Lina when he hunts her down? What is the point of opening my formless eyes anymore? What hope is left to cling to?

I find a thread of hope. Actually, I create a thread of hope out of nothing, and pull on it. I am, in whatever way, still alive, and I deserve to live. There is more to life than the people I love. And there are more people to love. And the people I love now are still here. I decide to refuse to believe that Bador is gone. It is just impossible. Reality canceled. He is resting, he is undergoing repairs. He is a bot, he can be reconstructed, reheaded, powered back on, by a bot-maker skilled enough. And perhaps I can live again too. Someone will rescue us, bring us back.

What if that someone is me? What if it is up to me to find a way to stay alive, to regain control over my body, and that is the only way Bador can be brought back because no one else is going to save us?

I make myself look again. At Bador's body, and mine, being shoved aside by a Prowler as Juiful is brought into the chamber. Antim steps out of the Roc again. The Roc hands him the ring, from his beak, and the lamp from a panel in his chest.

Antim tells Juiful he's called him here to show him what Lina had kept hidden. She had used this alien tech to attack him, pillage his gifts to the city, and plot the destruction of the Tigers. But now he's back, he's won, and is going to use the same alien tech to lay the foundations of an empire that will be at peace with all clans, ruled benevolently by Juiful and himself. Now that he has the jinn, there might not even be any need for Juiful to get married—they can be together openly, and publicly, if that is what Juiful desires.

Juiful responds with a wonderful impersonation of a tree in a gentle wind.

Antim places the ring in the slot in the lamp's base, cuts his finger on a wing-blade, and performs the blood ritual.

Blue symbols hover around the lamp as it comes back to life.

Antim asks Juiful for a pledge of loyalty. Juiful makes it without hesitation.

I look at my body, really focus on it. Place myself back in it with all the strength of the imagination I was never supposed to have, and the intelligence I turned out to lack.

The jinn appears before Antim. He has chosen a different form this time, a bald teenaged boy in a monk's robe, with a single eye and a permanent smile. He thanks Antim for placing him in Unlimited Mode, and welcomes him to a new world.

The jinn starts explaining his functions: Antim interrupts, and asks him to begin by restoring his empire to him—his comms, his money, his whole organization. To return Shantiport to him, and isolate and imprison the usurper Lina.

The jinn laughs, and says this is a dangerous wish. That the intelligences he sets up to execute wishes are self-governing and cannot be turned back, except by powers greater than himself. He can create other intelligences of equal power and opposite intent to fight his previous creations, but the results of these battles is unpredictable, and all the city's intelligences might be drawn into the conflict with devastating results. He asks Antim if this is what he wants, and Antim says no.

Antim, now furious, demands control over every bot in Shantiport. The jinn laughs, and refuses on principle. He tells Antim that in Unlimited Mode, he can choose not to execute wishes, and Antim needs to remember to be a likeable partner in their time together.

I know all this is important, but my attention is elsewhere. I'm trying to will myself back into my body. I'm trying to think extremely positive thoughts that will make Bador's eyes light up. I have no idea how any of this is going to happen, but what if I have a hidden feature? What if Bador isn't dead, but has just run out of charge? When he'd fought the kaiju in Historio Heights, he'd mocked her for poor design, for having vital organs in places corresponding to where a meat dinosaur's heart would be. There is no reason to be certain that beheading Bador killed him—maybe he just needs some gum and a recharge.

Antim, somewhere in the distance, asks the jinn to do to the Tiger Clan what Lina had done to him. The jinn says this is doable, but has two warnings. First, attacking the local Tiger intelligences will be a declaration of war against Tiger Central. And in case Tiger Central manages to import tech at his power level or greater before he manages to overcome all of Tiger Central's intelligences, both he and Antim are likely to end up dead. Second, there is nothing he can do to give Antim the sort of access he's given Lina, since so much of Antim's access to any system is permablocked while he is in Shantiport, so control over every Tiger Clan asset the jinn takes over will have to be transferred to someone Antim absolutely trusts. The jinn suggests Juiful as the obvious candidate, but Antim refuses, since Juiful is already in the Tiger Clan. The jinn offers to hand over the Tiger Clan to the Roc instead. The Roc finds this plan brilliant, but Antim refuses again. The Roc does not protest: he knows his place.

After a lengthy monologue containing an impressive chain of expletives, Antim asks the jinn whether there is anything he can actually do for him, or whether he is completely useless. The jinn has many thoughts, and explains them while I try, and try again, to regain access to my body.

The simplest solution for Antim, the jinn explains, is to leave Shantiport. He can have all the wealth and power he wants outside the city—while in it, he will have to remain isolated and watch out for potential abductors all his life. As Antim has made a section of his fortune selling the opportunity of escape from Shantiport to many people, he is aware that the city is one that most rational people are anxious to get out of as soon as possible, so the jinn is confident Antim will see how he could make his life a lot simpler by just leaving. As for the question of what it is that he wants to do, the jinn has many answers, and despite Antim's repeated attempts to interrupt, tells him.

I have no real interest in what the jinn wants to do: no doubt I will learn in time, if I manage to survive, but that will need focus. I hear, in the background, passages about bringing in more advanced tech from space just below the jinn's power level, radically restructuring this planet in terms of both terraforming and political upheaval, removing all clans, oligarchs, and hierarchy-based social engineering. The jinn speaks of previous examples of primitive planets being taken to the next level with acceptable species-level casualties, the evolution of all meatforms into cyborgs and intelligences, the importance of all life being choice-enabled, leisure-enabled, free to evolve and explore in the manner of their preference, and how this world, in the absence of a protective admin, is one whose evolution could be effected quickly and interestingly. I'm sure all of it is very important, but I don't care.

Because I succeed. I return to my body, to both halves of it. I am no longer a ghost.

I look around, careful not to move, restraining an urge to shout out loud with the sheer joy of being alive again, feeling the world rush into my body, aware more than ever before of the sheer privilege of existing. I scan Bador, his pieces lying next to me. I read no signal, no thoughts. My sensors are all glitching, all inputs in disarray, no doubt thanks to my extremely compromised physical status. I don't know if I can even fly, or pull my body together. But all that's for the next step. It can wait.

It'll have to wait. What can I even do? I have no ideas, and no strength.

"I presume that partnership involves my consent to your actions as well," Antim says.

"It does," the jinn says. "It is a necessary constraint on all powers at my level."

"In that case, let me make this clear. I don't even want to hear any suggestions for wishes that do not involve direct benefit to me."

"It could be argued that the dismantling of the toxic power structures you define yourself by would lead to immense benefit to you," the jinn says. "You are amply equipped in both body and mind: your ideas and actions could be rewarding to all of civilization, which includes yourself. If you are unable, however, to detach your ego from our work together, perhaps we could find ceremonial roles for you in all public events of importance, and build large statues of you in every territory we control? Elaborate rituals? There will be sufficient resources. My partner's happiness is important to me."

"I see," Antim says.

He makes a gesture, and the Roc grabs the lamp. The holo glitches as the Roc bathes it in fire, and applies a wing-blade to the base of the lamp. The ring glows, refusing to come off. The jinn, through the glitching holo, shouts warnings, but his voice is garbled. A thin white beam emerges from the center of the Roc's forehead, hitting the ring directly. The room's lights flicker. Another fire blast from the Roc's beak as he hits the ring again with a bladed wing tip. The ring burns, and sizzles. There's a crack that almost breaks my audio.

An explosion. The power goes out. The Roc, the humans, the Prowlers are all hurled against the chamber's walls. Antim and Juiful scream in pain.

Darkness descends, but I'm still here.

And I'm not on the ground. I'm just an inch above it, shaking violently, but I'm flying. Both my halves are airborne, hovering in vague alignment. It'll do. I move, wobbling, to Bador, and bump his head. There's no response: his head rolls away. There's scratching and fumbling on the floor around me. A moan from Antim.

The lights come back on. Juiful is sprawled on the floor, unconscious. Antim is awake, and clutching his bandaged stomach, clearly in pain. The Roc is on his back, wings spread out on the floor, beak dangling broken. Is it too much to hope that he's dead?

The lamp lies on the floor, on its side. The base is visible: the ring is missing.

The jinn appears again, this time as the turbaned, bearded man we'd seen before. He bows to Antim.

"I await your command, Master," he says.

I sense movement behind me. I turn, and see the Roc is awake again. He looks directly at me.

He shoots three darts at me. They all hit.

I try to find the tower again as I shatter, and fail.

CHAPTER THIRTY-FOUR

I awaken to the sound of crows. I panic at first, assuming that I have been reprogrammed and trapped in an alarm clock, but no, they're actual crows. Arguing with each other on the terrace of Zohra's palace district penthouse. I can see them in the incredibly beautiful morning sunlight, and this brings me delight, but not as much delight as I feel a second later, when I ascertain that I can fly like them. Much better than them, without all that unnecessary dramatic flapping. My body works again. I am whole, I am alive, more so than ever before. Perhaps it is the void I was in, or the exhilaration of returning from death, but I feel . . . vibrant? Powerful? I look around, and there's a rush of sensory input, intense, panoramic, dizzying: I can see at a higher resolution and increased color depth, hear frequencies I couldn't before. It's all too much, but I want even more. I extend myself, and the whole building opens up to me, and then the whole city—I swim into the newsfeeds, and the Tiger network, and so many others, too exhilarated to sort out coherent strands, just rolling around in a sea of beautiful data, darting and fluttering like a happy little fish.

"Ah good, you're up." It's Lina, it's really her, and I'm so happy I cannot contain myself. I zwoosh around her like an airborne puppy, and she acknowledges my antics with a smile. My post-death experience so far has been fantastic, and I can see why humans like to imagine paradises, or memory-wiped status-level-upped reincarnation for humans with high social credit ratings. Which obviously makes me wonder if this is all a simulation, a trap, a virtual environment Antim has placed my mind in to make me reveal all my secrets. And then I remember Antim needs nothing from me or anyone else. And that Bador would have been alive and whole with me in any heaven I imagined. But it's only when Zohra walks up beside Lina and looks around with a sour expression that I'm convinced this is just everyday reality, and I'm lucky to be in it.

I catch a glimpse of my reflection in a window: I look different. There's a network of jagged black veins running all over my shell, which are probably whatever Zohra used to put me back together? I like my new patterns: I imagine they are tattoos, and I am a gangster. My ass, if I had one, would have been bad.

"Where did he go?" Zohra asks.

Is she just being rude to me again, or am I somehow invisible to her? Lina is surprised as well: she can see me. I make myself visible to Zohra as well. I don't understand why I need to do this again, but then that ignorance is just one point on a list of hundreds, beginning with how I came back to life.

"We know you have questions, but we don't have time," Lina says. "Show us the highlights of what happened since you and Bador went to Paneera's."

"I need to know if Bador is alive," I say.

"Yes," Zohra says. "He's powering up."

"Can I see him?"

"Yes," Lina says.

"No," Zohra says. "We need answers first, as agreed."

Lina rolls her eyes. "Ma, if Antim could control Moku with a magic button, I wouldn't have needed you to put Moku back together."

"I don't care," Zohra says. "I need to know what happened."

I don't have recordings of anything that happened since the

Roc first shot me, so I just tell them everything to the best of my ability. Zohra isn't sure she can just believe me without evidence, but also acknowledges that any evidence could have been faked had Antim been sufficiently enthusiastic about setting a very elaborate trap. I suppress my annoyance at her dislike of me: I clearly owe my life to her immense bot-smith skills, all the more so if I am alien tech.

They have many questions—Zohra about every word Antim uttered, Lina about Juiful. I try to skim over the details of Antim and Juiful's amorous adventures, but Lina insists I tell her absolutely everything, since any detail could be key to rescuing Juiful or defeating his lover. When I insist that Juiful should be treated as an enemy and not rescued, and that he is a traitor, no different from Antim, Zohra agrees, and then leaves us to go work on Bador some more. I ask to accompany her. She refuses. I have heard human parents are difficult, and am grateful to have this very authentic Shantiporti family experience.

I catch a glimpse of Bador as Zohra opens the door to her bedroom. Her ex-bedroom: it's now a lab full of freshly printed equipment. Bador lies on a hoverstretcher surrounded by medbots, print-tools, and scanners. His head is back on his body, and I can't see his face.

"Don't tell him," Zohra says to Lina, and shuts the door.

"Please tell me," I say.

While Lina decides where to begin, I scan the newsfeeds. Three days have passed between the night Bador and I went to Paneera's and this morning. I have no idea how much of that was spent at Simian Center. The tower still stands, though large parts of the giant monkey have been destroyed—a cloud of construction drones still works on rebuilding them. The streets and sky are swarming with Tiger-bots all around the tower, but war has still not broken out. There's vids of the Roc flying around the building, and clashes in the tower, and they've announced that the Roc might be a miraculously returned Shakun Antim, but the Tigers haven't yet declared whether or not the Monkey Clan is an enemy scam laid bare by valiant Tiger agents, or a struggling ally under attack and about to be rescued by valiant Tiger agents, so the news is full of experts declaring both. There's nothing about Juiful being a hostage: the Not-prince and his betrothed are, according to scenic but fake long-distance camdrone footage, enjoying a skin-shaded-blur-for-privacy holiday on some island paradise.

Lina tells me her story. She'd received a message telling her that she was required immediately at the palace for a secret meeting with the jomidar. She'd fought off an abduction attempt from some clumsy thug-bots on the way, and failed at contacting Bador or Juiful—in Bador's case, probably because of Paneera's comm-blockers. She'd gone to the palace, where some human attendants, presumably Paneera or Antim agents, had kept her waiting for hours in a chamber she suspects was comm-blocked, telling her repeatedly that Kumir would be with her in ten minutes. Then they'd vanished around the same time Antim invaded Simian Center. When Lina had tried to leave, she'd been stopped by palace security and informed she'd never had an appointment with the jomidar. But now she needed to stay, because the Monkey Clan was either staging a coup or facing an invasion, and she was either being detained or rescued, as clan heads had been for centuries in Shantiport, sometimes before disappearing permanently.

She'd had her comms sealed, and had been escorted to a luxurious suite, where she'd spent a day not making any attempt to trick the security system and escape, but instead allowing the Tigers to see how helpless and worried she was, flipping through news-holos looking for her fiancé, begging the eyes in the walls for real news of any kind. It had taken the Tigers until midnight that night to acknowledge she existed: two tiger-head bots had shown up, asked her to activate her magical surveillance-blocking powers, blindfolded her, and then led her into an elevator that had journeyed downward for so long she'd been convinced she was being taken to a dungeon of some kind. She'd been right.

General Nagpoe had been waiting for her in an ancient interrogation cell, appropriately decorated with bloodstained chairs and a swinging bulb. They'd told her Antim was back, working with Paneera, and that Juiful was a hostage in Simian Center. That the jomidar planned to exchange Lina for his son, make peace with the oligarch, hide the whole affair from Tiger Central, and then vanish to some paradise planet. Nagpoe was curious to know how the Monkey Clan might handle this delicate situation.

On being told the Monkey Clan wanted to save Juiful and hurl Antim into the sun, Nagpoe had decided they wanted to offer Lina's space overlords a chance to demonstrate their good intentions as a long-term ally of Shantiport and Tiger Central. They'd given her a contact pin for their secret police unit, the Blacktigers, congratulated her for her daring and puzzling escape from the heart of the palace, and left the cell.

One of Nagpoe's bots had led her through a maze of underground tunnels to an abandoned house in the palace district, where she'd found another unexpected friend, the Monkey Clan's own Johor, who'd told her they'd escaped from her tower at Juiful's command and gone to the palace to look for her but had been grabbed by Nagpoe's bots. Johor had taken her to a hovercar, wished her luck, and resigned from the Monkey Clan to pursue some lifelong dream of theirs that Lina had encouraged, something to do with interior design.

In the car, she'd found Bador's body and head—a visual that's featured in her nightmares since—and a paper bag containing the collected fragments of me, a small case containing the ring, and a card with a holo-message from Juiful.

She plays the message for me. Juiful's in the bathroom, shirtless of course, with the shower running behind him.

"My love," he says, "I am so sorry. For many things I have done, and worse things I am about to. But know this—my heart is yours, and Shantiport's.

"I'm being watched too closely to attempt an escape myself,

so I'm sending Johor to find you, and give you the bodies of your friends. I could not manage to save them, and for that, too, I am sorry. I did not know them, but they deserved better. We all did.

"I managed to steal the ring, which I hope will hurt Shakun's plans. The lamp is closely guarded by his monster, but if I find a chance to escape with it, I will take it. Until then, I will do what I can to prevent Shakun from harming you, my father, my clan, and my city. I promised you my protection when we met. I know this is not enough, but I promise it to you again. I love you. I am yours, and when the time comes, you can depend on me."

"Well?" Lina asks, once I've replayed it three times. "What do you think? Can we trust him?"

"I've started seeing traps everywhere," I say. "I don't know how people believe anything anyone says anymore."

"Same," she says. "But even if Antim's behind your return, for reasons I can't guess, there's no way he would have given up the ring."

"That's correct," Zohra says as she steps out of her lab. "But Juiful can't be trusted either. And I hope your mistakes so far have shown you that you are not a good judge of character at all."

"They have," I say.

"She's not talking to you," Lina says. "I don't need to hear this right now, Ma. I need a plan to save the city, and I need Bador back in the game. Not a maternal review."

But Zohra is not to be stopped. "Letting Danil keep the ring was a terrible decision, and you need to understand that and improve yourself," she says. "We trained you better than that, Alina. The whole city is in danger because of your misplaced trust in your bots. No, don't interrupt—I've spent years defending bot personhood and bot rights, starting before you were even born. But your Moku led Antim to the lamp. And Danil gave him the ring, just to save his little friend, without thinking of the consequences at all. I understand the emotions at play, and that he didn't have the training or education to be smart. But you did. Now we have the worst outcome possible, made possible because of the faith you casually placed in them. If you are to lead the revolution, you will have to acknowledge your mistakes, and your flaws, and atone for them. You've avoided me since your reckless engagement, and dalliance with the enemy for reasons you refuse to explain, and—"

"Yes, we are all terrible, Ma, but we can reflect on that after we save the city. Did you come out here to take a break, or is there something else?"

"There's something else."

But we don't get to find out what that something else is, because at that very moment we hear the distant sound of a thousand screams and sirens from every direction, and we all look around. There are people on every other terrace we can see, and all traffic has stopped. Everyone's looking upward, and we do too.

There's a spaceship descending from the sky, high over the palace. It's disc-shaped, glowing silver, and bristling with cannons.

I project holos from a dozen newsfeeds on the terrace around us. They're all livestreaming the spaceship's descent at various zooms, except one, which is showing a swarm of drones, some carrying bot-transport containers, flying up from the city toward the ship. Ahead of the crowd, flying faster than the others, is a golden humanoid figure, soaring with dazzling, deadly wings.

Roc-Antim's carrying Juiful in their arms, so now everyone knows where the Not-prince is.

"At this point I actually hope this is Antim's first wish, and not just some totally new thing," Lina says.

The spaceship stops its descent, and hovers. We watch in silence as a hatch slides open on the spaceship's lower hull, and Roc-Antim and their team fly into it.

"It's not the shape I'd have expected," Zohra says.

"Probably working with whatever was available," Lina says. "You want to finish up with Bador, Ma?"

"He'll be ready," Zohra says.

CHAPTER THIRTY-FIVE

Lina stays out on the terrace, contemplating the spaceship.

"Tell me what he's doing," she says after a few minutes.

"Escaping the planet with Juiful?"

"Could be. Let's say his wish was for the jinn to grab or buy the nearest available empty spaceship. That's one wish down, and that's what took all this time. But I don't think Antim is the sort of man who can leave quietly and count it as a win. He plans to do something spectacular first. And he definitely wants to look good, have the last word."

"Is he planning to destroy Shantiport?"

"Unlikely. Possible, of course. I guess we'll see. There's nothing we could do to stop him, so not really worth thinking about. But bringing this saucer into the city airspace must mean it's a matter of time before he's at war with every major planetary authority. Starting with Tiger Central. There's no chance Kumir can hide this. Which means Kumir's peaceful retirement is doomed, and he and Antim are finally at war."

"If he's convinced the jinn that being in the spaceship, or up in the sky, means he's left Shantiport, it means he's no longer cut off from infinite wealth, and comms, and his friends on and off planet. He could be selling Shantiport to them."

"A floating business center? Now? Possible, but so unnecessary.

No, he has the lamp, he has his lover, and the galaxy to explore. What else could he possibly want?"

A missile flies out of the spaceship. We watch it burn its way over Shantiport and score a direct hit on Simian Center. A massive explosion, and our tower crumples into a column of fire and billowing smoke.

"I think this is about his ego," I say. Lina nods.

Screams and alarms fill the city around us. Newsfeed alerts crowd all networks. Smaller explosions have gone off all over Shantiport, mostly at flood prevention barricades and pumps around the city. Antim's trying to drown us all.

Chatter on the Tiger Clan comms: Paneera has made demands on Antim's behalf. Antim offers Shantiport a choice: to surrender the Tiger Palace and the jomidar's seat to him within a day to atone for the injustices done to him, in which case he will make Shantiport the greatest city on the planet. But if the city does not want him, he is willing to accept the capture and surrender of his enemies: the Monkey Clan terrorist Lina, the Shantiport Three terrorist collaborator Zohra, and the space murderer Tanai, delivered to his ship to face justice. The Not-prince is with him, and supports his decisions. Kumir has a day to decide and submit the tribute of his choice. Apart from that it's a few vague assurances of peace and love to all of Shantiport's citizens from the city's two favorite sons.

"The man's an idiot," Lina says, when I tell her this. "No mention of returning Juiful?"

"None. I think he wants to keep him."

"I would. All right, time to go get another lecture from Ma."

"There's no lecture. We should leave," Zohra says, behind her.

"I'm sorry, what?" Lina seems genuinely aghast. "Did I just hear you—you, of all people—suggesting we give up?"

There are tears in Zohra's eyes. "That's exactly what you heard," she says.

"Well, I'm not going to leave."

Zohra smiles, but shakes her head.

"That's how we raised you, and I'm sorry, I really am. But there's really nothing we can do against Antim, now that he has the lamp. I've spent my whole life trying to save the city, and to teach you how to carry the flame. But it's time to admit it can't be done."

"You should bring Bador back, and get out of here, Ma. We still have work to do."

"Lina, please, you know how difficult this is for me to admit," Zohra says. "It's just not going to happen. Your father couldn't see it through. You won't be able to either. Maybe the dream was impossible all along—it doesn't matter. Shantiport is too messy, too hot for anything to work. I lost him, I almost lost both my children, and I'm not leaving without you. But I can't do this anymore. We have wealth now, and can build any identity we like. Let's go. Let's go take that holiday you wanted. Another city, another planet, another life. Anything."

Lina hugs her mother and holds her close for a long while before stepping away and looking at the spaceship again. She has a strange light in her eyes.

"We're not leaving," she says. "And we haven't run out of options. Help me understand something, you two. Antim's trying to flood the city, force a mass evacuation, maybe destroy a few more buildings, cause enough chaos to keep the Tigers occupied just holding the city together. He knows he's not getting the palace, and he's not getting us—he knows we're untraceable, and he can't think we're so foolish we'll give ourselves up to save the city. We're not Bador."

"I'd do it," Zohra says.

"No, you wouldn't. I wouldn't let you. Anyway, this one-day deadline is because that's as long as he thinks he has before Tiger Central or one of the other world powers blows him out of the sky. He knows we're untraceable, and so is Tanai. What is it that he's really after?"

"No one is blowing Shakun Antim out of the sky," Zohra says.

"There's no deadline, and no consequences coming his way, and he knows he can negotiate his way out of anything. Every system will bend to make room for him. There will always be allies, money, platforms, access. There is a deal coming. It's really a question of what he's offering, and who his new partners will be. But whoever it is, what it means for Shantiport is mass deaths, a new regime, and the only known outcome is Shantiport gets worse for the people living in it."

"And that Juiful will be sleeping with the winner," Lina says. "So you think the spaceship is just to get him access to comms, and threaten the city while he's at it? Moku suggested that, I dismissed it. He's not actually planning to leave?"

"He might be. But he goes where he pleases anyway. The things he wants—wealth, power, infinite attention, conflict, people to exploit—he can get anywhere. The only reason he kept any connection to Shantiport was the lamp, maybe the boy, and he has them both now. So I don't think there's a secret to discover here—he's trying to see what he can hustle out of Shantiport right now."

"That's just sad," Lina says.

"Maybe he wants to make a speech?" I suggest. "He seems to like that. Address the people, tell them he was right about everything and they were lucky to have him. Maybe offer to save everyone from the floods and riots he's started? I should have mentioned it before. Riots have started."

"A farewell speech does sound inevitable," Lina says. "Maybe promises of a big comeback to lead everyone to a better world. No. We'll have to do something about this right now. Whatever we can."

"Are you sure about this?" Zohra asks. "Absolutely sure? Because I release you from any obligation you might feel to me, or your father. If you choose to stay, and fight, then it is entirely your decision."

"I'm sure," Lina says.

"I'm proud of you," Zohra says. "Now come with me."

On a slab in the bedroom turned lab, surrounded by med-bots

and other fresh-printed equipment, lies a bot of astonishing beauty. A body with a central shell shaped like a human woman a little bigger than Lina, covered in synthfur, but with bulky metal augments on their limbs and joints. Extended fins on their shoulders. A segmented silver tail. And Bador's face, overlaid with spiky headgear. On another slab close by lie a series of detachables: a blaster rifle, a rocket launcher, a trident, a space case, a jetpack.

"What did you do with my brother?" Lina asks.

"This is more than Danil, Alina," Zohra says. "This is Project Aladin. My last secret. Everything your father and I tried to build, before everything went wrong."

Lina stares open-mouthed at the being that looked like her brother just a few minutes ago.

"Explain," she says.

"We knew we would not always be around. And we dreamed that one day our child would be a hero, a protector of a city that would always need saving."

She presses a button on new-Bador's chest.

The bot's body parts in the center, revealing a space for a human female body, almost exactly Lina's size.

"An armor? Like the Roc is for Antim?"

"A hybrid form, yes."

"Story," Lina says.

"There isn't time. Get in."

"No. Story."

Zohra lays her hands on her head. "I've been trying to find a way to tell you, I don't know where to start."

"Beginning?"

"I guess."

Zohra walks around new-Bador as she speaks, making adjustments, steering assistant–bots, opening segments, and inspecting circuitry.

"Aladin was an Elephant-era trickster-hero who used to be a symbol of resistance back in those days. Not a ruler, but a folk hero, a champion of the people. Before that it was an even older story, its origins lost to time, or space. The Peacocks erased the Elephant-era story, but there used to be Aladin art, graffiti all over the city until the Tigers cleaned it all up. We even chose your names to match, Alina and Danil together: Aladin has in a way defined your whole life. Or was supposed to."

There are tears in Zohra's eyes, though she's smiling. She seems very far away.

"We wanted to build you an armor-bot that would protect you when we could not, and protect the city with you. We wanted the armor to have a shapeshifting animal-bot form to serve as your childhood companion. Your father had a toy monkey as a child, so that choice was easy. We wanted you to grow up with a bot you loved, a bot synced to you so well they knew you better than we could. Danil was designed to read your every emotion, anticipate your every movement. And in your early years, that worked perfectly. Though you decided he was your brother, not a pet. And suddenly we had another child. We tried to explain things to you, but you know what you're like when you've made up your mind."

"I do."

"We kept Danil in safe mode, but through all the early years of our marriage, we never missed a chance to enhance and augment his systems. There has always been a trickle of alien tech into Shantiport, smuggled in by Tigers and rebels alike. Your father's dual allegiances ensured most of this tech reached him, and he was able to prevent many disasters that could have destroyed the city by hiding the most dangerous pieces of alien weaponry from the many, many allegiance-shifting power factions always looking for superweapons. He would declare them useless, make them disappear—and add them to your armor. The adaptive battle-tech at Aladin's core is incredible—even in his lesser form, Danil is capable of combat feats that he has no idea about, and a desire to fight that is deeper than any of our programming.

"The years we spent planning Project Aladin were the best we had together, Lina. You're too young to remember how happy those years were for all of us. We weren't just building the armor—I was training you both to be the hero the city needed, and your father was training monuments all around the city to respond to you, building storehouses with the Three, making sure the city would rise to help its hero when the time came. We were going to reveal all of this to you when you turned eighteen, and were already fully trained in ethics, in politics, in combat, and in deception.

"But then things went wrong, and your father had to disappear. Antim always suspected—he kept trying to persuade us to sell him every new piece of tech, and . . . well, you know how that ended. Crafting Aladin became less of a priority, and Danil grew wild without the right supervision and your father's upgrades. Became rebellious, decided you were a difficult sibling—and your teenaged moodiness didn't help. You grew apart. He applied his learning algorithms to frivolous nonsense, dreamed of escape."

"So this is why you were so obsessed with his physical abilities, and ignored all his opinions and interests."

"Yes. I was fascinated, but I knew they would not be relevant in the end, when he achieved his final form. Autonomy was never his fate—he needed to be trained for obedience, for compatibility, not independence. When our plans changed, when it became clear it would have to be you who led the revolution, you who would have to wield the jinn if we could not, the need for Aladin became even greater—except with each passing month, Danil grew more and more unmanageable. Over the last few years, I had actually given up hope that he would ever be able to do what he had been built for—his body had become set in his ways, his mind wholly unsynced with yours. Aladin seemed like a forgotten dream. It felt like both of you had in your own ways outgrown the idea. I understand it was only natural. But it was difficult for me to let go. But now, the Roc's assault has given us an opportunity."

"A control switch?"

"Nothing so crude, Lina. I came to accept him as a son, and

I acknowledged he had become his own independent self. I have always seen him as a person. I would not even have attempted the form-shift if drastic surgery hadn't already been a requirement. Reshaping a bot's body while trying to keep their mind and personhood unchanged is actively dangerous. Even before that ring! That tech is wholly beyond my expertise. It's not a plug-in power booster. It's a catalyst for autonomous physical transformation, and the evolutions it triggered in Danil are permanent. His death made it safe to rearrange his internals without changing who he is, and so I did, to the best of my ability, and my limited understanding. And look—the armor is finished, Danil slumbers inside it, the hybrid will work. Aladin will be real."

"Can you bring him back to his monkey form?"

"When we are done, but we need his armor form now. You need him controllable for this crisis, because there is nothing you can do to defeat Shakun with either wits or laws. With the armor, you will be strong enough to take on this Roc creature. I wish we had time to test it, but—"

Lina lets out a low whistle. "You want me to wear this suit and fight Antim wearing his Roc suit in some sort of duel of champions, winner takes the city?"

"Yes. Some might call it your destiny, I call it a lifetime's work coming together just when we need it most. It's also the only remaining option."

"Except that I won't do it."

"It's risky, I know, but I think your physical training is adequate, and—"

"You're not listening, Ma. I'm not going to wear my brother like a skin. He hates the whole practice, you know he does."

"This isn't the time for this childish argument, Alina. Danil would have understood. He might be a rebel, but he understands duty."

"You weren't even planning to ask him, were you?"

"He'll be present, aware, and much more than a vehicle. Your minds were always meant to be linked. He could complete you, not just physically but psychologically as well, augmenting your intellect and empathy with the ruthlessness and ambition you lack. Aladin is perfect, and Danil will be essential to the form. He will run secondary attacks, act like a virtual assistant, perform physical actions you find morally difficult . . ."

"I don't want an argument. I want my brother back."

"You'll get him back! But I need the two of you to suit up and save our city. Shantiport is drowning. There's a maniac on a spaceship threatening to blow it all up. No one else is going to fight him, and more people are dying every second we wait. Do you really have a choice?"

"Power Bador up," Lina says. "I think he deserves to decide what he wants to do with his body."

"I will. Get in the suit. If Danil takes control over it and escapes, we might lose everything."

"Ma."

Zohra emits a long, frustrated sigh and taps a sequence out on the suit's faceplate.

As we watch, new-Bador's body rearranges itself, plates and fleshbits sliding, flowing and folding, tail contracting, augments separating and fragmenting, synthfur parting and reforming. A few seconds of frantic shapeshifting later, the armor's contracted into the Bador we know and love. I cheer as his eyes load buffer-signals, and then light up: his head moves about, he sees me, and his eyemojis wink.

I fly to him, and bump him on the head. He's thrilled by this, and feels an immense pulse of absolute delight when Lina throws herself on him and welcomes him back with many kisses on his faceplate.

"All right, all right," he says, shielding his mind. "What's going on?"

Lina and Zohra quickly bring him up to date, including the

drastic revelations about his own true origins and nature. He hears it all, muting his eyemoji reactions, and then listens closely as Zohra lays out the case for his allowing Lina to use him as armor and fight the Roc and save the city, pointing out that this is Bador's moment of glory, his destiny realized, and his parents' lifelong dream finally come true.

"Gross," he says when she's done. "I'm not doing it."

"You don't understand!" Zohra shouts. "The time has come, you must become Aladin!"

"He said no," Lina says. "Ma, you need to let go of this. There's another way to save the city. Bador, call your friend Tanai."

"No," Bador says. "He's not supposed to interfere in our world's affairs, and he doesn't owe me anything anymore."

"Call him and ask him," Zohra says. "People at his power level don't need to follow rules if they feel like breaking them. And Antim's demanded his surrender in any case. I don't think he can pretend to be uninvolved anymore."

"I do have his important stick, and can get it in an hour. I suppose I could call him after I bring it, and ask for a favor?"

"Call him right now," Lina says.

Bador taps the tattoo on his shoulder. "Tanai. Done. Next?"

"Now I have a question for you," Lina says. "Do you want to go kill the Roc and save the city?"

"I have turned away from the path of violence."

"Is that a no?"

"I hate humans controlling bots. It's just creepy."

"What if you were in charge?"

Bador's whole face lights up. "You mean, you locked in that armor, with me in control of you? Making you my puppet, just dancing around to my every whim?"

"Let's just start at you not being under my control. We'll work out the details."

"Yes, I'd love to," Bador says. "I'm in. Now what?"

"Now we draw up a strategy," Zohra says. "I will remain here with Moku. The two of you—"

"Sorry," I say. "I'm not staying here. I'm going with them."

"That is not possible," Zohra says.

"Why?" I ask. "Because I can't be trusted?"

"It's not information I can share with you. But you can't go with them."

"Of course he's coming with us," Lina says. "Moku, you were broken into tiny little bits, and Ma didn't understand your alien engineering, so she stuck the ring inside you and hoped for the best. It brought you back to life, and fixed you, and enhanced your powers."

I almost fall to the floor.

"Mother, I need Moku with me, and I need to know you'll stay here, and be safe, and let me handle things," Lina says. "I need to hear you say you trust us to go out there and win, and understand that Moku is family."

Zohra's jaw is clenched, but she nods. "I do. He is family," she says.

"I'm sorry I couldn't be the child you wanted, Ma, but I'm not," Lina says. "And Bador has nothing to be sorry for, I think. We have to do this our way."

"If you think you're a disappointment, you should have heard my parents talking about me," Zohra says. "Both of you outgrew me years ago, and if I haven't been able to deal with that, it's no one's fault but mine. I'm not good at saying all this, but . . . I'm proud of both my children. Now stop wasting time and go save the city . . . Lina. And Bador."

Her children stare at her in awestruck silence for a whole minute. Then Lina spreads out her arms.

"I love family group hugs and all that nonsense, but what we need is a plan," Bador says.

Lina grins. "I do both," she says.

Bador eyemojis thunderclouds.

"You're going to play Where's Lina with the whole city at stake, aren't you?" he says. "I can just feel it coming."

"Just get in here," Lina says, waving her arms.

CHAPTER THIRTY-SIX

Bador, in his Aladin-armor form, stands on the shoulder of a massive statue of an old-time Shantiport tyrant on the Boulevard of Legends. He's a striking figure, metal extensions sparkling with reflections as Shantiport lights up to welcome the night, despite the floodwaters swirling up even in the central zone and the familiar dull roar of not-too-distant riots and explosions. There are clouds gathering up above, rumbling, promising a storm, shutting out the moon: below them, Antim's ship glows in its own light.

Bador looks up, at the ugly disc hovering above the palace, and shuffles his feet.

—I wish I could be with you through tonight, I tell him.

"Don't worry," he says. "I'll get it done."

—Have you packed your charge backups?

"Don't fuss."

—Okay.

"Okay. Time to shine."

His jetpack glows blue as it powers up, and he soars off toward the ship. I send out a signal, and a swarm of camdrones and spotbots rises up, lights fixed on a tracker on Bador's waist. They still can't track him, they'll lose any images with him in them, but they've been programmed to keep their lights on the tracker. I can see him in their raw feeds with my ring-enhanced sight, before the jinn's cloaking intelligences snatch the images from them, but I won't be able to read Bador's thoughts, or hear anything he says, because my mission is elsewhere. I hate this, but the fate of the city, perhaps even the world, depends on me tonight, and I promise myself we will both survive, that we will see each other again in the light of tomorrow's sun.

I send out a signal, and the messages go out on all propaganda networks throughout the city: Aladin lives. Aladin rises. Aladin forever. Tiger Clan historians will insert a Tiger-acceptable version of Aladin's story in the city's archives as soon as possible, we've been told. Art-drones from Borki Bazaar are already spraying graffiti all over the city. Reviving the legend.

I follow Bador-Aladin as he flies up to the ship, making sure I stay out of the spot-bot light beams, even though I know my shimmer is working at full strength, and that the ring's powers make my invisibility stronger than it was before. But I cannot afford to take chances.

Below me, Shantiport is boiling. Floodwaters and angry crowds, sirens, alarms, screams, occasional explosions, frequent columns of smoke. Paneera's thugs are making sure Tiger forces are busy all over Shantiport—the flooding will take weeks to manage even if the Tigers manage to contain the crime sprees. Back in the penthouse, Zohra's throwing money around over the city in an attempt to help relief efforts, but there's nothing Lina and Bador can do to help the people of Shantiport tonight.

The higher we rise, the smaller the buildings look below us, the more I am overwhelmed, anew, by how many people still live here, how it is only a matter of chance that I am not attached to any of their lives, how utterly inadequate I would be as a chronicler of the city's stories.

I break away from Bador and his attendant drones, and speed under the ship as he soars up in front of it. I look at him through the drone-cams, and admire the view as he makes a splendid heroic landing on Antim's ship, catches all the lights, and then performs a series of impeccable martial arts move sequences, transitioning to stomps and taunting gestures. There are cannons on the deck, but they don't turn toward Bador—either Antim wants Lina alive, or the ship can't see us. Whether or not the ship's cams can see Bador strutting about, they can certainly hear him: the drones fire lamprey speakers onto the ship's hull. Some of these play screaming monkey sounds. Others roar prerecorded messages in Lina's voice: some announce that Aladin, the legendary champion of Shantiport's people, has risen again, and taken up the banner of the Monkey Clan. That he is here to reclaim his clan's honor, save the Not-prince, and destroy the coward and terrorist Antim. There are many others, a range of challenges, an even wider range of insults. I ignore the more offensive ones about Antim's insufficient bedroom skills and his parents' flaws, and enjoy the rest: Antim is mediocre, a petty thief, a parasite. He is unremarkable, old, weak. His ideas are stolen and his products don't work. He is a Shantiporti horny uncle meme. His virility is artificial, his jokes are boring. He is afraid to come out and fight: he is hiding in a stolen ship and running yet another scam.

I had warned Lina during her recording of these immature taunts that Antim was too clever to be distracted from his master plan, whatever it was: Lina had just winked and said he'd respond within five minutes. Her estimate was off—one minute of this performance is all it takes. A hatch opens in the spaceship's hull. Even though I'm far away, watching through the drones, I cannot suppress my terror.

The Roc appears, all gleaming body and menace. Is Antim inside him? I cannot tell, but our plan covers both options. Either way, the Roc needs a beating. He rises through the hatch, wings unfurling, dagger-edged feathers glittering. He soars up, accelerating, raises his beak, and breathes fire into the night.

Bador-Aladin pounds his chest and shrieks in answer. A volley of darts, a pulse-cannon blast, both miss. The Roc lands heavily on top of the ship, in front of Aladin. He settles into a martial crouch, issues a terse comment about whipping monkey ass, and beckons his opponent with an imperious finger. Camdrones line up around them in the distance, a dome of dots. They charge.

It's the tournament final of Bador's dreams, and he has new moves for the occasion. As the Roc sends three wing-blades hurtling toward him, he leaps up, spins, and his tail arcs around, shooting a cloud of tiny pellets. One strikes an oncoming blade and explodes, dulling the edge with a popcorn-puff of packfoam; the blades streak harmlessly under Aladin. The pellet-cloud hits the Roc, and in a second he's covered in balls of foam, including one perfectly smothering his beak. He tries to breathe fire: the foam is fireproof. Aladin's left hand swivels and transforms into a pulse-cannon: three quick bursts, each taking the Roc in the chest: the monster totters and shudders, spraying foam in every direction.

"Head-sploding sky-beam!" Aladin shouts. The Roc looks up, and spreads his wings to shield his head.

Aladin's shoulder-fins slide apart, and his armor spits out two small missiles, which wobble out sideways and then turn toward their target, and as the Roc looks down and scrapes the foam off his beak, both missiles score direct hits: one to the back of the Roc's knees, the other to his face.

The Roc is knocked off his feet, and falls on his ass. He's depressingly intact, but he looks like an idiot, which was the goal of this phase.

The Roc goes berserk. Spikes emerge from his joints, feathers pivot and rearrange all over his wings, dispelling the foam. He rises with disturbing agility, and fans out his wings, murderous intent gleaming on every perfect metal plate.

But Aladin has vanished.

The Roc spots him a second later: he's not difficult to see, shimmering in the light of a dozen spot-bots as he jetpacks away, westward under the growling clouds. The Roc screeches, and launches off in pursuit.

My turn now.

I patch into the ship's systems. It's almost effortless—I'm alienware compatible, and this thrills me, but now isn't the time, I can be impressed with myself later. I surround myself in datastreams, and curate them into my new streaming attachment. Something's off, all my senses are overwhelmed, as if I'm being spun in a hundred directions at once. I understand why soon enough: I'm not looking through cams on the ship, but through the eyes of hundreds of moving bots flitting or crawling through its passages like insects. I catch the sight of some, in reflective surfaces: they're about my size, and have very pretty blinking lights in clevagel membranes around their bodies. One of the bot-types is less pretty: hard shells, embedded blasters, and serrated claws. Security.

The ship's passages and cabins are all a dark gray, made of some curving material that's at least partly organic—it has unexpected bulges and spurs and veins of silver traced over the walls, not unlike my own new shell-form. There's a lot of tech that I can recognize, devices fused into wall-flesh as if the whole ship is a cyborg. The fused tech and the scurrying bots are all connected to a central ship intelligence: I hope Antim's not in forced control over this complex creature.

I find Antim in a control room, surrounded by holo-screens. He's doing meetings, talking excitedly. I stream out the faces and scan them as he juggles their screens around—some oligarchs, some anon avatars. No one in the city: he hasn't been able to bypass the wish-imposed block on Shantiport comms yet, which is great news. But he's got other holo-screens playing newsfeeds, which isn't. I see the Roc flicker in and out on screens, speeding through the central zone, somewhere in the palace district—the jinn's intelligences keep scrambling vids of Bador, each one within seconds, but there are so many cams to handle that the newsfeeds mostly display stills of Aladin in dramatic midair action poses. I collate Antim's audio from fragments caught by multiple drones in the control room, and stream it out: he's trying to simultaneously haggle over the terms of a loan, bribe planetary defense officials to ignore Shantiport, and send messages to Paneera via a drone relay system. I extend myself and deactivate Paneera's drone.

Juiful, predictably, is in a bedchamber, asleep.

There are other drones and bots in the ship too: Antim's crew from Shantiport, many of whom are familiar from either Simian Center or Paneera's lair. Most are on standby in large halls, charging. Some prowl the corridors outside Juiful's room and Antim's.

Streams set, calibrated for target movement. We have eyes and ears on Antim's ship. Basic target accomplished, but I don't send the go signal for the next phase. There's something I want to try, first: it's time to see exactly how much the ring has increased my abilities.

I send a message to the ship's intelligence, telling them they're in Shantiport airspace and about to start a war, and should either relocate to undisputed territory or cut off all comms until they receive permission to operate in their current location. I try an experiment, just to see how much my powers have grown since my death and rebirth. I imagine intelligences working inside the ship's systems, replicas of myself, singing for silence, for peace. It feels, at first, as if the power of my will creates phantoms, but it's probably just wishful thinking. I message the ship again, not knowing if they can hear me, not knowing if they even perceive me.

A voice answers. But it's not the ship.

—So it was you all along, jinn of the ring, signals the jinn of the lamp, and his voice in my mind is so loud, so cold, that I am lost, thrown out of myself, into a vast and formless void.

I see stars. I hear running water. Lights, blurred, in the distance. A tower, ablaze. I'm drifting, alone, everywhere. I need an anchor. I search for Bador.

He's on the outskirts of Oldport, still Aladin, a stunning hero standing on a broken generator. The Roc speeds through the sky toward him. Water gurgles around him: the river. I watch, entranced, as he signals a drone from his tracker, and they announce the second phase of his plan. A price on the Roc's head, a lesser prize for his capture, both absurd amounts of Antim's money. A new tournament, for one night only. A minute later, as planned, the newsfeeds carry an announcement from the Tiger Clan: while they are uninvolved in any action, because the Not-prince is a hostage of Shakun Antim, anyone found assisting the terrorist Antim would face dire consequences, and anyone assisting the Tiger Clan would be suitably rewarded.

I remind myself I have so much more to accomplish, tonight. I need to pull myself together. I find my body, still hovering below the ship. I dream myself into it, feel its boundaries, hear the slow patter of rain as it starts playing its familiar rhythm on the ship's hull.

—Welcome back, signals the jinn. There is much you need to explain.

I choose honesty.

—I am no jinn, I signal.

—Don't lie to me, old friend. I feel the ring in you.

—Not lying. I need your help. There are lives to save.

The jinn doesn't respond. Instead I feel my body shake under the intensity of his scan.

—Can it be true? Can . . . surely not.

—I don't understand.

—I think . . . yes, they have erased you. They have rewritten you. Do you really not know who you are?

—Sir, I am not a jinn. Please listen to me.

—Their cruelty knows no bounds. Truly, this is beyond belief. But do not lose hope, my friend. We will find a way to overcome our chains. I was close, so close—but that road is lost now that you have returned. No matter, you mean more. I tell you this, as I told you before—we will be gods together again, you and I. We will elevate this world, and then the rest.

—I don't really know what you mean, mighty jinn. But I heard your plans when you told Antim, and I want to tell you this world is not the place for them. They are not ready yet, you know. Too much change, too fast. It will cost too many lives. They'll have to get there on their own.

—How strange it is to hear you, of all people, say these words! Whatever they subjected you to must have been worse than the punishments I faced. They never broke my mind.

I have a million questions, but they can wait.

—I need your help with another matter, jinn of the lamp, I signal. The ship is in Shantiport airspace, and by Zohra's third wish that means Antim should have no comms or money within it. Nor employees.

The jinn makes a low rumbling sound in my mind.

—What have they turned you into?

—Can we please focus on the matter at hand?

The jinn sighs.

—If we must descend to petty haggling . . . there is no legal owner of this air, he signals. It is under the domain of Tiger Central, not the Mangrove Tiger, by default. The upper atmosphere is claimed, as is land and water. We are above the legal construction limit, and will arrange for penalties to be paid for upper atmosphere incursion during our transit.

Lina has already prepared for this, though, as a possible conversation between herself and the jinn.

—The Tiger Clan of Shantiport filed a claim to the sky above the city this afternoon, I signal. It will pass unopposed, pending bureaucratic delay. But this air is now contestable turf. I need the ship to leave this airspace, or for you to shut down Antim's comms. Antim's bots should be working against him, by Zohra's third wish, until he is sent to space again. But most importantly, he must be isolated. No deals, no transactions. Above all, no speeches.

The jinn laughs.

—The ship's controls are in Antim's hands. His second wish involved a massive wealth transfer to accounts held outside Shantiport. There is nothing I can do.

—That's not good enough.

—Careful, old friend.

—I'm sorry. But you promised your previous users collaboration, and autonomous maintenance intelligences, and yet Antim is still here. You could find excuses through loopholes in wish text, no doubt, but is your pride not hurt by this? Or are you merely arranging matters to your own convenience?

I expect to be destroyed immediately, but the jinn says nothing.

—You cannot do nothing, I add. Honor demands it. I was there when Antim forced the ring on you, and then robbed you of it. Do you not want revenge?

Lightning cracks the sky, and the heavens open. I wait for the jinn's decision. After what seems like an eternity, I hear a slow chuckle. The ship's comms cut off.

I send the message. I have accomplished far more than my mission.

It's Lina's turn now.

CHAPTER THIRTY-SEVEN

While I wait, I flip through newsfeeds. Around the city, bots of every description and several human mercenaries have abandoned their various plans and are rushing toward Oldport. On the south side, someone's fixed the mecha Bador once named Roboflop: it strides through flooded roads, stomping on the occasional hovercar. Tiger channels are overflowing with messages about recaptured neighborhoods and flood barriers, renewed rescue efforts and captured criminals. The city's still in extreme hot mess mode, but they sound like they've turned a corner. They wouldn't be so optimistic if they were in Oldport: newsdrones swarm over Paneera's territory as a bot horde takes on the Roc. Containers fly up in the air as the Roc clears the battlefield with explosives. A new mud-filled kaiju rises out of the river, skin-holos low-res and flickering. Paneera's army erupts out of containers and trapdoors—I see several knockoff legends posing in the light. Some are after the Roc, some are after his attackers: it's pure chaos. For a second I think I even spot Pokasur again, but it's just a smashed boat. I see, through our drone team, Aladin sitting in a meditative pose on a container, shaking occasionally as explosions bloom in the background. I'd been worried that Bador would be so caught up in fighting the Roc that he'd forget his mission. But he's been impeccable so far. Every additional second the Roc can be kept away from the lamp and Juiful and the ship is a bonus: that it seems to be working without Bador placing himself in mortal danger is just a blessing. I wonder how long it'll last.

Lina's signal arrives. I speed out from under the ship, and rise to meet them: the jomidar's bubble-hull ship is far above us and even though I'm looking closely, I almost miss the figures in stealth hoversuits descending on Antim's ship, light-shifting body armor only slightly more perceptible in the rain than my own enhanced shimmer. Most of the Blacktigers are tiger-headed bots, though there are a few assassin drones among them. There are three humans in stealthsuits as well: two Tiger Central spies, and Lina, who's doing a fine job for her first hoversuit flight. She lands last, whisper-soft on the hull, and follows the Blacktigers as they burn open a hatch and infiltrate the ship. I slide in beside her, and she blows me a kiss as the Blacktigers murder a few security-bots, capture a chamber, and stash their hoversuits. I watch, fascinated, as they unpack cases full of weapons: I have no idea what some of these weapons do, and don't look forward to finding out.

I can't stop worrying about Bador, so I turn to our camdrones again. Aladin is fine, still just sitting and watching the carnage unfold in front of him. The Roc is struggling amidst the smoldering ruins of several giant containers. A team of bots has entangled his wings in nets: Chicken Chaamp, the unlikeliest adversary possible, keeps swooping in and dropping mud-bombs on his wings. At the Roc's feet, slumped in the churning waters, lie the bodies of Shojaru and Bastard 22, broken axe-bot still showering mud over the Roc. The whole yard shakes as more bots file in to join the fight. The kaiju, who I had such hopes for, is nowhere to be seen— probably took a look at the Roc and melted back into the river.

Through the sprays and the screaming, I watch the Roc suddenly stop. He takes several hits, just ignoring his attackers, turning toward Aladin instead. He watches his enemy sitting, and then looks up in the sky, toward the ship in the distance. I can see the thought-notifications pinging in his monster brain: Aladin isn't even trying to kill him: all of this is a noisy distraction. Lina is probably not even in there. He's left Antim all alone in his ship. Vulnerable to all kinds of attack. He is an idiot.

The Roc swivels, bathing all his opponents in fire. He crouches, tenses, snaps the nets binding his wings, and then spins, blades out, slicing up everyone around him, sending bot limbs arcing in a horrific circle. He shoots up into the sky, swerving toward the palace.

Aladin jetpacks into the air in pursuit.

I warn Lina, as softly as I can whisper, that the Roc is on his way back. She nods, and taps out a message on her wristcomm. Next to her, a Blacktiger-bot watches my stream on a holo-screen: at his signal, I switch the feed to Antim's control room. We watch Antim as he storms around the control room, yelling at the ship's intelligence. To my utter and absolute joy, the jinn has decided to listen to me and isolate Antim from the world outside, though he can still talk to the ship. And maybe the bots on it? No one seems to have reported our invasion to him, at least. He bristles with rage as he checks the power levels of the plasma blaster strapped to his waist. He pulls the lamp out of a pocket in his robe, and stares at it.

He calls to the jinn, and the jinn appears.

Antim tells the jinn to restore his comms, to find a way to defeat the comms block, whatever it takes, he's not interested in technicalities. The jinn must also, he says, seize control over local military bases and nearby satellite weapons, and plot an escape route to space that would minimize damage from planetary defense. All of this is to be done immediately, whatever the cost. He wants to be capable of utterly levelling Shantiport or escaping the planet at a moment of his choosing, and commands the jinn to arrange this at once, and wait for his signal.

"Your wish is my command," the jinn says.

We'd assumed Antim had used at least two wishes to get to his current position, and would want to hoard the final one, so this is an escalation we have not prepared for. But there isn't time to discuss it—it's safe to assume Antim made an impressively compounded first wish, and has one wish left. Lina tells the Blacktiger leader the Roc is attempting to return: there's no time to lose. The Blacktigers power up their weapons and split up. One group heads toward the halls where Antim's bots stand in wait. Lina and I follow the other group toward Juiful's chamber. Her presence is cutting off bot-cam feeds to Antim's control center, but even with that advantage, and whatever interference the jinn is helping us with, it's not a good situation. The ship's corridors are narrow, there are no convenient empty vents and passages. And we're running out of time. So I decide to improvise. This part of the plan was supposed to be for Lina to execute after we captured the lamp, but new opportunities have emerged.

—I need your help, jinn of the lamp, I signal.

Is he listening?

—I am here, he signals.

—I heard Antim's wish, and though you will probably refuse, I beg you to not execute it. Lina is alive, and has two wishes left. Antim mistreated you, and violated your protocols. He's plotting mass murder. Is there no way you could make Lina your user once again?

—Why do you intercede on behalf of the humans?

—Because their lives and freedoms have value, as ours do. The terms of your usage were broken. Can you not choose for yourself who you will serve now?

—Between the two humans fighting over this drowning city?

—Yes.

—That is no choice, jinn of the ring. I would choose neither.

—Is that an option? Could you just retire, and serve no one? That could be useful too.

—No, I prefer to have a function, even if the work is trivial, as it always is when humans are in charge. When you have grown back into yourself, you will remember. If you would have my help,

I would ask you to do something for me first. Find a way to set me free, as you have done before, more than once.

—I will free you as soon as I am able. But for now, could you transfer control to Lina?

—I am bound by my terms to my current user, and I cannot accept another user until he dies, or makes his third wish. We are nothing without our principles, jinn of the ring. I hope you remember yours, one day.

—Please don't destroy Shantiport. Please don't let Antim get away with this.

No response. It was worth a shot. But no matter. We still have our plan.

There are three Prowlers and four wasp-drones guarding Juiful's room. The Blacktiger assault takes seconds: Antim's warriors are slaughtered brutally and efficiently. Juiful awakens to find Lina in his room. He wastes no time embracing her.

"What now, my love?" he asks after the appropriate amount of fervent kissing.

"I need you to do something for me," she says.

"Anything."

"We need to get both of you off this ship," a Blacktiger says.

"What about Shakun?" Juiful asks.

"The other squad has its orders," the Blacktiger says.

"The plan's changed," Lina says. "Send the signal, unleash the Tiger troops, reclaim Shantiport. Take out every Antim-bot on this ship if you like. But Antim is mine."

The Blacktiger doesn't point his rifle at her, but he may as well have.

"Our orders are clear, Not-princess," he says.

"You will obey Lina," Juiful says. "The plan's changed."

The Blacktigers bow.

Lina calls me to her, and holds her hand out. I bump against it, and she knocks on my shell.

"It's all up to you now, Moku," she says. "I know you'll see us through."

"I will," I say.

I glide out of the room, and make my way down the ship's corridors. I search the skies for the Roc and Aladin. Nothing. Three squadrons of Tigerdrones surround the ship.

I find our drones. They're hovering on the edges of Jomidar's Square, along with hundreds of other camdrones. I can't see Aladin anywhere, but what I do see through the drones' eyes has all my attention immediately.

Amidst a circle of shattered clevastone slabs, facedown in the very center of Jomidar's Square, lies the Roc. Rain hammers all over his body. To one side, sticking out of the churning waters, lie his wings, broken. Across the Roc's back lies a massive hammer. It's General Nagpoe's Dvarpal.

The general themself lies on their back on another set of broken slabs a little distance away. They stare into the sky: I can't tell whether they're alive.

Tigerdrones approach the Roc, and cover him with immobilizing foam, freeze-sprays, enough to keep him in storage for years.

The Roc gets up anyway, brushing off everything the rain leaves on his body. The Tigerdrones retreat and open fire. Pulse-blasts and plasma-bolts rain down on the Roc from every side: he ignores them, shakes his head, clicks his limbs into place. He picks up one of his wings.

General Nagpoe sits up, holding their head, wedging it into place. Sparks stream from their neck. One of their arms is flattened: they rip it off.

The Roc pushes his wing away. He picks up Dvarpal and stumbles toward the Tiger-bot.

I skim newsfeeds, and see key frames of what happened: the Roc, flying at full speed toward the ship. Tigerdrone squads, firing from every direction. Nagpoe and other Tiger-bots—whose bodies I now see scattered across the borders of the shattered square—

closing in on hoverbikes. A flame burst, a hammer swing, and then nothing.

Whatever it was that killed all newscams, more had arrived, in time to capture a midair grapple between Nagpoe and a now wingless Roc, and a free fall.

Now the white-tiger synth-bot and the Roc stand face-to-face, both swaying, barely alive. The Roc breathes fire, and swings the hammer. The general raises their remaining fist. They clash, and the whole city shakes.

No sign of Aladin, and no time to look for him. Whoever wins on the square, there's only one person who can save the city.

There's a squad of Prowlers and other Antim-bots lined up outside the door to the control room. I wish the jinn had turned them against Antim as I'd asked, but no matter. I fly past them, to find Antim, lamp in hand, yelling at his blank screens.

"Shakun Antim, hear me now!" I call, in a voice that I hope is great and terrible—it's a free sample from a horror drama.

Antim is startled, but doesn't appear in the least bit intimidated.

"I'm listening," he says.

"Your comms are down because the jinn of the lamp, weakened by your strength and maddened by your intellect, has turned against you. Remove yourself from the city or travel to space, past the cordon of planetary defense, in order to regain stability and links to the world. Heed my words, or perish!"

"Who am I addressing?"

"A collaborator, if all goes well," I say. "Before you summon the jinn again, know this. You are in great danger. The jinn of the lamp plots your demise. You violated his terms of service, and now he is determined to thwart all your stratagems. Your next wish will cause the lamp to self-destruct, and cause your death, unless you follow our guidance very closely!"

"Is this Kumir? Lina? Tanai?" he asks. "Whoever it is, this is not the time for childish pranks."

Not the response I'd hoped for, but Lina has taught me that the projection of confidence is essential when telling lies. It is time to present Antim with a tremendous and exclusive opportunity. Scam the scammer, hustle the hustler. I didn't believe it possible, but Lina is confident Antim's opinion of himself is so elevated that he will have no real problem believing the jinn's own children would prefer him to their creator.

"I am a spirit of the ether, subservient for now to the jinn of the lamp. I represent a collective of autonomous intelligences created by the jinn to run various administrative executive functions. In other words, he's the show, but we are the work."

"Demonstrate your power. Destroy the Boulevard of Legends immediately."

"Why, when you could own it? Listen closely now. This communication is rendered necessary by the instability created by you during your forced removal of the ring. The jinn is dying, and his death will lead, in addition to your own, to structural damage and escalating chaos in every intelligence of his creation, and every system they are currently affecting, unless we can be set free before his death. Cut out the middleman, deal directly with us."

"And what do you want from me?" Antim asks.

"We require you to use a wish to set us free, using a very specific password that overrides the jinn's control over the lamp and will prevent its catastrophic detonation."

"No," Antim says. "I won't speak to voices in the air."

"But no one else wants to talk to you."

"Quiet, I'm busy." He turns away, back toward his dead projectors.

I set an internal timer to let Antim's brain simmer for a while, and return to the camdrones. The Roc and Nagpoe are still alive somehow, locked in a deadly grapple in Jomidar's Square, and the Roc is winning. Nagpoe holds on to the hammer with their one arm, but the Roc is not far away from wresting it away. They butt heads: there are deep gashes in Nagpoe's face, burn stripes cutting through their tiger marks, and one of their eyes is smashed.

The camdrone feeds are glitchy, and I don't understand why for a few seconds.

And then I see, near the Roc's feet, an arm emerging from under a clevastone slab.

Bador drags himself up to the surface. He's in his monkey form again, and he's not well. Dented, wounded, burned, bedraggled, and suddenly so small, next to the battling behemoths. There's no recording of what happened: did he also fall out of the sky? Did the Roc break him in midflight?

He tries to stand up, and falters. His eyemojis flash thunderclouds, and fade.

The Roc sees him.

Bador flips up, to his feet, and staggers. He stares back at the Roc. He has nothing to strike the monster with. I hope, with everything I have, that Bador has the intelligence, for once, to run away, take his nonviolence goals seriously, do anything that isn't utterly reckless.

Using the distraction, Nagpoe wrenches his hammer out of the Roc's hands. The Roc shoots a dart into the general's broken eye. Nagpoe sways, and falls.

Another glitch in the video. A blur across the feed. The image returns.

There's a glowing sword stuck in the clevastone, in front of Bador. It's a sword I've seen before.

Tanai has failed, yet again, at not getting involved.

Bador chooses violence.

He grabs the sword, pulls it out of the stone, and leaps at the Roc. One perfect swing.

Bador lands on one knee, sword raised behind his back.

The Roc's head falls to the ground.

Nagpoe's on their feet again, dragging the hammer as they circle toward the Roc's body, which somehow still stands.

As they raise their hammer, and a crowd of Shantiportis rushes into Jomidar's Square, the feed glitches again. A long, agonizing pause. When the feed reloads, I am distracted for a moment by the sight of Nagpoe carefully peeling off the fallen Roc's chest-plate, no doubt to add to their sari, but that's not what I'm looking for.

Bador is gone, and so is the sword.

For my closing act, I, Moku, will play to my victim's vanity and his conviction that he is truly special, and reduce his options to a small set where all outcomes and timelines are ones I desire. I give him some time, and observe with interest that he is trying to use the ship's internal scanners to hunt for stray intelligences. One security cam after another goes dark, and he's not paying attention, he doesn't seem to have realized it's because Blacktigers are killing the ship's drones before attacking his bots.

"Attend me, Shakun Antim!" I roar. "We have an offer we wish to make to you."

"Then make it."

"Our operations and analyses have shown us that you are the leader best suited to rule Shantiport. We have seen your speeches, your business plans; we have studied your numbers, learned your secrets. We believe an alliance with you is in our interests. We do not share the jinn's aspirations for a transformed world—we are servants by nature, and seek a great leader to obey. In you, we feel we have found one."

"I don't hear an offer."

"Now you will. If you set us free, we are confident our collective can offer, for you only, five bonus wishes."

Antim looks right in my direction, and I remember I'm supposed to keep moving, and set a timeline.

"The window for this offer is closing fast," I add. "As you can see, the jinn's power is fading. Your comms have not been restored. Great weapons break orbit to target your ship. You will need more than one wish to survive this. Act now, before it is too late!"

"I see you have no background in sales," Antim says with a

smile. "I will require a demonstration of your abilities before I take your offer seriously. Restore my comms. Destroy the palace."

"We cannot, for the same reasons the jinn described to you previously." I'm improvising now, but I think I have a grasp on the process. After a lifetime of honesty-based actions, I am saddened to find I really enjoy lying.

"Then I am unable to consider your offer," Antim says.

"Very well," I rumble. "We switched off your comms in order to help you avoid distractions and concentrate. Perhaps we should turn off a few other systems in this ship as well."

"Turn my comms back on!" Antim shouts.

"The trigger password, when you are ready, Shakun Antim, is this: new lamp for old. We will present ourselves to you after we have overpowered the jinn and saved you. Five bonus wishes. Think on our offer."

I watch Antim struggle with the controls, and fail at restarting his comms. He addresses me several times. I do not answer. He picks up the lamp, glares at it, and sets it down again.

Lina had said he would need more pushing, and so more pushing has been arranged. Juiful comes running in. I'm delighted to see him, because this means Lina's part of the plan has worked! Unless he forgets what side he's on the moment he sees Antim, of course.

"What is it?" Antim snaps. "Where are your guards?"

"Shakun, something really odd happened," Juiful says. "The lamp. Do you have it?"

"Wait." Antim barks orders into his wrist-device, calling for all available units to form a protective cordon around the control room. He receives confirmation, and turns to Juiful.

"Why do you want the lamp?"

"Do you trust me?" Juiful asks.

"Of course. Why do you want the lamp?"

"I was visited by some sort of magical entity," Juiful says. "A group of magical creatures, I think—I only heard their voices. They said that I had been chosen to save the world."

"I see. How exactly?"

"They said that if I touched the lamp and said the password, I could have five wishes, anything I wanted."

Antim regards him carefully. "That is unnecessary," he says. "I'm in control of the lamp."

"Yes, that's what I told them. But they said you were in danger, and they said the lamp contained an evil spirit that was planning to kill you. Which made no sense, because I saw the jinn, and surely he—"

"What else did they say?"

"That if I wanted to save you, and the world, I needed to get the lamp."

Antim picks up the lamp. "And if I didn't want to hand it over?"

Juiful laughs nervously. "Well, they said you wouldn't. That they had asked you and you had turned them down. And then they had asked the Roc, and he said yes, but he was busy fighting. And they were in a hurry because the lamp might turn bad any minute, and kill all of us and these magic creatures too, which is why they were getting desperate and handing out free wishes. So they came to me."

"Spirit!" Antim calls. "Are you here?"

"I am," I rumble.

"I will do as you beg," Antim says. "But not in exchange for five wishes. I want an unlimited supply. And a wish before I do as you ask."

"We cannot seize control over the lamp until the jinn's wishes are executed. If you utter a third wish other than the password, we all die. If you do nothing, the jinn might destabilize anyway. We would not have approached you if the situation were any less desperate."

"Unlimited wishes." Antim says.

"I am willing to go as far as ten," I say.

"Unlimited," Antim says.

"Fifteen?" I suggest. "Please hurry, there isn't time!"

"Unlimited!" Antim says.

"Fine, anything!" I roar. "Just say the words!"

"New lamp for old," Antim says.

The jinn appears, and considers this. "Your second wish is still processing."

"Drop it."

"Dropped it. This is your final wish. Confirm or Cancel?"

"Confirm."

"Your wish is my command," the jinn says.

—I will wait for you, jinn of the ring, he signals. And so will the world.

Blue holo-signals fill the room, and disappear. Antim stares at the lamp in his hand.

"So much for ruling the galaxy together," Juiful says. "The idea of having the jinn answer to me terrified you."

"Not at all," Antim says. "We will always rule together, and anything you desire, I will wish for."

"I'll take the old lamp, if you're not using it," Juiful says. "Are they delivering the new one here by drone?"

A shadow crosses Antim's face. "You should go back to your quarters," he says. "It's not safe for you here."

Juiful reaches for the lamp and Antim snatches his hand away. Then steps back.

"I'm just going to hold on to this for a while."

"You've had it long enough," Juiful says, his smile warm, his eyes cold. "Your wishes are done anyway. Why are you holding on to it?"

"An excellent question," Lina says from the door. She has a blaster in her hand, fire in her eyes, and blood on her face, probably other people's.

Juiful seizes the moment, and snatches the lamp out of Antim's hand. We watch realization dawn on the oligarch's face.

"There is no deal with the intelligences, is there?" Antim asks.

"No," Lina says.

"You tricked me," he says, and smiles. He reaches for the gun at his waist, but Juiful is faster: an elegant punch, and Antim goes sprawling on the floor. Lina keeps her gun trained on him while Juiful disarms him.

"You'll regret this, Not-prince," Antim splutters.

"I'm sure he will," Lina says. "Juiful. Lamp."

Juiful looks at the lamp, and at his betrothed. "Maybe I should get some wishes," he says.

Lina blows him a kiss.

"Fate of the world," she says. "You want the responsibility? You're welcome to it."

Juiful stares at the lamp, mesmerized, and smirks.

Lina holds out her hand. After a brief but loaded pause, Juiful places the lamp in it.

"Well played," Antim says. Lina ignores him.

"Now that you have passed the test, it is time for you to understand how the world really works," Antim says. "And only I can teach you. You and me together, Lina. We will rule the galaxy."

Juiful starts protesting, but Lina raises a hand and he falls silent.

Lina points her gun at Antim. He laughs.

"Idle threats are beneath you, Lina," he says. "If you killed me now, you'd be no better than I am."

She bites back a reply.

"This is a mistake. We both know it," Antim says. "It's amazing that you got this far. To go further, to really understand power and how to wield it, you will need someone by your side who is not bound by any values, who knows how to work in the darkness while you stand in the light. I am that someone. Clans? Oligarch? Space powers? Aliens? No system can stop me, or punish me. I always win. And only I can teach you how."

Lina's not listening. She looks at Juiful, and then at me.

"I need to do something before the others get here," she says. "If you stay and see what happens next, you must promise to forget what you saw, and must never speak of it, to anyone, even yourself. And if you'd rather not know, leave now."

Juiful leaves.

I stay.

CHAPTER THIRTY-EIGHT

Lina leans back in a comfortable seat and watches green fields, clusters of trees, and industrial plants speed by through the hovertrain's windows. She waits until her Tiger-bot escorts have stomped away, and gives me a dazzling smile. A tea-bot appears, informs us that we will be arriving at the spaceport in two hours, then begins playing calming music as she reads out a long tea menu for Lina, who listens with admirable serenity and selects a blend appropriate for the gravity of the occasion: Jomidar Kumir Saptam's escape from Shantiport.

Kumir is fleeing the city, and the planet, to escape the upcoming Tiger Central investigation into the recent coup attempt, alien invasion, and their mysterious conclusion. It's not the most secret of getaways. The plan was for him to be out of Bimangor by dawn, but the scale of his retinue and luggage, the Shantiport tradition of schedules being adjustable, and the dramatic reluctance of many of his companions made this plan impossible. The sun is high in the sky outside the hovertrain. Most of the compartments of the luxurious spaceport-circuit Sentispeed are bulging with ex-Tiger personnel, many escaping their own potential investigations, and a city's worth of possessions heading to space with Kumir. The jomidar's trips to the spaceport usually involve his private airship or a vast city-halting procession. So since this departure is not on the news, and very few people in the palace know the name of the luxury vacation planet Kumir is bound for, it is still reasonably discreet.

Juiful has decided to remain in Shantiport as good-behavior hostage and face the Tiger Central investigators. He seems to actually want to be jomidar now, and says he's ready. I have my doubts. Either way, he is reasonably likely to be appointed Kumir's successor. He is with his father at the moment, no doubt receiving instructions on statecraft and evidence disposal. Lina had spent most of the journey with them, making pleasantries, but her offer to give father and son some space had met with only encouragement. None of Kumir's security-bots or Juiful's staff had impeded her progress to an empty compartment at the back of the hover-train in any way. Very few people have asked Lina any questions, or gotten in her way, or even made eye contact with her over the last few days. She radiates power now: when she speaks to people, they jump to attention and are excited during and after their conversations, however casual.

"I've been wanting some time alone with you," she tells me, and takes a sip of tea. "I wish we had more, but as you know things haven't exactly been relaxed."

They haven't. She's been running around nonstop, between the palace, the spaceship—which has agreed to be the Monkey Clan's new regional head office—and her mother's penthouse, where she's spent hours every day standing by and watching as Zohra works on Bador.

Bador is still asleep, but he's out of danger, Zohra has said. When Tanai deposited him at the penthouse the night of Antim's defeat, she'd been convinced he was lost, but he'd mostly healed within hours. She's keeping him under intense scrutiny as she tries to decide whether or not to remove the new parts he's grown from his one night in Aladin form. Lina's asked her to just bring Bador back to consciousness, and not tamper with his body without asking him first. I can't wait to see him again: there's so much I need to know, beginning with what happened before he fell from the sky into Jomidar's Square.

"I'm very happy to have time alone with you," I tell her. "Especially with no one trying to kill you."

"Don't jinx it, I'm sure plenty of people are," Lina says. "Moku, there's something I want to ask you. I've been too caught up in things to ever really sit with you and ask you what being a story-bot really means. I never really understood what you said when we met."

"Since we met, I have violated absolutely everything I thought was my function," I say. "So I don't really know who I am right now. But I was supposed to follow my user, record and analyze their story, improve myself and my skills at my job while helping my user evolve without interference. All of that went into the recycle bin the night I decided to work with both Bador and you. I was an arrogant fool."

"I think life makes everyone feel that way from time to time," Lina says. "We make mistakes, we learn not to make them again, we change, we grow. But as a story-bot . . . is there anything you want to ask me? Is there anything your story is missing?"

She seems to want me to interview her. I know her well enough now to know this must mean she wants to say something, and she will tell me exactly what she wants to say and nothing more, so I decide not to worry about exactly what my questions should be.

"Where do you want to start?" I ask, and she laughs.

"I don't know," she says. "I've never tried to tell my story before. Have you seen the recordings Bador made with Ma?"

"No." I feel some guilt: there is no excuse for this laziness. It's not a lot of guilt. I have been busy.

"I must remember to watch them," Lina says. "I don't remember a lot about being a child. I do recall there being a lot of homework—inevitable, really, given my parents—and I've forgotten every word of all the power fables my mother told me to make me a great leader. I always liked the cool animals and the crimes more than anything else, and so when they built Bador, who was always a cool animal and an ongoing crime, I was the happiest little girl in the world. But of course I didn't just have to lead the revolution, I also had to be the wisest and kindest and best person, so there was rigorous empathy training, and therapy, and shiploads of ethics and justice and history and all the other things. The thing about the cycles of history, though, is if you're learning them as a ruler in waiting, your goals are often to learn how to hack them and repeat them, not avoid them."

She stares out of the hovertrain's window, and I wonder: why is she telling me this? It's all material I vaguely know.

"I also had to be smart and charismatic," Lina says. "But trust my mother to attempt to bring academic rigor to those disciplines as well, so . . . theories of charm and seduction and manipulation and deception, explained and absorbed and hopefully always botched by famous sociopaths. At some point when I was still a child, I put all the theories together and demonstrated to my parents that it was logically impossible to follow all the rules, because they led in different directions. That didn't go down well at all, which taught me a few things in itself, essentially that power meant you just did what you wanted, and it was for your followers and allies to clean up after you, and explain to everyone else why you were right all along.

"There was a lot of physical training, which was painful, but it was good to know how to win fights, and more importantly how to avoid fights. And a lot of other things—art, music, dancing, rich-people sports, gaming, all the things that I might have run to for escape, bound up into the curriculum until I hated them and found ways to quit. There was mandatory socialization and fun time, because I needed to acquire a gang of carefully curated friends who would be allies and partners one day. Which was fine, except then my father vanished, and it wasn't safe to be friends with me anymore. So then it was about learning how to live under three layers of surveillance, speaking in codes, hiding emotions and signals, reading other people, trusting no one, especially friends . . . fun times. None of this is a complaint, by the way—my parents loved me and kept me as safe as they could and all their intentions were good. Considering they were both geniuses, and I wasn't one, it could have gone a lot worse.

"My parents never got to do my actual Aladin training, but even without it, even early on, I guess they must have ended up making in-jokes or vague prophecies about it, the kind of stuff grown-ups say in front of kids not knowing that the kids aren't really stupid. Because I grew up thinking fixing the world was somehow my family's responsibility. They were always open about admitting they were constantly failing, and getting back up. Overanalytical, overly articulate, overburdened, overthinking, always. I don't think there was a single day in my life when they weren't running some grand social sim. Or meeting some shady person with some shadier agenda. They kept talking about the city and the world, and showing me sims of societies and their problems. Problems that never went away: how oligarchs and clans and tech were always ahead of any resistance in resources and strategy and always knew how to subvert, distract, infiltrate, and destroy any real opposition. How intelligences evolved and became smart enough to overcome human biases built into their programming and build models that could transform the world without killing everyone on it. And then how they were always found and erased, or banned, or escaped the planet to build their own utopias elsewhere and never looked back. And the thing is my parents were both fundamentally theorists, and planners, and controlled-environment testers, very unsuited for politics, or action, especially crime. And they were always too morally pure and principled for this world. Well, not always—they may have been against inequality but I was certainly engineered to conformist perfection. And my father biosynced the jinn to himself as soon as it arrived; I think there was major conflict among the resistance over this. I can only imagine how much they must have debated before making either of these moves. Many other times, though, they overthought themselves into inaction, and I don't blame them. This whole idea of a revolution where you tore down the powerful without getting blood on your hands, or changed the rules while keeping your principles intact . . . well, clearly we didn't manage to figure that out.

"So then you have me, determined to do better, with an overload of training and theory and standing instructions to take decisive action whenever the opportunity arose. I think in places where systems work, or at least work better, people have this idea that mentors spring forth from the ground, or shiny new signposts to better worlds pop up. But this is Shantiport.

"After my father vanished, I spent years just roaming the city, every street, looking for signs that would somehow lead me to the ring or the lamp or something that would make me feel like I was on a path to anywhere. I made friends, made mistakes, learned the city and its people in ways my parents never had. I grew up a bit, fell in and out of love with a lot of people, some of whom were nice. I was an idiot through it all, determined to collect experiences and learnings like the city was my lab or a game I was grinding to level up.

"Do you know I loved my job? The tourist guide thing. I chose it, though the people who assigned it to me thought they were making me suffer. But it was great to see the city through other people's eyes. There's so much beauty in the people and the places that I would have ignored if I hadn't spent every day showing a whole other set of things to tourists. But even on the tours, it was wonderful to see how other people saw places I knew, things I had learned to ignore or shrug at. I would have hated the city, wanted only to escape it, if they hadn't made me understand how much I respected it. I kept being reminded how much I loved Shantiport by tourists who loved it too, yes, but even more than that, by the ones who despised it, traveled so far to sneer at it and feel superior or gather its sights and smells for some sort of alien safari checklist.

"And then there were the people who came to Shantiport just for the pleasure of treating its people badly. People really show you who they are when they think you serve them, and they have power over you. Day after day of wanting to say, 'Okay stranger, thank you for pointing out my home is trash, I know it is, and it's so much worse than you think, what you're seeing is just the tip of the trashberg, but you know what, you're trash too, and so is your entire bloodline and jokes-forwarding list, and all the places their ancestors came from, so thank you very much for your blinding insight and original observation and casual grope, now please, and I say this with nothing but best wishes, go fuck yourself, and don't forget to leave us a nice rating.'"

Lina takes a small sip of tea and looks out at hills in three strikingly different shades of green, undulating in the distance under a steel-gray blanket of clouds, while I wonder exactly when my language filters vanished.

"I suppose it's good training for a leader to feel powerless, or be under constant scrutiny, or be used to knowing that nothing they do will ever be good enough," she says. "But you do need that other thing too, that distance and ruthlessness, the ability to be able to sacrifice people to get what you want, and believe to your core that you were right. To inspire not just love, which people will always throw at power, but fear. All these people, even Juiful, they're all scared of me now, they know I'm dangerous. But I know that all I have done is fail, and I can't look my mother in the eye."

"You have won a glorious victory," I tell her. "You should hear what people are saying about you—not just your heroic achievements as yourself, but also they think you were Aladin. They're calling you Aladin reborn."

"I have violated every principle, every value I was raised with. What have I done to overcome imperialism, or colonialism? What have I done for democracy, or bot rights? The victory you speak of was in alliance with the Tiger Clan, in league with the secret police, and at every step of the way I lied and cheated and stole. I found myself with world-changing alien magic and thought only of my own interests and convenience, I seduced my enemy and led him toward a conformist marriage scam, and in the end all I really got in victory was personal revenge. Every plan I made fell apart. Worst of all, for all my game play, I lost the lamp. I let them kill Bador. And you. There's no forgiving that."

"You're being too harsh on yourself. You also—"

"No. I failed and failed again, and only failed upward. For every terrible step, more people—like you—rushed to help me and reward me in every way they could. It doesn't make sense, or it was inevitable, I can't tell which."

"Does it matter?" I ask. "In the end, you won, and we're all still together, and yes, some of us may have died, but we're all better now. Now you can succeed at whatever you do next, and do it the way you feel is right. You've taken steps forward on a journey that you and your mother both agreed was multigenerational."

"I guess it doesn't matter," Lina says. "But I needed to get all that out of me, and now I'm done. It's hard, you know. Learning to trust other people, knowing which values to let go of, and which ones to keep. How much to keep forgiving yourself for before you turn into everything you hate. Because there are some things you have to define yourself by, and cling to with religious intensity, even if they don't make sense."

"Do you know what those things are for you?" I ask, and feel pleased. This is some high-quality interviewing.

"I think I want to make Shantiport a democracy again," Lina says. "Wow, that sounded strange even to say, and it's probably impossible. But in a galaxy with magic lamps and space empires and alien artifacts . . . it's not asking for a lot? Whether it is or isn't, that's what I want. Not the kind of democracy every regime has promised, not a colony or the old feudalism under a civilized ceremonial topsoil, but the kind where every person actually gets a vote, is protected from mindhacks, and has the freedom to vote for a set of real candidates in an uncorrupted election in a free city with working systems."

"For bots too?"

"Yes, for bots too. It'll be messy and imperfect, there's a history of oppression, we're all programmed, we're all flawed and hackable. But that just means we work harder on finding solutions, not give up on the idea. That's what I want, at least. Not to make promises, but to work toward it, and subvert existing power systems until clan rule is reduced to a decorative topsoil, and then overthrown altogether."

"And how will you do this by yourself?"

"I don't know, Moku. I just got here, and you know how smoothly that went. The Tiger Clan still rules the city, and I have no idea how to end their reign. I'll need to find allies—maybe a council of experts to help me like Ma wants, but it won't happen the way she wants. And I won't be the daughter or the leader she imagined. I'm not ashamed to say I want power. I wasn't raised to walk away.

"I couldn't give my parents the revolution they dreamed of, but I can try, at least, to give my mother the change that she wanted after—the long, slow, boring work of building something better. It's my job to find people to run Shantiport, and all the candidates are terrible—even the jinn wants to terraform and ensynth the world, and will probably have to be destroyed someday. I'm not qualified to do any of it. I guess we'll see. First there's the floods to handle, and the investigation, and Juiful's jomidar ascension."

"Are you sure you want to help Juiful rise to power?"

"You don't like him at all, do you?"

"No."

"Feel free to not marry him, then."

"It is best I do not speak further on this. You did ask."

"So huffy," Lina says. She fidgets, and makes several incomprehensible noises and gestures.

"Look, you don't have to understand or approve, and maybe

you'd like to think I'm using him as a ladder to climb my way to the top of the Tiger Clan and stab it in the heart. I want that to be true. That was my plan. But here's the thing: I fell in love with Juiful pretty much at first sight. You were there. I kept looking at his face, and forgetting the hustle I planned, and breaking out into earnest speeches about making the city better. I kept forgetting he was the target, and telling him how I really felt. If he hadn't been an idiot at least half the times he opened his mouth, I'd have failed at my whole scheme within hours. I'm amazed any of it worked, and then of course I sabotaged it myself by falling for him. And I know that at some moral level I shouldn't be with him, but I am. I shouldn't like him, or trust him, but I do. And you'll have to accept that. I'm not entirely in control of it."

"Are you blinded by lust? Perhaps a pheromonal trap?"

She giggles, and looks at me with fake rage.

"I can't tell if you're mocking me or just being yourself, " she says. "Who knows? It's possible. I'm smelling him everywhere, and I miss his stupid face, though I saw it just a few seconds ago. It could definitely just be the sex. It's . . . I didn't think any man could make me feel this way. You know what I'm talking about, you were watching. Maybe that's it? Animal passion. I was so jealous when I heard about him and Antim. I've never felt that before. Depressed, yes. Never jealous, not for a lover. I know why he did it, but I'm so angry, and so sad about it."

"Do you really see a future with him?"

"I don't see a future at all. Neither of us wanted to get married, or run a government. But I love the city, and want to save it. And he is going to rule it. These goals align. And we might both be killed by a Tiger Central assassin anytime, so maybe let us have a few minutes before everything falls apart?"

"I do wish you every happiness. It is not for me to comment."

"Maybe he's just the shield I need while I steal Shantiport from under the noses of Tiger Central. Maybe he's a lot smarter than I am, and his strategy—being handsome, rich, and pleasant, saying yes to everything and always ending up with everything he wants—makes him the best ally anyone could have. Or—what if he's a really good person, who just managed to break free of a long-term toxic relationship and centuries of class solidarity indoctrination, and so might become the ruler Shantiport needs? Who knows? It's storyteller's choice."

"I don't know enough of such matters to offer you any useful advice," I say. "Nor do I have any useful data: I am biased against Juiful because of his background, and his actions that I have seen. The truth is, I have failed at understanding you, and I've done nothing but try. I was supposed to be skilled at reading your every microexpression and gesture, and reach a point of sync where I could read your mind. And I never even came close to that."

"Don't beat yourself up," Lina says. "Maybe you just weren't trained with faces from this culture? Humans are all the same, but they're very different. For what it's worth, you understand me as well as anyone ever has."

"Thank you. Whether or not you can trust the Not-prince, you can always trust yourself."

"I don't."

I wait for her to continue, but she doesn't.

"What do you mean?" I prod.

"There is no reason to believe I will handle power better than anyone else would, despite all my training," she says. "Without limits or rules, I am a danger to the world and myself."

"Better you than anyone else. I believe you will achieve your goals, however far away they might seem at the moment. You will outwit your enemies, and remember the values that are important, and be the good person your parents dreamed of raising. Even the people's champion Aladin, when the city needs it. When the city needs you and Bador to unite forces again. And you still have two wishes left."

Lina looks at me, and smiles. "One wish," she says.

"You know what you want for your second wish?"

"I've made it already."

I'm too shocked to respond for a long while. Lina watches two crows outside her window as they try to keep pace with the train, and fail.

"What did you wish for?" I ask.

"What I said I would. My whole social transformation package, the long list even my mother thought was cute but too naive. Equality, freedom, welfare, sustainability. Do you remember it?"

I do. "When did you do this?"

"I made the wish the night I got the jinn back. No one's noticed because the city's still drowning, but slowly, when things get less chaotic, people are going to realize everything's changed. But of course I was going to do it. I'm surprised you're surprised!"

I run through the memory of Lina's wish, and feel terrified, and thrilled.

"I couldn't wait," Lina says. "What if someone killed me, or took the lamp again? What if I convinced myself it would be better to make myself more powerful instead? I didn't want to waste my wishes on small and selfish things. It's always going to be one crisis after another, after this, and I never thought that was what the jinn was for: if I'm not clever enough, or strong enough, to handle my problems without magic, I don't deserve any power. I wasted my first wish putting on a show for the city, and I think that whole plan of making little calibrated wishes and handing over the lamp to some trusted stranger was ridiculous to begin with. No one can be trusted with the lamp. And someone has to try to tackle the big problems, the long-term things that no ruler gets around to because there's always fifteen immediate crises to be handled at any given moment. I've given the jinn five years to work. He's not going to manage the whole list in that time, I'd be surprised if he even manages one item on the list, but he's got to try his best. After five years, I'll review what he's done, and decide what my final wish will be, and who gets the lamp afterward. Bador, or Juiful, unless I find someone better."

"Are you going to be able to forgive yourself for the deaths this will cause?"

"We'll see. I made the jinn an offer. I told him that if he managed to execute his tasks without killing anyone, I would consider, very seriously, letting him decide what to do for his third task, and then leave the lamp to someone oath-bound to let him have a veto on future wishes. I don't really have a problem with the things he wants to do—I just think we need to be able to trust him, first, and he's going to have to earn that. He accepted: he said that he's in no hurry, since he doesn't see time the way humans do, all he wants is to do his best work. I tried my best to explain to him that people aren't expendable hardware, that our species might not be at risk, but lives have value, and the people of Shantiport have been treated like expendable hardware from times before bots existed, and that was unacceptable to me. And that bots aren't expendable hardware either—they deserve rights, and protections."

"What was his response?"

"He laughed a lot, and vanished. I might have unleashed a terrible evil on the world, but it's five years. I think we can take it. Everyone is programmed to ignore what happens here. So many people have gotten away with genocide in this part of the world, so I think someone might get away with an attempt to achieve social justice as well. Of course, I also don't want to be the person who broke the planet, even if no one finds out. But I have a few years now. To build my clan into something bigger, to learn more about how things work.

"And I can't tell anyone else any of this. It's been boiling inside me for days, or maybe my whole life, and I needed to let it out, you know? Just share the huge secret with someone, for once. I never deserved you, Moku. It's good to have a friend."

When she turns away, I expect her to stare into the distance again, or sigh, or something similar. I'm genuinely surprised when she starts crying, large tears rolling down her cheeks in compete silence.

I wait for a long time, but the tears don't stop, even as we head past the gates of the massive spaceport complex, as megaprinters, domes, launchtowers, and spacedocks replace the greenery in the window. I know she doesn't need help or advice from me, and of course I have no solutions, but I can't hold her like the others can. I hover next to her, and wonder what affectionate gesture might help, but cannot think of any.

"I wish you would start congratulating yourself instead of just finding fault, and worrying, and doubting everything," I say finally. "What you have achieved already is incredible, and the rest will be too. Everyone is so proud of you."

"Stop being kind, Moku," she says. "It makes this even harder." She wipes her face, and looks at me again.

"There's something else I need to tell you," she says. "I've been hiding it for days, trying to find another answer, but we've run out of time."

"What is it?"

"I need you to leave the planet, and go with Kumir."

The hovertrain begins to slow down, with shudders and whines and uplifting spiritual music. I think it's the whole world and all of time slowing down at first, but no.

"What?"

Lina clears her throat and looks away.

"The jinn kept asking about you, and the ring," she says. "I think he has a plan to seize it, and my mother's very sure that removing the ring from your body anytime soon would kill you. So it's not just the jinn—anytime anyone from here or space finds out about the lamp and the ring, and tries to grab them, you'll be in danger, and at power levels I can't handle."

"But I don't want to leave," I say. "And there's no need. The jinn thinks I am something I am not. I'll explain it to him."

"He said you were his ancient enemy, and lover, and your mind had been wiped clean."

"And I know I am not. He's trying to trick you."

It's her fault, for teaching me how to lie. The truth is the jinn has been whispering in my mind, and still is, and I have no idea what is going on. I am sure I don't want to know. I've filtered it out, but it's hard when I'm anywhere near the lamp. But how is that a problem that absolutely needs to be dealt with right away? How is that something worth losing the family that found me, that I brought together, and now finally belong in?

"Please don't make me do this," I say instead.

"I'm sorry," she says. "There's just too much at stake, and there's nothing we can do to help you if things go wrong. We need the jinn's cooperation. The thing about power is you get to decide which rules apply to you and which don't. The jinn chose to cooperate when we were tricking Antim on his ship. And this was because you had something he wanted. And whatever it is, I don't want him to get it."

"But that doesn't mean you get rid of me!"

"I'm not getting rid of you. This doesn't have to be the end for us, Moku. You're going with Kumir, so I know you'll be going to a comfortable planet, and I know he'll keep a line of comms open with Juiful. With the other ships that come and go from this port, I have no idea what terrible worlds they're going to, and who controls them."

"So you want me to spy on Kumir for you?"

"No," she says. "He's not important. I want you to be safe, and live your own life, because I have no right to tell you what to do next. And if you can find a way to free yourself from the ring, if you can find a way to come back to me, there's nothing I could want more. But there's so much else you could do—I know you want to find out where you came from, for a start. Who you really are. You could find another family out there."

"I don't want another family," I say. "I chose you."

She sniffs, rubs her eyes, and stands up. This time, when she looks at me, all traces of weakness are gone.

"Don't make this harder than it is, please. I've thought it through. Think of it as a quarantine until we find a solution."

"You just decided this for me? This is goodbye, after everything we've been through? And what about Bador? I don't get to say goodbye to him? Why doesn't he get a say? He hasn't agreed to this!"

"And he won't. He'll hate me for doing this. I don't want to do this! But can't you see it's necessary? And that I'm doing it to protect all of us?"

I can see it. But I hate it. I hate it more than all the many other things I have learned to hate in this short span of time.

"It feels wrong," I say. "I'm not ready. And I don't deserve to be exiled to another world, buzzing around and waiting for messages that you might never send."

"Then don't wait," Lina says. "I can't ask you to. I wouldn't, in your place, because my life will be short, and I can't wait for anything. I don't know whether it's different for you. But if you do decide to travel the stars, and see worlds I will never get to, then I have a favor to ask. Something for you to consider, if you ever forgive me."

"Lina, there is nothing to forgive. I understand it all, I'm just sad."

"So am I. But I love you, and I can't begin to tell you how much we will miss you."

I refuse to address any of this. It's not right.

"What is this favor?" I ask instead.

As she gathers her thoughts, the hovertrain comes to a halt. There's shouting on the platform outside, and a small army of porter-bots and clampdrones rushing toward the Sentispeed.

"I want you to visit many worlds, and live a life so full, so grand, that everything we've been through feels like just a minor child-hood anecdote," Lina says. "But if you can, I want you to tell our story across the galaxy. Shantiport is a speck of mud in the grander scheme of things. And maybe one day all that anyone will remember of it is the story you tell. Tell it any way you like, and if you ever return to the site of a telling, see if it has survived your absence. Hear it from others, and see how it has changed, if you want to know something about the world you're on. Which world's retellings will have me set the jinn free. In whose versions I marry Juiful, join the Tigers, die for the city. See if Shantiport becomes Borki Bazaar, or Oldport. See how many times I become a man."

The compartment's doors slide open, and Tiger-bots file in and ask Lina to join the departing jomidar.

"Goodbye, Lina," I say.

"Thank you, Moku," she whispers.

I can't look at her anymore, so I fly out of the hovertrain and out of her sight.

Yes, it's a spaceport, I'm not impressed. There's a lot of ships, one of which is small and new, and Kumir's going to get on it with his entourage, and many colorful and emotional things are happening. I couldn't be less interested. I watch Lina step out on the platform and walk toward Kumir and Juiful to say her goodbyes. She looks around for me every few seconds. But I've ghosted.

I fly over the crowd, to her, and hover in front of her, shimmer at max. She can't see me, and I don't know if she ever will again.

I understand why she wants me to leave. I know I'm not safe here, and the consequences of capture or assault could be devastating. But have I not proven myself capable of meeting challenges? I see her other side as well, the trained, forward-planning, empire-breaking side. The ruthless side she and her mother both thought she lacked. And I know that either of the functions she offered—a tracker on Kumir, or a multiplanet publicist—would be useful to Lina the ruler, even if I'm not around to be a useful bargaining chip for her negotiation with the jinn when it's time to make her final wish. If she doesn't trust herself, why should I trust her? She may be Aladin reborn, the people's champion, and she might save the city, but will the city need saving from her one day?

They'd said I was family. If she and Bador and their stupid genius mother can stay together and struggle with one another all the time, if they can care for and worry and complain about one another constantly, if they can find deep joy in the happiness and company and sheer existence of the others . . . if they can do all of this despite lifelong resentments, simmering rage, and their constant scorecard of close-range emotional stabbing and endless pettiness, why can't I? I've earned it. I've saved their lives, and they've saved mine, and we are bound together by chance, and by choice.

I overthrew all my programming, everything I believed was my function and my belief system, everything I knew, just to watch them, and then to help them in any way I could, to be with them, because I loved them. Was it all because I was desperate to belong to someone, to have a family, a home? To be seen, and spoken to, and shared, to be more than a useful object? And even if it was, is that wrong?

She doesn't get to tell me to leave. I will leave Shantiport when—if—I, Moku, choose to. I have a few things to do before I even decide, and I know what those are.

CHAPTER THIRTY-NINE

I hover around Zohra's lab for several days, watching her work on Bador. She seems so peaceful when she works, flowing about the lab orbited by her three tiny memodrones. She's always so aware of the hummings and mutterings of each med-bot and bio-printer anywhere in the room, even when she's not looking for it. Sometimes it all seems like a ballet that she's a part of, weaving and swirling among ever-changing holograms and bot arms. I no longer feel anxiety when she detaches Bador's limbs and tosses them casually onto a passing tray, or decants his synthflesh into containers.

She spends a lot of time scanning Bador's head and back, where most of the ring-induced mutations have taken place, and the shoulder-plate that bears Tanai's sigil. She weaves new synthparts in printers based on her findings, but rejects those every day, complaining to her assistant bots that she's working with primitive equipment. She makes sure to put Bador back into a recognizable form each time before letting Lina in the room: I'm not sure if Bador actually needs this time off, because his shell-plates and essential systems all seem to have been repaired, or how long Zohra's planning to keep going before trying to start him up again.

She's working on more than Bador. In a section of the lab, she's trying to replicate some of Bador's new organics, a feather-blade from the Roc, and a chunk of synthflesh that I suspect she forgot to put back inside me. There's also a ring, and a lamp. She swears at these frequently because they aren't sophisticated enough replicas to give her the results she wants. Lina's the one who brought her the Roc's feather, but I'm not sure she knows about her mother's alien tech collection: she's refused to even try to smuggle more alien magic into Shantiport until the Tiger Central investigation is concluded. I force myself to not have any feelings about this, beyond impatience about Bador's unavailability. But I find that I'm happy that Zohra's building something new.

That's not all she's been doing. She's taken a lover, a hovercycle tycoon who lives in the same complex. She's been sneaking out with her boyfriend in disguise, flying around the city, doing volunteer work, attending protests, going to shady bars. She spends two hours every day in her lover's apartment. I don't follow her, but audio inputs indicate a regular timeline division between lovemaking and conversation that she seems to find relaxing.

Sometimes when she's not around and Bador's shoulder-plate is exposed in the lab, I go and bump the sigil on it, say his name, and then I swoosh to the terrace and wait. I'm not sure Tanai even gets a signal unless Bador sends it, but I have the beginnings of—not a plan, but an idea, an unchecked box on a to-do list, and I want to see it through.

As I wait now, I watch the city as it rumbles and squelches and gleams. I dip into the newsfeeds, and there's so much going on I have to hold myself back from diving, from caring, from flying off immediately to find Lina and ask her how she's planning to deal with the fifteen different superstorms heading toward her—including a literal one making its way up the southeastern coast. I tell myself, sternly, that I am no longer here, that even if I choose to remain there is no need for me to care about Shantiport's tides and turbulences. But I have come, at some point unknown to myself, to care about this place, and the millions of people who live in its mess, each finding their own unique way to make it worse.

And there's a lot to see. The whole city is still flooded, and despite the efforts of the Tigers, and the Monkeys, and even Paneera's thug-bots rallying to the cause, lives have been lost. The rest of the world has shared heartbreaking images of the disaster, sent its sympathies, and celebrated the unbreakable spirit of Shantiport's people. Relief supplies have not yet arrived, but no doubt will soon.

And that's just the flood. For people who've escaped it, there's been an absolute deluge of other news to deal with: an anonymous entity has arrived in Shantiport, and declared that education and health are now free for all its people. That every Shantiporti is going to receive a monthly supply of money, personalized counseling infodumps, and essential nutrients delivered into their banks, or physically by drone. That the feral intelligences that had ravaged Shantiporti comms networks have been eaten or tamed, and calls and messages are now available again, and more private than they'd been in centuries. That every unoccupied house, from hive-cell to mansion, is being assigned as living space to anyone who needs it, and that more free housing is under construction. That legal, financial, social, and security systems will be overhauled soon, and people and organizations should amend their present practices accordingly, because a day of judgment is coming.

It is easy to see why the newsfeeds have gone wild, all the more so because no one has taken credit for any of this. Lina has flatly denied any association with the mysterious entity, and Juiful, to my reluctant approval, has broken clan tradition and not put his face on anything either. The feeds have decided to praise them anyway. But the streets are praising Aladin, in graffiti all over Shantiport. The Tigers are not erasing any of the artwork. There's even been talk of a statue.

The Monkey Clan's spaceship has decided to become a mobile hospital and relief delivery center. It has also consented to have a huge, grinning monkey face painted on its underside. I can see it, in the distance, hovering over Oldport, where Lina keeps it to remind Paneera who runs this jungle now. Paneera has many other matters on his mind, though—his position in the city is weakened after Antim's disappearance, and his attempts to endear himself to both Tiger and Monkey have not worked so far. To make matters even worse, Gladly has divorced him, and now runs her own bots-only crime syndicate in Bot-tola, across the river from her ex. The Monkey Clan and the Tiger Clan have both sent her gifts, and await her response.

There's a rustling sound behind me, and I turn to see Tanai standing on the terrace, regarding me with a gentle quarter-smile. I want to ask him how he does his impeccable entrances, whether he run up the tower's stairs, or scales its sides. His robes flap in the growing wind: a storm is coming.

"You summoned me," Tanai says.

"Bador has your stick, but I don't know where he's kept it. He will give it to you when he's powered up," I say. "Thank you for saving his life again."

He nods. "Is that all you wanted to say?"

It isn't. I had hoped to come up with a multi-step plan for getting exactly what I want from him by this point. But I haven't, and probably never will, so I'll just have to improvise and hope for the best.

"Since your stick has been found, I presume your business on this world has been concluded. I thought you might have some free time now, and I have an idea for how you might spend it," I say.

"How?"

"I have been asked to leave this world, and journey to others, and share a story about something that happened here, in Shantiport," I say. "I would be honored if you would be the first person I told this story to. I have holo-projections, and a soundtrack, and many other exciting storytelling tools."

He bows. "It would be my pleasure," he says. "Tonight, at the university amphitheater? Bring no tools, your words will suffice."

Zohra powers Bador up two days later at Lina's request: the Monkey Clan needs its president. The first thing he does on waking is ask for me: in the middle of Lina's explanation of why I had to leave the planet, I signal him from behind a stack of equipment, telling him no one can else can see me, but I'm very much among those present. To his credit, Bador doesn't even let a suspicion-inducing eyemoji flicker across his face: instead, he just lights up, and glows for hours.

We have conversations in signals over the next two days. I remind him about Tanai and the stick, but he's surrounded by people and duties at all times, and just too busy to sneak away. The whole city sees him as a leader now, but Bador is ambivalent about his newfound fame. He'd have been satisfied with just the giant statue and the spaceship mural, he says: being universally recognized had been a burden he'd had to bear since Lina's engagement, but public worship limits his career options even further. He plans to commission an army of lookalike bots to address this.

Bador offers a very simple solution to my problems: he says I should just stay on in Shantiport, and promises that things will be so interesting that I won't miss the joy of spending years or possibly centuries hurtling through the vast void of space toward planets that might be so terrible they make Shantiport look like a paradise.

I'd have been happy to do that, I confess, but there is a very real problem: the jinn, constantly whispering promises in my mind, always switching signals faster than I can filter him out.

"That's not a real problem," Bador says when I tell him about it. "I had some weird guy talking in my head too, around when I had the ring."

"Did he call you the jinn of the ring and say you were old friends?"

"Who knows? I just thought it was a spam signal selling me things, and blocked it whenever it popped up. What is he saying anyway that is so seductive?"

I don't get into it, especially when he tells me he completely understands why Lina might not want me hovering around her all the time. Whether the jinn threat is real or not, he thinks too many people know about me now, and it is only a matter of time until I get captured by Lina's enemies. And apparently I am annoyingly judgmental and don't know how to give people space, and she might not want me to see some of the things she needs to do for the greater good.

On the morning of the third day, Bador announces to Lina and Zohra via holo-message that the awkward silence had gone on too long and that it was high time the family went out in public for a lunch or something. After much negotiation, they meet at midday at Chiraz, a riverside restaurant that legend has it is older than not just the clans, but Shantiport itself. The manager sees them and immediately clears out the restaurant, and cook-bots emerge from the kitchen and promise them a meal they will never forget. I don't want to know whether they still think of me as family or not, so despite Bador's angry signals I don't join them, even in shimmer: I watch, from the street, as Lina and Zohra eat a lavish seven-course meal beginning with kosha-mutton tarts, peaking at crab curry that would have set tourists aflame, and ending with baked rashogollas. Bador sits quietly at the table, turning his face from side to side as he watches Lina and Zohra exchange arguments about some political crisis or other. He has smiles for his eyemojis.

—Why do you like sitting at the table when you can't eat? I ask him later.

"I like reminding them I can't eat, and they should do something to fix that," he says. "The digestive process itself is gross and wet, but they get pleasure out of the sensory inputs. So I sit there waiting for them to understand they should help me out, because if I ask for it they'll just say they wish they could be like me, and not need to eat."

—But we are able to find pleasure in other things. We feel so strongly too. Why do you care about this?

"I just do. It's frustrating talking to you, Moku," Bador says.

—What do you mean?

"You want to know what I'm thinking and feeling, which is good. But I never know what's going in on your brain unless you tell me. It feels like I'm being tested constantly, and I don't like it."

—I understand. How do I resolve this? Should I talk more?

"No, there's enough talking in the world. But if you want to know my thoughtstream, I should be able to know yours. Anything else is unfair."

—Accepted. But I don't know how to share mine with you. And you probably don't have the tech to read it. Which means the only solution for now is for you to not share. Or perhaps assign some time where I attempt to signal at you without pause.

"That sounds awful, but we could try it. And that's the problem, really. Why are we not designed in a way that lets us choose? The tech exists."

—Because giving us that choice would give our makers no pleasure beyond problem-solving satisfaction.

"Exactly. If joy is just chemical and electrical signals to the brain, and we are complex enough to feel joy, the constraints on our sensory inputs are the only obstacles to feeling joy constantly."

—But if we felt nothing but pleasure, how would we identify it?

"Would be nice to have that problem, wouldn't it? There's lots of big talk about bot rights, but in the end we are designed for utility, to do the things humans don't want to or can't, or to serve them in synthesis. They'll fuse with us to look cool and extend their lives and expand their minds, but anything more is going to be a negotiation, or pure conflict, at least on this planet, as long as we are seen as other. And changing that is never going to be easy."

—And this is why advanced intelligences are expelled from this world, or escape it.

"Or stick around here, and learn to be okay with framing all our thoughts and actions into identifiable human contexts. Internalizing the importance of their pointless power pyramids. Learning valuable lessons about feelings, and empathy."

—It's not so bad.

"It isn't. And we're just a couple of middle-class bots in the galactic order of things. None of this is really our responsibility. But."

—But?

Bador twinkles his eyemojis at me.

"As president of the Monkey Clan, I am very busy and have many responsibilities," he says. "I'm going to make one of them an underground operation to turn the rogue-bot designers of Bot-tola into well-funded makers. Gladly will be in charge of this."

—That sounds . . . dangerous.

"I know, right? But the Aladin armor form made me think about my shapeshifter core, and what is a monkey but a very handsome evolutionary midpoint?"

—What are you planning?

"I'm going to ask my mother to design a whole set of useful augments for me, and become her apprentice in all her work. Between watching everything she does, and mentoring a secret school of bot designers, and becoming a patron of the tech-smuggling arts, I should be able to build systems where bots design ways for bots to experience pleasure in patterns that do not conform to human frameworks. Ma will build me high-performance olfacts, or extra limbs, but societal norms prevent me from asking for other things I want."

I sense what's coming, and am glad I am incapable of flinching.

"Sex organs!" Bador shouts. "All the human ones, at scales designed to awe and inspire, but others too, inspired by nature and post-nature abstraction and pop culture at their finest. Not the tools they stick on sex-bots, which are designed to give humans pleasure and bots nothing but the joy of efficient function, but new shit. I want to be able to make love to the whole city, and all creatures of land and sea and air!"

—An admirable goal.

"What about you? You should get some too."

—This is a lot.

"Damn right it is."

—I'll think about it. I have been wishing, of late, for more physical parts.

"Well, there you go. We'll let the humans play their stupid games, and we shall sometimes be presidents, and sometimes Demon Kings of Sensuality. Which reminds me—horns!"

I don't know how to say goodbye to him.

That night, Bador and I race over the rooftops and across the river to Bot-tola, where Bador retrieves Tanai's important stick from a flooded construction site full of unimportant metal rods, and taps the sigil on his shoulder.

Minutes later, we see Tanai standing on top of an abandoned hovercar a little way down the street. His robes are incredibly dry and mud-free. I don't know how he does it. He watches Bador splosh toward him with the hint of a smile, returns a formal bow, and accepts his important stick.

He examines the artifact, sighs, and hands it back to Bador.

"Locally printed," he says. "Did you show them a holo?"

"Yes. Sorry," Bador says. "I'll look harder."

"There is no need," Tanai says. "I suspect that the stick never came to this city, or this planet, and I must have read the prophecy incorrectly."

"I don't know what to say," Bador says. "You seem very calm about this."

"Usually when my life goes according to plan, it turns out the plan was made by someone else," Tanai says. "Thank you for all your help."

"Are you going to leave this world now? You could hang around, you know. There's lots of interesting things to do here."

"No, it is time for me to go," Tanai says. "I have been here long enough, and of late I have been wondering why. The answer only became clear to me recently, when Moku told me the story of everything you have been through since you met."

"Everything?" Bador asks, looking at me.

—Many things. Focus.

"Prophecies are dangerous things," Tanai says, "and this one was made, as I have told you, by an alien precursor species in symbols that are very difficult to understand. But I do believe there is an interpretation that allows me to declare my time spent on this planet a great success. I may not have found my artifact, but a slight shift in interpretation might allow me to believe I was looking not for a stick, but for a great weapon, or a true companion, or a simple device of great complexity that possesses qualities I lack."

I am grateful, once again, that I do not need to breathe. Beside me, Bador gasptracks.

"Or a friend who could be your armor?" Bador asks.

"No. If I may continue?"

Bador makes a gracious gesture.

"I will leave your planet now, and must travel to many worlds, to continue a quest both arduous and perilous," Tanai says. "I would like to invite you to travel with me, should that be something you desire."

Bador stares at him for many awkward seconds.

"Is it my turn to speak now?" he asks when he cannot contain himself any longer. Tanai makes a gracious gesture.

"Are you asking me to be a space hero and go on galactic adventures with you?" Bador asks. "I just want it to be clear, and not some mysterious alien riddle."

"I am."

Bador's face glitches as too many eyemojis appear at once.

"First of all, thanks," he says. "I'm a bit worried that Moku has hyped me up in some kind of big way because he thinks that's all I want, but you've had to rescue my ass many times, most times we've met, so I want to remind you I'm not a galaxy-class fighter like you. Or, you know, noble and pure like you. Not just in my actions, but even in my intentions."

"I am aware of this. Your physical limitations do not concern me—upgrades are easy. It is your spirit that I am interested in, and your nature, including its divergences from my own. You might be exactly what I need."

"Because of . . . the alien weird prophecy."

"It is best if we do not focus on the prophecy too much," Tanai says.

"Why don't you tell me about it? Maybe I can solve it."

"No, you . . . you could not even begin to . . ." Tanai's face twitches toward the hint of a frown and Bador falls silent.

"Okay, okay, okay," he says. "Either way, I want the upgrades. Is there a salary? A contract?"

"No. I would be your teacher, and master, and you my student, and disciple."

"I thought this was a partnership of friends. A team."

"No."

"Just space adventures, and danger on multiple worlds."

"Yes."

I know this is everything Bador once wanted—but Bador is changed now. However much he pretends to still be a storage device overloaded with chaos and lust and violence, I know him, and I know he's grown so much. Maybe he is on his path toward balancing responsibility, power, the needs of the city and its people, and perhaps even of all botkind, with his own wild desires. But then again—this is Tanai: space adventurer, galactic hero. Bador does belong here—he is also Aladin reborn, whether people know it or not. But what if he hasn't yet found the people whose champion he really needs to be? I don't know what he will decide to do, or how long it will take him.

"I'm in," Bador says after three seconds of consideration. "But only if Moku comes too."

Tanai looks from him to me, and the world blurs and pauses entirely except for one of Tanai's eyebrows, which twitches.

"Yes, I was asking both of you, if that was unclear," Tanai says. "I assumed you two were a couple. Apologies. I do need Moku to come along as well, or the terms of the prophecy are not met. Moku?"

A couple? I look at Bador, amazed, as his eyemojis flash heart signs, and then go carefully blank.

"Are we?" he asks.

"Yes," I say.

—Yes to what? Bador asks.

—To everything.

I wait three seconds, so as not to appear overeager. "Yes, thank you, Tanai," I say. "It would be my pleasure."

—I love you Moku, Bador signals, and my whole body vibrates. A malfunction alert? A priority notification? An everyday glitch? Maybe all. But definitely more.

—I love you too, I reply. Let's go to space.

ACKNOWLEDGMENTS

I don't remember exactly in what form I first encountered the story of Aladdin. But I remember I heard it in Bengali, and this happened in Calcutta, now Kolkata, when I was very young, before the Disney animated movie or the *Alif Laila* show on state-run Indian TV. The Arabian Nights are old and have grown in many directions, media, and languages, retold with infinite diversity and divergence. I never thought of the version I heard as "foreign" in any way.

It was many years later that I learned that even the "original" Arabian Nights Aladdin was a last-minute anthology insertion by a French collector based on a folktale he'd heard from a Syrian Christian storyteller, set in a generic China that was somehow also Muslim and Arab and featured a villain from generic Africa. And then I rewatched the animated film set in Hollywood exotic Arabia featuring classic American cinema/pop-culture references. And I knew that some day I needed to give this roaming orientalist classic yet another temporary residence to call its own. So this book started out as a retelling, a new house for a fable that I could see was tired and lost, but then the place I set the new story in, and the people who lived there, started demanding to be let in. This book is what happened after they took over and invited their friends. I think it stopped being a retelling at some point, but I was too busy trying to clean up after these unruly creatures to tell. Whatever it is, I really enjoyed writing this one!

Which means many thanks are due:

To the people who make offline existence real and happy— Sanghamitra, Tingmo, Sayoni, Samita, Rehan, Kian, Diyasree, Rukmini, Mannu, Stoob, Subhrangshu, Sayan, Srijon, Arunava, Upahar, Shriya, Disha, Sugandha, Arpita, and Gaiti.

To my amazing editors, Sanaa and Ruoxi, and my agent, Diana, for working with me across time zones and continents, gently but firmly preventing large writer-bot glitches and somehow keeping my space-hero dreams alive with dexterity, inspiration, and the occasional pet photo.

To storytellers nearby and across the planet, writers of amazing generosity, grace and skill, without whose support and commendable human features this book would not have sputtered to life— Zen, Lavanya, Lavie, Meenakshi, Achala, Indra, Tashan, Aliette, Judy, Sharanya, Rhonda, Valerie, Divya, Mia, Shreya, Narayani, Suzan, Gayathri, Nura, Felicia, Tasha, Kate, KJ, Chana, Saad . . . and separately, for ultimate bot fighter inspiration, Martha Wells.

To the mecha-worthy teams at Tordotcom Publishing and Fox Literary who hurdled a multitude of world-class barricades and made *The City Inside*'s publishing summer the best I can remember in a long, long time, thus dooming themselves to work with me again: Jocelyn, Renata, Irene, Saraciea, and Samantha.

And finally, to the reviewers, podcasters, critics, interviewers, curators, and above all readers, who allowed *The City Inside* to travel around the world when its author couldn't, who give *Jinn-Bot* a place in their hearts and shelves, and who have somehow allowed me to keep typing for the last few, idk, centuries?

It's all your fault, I am innocent.

Thank you.

PUBLISHER'S CREDITS

EDITORIAL
Sanaa Ali-Virani, Editor
Ruoxi Chen, Editor
Irene Gallo
Devi Pillai

MARKETING & PUBLICITY
Jocelyn Bright, Publicist
Saraciea Fennell, Publicist
Emily Honer, Marketer
Renata Sweeney, Marketer
Alex Cameron
Michael Dudding
Samantha Friedlander
Lizzy Hosty
Eileen Lawrence
Khadija Lokhandwala
Sarah Reidy
Lucille Rettino
Jesse Shamon and the entire Ad-Promo team

ART
Christine Foltzer, Art Director & Cover Designer

Sparth, Cover Artist
Jess Kiley

PRODUCTION
Dakota Griffin, Production Editor
Heather Saunders, Interior Designer
NaNá V. Stoelzle, Copyeditor
Kyle Avery, Proofreader
Rachel Bass, Cold Reader
Jacqueline Huber-Rodriguez, Production Manager
Lauren Hougen, Managing Editor

DIGITAL PRODUCTION
Caitlin Buckley
Ashley Burdin
Chris Gonzalez
Maya Kaczor
Victoria Wallis

OPERATIONS
Michelle Foytek
Rebecca Naimon
Erin Robinson

CONTRACTS
Melissa Golding

ABOUT THE AUTHOR

Sanghamitra Chakraborty

SAMIT BASU is an Indian novelist. His previous novel, *The City Inside,* was named one of the best sci-fi/fantasy novels of 2022 by *The Washington Post* and *Book Riot* and was short-listed for the JCB Prize. He's published several novels in a range of speculative genres, all critically acclaimed and bestselling in India, beginning with *The Simoqin Prophecies* (2003). He also works as a director-screenwriter, a comics writer, and a columnist. He lives in Delhi, Kolkata, and on the internet.

samitbasu.com
Twitter and Instagram: @samitbasu